EVERYMAN, *I will go with thee,*

and be thy guide,

In thy most need to go by thy side

GIOVANNI BOCCACCIO

Born in Paris in 1313, the illegitimate son of
a Florentine merchant and a French woman.
Spent his youth in Florence; met 'Fiammetta' at Naples in 1336, returning to
Florence in 1341. Met Petrarch, 1350. Died
in poverty, 21st December 1375.

GIOVANNI BOCCACCIO

The Decameron

IN TWO VOLUMES · VOLUME TWO

TRANSLATED BY
J. M. RIGG

INTRODUCTION BY
EDWARD HUTTON

DENT: LONDON
EVERYMAN'S LIBRARY
DUTTON: NEW YORK

All rights reserved
Made in Great Britain
at the
Aldine Press · Letchworth · Herts
for
J. M. DENT & SONS LTD
Aldine House · Albemarle Street · London
This edition was first published in
Everyman's Library in 1930
Reprinted 1973

Published in the U.S.A. by arrangement
with J. M. Dent & Sons Ltd

No. 846   Hardback ISBN 0 460 00846 3
No. 1846 Paperback ISBN 0 460 01846 9

CONTENTS

CONTENTS

CONTENTS

VILLA PALMIERI
The villa and terrace from the Lower Garden

Endeth here the fourth day of the Decameron, beginneth the fifth, in which under the rule of Fiammetta discourse is had of good fortune befalling lovers after divers direful or disastrous adventures.

ALL the east was white, nor any part of our hemisphere un-illumined by the rising beams, when the carolling of the birds that in gay chorus saluted the dawn among the boughs induced Fiammetta to rise and rouse the other ladies and the three gallants ; with whom adown the hill and about the dewy meads of the broad champaign she sauntered, talking gaily of divers matters, until the sun had attained some height. Then, feeling his rays grow somewhat scorching, they retraced their steps, and returned to the villa ; where, having repaired their slight fatigue with excellent wines and comfits, they took their pastime in the pleasant garden until the breakfast hour ; when, all things being made ready by the discreet seneschal, they, after singing a stampita,[1] and a balladette or two, gaily, at the queen's behest, sat them down to eat. Meetly ordered and gladsome was the meal, which done, heedful of their rule of dancing, they trod a few short measures with accompaniment of music and song. Thereupon, being all dismissed by the queen until after the siesta, some hied them to rest, while others tarried taking their pleasure in the fair garden. But shortly after none, all, at the queen's behest, reassembled, according to their wont, by the fountain ; and the queen, having seated herself on her throne, glanced towards Pamfilo, and bade him with a smile lead off with the stories of good fortune. Whereto Pamfilo gladly addressed himself, and thus began.

[1] A song accompanied by music, but without dancing.

NOVEL I

Cimon, by loving, waxes wise, wins his wife Iphigenia by capture on the high seas, and is imprisoned at Rhodes. He is delivered by Lysimachus; and the twain capture Cassandra and recapture Iphigenia in the hour of their marriage. They flee with their ladies to Crete, and having there married them, are brought back to their homes.

MANY stories, sweet my ladies, occur to me as meet for me to tell by way of ushering in a day so joyous as this will be: of which one does most commend itself to my mind, because not only has it one of those happy endings of which to-day we are in quest, but 'twill enable you to understand how holy, how mighty and how salutary are the forces of Love, which not a few, witting not what they say, do most unjustly reprobate and revile: which, if I err not, should to you, for that I take you to be enamoured, be indeed welcome.

Once upon a time, then, as we have read in the ancient histories of the Cypriotes, there was in the island of Cyprus a very great noble named Aristippus, a man rich in all worldly goods beyond all other of his countrymen, and who might have deemed himself incomparably blessed, but for a single sore affliction that Fortune had allotted him. Which was that among his sons he had one, the best grown and handsomest of them all, that was well-nigh a hopeless imbecile. His true name was Galesus; but, as neither his tutor's pains, nor his father's coaxing or chastisement, nor any other method had availed to imbue him with any tincture of letters or manners, but he still remained gruff and savage of voice, and in his bearing liker to a beast than to a man, all, as in derision, were wont to call him Cimon, which in their language signifies the same as " bestione " (brute) [1] in ours. The father, grieved beyond measure to see his son's life thus blighted, and having abandoned all hope of his recovery, nor caring to have the cause of his mortification ever before his eyes, bade him betake him to the farm, and there keep with his husbandmen. To Cimon the change was very welcome, because the manners and habits of the uncouth hinds were more to his taste than those of the citizens. So to the farm Cimon hied him, and addressed himself to the work thereof; and being thus employed, he chanced one afternoon as he passed,

---

[1] One of the augmentative forms of bestia.

staff on shoulder, from one domain to another, to enter a planta-
tion, the like of which for beauty there was not in those parts,
and which was then—for 'twas the month of May—a mass of
greenery ; and, as he traversed it, he came, as Fortune was
pleased to guide him, to a meadow girt in with trees exceeding
tall, and having in one of its corners a fountain most fair and
cool, beside which he espied a most beautiful girl lying asleep
on the green grass, clad only in a vest of such fine stuff that it
scarce in any measure veiled the whiteness of her flesh, and
below the waist nought but an apron most white and fine of
texture ; and likewise at her feet there slept two women and a
man, her slaves. No sooner did Cimon catch sight of her, than,
as if he had never before seen form of woman, he stopped short,
and leaning on his cudgel, regarded her intently, saying never a
word, and lost in admiration. And in his rude soul, which,
despite a thousand lessons, had hitherto remained impervious
to every delight that belongs to urbane life, he felt the awakening
of an idea, that bade his gross and coarse mind acknowledge,
that this girl was the fairest creature that had ever been seen
by mortal eye. And thereupon he began to distinguish her
several parts, praising her hair, which shewed to him as gold,
her brow, her nose and mouth, her throat and arms, and above
all her bosom, which was as yet but in bud, and as he gazed,
he changed of a sudden from a husbandman into a judge of
beauty, and desired of all things to see her eyes, which the
weight of her deep slumber kept close shut, and many a time
he would fain have awakened her, that he might see them.
But so much fairer seemed she to him than any other woman
that he had seen, that he doubted she must be a goddess ; and
as he was not so devoid of sense but that he deemed things
divine more worthy of reverence than things mundane, he
forbore, and waited until she should awake of her own accord ;
and though he found the delay overlong, yet, enthralled by so
unwonted a delight, he knew not how to be going. However,
after he had tarried a long while, it so befell that Iphigenia—
such was the girl's name—her slaves still sleeping, awoke, and
raised her head, and opened her eyes, and seeing Cimon standing
before her, leaning on his staff, was not a little surprised, and
said :—" Cimon, what seekest thou in this wood at this hour ? "
For Cimon she knew well, as indeed did almost all the country-
side, by reason alike of his uncouth appearance as of the rank
and wealth of his father. To Iphigenia's question he answered
never a word : but as soon as her eyes were open, nought could

he do but intently regard them, for it seemed to him that a soft influence emanated from them, which filled his soul with a delight that he had never before known. Which the girl marking began to misdoubt that by so fixed a scrutiny his boorish temper might be prompted to some act that should cause her dishonour : wherefore she roused her women, and got up, saying :—" Keep thy distance, Cimon, in God's name." Whereto Cimon made answer :—" I will come with thee." And, albeit the girl refused his escort, being still in fear of him, she could not get quit of him ; but he attended her home ; after which he hied him straight to his father's house, and announced that he was minded on no account to go back to the farm : which intelligence was far from welcome to his father and kinsmen ; but nevertheless they suffered him to stay, and waited to see what might be the reason of his change of mind. So Cimon, whose heart, closed to all teaching, love's shaft, sped by the beauty of Iphigenia, had penetrated, did now graduate in wisdom with such celerity as to astonish his father and kinsmen, and all that knew him. He began by requesting his father to let him go clad in the like apparel, and with, in all respects, the like personal equipment as his brothers : which his father very gladly did. Mixing thus with the gallants, and becoming familiar with the manners proper to gentlemen, and especially to lovers, he very soon, to the exceeding great wonder of all, not only acquired the rudiments of letters, but waxed most eminent among the philosophic wits. After which (for no other cause than the love he bore to Iphigenia) he not only modulated his gruff and boorish voice to a degree of smoothness suitable to urbane life, but made himself accomplished in singing and music ; in riding also and in all matters belonging to war, as well by sea as by land, he waxed most expert and hardy. And in sum (that I go not about to enumerate each of his virtues in detail) he had not completed the fourth year from the day of his first becoming enamoured before he was grown the most gallant, and courteous, ay, and the most perfect in particular accomplishments, of the young cavaliers that were in the island of Cyprus. What then, gracious ladies, are we to say of Cimon ? Verily nought else but that the high faculties, with which Heaven had endowed his noble soul, invidious Fortune had bound with the strongest of cords, and circumscribed within a very narrow region of his heart ; all which cords Love, more potent than Fortune, burst and brake in pieces ; and then with the might, wherewith he awakens dormant powers, he brought them forth of the cruel obfuscation, in which they lay, into clear light, plainly shewing thereby, whence he may draw, and whither he may guide, by his beams the souls that are subject to his sway.

Now, albeit by his love for Iphigenia Cimon was betrayed, as young lovers very frequently are, into some peccadillos, yet Aristippus, reflecting that it had turned him from a booby into a man, not only bore patiently with him, but exhorted him with all his heart to continue steadfast in his love. And Cimon, who still refused to be called Galesus, because 'twas as Cimon that Iphigenia had first addressed him, being desirous to accomplish his desire by honourable means, did many a time urge his suit upon her father, Cipseus, that he would give her him to wife : whereto Cipseus always made the same answer, to wit, that he had promised her to Pasimondas, a young Rhodian noble, and was not minded to break faith with him. However, the time appointed for Iphigenia's wedding being come, and the bride-groom having sent for her, Cimon said to himself :—'Tis now for me to shew thee, O Iphigenia, how great is my love for thee : 'tis by thee that I am grown a man, nor doubt I, if I shall have thee, that I shall wax more glorious than a god, and verily thee will I have, or die. Having so said, he privily enlisted in his cause certain young nobles that were his friends, and secretly fitted out a ship with all equipment meet for combat, and put to sea on the look-out for the ship that was to bear Iphigenia to Rhodes and her husband. And at length, when her father had done lavishing honours upon her husband's friends, Iphigenia embarked, and, the mariners shaping their course for Rhodes, put to sea. Cimon was on the alert, and overhauled them the very next day, and standing on his ship's prow shouted amain to those that were aboard Iphigenia's ship :—" Bring to ; strike sails, or look to be conquered and sunk in the sea." Then, seeing that the enemy had gotten their arms above deck, and were making ready to make a fight of it, he followed up his words by casting a grapnel upon the poop of the Rhodians, who were making great way ; and having thus made their poop fast to his prow, he sprang, fierce as a lion, reckless whether he were followed or no, on to the Rhodians' ship, making, as it were, no account of them, and animated by love, hurled himself, sword in hand, with prodigious force among the enemy, and cutting and thrusting right and left, slaughtered them like sheep ; insomuch that the Rhodians, marking the fury of his onset, threw down their arms, and as with one voice did all

acknowledge themselves his prisoners. To whom Cimon :—
"Gallants," quoth he, "'twas neither lust of booty nor enmity
to you that caused me to put out from Cyprus to attack you
here with force of arms on the high seas. Moved was I thereto
by that which to gain is to me a matter great indeed, which
peaceably to yield me is to you but a slight matter ; for 'tis
even Iphigenia, whom more than aught else I love ; whom, as
I might not have her of her father in peaceable and friendly sort,
Love has constrained me to take from you in this high-handed
fashion and by force of arms ; to whom I mean to be even
such as would have been your Pasimondas : wherefore give her
to me, and go your way, and God's grace go with you."

Yielding rather to force than prompted by generosity, the
Rhodians surrendered Iphigenia, all tears, to Cimon ; who,
marking her tears, said to her :—" Grieve not, noble lady ; thy
Cimon am I, who, by my long love, have established a far better
right to thee than Pasimondas by the faith that was plighted
to him." So saying, he sent her aboard his ship, whither he
followed her, touching nought that belonged to the Rhodians,
and suffering them to go their way. To have gotten so dear a
prize made him the happiest man in the world, but for a time
'twas all he could do to assuage her grief : then, after taking
counsel with his comrades, he deemed it best not to return to
Cyprus for the present : and so, by common consent they
shaped their course for Crete, where most of them, and especially
Cimon, had alliances of old or recent date, and friends not a few,
whereby they deemed that there they might tarry with Iphigenia
in security. But Fortune, that had accorded Cimon so gladsome a capture of the lady, suddenly proved fickle, and converted the boundless joy of the enamoured gallant into woeful
and bitter lamentation. 'Twas not yet full four hours since
Cimon had parted from the Rhodians, when with the approach
of night, that night from which Cimon hoped such joyance as
he had never known, came weather most turbulent and tem-
pestuous, which wrapped the heavens in cloud, and swept the
sea with scathing blasts ; whereby 'twas not possible for any
to see how the ship was to be worked or steered, or to steady
himself so as to do any duty upon her deck. Whereat what
grief was Cimon's, it boots not to ask. Indeed it seemed to
him that the gods had granted his heart's desire only that it
might be harder for him to die, which else had been to him but
a light matter. Not less downcast were his comrades ; but
most of all Iphigenia, who, weeping bitterly and shuddering at

every wave that struck the ship, did cruelly curse Cimon's love and censure his rashness, averring that this tempest was come upon them for no other cause than that the gods had decreed, that, as 'twas in despite of their will that he purposed to espouse her, he should be frustrate of his presumptuous intent, and having lived to see her expire, should then himself meet a woeful death.

While thus and yet more bitterly they bewailed them, and the mariners were at their wits' end, as the gale grew hourly more violent, nor knew they, nor might conjecture, whither they went, they drew nigh the island of Rhodes, albeit that Rhodes it was they wist not, and set themselves, as best and most skilfully they might, to run the ship aground. In which enterprise Fortune favoured them, bringing them into a little bay, where, shortly before them, was arrived the Rhodian ship that Cimon had let go. Nor were they sooner ware that 'twas Rhodes they had made, than day broke, and, the sky thus brightening a little, they saw that they were about a bow-shot from the ship that they had released on the preceding day. Whereupon Cimon, vexed beyond measure, being apprehensive of that which in fact befell them, bade make every effort to win out of the bay, and let Fortune carry them whither she would, for nowhere might they be in worse plight than there. So might and main they strove to bring the ship out, but all in vain : the violence of the gale thwarted them to such purpose as not only to preclude their passage out of the bay but to drive them, willing nilling, ashore. Whither no sooner were they come, than they were recognized by the Rhodian mariners, who were already landed. Of whom one ran with all speed to a farm hard by, whither the Rhodian gallants were gone, and told them that Fortune had brought Cimon and Iphigenia aboard their ship into the same bay to which she had guided them. Whereat the gallants were overjoyed, and taking with them not a few of the farm-servants, hied them in hot haste to the shore, where, Cimon and his men being already landed with intent to take refuge in a neighbouring wood, they took them all (with Iphigenia) and brought them to the farm. Whence, pursuant to an order of the Senate of Rhodes, to which, so soon as he received the news, Pasimondas made his complaint, Cimon and his men were all marched off to prison by Lysimachus, chief magistrate of the Rhodians for that year, who came down from the city for the purpose with an exceeding great company of men at arms. On such wise did our hapless and enamoured Cimon lose

his so lately won Iphigenia before he had had of her more than
a kiss or two.   Iphigenia was entertained and comforted of the
annoy, occasioned as well by her recent capture as by the fury
of the sea, by not a few noble ladies of Rhodes, with whom she
tarried until the day appointed for her marriage.   In recompense of the release of the Rhodian gallants on the preceding
day the lives of Cimon and his men were spared, notwithstanding
that Pasimondas pressed might and main for their execution ;
and instead they were condemned to perpetual imprisonment :
wherein, as may be supposed, they abode in dolorous plight,
and despaired of ever again knowing happiness.

However, it so befell that, Pasimondas accelerating his
nuptials to the best of his power, Fortune, as if repenting her
that in her haste she had done Cimon so evil a turn, did now
by a fresh disposition of events compass his deliverance.   Pasimondas had a brother, by name Hormisdas, his equal in all
respects save in years, who had long been contract to marry
Cassandra, a fair and noble damsel of Rhodes, of whom Lysimachus was in the last degree enamoured ; but owing to divers
accidents the marriage had been from time to time put off.
Now Pasimondas, being about to celebrate his nuptials with
exceeding great pomp, bethought him that he could not do
better than, to avoid a repetition of the pomp and expense,
arrange, if so he might, that his brother should be wedded on
the same day with himself.   So, having consulted anew with
Cassandra's kinsfolk, and come to an understanding with them,
he and his brother and they conferred together, and agreed that
on the same day that Pasimondas married Iphigenia, Hormisdas
should marry Cassandra.   Lysimachus, getting wind of this
arrangement, was mortified beyond measure, seeing himself
thereby deprived of the hope which he cherished of marrying
Cassandra himself, if Hormisdas should not forestall him.   But
like a wise man he concealed his chagrin, and cast about how he
might frustrate the arrangement : to which end he saw no other
possible means but to carry Cassandra off.   It did not escape
him that the office which he held would render this easily
feasible, but he deemed it all the more dishonourable than if
he had not held the office ; but, in short, after much pondering,
honour yielded place to love, and he made up his mind that,
come what might, he would carry Cassandra off.   Then, as he
took thought what company he should take with him, and how
he should go about the affair, he remembered Cimon, whom he
had in prison with his men, and it occurred to him that he could

not possibly have a better or more trusty associate in such an enterprise than Cimon. Wherefore the same night he caused Cimon to be brought privily to him in his own room, and thus addressed him:—" Cimon, as the gods are most generous and liberal to bestow their gifts on men, so are they also most sagacious to try their virtue; and those whom they find to be firm and steadfast in all circumstances they honour, as the most worthy, with the highest rewards. They have been minded to be certified of thy worth by better proofs than thou couldst afford them, as long as thy life was bounded by thy father's house amid the superabundant wealth which I know him to possess: wherefore in the first place they so wrought upon thee with the shrewd incitements of Love that from an insensate brute, as I have heard, thou grewest to be a man; since when, it has been and is their intent to try whether evil fortune and harsh imprisonment may avail to change thee from the temper that was thine when for a short while thou hadst joyance of the prize thou hadst won. And so thou prove the same that thou wast then, they have in store for thee a boon incomparably greater than aught that they vouchsafed thee before: what that boon is, to the end thou mayst recover heart and thy wonted energies, I will now explain to thee. Pasimondas, exultant in thy misfortune and eager to compass thy death, hastens to the best of his power his nuptials with thy Iphigenia; that so he may enjoy the prize that Fortune, erstwhile smiling, gave thee, and forthwith, frowning, reft from thee. Whereat how sore must be thy grief, if rightly I gauge thy love, I know by my own case, seeing that his brother Hormisdas addresses himself to do me on the same day a like wrong in regard of Cassandra, whom I love more than aught else in the world. Nor see I that Fortune has left us any way of escape from this her unjust and cruel spite, save what we may make for ourselves by a resolved spirit and the might of our right hands: take we then the sword, and therewith make we, each, prize of his lady, thou for the second, I for the first time: for so thou value the recovery, I say not of thy liberty, for without thy lady I doubt thou wouldst hold it cheap, but of thy lady, the gods have placed it in thine own hands, if thou art but minded to join me in my enterprise."

These words restored to Cimon all that he had lost of heart and hope, nor pondered he long, before he replied:—" Lysimachus, comrade stouter or more staunch than I thou mightst not have in such an enterprise, if such indeed it be as thou sayst : wherefore lay upon me such behest as thou shalt deem meet, and thou shalt marvel to witness the vigour of my performance." Whereupon Lysimachus :—" On the third day from now," quoth he, " their husbands' houses will be newly entered by the brides, and on the same day at even we too will enter them in arms, thou with thy men, and I with some of mine, in whom I place great trust, and forcing our way among the guests and slaughtering all that dare to oppose us, will bear the ladies off to a ship which I have had privily got ready." Cimon approved the plan, and kept quiet in prison until the appointed time ; which being come, the nuptials were celebrated with great pomp and magnificence, that filled the houses of the two brothers with festal cheer.   Then Lysimachus having made ready all things meet, and fired Cimon and his men and his own friends for the enterprise by a long harangue, disposed them in due time, all bearing arms under their cloaks, in three companies ; and having privily despatched one company to the port, that, when the time should come to embark, he might meet with no let, he marched with the other two companies to the house of Pasimondas, posted the one company at the gate, that, being entered, they might not be shut in or debarred their egress, and, with the other company and Cimon, ascended the stairs, and gained the saloon, where the brides and not a few other ladies were set at several tables to sup in meet order : whereupon in they rushed, and overthrew the tables and seized each his own lady, and placed them in charge of their men, whom they bade bear them off forthwith to the ship that lay ready to receive them.   Whereupon the brides and the other ladies and the servants with one accord fell a-sobbing and shrieking, insomuch that a confused din and lamentation filled the whole place.   Cimon, Lysimachus and their band, none withstanding, but all giving way before them, gained the stairs, which they were already descending when they encountered Pasimondas, who, carrying a great staff in his hand, was making in the direction of the noise ; but one doughty stroke of Cimon's sword sufficed to cleave his skull in twain, and lay him dead at Cimon's feet, and another stroke disposed of hapless Hormisdas, as he came running to his brother's aid.   Some others who ventured to approach them were wounded and beaten off by the retinue.   So forth of the house, that reeked with blood and resounded with tumult and lamentation and woe, sped Cimon and Lysimachus with all their company, and without any let, in close order, with their fair booty in their midst, made good

their retreat to the ship ; whereon with the ladies they one and
all embarked, for the shore was now full of armed men come to
rescue the ladies, and, the oarsmen giving way, put to sea elate.
Arrived at Crete, they met with a hearty welcome on the part
of their many friends and kinsfolk ; and, having married their
ladies, they made greatly merry, and had gladsome joyance of
their fair booty.   Their doings occasioned, both in Cyprus and
in Rhodes, no small stir and commotion, which lasted for a long
while : but in the end, by the good offices of their friends and
kinsfolk in both islands, 'twas so ordered as that after a certain
term of exile Cimon returned with Iphigenia to Cyprus, and in
like manner Lysimachus returned with Cassandra to Rhodes ;
and long and blithely thereafter lived they, each well contented
with his own wife in his own land.

NOVEL II

Gostanza loves Martuccio Gomito, and hearing that he is dead,
gives way to despair, and hies her alone aboard a boat, which
is wafted by the wind to Susa.   She finds him alive in Tunis,
and makes herself known to him, who, having by his counsel
gained high place in the king's favour, marries her, and
returns with her wealthy to Lipari.

PAMFILO'S story being ended, the queen, after commending it
not a little, called for one to follow from Emilia ; who thus
began :—

Meet and right it is that one should rejoice when events so
fall out that passion meets with its due reward : and as love
merits in the long run rather joy than suffering, far gladlier obey
I the queen's than I did the king's behest, and address myself
to our present theme.   You are to know then, dainty ladies,
that not far from Sicily there is an islet called Lipari, in which,
no great while ago, there dwelt a damsel, Gostanza by name,
fair as fair could be, and of one of the most honourable families
in the island.   And one Martuccio Gomito, who was also of the
island, a young man most gallant and courteous, and worthy
for his condition, became enamoured of Gostanza ; who in like
manner grew so afire for him that she was ever ill at ease,
except she saw him.   Martuccio, craving her to wife, asked her
of her father, who made answer that, Martuccio being poor,
he was not minded to give her to him.   Mortified to be thus

rejected by reason of poverty, Martuccio took an oath in presence of some of his friends and kinsfolk that Lipari should know him no more, until he was wealthy. So away he sailed, and took to scouring the seas as a rover on the coast of Barbary, preying upon all whose force matched not his own. In which way of life he found Fortune favourable enough, had he but known how to rest and be thankful: but 'twas not enough that he and his comrades in no long time waxed very wealthy; their covetousness was inordinate, and, while they sought to gratify it, they chanced in an encounter with certain Saracen ships to be taken after a long defence, and despoiled, and, most part of them, thrown into the sea by their captors, who, after sinking his ship, took Martuccio with them to Tunis, and clapped him in prison, and there kept him a long time in a very sad plight.

Meanwhile, not by one or two, but by divers and not a few persons, tidings reached Lipari that all that were with Martuccio aboard his bark had perished in the sea. The damsel, whose grief on Martuccio's departure had known no bounds, now hearing that he was dead with the rest, wept a great while, and made up her mind to have done with life; but, lacking the resolution to lay violent hands upon herself, she bethought her how she might devote herself to death by some novel expedient. So one night she stole out of her father's house, and hied her to the port, and there by chance she found, lying a little apart from the other craft, a fishing boat, which, as the owners had but just quitted her, was still equipped with mast and sails and oars. Aboard which boat she forthwith got, and being, like most of the women of the island, not altogether without nautical skill, she rowed some distance out to sea, and then hoisted sail, and cast away oars and tiller, and let the boat drift, deeming that a boat without lading or steersman would certainly be either capsized by the wind or dashed against some rock and broken in pieces, so that escape she could not, even if she would, but must perforce drown. And so, her head wrapped in a mantle, she stretched herself weeping on the floor of the boat. But it fell out quite otherwise than she had conjectured: for, the wind being from the north, and very equable, with next to no sea, the boat kept an even keel, and next day about vespers bore her to land by a city called Susa, full a hundred miles beyond Tunis. To the damsel 'twas all one whether she were at sea or ashore, for, since she had been aboard, she had never once raised, nor, come what might, meant she ever to raise, her head.

Now it so chanced, that, when the boat grounded, there was on the shore a poor woman that was in the employ of some fishermen, whose nets she was just taking out of the sunlight. Seeing the boat under full sail, she marvelled how it should be suffered to drive ashore, and conjectured that the fishermen on board were asleep. So to the boat she hied her, and finding therein only the damsel fast asleep, she called her many times, and at length awakened her; and perceiving by her dress that she was a Christian, she asked her in Latin how it was that she was come thither all alone in the boat. Hearing the Latin speech, the damsel wondered whether the wind had not shifted, and carried her back to Lipari: so up she started, gazed about her, and finding herself ashore and the aspect of the country strange, asked the good woman where she was. To which the good woman made answer:—" My daughter, thou art hard by Susa in Barbary." Whereupon the damsel, sorrowful that God had not seen fit to accord her the boon of death, apprehensive of dishonour, and at her wits' end, sat herself down at the foot of her boat, and burst into tears. Which the good woman saw not without pity, and persuaded her to come with her into her hut, and there by coaxing drew from her how she was come thither; and knowing that she could not but be fasting, she set before her her own coarse bread and some fish and water, and prevailed upon her to eat a little. Gostanza thereupon asked her, who she was that thus spoke Latin; whereto she answered that her name was Carapresa, and that she was from Trapani, where she had served some Christian fishermen. To the damsel, sad indeed though she was, this name Carapresa, wherefore she knew not, seemed to be of happy augury, so that she began to take hope, she knew not why, and to grow somewhat less fain of death: wherefore without disclosing who or whence she was, she earnestly besought the good woman for the love of God to have pity on her youth, and advise her how best to avoid insult. Whereupon Carapresa, good woman that she was, left her in her hut, while with all speed she picked up her nets; and on her return she wrapped her in her own mantle, and led her to Susa. Arrived there, she said to her:—" Gostanza, I shall bring thee to the house of an excellent Saracen lady, for whom I frequently do bits of work, as she has occasion: she is an old lady and compassionate: I will commend thee to her care as best I may, and I doubt not she will right gladly receive thee, and entreat thee as her daughter: and thou wilt serve her, and, while thou art with her, do all thou canst to gain her favour, until such time as God may send thee better fortune ; " and as she said, so she did.

The old lady listened, and then, gazing steadfastly in the damsel's face, shed tears, and taking her hand, kissed her forehead, and led her into the house, where she and some other women dwelt quite by themselves, doing divers kinds of handiwork in silk and palm leaves and leather. Wherein the damsel in a few days acquired some skill, and thenceforth wrought together with them ; and rose wondrous high in the favour and good graces of all the ladies, who soon taught her their language.

Now while the damsel, mourned at home as lost and dead, dwelt thus at Susa, it so befell that, Mariabdela being then King of Tunis, a young chieftain in Granada, of great power, and backed by mighty allies, gave out that the realm of Tunis belonged to him, and having gathered a vast army, made a descent upon Tunis with intent to expel the King from the realm. Martuccio Gomito, who knew the language of Barbary well, heard the tidings in prison, and learning that the King of Tunis was mustering a mighty host for the defence of his kingdom, said to one of the warders that were in charge of him and his comrades :—" If I might have speech of the King, I am confident that the advice that I should give him would secure him the victory." The warder repeated these words to his chief, who forthwith carried them to the King. Wherefore by the King's command Martuccio was brought before him, and being asked by him what the advice, of which he had spoken, might be, answered on this wise :—" Sire, if in old days, when I was wont to visit this country of yours, I duly observed the manner in which you order your battle, methinks you place your main reliance upon archers ; and therefore, if you could contrive that your enemy's supply of arrows should give out and your own continue plentiful, I apprehend that you would win the battle."
" Ay indeed," replied the King, " I make no doubt that, could I but accomplish that, I should conquer." " Nay but, Sire," returned Martuccio, " you may do it, if you will. Listen, and I will tell you how. You must fit the bows of your archers with strings much finer than those that are in common use, and match them with arrows, the notches of which will not admit any but these fine strings ; and this you must do so secretly that your enemy may not know it, else he will find means to be even with you. Which counsel I give you for the following reason :—When your and your enemy's archers

have expended all their arrows, you wot that the enemy will fall to picking up the arrows that your men have shot during the battle, and your men will do the like by the enemy's arrows ; but the enemy will not be able to make use of your men's arrows, by reason that their fine notches will not suffice to admit the stout strings, whereas your men will be in the contrary case in regard of the enemy's arrows, for the fine string will very well receive the large-notched arrow, and so your men will have an abundant supply of arrows, while the enemy will be at a loss for them."

The King, who lacked not sagacity, appreciated Martuccio's advice, and gave full effect to it ; whereby he came out of the war a conqueror, and Martuccio, being raised to the chief place in his favour, waxed rich and powerful. Which matters being bruited throughout the country, it came to the ears of Gostanza that Martuccio Gomito, whom she had long supposed to be dead, was alive ; whereby her love for him, some embers of which still lurked in her heart, burst forth again in sudden flame, and gathered strength, and revived her dead hope. Wherefore she frankly told all her case to the good lady with whom she dwelt, saying that she would fain go to Tunis, that her eyes might have assurance of that which the report received by her ears had made them yearn to see. The lady fell heartily in with the girl's desire, and, as if she had been her mother, embarked with her for Tunis, where on their arrival they were honourably received in the house of one of her kinswomen. Carapresa, who had attended her, being sent to discover what she might touching Martuccio, brought back word that he was alive, and high in honour and place. The gentlewoman was minded that none but herself should apprise Martuccio of the arrival of his Gostanza : wherefore she hied her one day to Martuccio, and said :—" Martuccio, there is come to my house a servant of thine from Lipari, who would fain speak with thee here privily, and for that he would not have me trust another, I am come hither myself to deliver his message." Martuccio thanked her, and forthwith hied him with her to her house : where no sooner did the girl see him than she all but died for joy, and carried away by her feelings, fell upon his neck with open arms and embraced him, and, what with sorrow of his past woes and her present happiness, said never a word, but softly wept. Martuccio regarded her for a while in silent wonder ; then, heaving a sigh, he said :—" Thou livest then, my Gostanza ? Long since I heard that thou wast lost ; nor was aught known of thee

at home." Which said, he tenderly and with tears embraced
her. Gostanza told him all her adventures, and how honourably
she had been entreated by the gentlewoman with whom she had
dwelt. And so long time they conversed, and then Martuccio
parted from her, and hied him back to his lord the King, and
told him all, to wit, his own adventures and those of the girl,
adding that with his leave he was minded to marry her according
to our law. Which matters the King found passing strange;
and having called the girl to him, and learned from her that
'twas even as Martuccio had said:—" Well indeed," quoth he,
" hast thou won thy husband." Then caused he gifts most
ample and excellent to be brought forth, part of which he gave
to Gostanza, and part to Martuccio, leaving them entirely to
their own devices in regard of one another. Then Martuccio,
in terms most honourable, bade farewell to the old lady with
whom Gostanza had dwelt, thanking her for the service she had
rendered to Gostanza, and giving her presents suited to her
condition, and commending her to God, while Gostanza shed
many a tear: after which, by leave of the King, they went
aboard a light bark, taking with them Carapresa, and, sped by a
prosperous breeze, arrived at Lipari, where they were received
with such cheer as 'twere vain to attempt to describe. There
were Martuccio and Gostanza wedded with all pomp and
splendour; and there long time in easeful peace they had
joyance of their love.

NOVEL III

*Pietro Boccamazza runs away with Agnolella, and encounters a
gang of robbers : the girl takes refuge in a wood, and is guided
to a castle. Pietro is taken, but escapes out of the hands of
the robbers, and after some adventures arrives at the castle
where Agnolella is, married her, and returns with her to Rome.*

ENDED Emilia's story, which none of the company spared to
commend, the queen, turning to Elisa, bade her follow suit;
and she, with glad obedience, thus began:—

'Tis a story, sweet ladies, of a woeful night passed by two
indiscreet young lovers that I have in mind; but, as thereon
ensued not a few days of joy, 'tis not inapposite to our arguments
and shall be narrated.

'Tis no long time since at Rome, which, albeit now the tail,[1] was of yore the head, of the world, there dwelt a young man, Pietro Boccamazza by name, a scion of one of the most illustrious of the Roman houses, who became enamoured of a damsel exceeding fair, and amorous withal—her name Agnolella—the daughter of one Gigliuozzo Saullo, a plebeian, but in high repute among the Romans. Nor, loving thus, did Pietro lack the address to inspire in Agnolella a love as ardent as his own. Wherefore, overmastered by his passion, and minded no longer to endure the sore suffering that it caused him, he asked her in marriage. Whereof his kinsfolk were no sooner apprised, than with one accord they came to him and strongly urged him to desist from his purpose : they also gave Gigliuozzo Saullo to understand that he were best to pay no sort of heed to Pietro's words, for that, if he so did, they would never acknowledge him as friend or relative. Thus to see himself debarred of the one way by which he deemed he might attain to his desire, Pietro was ready to die for grief, and, all his kinsfolk notwithstanding, he would have married Gigliuozzo's daughter, had but the father consented. Wherefore at length he made up his mind that, if the girl were willing, nought should stand in the way ; and having through a common friend sounded the damsel and found her apt, he brought her to consent to elope with him from Rome. The affair being arranged, Pietro and she took horse betimes one morning, and sallied forth for Anagni, where Pietro had certain friends, in whom he placed much trust ; and as they rode, time not serving for full joyance of their love, for they feared pursuit, they held converse thereof, and from time to time exchanged a kiss. Now it so befell, that, the way being none too well known to Pietro, when, perhaps eight miles from Rome, they should have turned to the right, they took instead a leftward road. Whereon when they had ridden but little more than two miles, they found themselves close to a petty castle, whence, so soon as they were observed, there issued some dozen men at arms ; and, as they drew near, the damsel, espying them, gave a cry, and said :—" We are attacked, Pietro, let us flee ; " and guiding her nag as best she knew towards a great forest, she planted the spurs in his sides, and so, holding on by the saddle-bow, was borne by the goaded creature into the forest at a gallop. Pietro, who had been too engrossed with her face to give due heed to the way, and thus had not

---

[1] In reference to the forlorn condition of the city while the seat of the papacy was at Avignon, 1308–1377.

been ware, as soon as she, of the approach of the men at arms, was still looking about to see whence they were coming, when they came up with him, and took him prisoner, and forced him to dismount. Then they asked who he was, and, when he told them, they conferred among themselves, saying :—" This is one of the friends of our enemies : what else can we do but relieve him of his nag and of his clothes, and hang him on one of these oaks in scorn of the Orsini ? " To which proposal all agreeing, they bade Pietro strip himself : but while, already divining his fate, he was so doing, an ambuscade of full five-and-twenty men at arms fell suddenly upon them, crying :—" Death, death ! " Thus surprised, they let Pietro go, and stood on the defensive ; but, seeing that the enemy greatly outnumbered them, they took to their heels, the others giving chase. Whereupon Pietro hastily resumed his clothes, mounted his nag, and fled with all speed in the direction which he had seen the damsel take. But finding no road or path through the forest, nor discerning any trace of a horse's hooves, he was—for that he found not the damsel—albeit he deemed himself safe out of the clutches of his captors and their assailants, the most wretched man alive, and fell a-weeping and wandering hither and thither about the forest, uttering Agnolella's name. None answered ; but turn back he dared not : so on he went, not knowing whither he went ; besides which, he was in mortal dread of the wild beasts that infest the forest, as well on account of himself as of the damsel, whom momently he seemed to see throttled by some bear or wolf. Thus did our unfortunate Pietro spend the whole day, wandering about the forest, making it to resound with his cries of Agnolella's name, and harking at times back, when he thought to go forward ; until at last, what with his cries and his tears and his fears and his long fasting, he was so spent that he could go no further. 'Twas then nightfall, and, as he knew not what else to do, he dismounted at the foot of an immense oak, and having tethered his nag to the trunk, climbed up into the branches, lest he should be devoured by the wild beasts during the night. Shortly afterwards the moon rose with a very clear sky, and Pietro, who dared not sleep, lest he should fall, and indeed, had he been secure from that risk, his misery and his anxiety on account of the damsel would not have suffered him to sleep, kept watch, sighing and weeping and cursing his evil luck.

Now the damsel, who, as we said before, had fled she knew not whither, allowing her nag to carry her whithersoever he would, strayed so far into the forest that she lost sight of the place where she had entered it, and spent the whole day just as Pietro had done, wandering about the wilderness, pausing from time to time, and weeping, and uttering his name, and bewailing her evil fortune. At last, seeing that 'twas now the vesper hour and Pietro came not, she struck into a path, which the nag followed, until, after riding some two miles, she espied at some distance a cottage, for which she made with all speed, and found there a good man, well stricken in years, with his wife, who was likewise aged. Seeing her ride up alone, they said :—" Daughter, wherefore ridest thou thus alone at this hour in these parts ? " Weeping, the damsel made answer that she had lost her companion in the forest, and asked how far might Anagni be from there ? " My daughter," returned the good man, " this is not the road to Anagni , 'tis more than twelve miles away." " And how far off," inquired the damsel, " are the nearest houses in which one might find lodging for the night ? " " There are none so near," replied the good man, " that thou canst reach them to-day." " Then, so please you," said the damsel, " since go elsewhither I cannot, for God's sake let me pass the night here with you." Whereto the good man made answer :—" Damsel, welcome art thou to tarry the night with us ; but still thou art to know that these parts are infested both by day and by night by bands, which, be they friends or be they foes, are alike ill to meet with, and not seldom do much despite and mischief, and if by misadventure one of these bands should visit us while thou wert here, and marking thy youth and beauty should do thee despite and dishonour, we should be unable to afford thee any succour. This we would have thee know, that if it should so come to pass, thou mayst not have cause to reproach us." The damsel heard not the old man's words without dismay ; but, seeing that the hour was now late, she answered :—" God, if He be so pleased, will save both you and me from such molestation, and if not, 'tis a much lesser evil to be maltreated by men than to be torn in pieces by the wild beasts in the forest." So saying, she dismounted, and entered the cottage, where, having supped with the poor man and his wife on such humble fare as they had, she laid herself in her clothes beside them in their bed. She slept not, however ; for her own evil plight and that of Pietro, for whom she knew not how to augur aught but evil, kept her sighing and weeping all night long. And towards matins she heard a great noise as of men that marched ; so up she got and hied her into a large courtyard that was in rear of the cottage, and part of which was covered with a great heap of hay, which she espying, hid herself therein, that, if the men came there, they might not so readily find her. Scarce had she done so than the men, who proved to be a strong company of marauders, were at the door of the cottage, which they forced open; and having entered, and found the damsel's nag, still saddled, they asked who was there. The damsel being out of sight, the good man answered:—"There is none here but my wife and I; but this nag, which has given some one the slip, found his way hither last night, and we housed him, lest he should be devoured by the wolves." "So!" said the chief of the band, "as he has no owner, he will come in very handy for us."

Whereupon, in several parties, they ransacked the cottage from top to bottom; and one party went out into the courtyard, where, as they threw aside their lances and targets, it so befell that one of them, not knowing where else to bestow his lance, tossed it into the hay, and was within an ace of killing the damsel that lay hid there, as likewise she of betraying her whereabouts, for the lance all but grazing her left breast, insomuch that the head tore her apparel, she doubted she was wounded, and had given a great shriek, but that, remembering where she was, she refrained for fear. By and by the company cooked them a breakfast of kid's and other meat, and having eaten and drunken, dispersed in divers directions, as their affairs required, taking the girl's nag with them. And when they were gotten some little way off, the good man asked his wife:— "What became of the damsel, our guest of last night, that I have not seen her since we rose?" The good woman answered that she knew not where the damsel was, and went to look for her. The damsel, discovering that the men were gone, came forth of the hay, and the good man, seeing her, was overjoyed that she had not fallen into the hands of the ruffians, and, as day was breaking, said to her:—"Now that day is at hand, we will, so it like thee, escort thee to a castle, some five miles hence, where thou wilt be in safety; but thou must needs go afoot, because these villains, that are but just gone, have taken thy nag with them." The damsel, resigning herself to her loss, besought them for God's sake to take her to the castle: whereupon they set forth, and arrived there about half tierce. Now the castle belonged to one of the Orsini, Liello di Campo di Fiore by name, whose wife, as it chanced, was there. A most kindly and good woman she was, and, recognizing the damsel as soon

as she saw her, gave her a hearty welcome and would fain have
from her a particular account of how she came there. So the
damsel told her the whole story. The lady, to whom Pietro
was also known, as being a friend of her husband, was distressed
to hear of his misadventure, and being told where he was taken,
gave him up for dead. So she said to the damsel:—" Since so
it is that thou knowest not how Pietro has fared, thou shalt
stay here with me until such time as I may have opportunity
to send thee safely back to Rome."

Meanwhile Pietro, perched on his oak in as woeful a plight as
might be, had espied, when he should have been in his first
sleep, a full score of wolves, that, as they prowled, caught sight
of the nag, and straightway were upon him on all sides. The
horse, as soon as he was ware of their approach, strained on the
reins till they snapped, and tried to make good his escape; but,
being hemmed in, was brought to bay, and made a long fight
of it with his teeth and hooves; but in the end they bore him
down and throttled him and forthwith eviscerated him, and,
the whole pack falling upon him, devoured him to the bone
before they had done with him. Whereat Pietro, who felt that
in the nag he had lost a companion and a comfort in his travail,
was sorely dismayed, and began to think that he should never
get out of the forest. But towards dawn, he, perched there in
the oak, almost dead with cold, looking around him as he frequently did, espied about a mile off a huge fire. Wherefore, as
soon as 'twas broad day, he got down, not without trepidation,
from the oak, and bent his steps towards the fire; and being
come to it, he found, gathered about it, a company of shepherds,
eating and making merry, who took pity on him and made
him welcome. And when he had broken his fast and warmed
himself, he told them the mishap that had befallen him, and
how it was that he was come there alone, and asked them if
there was a farm or castle in those parts, whither he might
betake him. The shepherds said that about three miles away
there was a castle belonging to Liello di Campo di Fiore, where
his lady was then tarrying. Pietro, much comforted, requested
to be guided thither by some of their company; whereupon two
of them right gladly escorted him. So Pietro arrived at the
castle, where he found some that knew him; and while he was
endeavouring to set on foot a search for the damsel in the forest,
the lady summoned him to her presence, and he, forthwith
obeying, and seeing Agnolella with her, was the happiest man
that ever was. He yearned till he all but swooned to go and

embrace her, but refrained, for bashfulness, in the lady's presence. And overjoyed as he was, the joy of the damsel was no less. The lady received him with great cheer, and though, when she had heard the story of his adventures from his own lips, she chid him not a little for having set at nought the wishes of his kinsfolk ; yet, seeing that he was still of the same mind, and that the damsel was also constant, she said to herself :— To what purpose give I myself all this trouble ? they love one another, they know one another ; they love with equal ardour ; their love is honourable, and I doubt not is well pleasing to God, seeing that the one has escaped the gallows and the other the lance, and both the wild beasts : wherefore be it as they would have it. Then, turning to them, she said :—" If 'tis your will to be joined in wedlock as man and wife, mine jumps with it : here shall your nuptials be solemnized and at Liello's charges, and for the rest I will see that your peace is made with your kinsfolk." So in the castle the pair were wedded, Pietro only less blithe than Agnolella, the lady ordering the nuptials as honourably as might be in her mountain-home, and there they had most sweet joyance of the first fruits of their love. So some days they tarried there, and then accompanied by the lady with a strong escort, they took horse and returned to Rome, where, very wroth though she found Pietro's kinsfolk for what he had done, the lady re-established solid peace between him and them ; and so at Rome Pietro and Agnolella lived together to a good old age in great tranquillity and happiness.

NOVEL IV

Ricciardo Manardi is found by Messer Lizio da Valbona with his daughter, whom he marries, and remains at peace with her father.

In silence Elisa received the praise bestowed on her story by her fair companions ; and then the queen called for a story from Filostrato, who with a laugh began on this wise :— Chidden have I been so often and by so many of you for the sore burden, which I laid upon you, of discourse harsh and meet for tears, that, as some compensation for such annoy, I deem myself bound to tell you somewhat that may cause you to laugh a little : wherefore my story, which will be of the briefest, shall be of a love, the course whereof, save for sighs and a brief passage of fear mingled with shame, ran smooth to a happy consummation.

Know then, noble ladies, that 'tis no long time since there dwelt in Romagna a right worthy and courteous knight, Messer Lizio da Valbona by name, who was already verging upon old age, when, as it happened, there was born to him of his wife, Madonna Giacomina, a daughter, who, as she grew up, became the fairest and most debonair of all the girls of those parts, and, for that she was the only daughter left to them, was most dearly loved and cherished by her father and mother, who guarded her with most jealous care, thinking to arrange some great match for her. Now there was frequently in Messer Lizio's house, and much in his company, a fine, lusty young man, one Ricciardo de' Manardi da Brettinoro, whom Messer Lizio and his wife would as little have thought of mistrusting as if he had been their own son : who, now and again taking note of the damsel, that she was very fair and graceful, and in bearing and behaviour most commendable, and of marriageable age, fell vehemently in love with her, which love he was very careful to conceal. The damsel detected it, however, and in like manner plunged headlong into love with him, to Ricciardo's no small satisfaction. Again and again he was on the point of speaking to her, but refrained for fear ; at length, however, he summoned up his courage, and seizing his opportunity, thus addressed her :—
" Caterina, I implore thee, suffer me not to die for love of thee." Whereto the damsel forthwith responded :—" Nay, God grant that it be not rather that I die for love of thee." Greatly exhilarated and encouraged, Ricciardo made answer :—" 'Twill never be by default of mine that thou lackest aught that may pleasure thee ; but it rests with thee to find the means to save thy life and mine." Then said the damsel :—" Thou seest, Ricciardo, how closely watched I am, insomuch that I see not how 'twere possible for thee to come to me ; but if thou seest aught that I may do without dishonour, speak the word, and I will do it." Ricciardo was silent a while, pondering many matters : then, of a sudden, he said :—" Sweet my Caterina, there is but one way that I can see, to wit, that thou shouldst sleep either on or where thou mightst have access to the terrace by thy father's garden, where, so I but knew that thou wouldst be there at night, I would without fail contrive to meet thee, albeit 'tis very high." " As for my sleeping there," replied Caterina, " I doubt not that it may be managed, if thou art sure that thou canst join me." Ricciardo answered in the

affirmative. Whereupon they exchanged a furtive kiss, and parted.

On the morrow, it being now towards the close of May, the damsel began complaining to her mother that by reason of the excessive heat she had not been able to get any sleep during the night. "Daughter," said the lady, "what heat was there? Nay, there was no heat at all." "Had you said, ' to my thinking,' mother," rejoined Caterina, "you would perhaps have said sooth; but you should bethink you how much more heat girls have in them than ladies that are advanced in years." "True, my daughter," returned the lady, "but I cannot order that it shall be hot and cold, as thou perchance wouldst like; we must take the weather as we find it, and as the seasons provide it: perchance to-night it will be cooler, and thou wilt sleep better." "God grant it be so," said Caterina, "but 'tis not wonted for the nights to grow cooler as the summer comes on." "What then," said the lady, "wouldst thou have me do?" "With your leave and my father's," answered Caterina, "I should like to have a little bed made up on the terrace by his room and over his garden, where, hearing the nightingales sing, and being in a much cooler place, I should sleep much better than in your room." Whereupon:—"Daughter, be of good cheer," said the mother; "I will speak to thy father, and we will do as he shall decide." So the lady told Messer Lizio what had passed between her and the damsel; but he, being old and perhaps for that reason a little morose, said:—"What nightingale is this, to whose chant she would fain sleep? I will see to it that the cicalas shall yet lull her to sleep." Which speech, coming to Caterina's ears, gave her such offence, that for anger, rather than by reason of the heat, she not only slept not herself that night, but suffered not her mother to sleep, keeping up a perpetual complaint of the great heat. Wherefore her mother hied her in the morning to Messer Lizio, and said to him:—"Sir, you hold your daughter none too dear; what difference can it make to you that she lie on the terrace? She has tossed about all night long by reason of the heat; and besides, can you wonder that she, girl that she is, loves to hear the nightingale sing? Young folk naturally affect their likes." Whereto Messer Lizio made answer:—"Go, make her a bed there to your liking, and set a curtain round it, and let her sleep there, and hear the nightingale sing to her heart's content." Which the damsel no sooner learned, than she had a bed made there with intent to sleep there that same night; wherefore she watched until she saw Ricciardo, whom by a concerted sign she gave to understand what he was to do. Messer Lizio, as soon as he had heard the damsel go to bed, locked a door that led from his room to the terrace, and went to sleep himself. When all was quiet, Ricciardo with the help of a ladder got upon a wall, and standing thereon laid hold of certain toothings of another wall, and not without great exertion and risk, had he fallen, clambered up on to the terrace, where the damsel received him quietly with the heartiest of cheer. Many a kiss they exchanged; and then got them to bed, where well-nigh all night long they had solace and joyance of one another, and made the nightingale sing not a few times. But, brief being the night and great their pleasure, towards dawn, albeit they wist it not, they fell asleep, Caterina's right arm encircling Ricciardo's neck, while with her left hand she held him by that part of his person which your modesty, my ladies, is most averse to name in the company of men. So, peacefully they slept, and were still asleep when day broke and Messer Lizio rose; and calling to mind that his daughter slept on the terrace, softly opened the door, saying to himself:—Let me see what sort of night's rest the nightingale has afforded our Caterina? And having entered, he gently raised the curtain that screened the bed, and saw Ricciardo asleep with her and in her embrace as described, both being quite naked and uncovered; and having taken note of Ricciardo, he went away, and hied him to his lady's room, and called her, saying:—"Up, up, wife, come and see; for thy daughter has fancied the nightingale to such purpose that she has caught him, and holds him in her hand." "How can this be?" said the lady. "Come quickly, and thou shalt see," replied Messer Lizio. So the lady huddled on her clothes, and silently followed Messer Lizio, and when they were come to the bed, and had raised the curtain, Madonna Giacomina saw plainly enough how her daughter had caught, and did hold the nightingale, whose song she had so longed to hear. Whereat the lady, deeming that Ricciardo had played her a cruel trick, would have cried out and upbraided him; but Messer Lizio said to her:—"Wife, as thou valuest my love, say not a word; for in good sooth, seeing that she has caught him, he shall be hers. Ricciardo is a gentleman and wealthy; an alliance with him cannot but be to our advantage: if he would part from me on good terms, he must first marry her, so that the nightingale shall prove to have been put in his own cage and not in that of another." Whereby the lady was reassured, see-

ing that her husband took the affair so quietly, and that her
daughter had had a good night, and was rested, and had caught
the nightingale. So she kept silence; nor had they long to
wait before Ricciardo awoke; and, seeing that 'twas broad
day, deemed that 'twas as much as his life was worth, and
aroused Caterina, saying :—" Alas! my soul, what shall we do,
now that day has come and surprised me here?" Which
question Messer Lizio answered by coming forward, and saying :—" We shall do well." At sight of him Ricciardo felt as
if his heart were torn out of his body, and sate up in the bed,
and said :—" My lord, I cry you mercy for God's sake. I wot
that my disloyalty and delinquency have merited death;
wherefore deal with me even as it may seem best to you: however, I pray you, if so it may be, to spare my life, that I die
not." " Ricciardo," replied Messer Lizio, " the love I bore
thee, and the faith I reposed in thee, merited a better return;
but still, as so it is, and youth has seduced thee into such a
transgression, redeem thy life, and preserve my honour, by
making Caterina thy lawful spouse, that thine, as she has been
for this past night, she may remain for the rest of her life. In
this way thou mayst secure my peace and thy safety; otherwise
commend thy soul to God." Pending this colloquy, Caterina
let go the nightingale, and having covered herself, began with
many a tear to implore her father to forgive Ricciardo, and
Ricciardo to do as Messer Lizio required, that thereby they
might securely count upon a long continuance of such nights of
delight. But there needed not much supplication; for, what
with remorse for the wrong done, and the wish to make amends,
and the fear of death, and the desire to escape it, and above all
ardent love, and the craving to possess the beloved one, Ricciardo
lost no time in making frank avowal of his readiness to do as
Messer Lizio would have him. Wherefore Messer Lizio, having
borrowed a ring from Madonna Giacomina, Ricciardo did there
and then in their presence wed Caterina. Which done, Messer
Lizio and the lady took their leave, saying :—" Now rest ye a
while; for so perchance 'twere better for you than if ye rose."
And so they left the young folks, who forthwith embraced, and
not having travelled more than six miles during the night, went
two miles further before they rose, and so concluded their first
day. When they were risen, Ricciardo and Messer Lizio discussed the matter with more formality; and some days afterwards Ricciardo, as was meet, married the damsel anew in
presence of their friends and kinsfolk, and brought her home

with great pomp, and celebrated his nuptials with due dignity
and splendour. And so for many a year thereafter he lived
with her in peace and happiness, and snared the nightingales
day and night to his heart's content.

NOVEL V

*Guidotto da Cremona dies leaving a girl to Giacomino da Pavia.
She has two lovers in Faenza, to wit, Giannole di Severino and
Minghino di Mingole, who fight about her. She is discovered
to be Giannole's sister, and is given to Minghino to wife.*

ALL the ladies laughed so heartily over the story of the nightingale, that, even when Filostrato had finished, they could not
control their merriment. However, when the laughter was
somewhat abated, the queen said :—" Verily if thou didst
yesterday afflict us, to-day thou hast tickled us to such purpose
that none of us may justly complain of thee." Then, as the
turn had now come round to Neifile, she bade her give them a
story. And thus, blithely, Neifile began :—As Filostrato went
to Romagna for the matter of his discourse, I too am fain to
make a short journey through the same country in what I am
about to relate to you.

     I say, then, that there dwelt of yore in the city of Fano two
Lombards, the one ycleped Guidotto da Cremona and the other
Giacomino da Pavia, men advanced in life, who, being soldiers,
had spent the best part of their youth in feats of arms. Now
Guidotto, being at the point of death, and having no son or
any friend or kinsman in whom he placed more trust than in
Giacomino, left him a girl of about ten years, and all that he
had in the world ; and so, having given him to know not a little
of his affairs, he died. About the same time the city of Faenza,
which had long been at war and in a most sorry plight, began
to recover some measure of prosperity ; and thereupon liberty
to return thither on honourable terms was accorded to all that
were so minded. Whither, accordingly, Giacomino, who had
dwelt there aforetime, and liked the place, returned with all
his goods and chattels, taking with him the girl left him by
Guidotto, whom he loved and entreated as his daughter. The
girl grew up as beautiful a maiden as was to be found in the
city ; and no less debonair and modest was she than fair.
Wherefore she lacked not admirers ; but above all two young

men, both very gallant and of equal merit, the one Giannole di
Severino, the other Minghino di Mingole, affected her with so
ardent a passion, that, growing jealous, they came to hate one
another with an inordinate hatred. Right gladly would each
have espoused her, she being now fifteen years old, but that his
kinsmen forbade it ; wherefore seeing that neither might have
her in an honourable way, each determined to compass his end
as best he might.

Now Giacomino had in his house an ancient maid, and a man,
by name Crivello, a very pleasant and friendly sort of fellow,
with whom Giannole grew familiar, and in due time confided
to him all his love, praying him to further the attainment of his
desire, and promising to reward him handsomely, if he did so.
Crivello made answer :—" Thou must know that there is but
one way in which I might be of service to thee in this affair :
I might contrive that thou shouldst be where she is when
Giacomino is gone off to supper ; but, were I to presume to say
aught to her on thy behalf, she would never listen to me. This,
if it please thee, I promise to do for thee, and will be as good as
my word ; and then thou canst do whatever thou mayst deem
most expedient." Giannole said that he asked no more ; and
so 'twas arranged.

Meanwhile Minghino on his part had made friends with the
maid, on whom he had so wrought that she had carried several
messages to the girl, and had gone far to kindle her to his love,
and furthermore had promised to contrive that he should meet
her when for any cause Giacomino should be from home in the
evening. And so it befell that no long time after these parleys,
Giacomino, by Crivello's management, was to go sup at the
house of a friend, and by preconcert between Crivello and
Giannole, upon signal given, Giannole was to come to Giacomino's house and find the door open. The maid, on her part,
witting nought of the understanding between Crivello and Giannole, let Minghino know that Giacomino would not sup at
home, and bade him be near the house, so that he might come
and enter it on sight of a signal from her. The evening came ;
neither of the lovers knew aught of what the other was about ;
but, being suspicious of one another, they came to take possession, each with his own company of armed friends. Minghino,
while awaiting the signal, rested with his company in the house
of one of his friends hard by the girl's house : Giannole with his
company was posted a little farther off. Crivello and the maid,
when Giacomino was gone, did each their endeavour to get the

other out of the way. Crivello said to the maid :—" How is it thou takest not thyself off to bed, but goest still hither and thither about the house ? " And the maid said to Crivello :— " Nay, but why goest thou not after thy master ? Thou hast supped ; what awaitest thou here ? " And so, neither being able to make the other quit the post, Crivello, the hour concerted with Giannole being come, said to himself :—What care I for her ? If she will not keep quiet, 'tis like to be the worse for her. Whereupon he gave the signal, and hied him to the door, which he had no sooner opened, than Giannole entered with two of his companions, and finding the girl in the saloon, laid hands on her with intent to carry her off. The girl struggled, and shrieked amain, as did also the maid. Minghino, fearing the noise, hasted to the spot with his companions ; and, seeing that the girl was already being borne across the threshold, they drew their swords, and cried out in chorus :—" Ah ! Traitors that ye are, ye are all dead men ! 'Twill go otherwise than ye think for. What means this force ? " Which said, they fell upon them with their swords, while the neighbours, alarmed by the noise, came hurrying forth with lights and arms, and protested that 'twas an outrage, and took Minghino's part. So, after a prolonged struggle, Minghino wrested the girl from Giannole, and set her again in Giacomino's house. Nor were the combatants separated before the officers of the Governor of the city came up and arrested not a few of them ; among them Minghino and Giannole and Crivello, whom they marched off to prison. However, peace being restored and Giacomino returned, 'twas with no little chagrin that he heard of the affair ; but finding upon investigation that the girl was in no wise culpable, he was somewhat reassured ; and determined, lest the like should again happen, to bestow the girl in marriage as soon as might be.

On the morrow the kinsfolk of the two lovers, having learned the truth of the matter, and knowing what evil might ensue to the captives, if Giacomino should be minded to take the course which he reasonably might, came and gave him good words, beseeching him to let the kindly feeling, the love, which they believed he bore to them, his suppliants, count for more with him than the wrong that the hare-brained gallants had done him, and on their part and their own offering to make any amend that he might require. Giacomino, who had seen many things in his time, and lacked not sound sense, made answer briefly :— " Gentlemen, were I in my own country, as I am in yours, I hold myself in such sort your friend that nought would I do in this matter, or in any other, save what might be agreeable to you : besides which, I have the more reason to consider your wishes, because 'tis against you yourselves that you have offended, inasmuch as this damsel, whatever many folk may suppose, is neither of Cremona nor of Pavia, but is of Faenza, albeit neither I nor she, nor he from whom I had her, did ever wot whose daughter she was : wherefore, touching that you ask of me, I will even do just as you bid me." The worthy men found it passing strange that the girl should be of Faenza ; and having thanked Giacomino for his handsome answer, they besought him that he would be pleased to tell them how she had come into his hands, and how he knew that she was of Faenza. To whom Giacomino replied on this wise :—" A comrade and friend I had, Guidotto da Cremona, who, being at the point of death, told me that, when this city of Faenza was taken by the Emperor Frederic, he and his comrades, entering one of the houses during the sack, found there good store of booty, and never a soul save this girl, who, being two years old or thereabouts, greeted him as father as he came up the stairs ; wherefore he took pity on her, and carried her with whatever else was in the house away with him to Fano ; where on his deathbed he left her to me, charging me in due time to bestow her in marriage, and give her all his goods and chattels by way of dowry : but, albeit she is now of marriageable age, I have not been able to provide her with a husband to my mind ; though right glad should I be to do so, that nought like the event of yesterday may again befall me."

Now among the rest of those present was one Guglielmo da Medicina, who had been with Guidotto on that occasion, and knew well whose house it was that Guidotto had sacked ; and seeing the owner there among the rest, he went up to him, and said :—" Dost hear, Bernabuccio, what Giacomino says ? " " Ay," answered Bernabuccio, " and I gave the more heed thereto, for that I call to mind that during those disorders I lost a little daughter of just the age that Giacomino speaks of." " 'Tis verily she then," said Guglielmo, " for once when I was with Guidotto I heard him describe what house it was that he had sacked, and I wist that 'twas thine. Wherefore search thy memory if there be any sign by which thou thinkest to recognize her, and let her be examined that thou mayst be assured that she is thy daughter." So Bernabuccio pondered a while, and then recollected that she ought to have a scar, shewing like a

tiny cross, above her left ear, being where he had excised a
tumour a little while before that affair : wherefore without
delay he went up to Giacomino, who was still there, and besought
him to let him go home with him and see the damsel. Giacomino gladly did so, and no sooner was the girl brought into
Bernabuccio's presence, than, as he beheld her, 'twas as if he
saw the face of her mother, who was still a beautiful woman.
However, he would not rest there, but besought Giacomino of
his grace to permit him to lift a lock or two of hair above her
left ear ; whereto Giacomino consented. So Bernabuccio
approached her where she stood somewhat shamefast, and with
his right hand lifted her locks, and, seeing the cross, wist that
in very truth she was his daughter, and tenderly wept and
embraced her, albeit she withstood him ; and then, turning to
Giacomino, he said :—" My brother, the girl is my daughter ;
'twas my house that Guidotto sacked, and so sudden was the
assault that my wife, her mother, forgot her, and we have
always hitherto supposed, that, my house being burned that
same day, she perished in the flames." Catching his words,
and seeing that he was advanced in years, the girl inclined to
believe him, and impelled by some occult instinct, suffered his
embraces, and melting, mingled her tears with his. Bernabuccio forthwith sent for her mother and her sisters and other
kinswomen and her brothers, and having shewn her to them all,
and told the story, after they had done her great cheer and
embraced her a thousand times, to Giacomino's no small delight,
he brought her home with him. Which coming to the ears of
the Governor of the city, the worthy man, knowing that Giannole, whom he had in ward, was Bernabuccio's son and the girl's
brother, made up his mind to deal leniently with Giannole :
wherefore he took upon himself the part of mediator in the
affair, and having made peace between Bernabuccio and Giacomino and Giannole and Minghino, gave Agnesa—such was the
damsel's name—to Minghino to wife, to the great delight of all
Minghino's kinsfolk, and set at liberty not only Giannole and
Minghino but Crivello, and the others their confederates in the
affair. Whereupon Minghino with the blithest of hearts wedded
Agnesa with all due pomp and circumstance, and brought her
home, where for many a year thereafter he lived with her in
peace and prosperity.

NOVEL VI

*Gianni di Procida, being found with a damsel that he loves, and
who had been given to King Frederic, is bound with her to a
stake, so to be burned.　He is recognized by Ruggieri dell'
Oria, is delivered, and marries her.*

NEIFILE'S story, with which the ladies were greatly delighted,
being ended, the queen called for one from Pampinea ; who
forthwith raised her noble countenance, and thus began :—
Mighty indeed, gracious ladies, are the forces of Love, and great
are the labours and excessive and unthought-of the perils which
they induce lovers to brave ; as is manifest enough by what we
have heard to-day and on other occasions : howbeit I mean to
shew you the same once more by a story of an enamoured youth.

Hard by Naples is the island of Ischia, in which there dwelt
aforetime with other young damsels one, Restituta by name,
daughter of one Marin Bolgaro, a gentleman of the island.　Very
fair was she, and blithe of heart, and by a young gallant, Gianni
by name, of the neighbouring islet of Procida, was beloved
more dearly than life, and in like measure returned his love.
Now, not to mention his daily resort to Ischia to see her, there
were times not a few when Gianni, not being able to come by
a boat, would swim across from Procida by night, that he might
have sight, if of nought else, at least of the walls of her house.
And while their love burned thus fervently, it so befell that
one summer's day, as the damsel was all alone on the seashore,
picking her way from rock to rock, detaching, as she went,
shells from their beds with a knife, she came to a recess among
the rocks, where for the sake, as well of the shade as of the
comfort afforded by a spring of most cool water that was there,
some Sicilian gallants, that were come from Naples, had put in
with their felucca.　Who, having taken note of the damsel,
that she was very fair, and that she was not yet ware of them,
and was alone, resolved to capture her, and carry her away ;
nor did they fail to give effect to their resolve ; but, albeit she
shrieked amain, they laid hands on her, and set her aboard
their boat, and put to sea.　Arrived at Calabria, they fell a-
wrangling as to whose the damsel should be, and in brief each
claimed her for his own : wherefore, finding no means of coming
to an agreement, and fearing that worse might befall them, and
she bring misfortune upon them, they resolved with one accord

to give her to Frederic, King of Sicily, who was then a young man, and took no small delight in commodities of that quality ; and so, being come to Palermo, they did.

Marking her beauty, the King set great store by her ; but as she was somewhat indisposed, he commanded that, till she was stronger, she should be lodged and tended in a very pretty villa that was in one of his gardens, which he called Cuba ; and so 'twas done. The purloining of the damsel caused no small stir in Ischia, more especially because 'twas impossible to discover by whom she had been carried off. But Gianni, more concerned than any other, despairing of finding her in Ischia, and being apprised of the course the felucca had taken, equipped one himself, and put to sea, and in hot haste scoured the whole coast from Minerva to Scalea in Calabria, making everywhere diligent search for the damsel, and in Scalea learned that she had been taken by Sicilian mariners to Palermo. Whither, accordingly, he hied him with all speed ; and there after long search discovering that she had been given to the King, who kept her at Cuba, he was sore troubled, insomuch that he now scarce ventured to hope that he should ever set eyes on her, not to speak of having her for his own, again. But still, holden by Love, and seeing that none there knew him, he sent the felucca away, and tarried there, and frequently passing by Cuba, he chanced one day to catch sight of her at a window, and was seen of her, to their great mutual satisfaction. And Gianni, taking note that the place was lonely, made up to her, and had such speech of her as he might, and being taught by her after what fashion he must proceed, if he would have further speech of her, he departed, but not till he had made himself thoroughly acquainted with the configuration of the place ; and having waited until night was come and indeed far spent, he returned thither, and though the ascent was such that 'twould scarce have afforded lodgment to a woodpecker, won his way up and entered the garden, where, finding a pole, he set it against the window which the damsel had pointed out as hers, and thereby swarmed up easily enough.

The damsel had aforetime shewn herself somewhat distant towards him, being careful of her honour, but now deeming it already lost, she had bethought her that there was none to whom she might more worthily give herself than to him ; and reckoning upon inducing him to carry her off, she had made up her mind to gratify his every desire ; and to that end had left the window open that his ingress might be unimpeded.

So, finding it open, Gianni softly entered, lay down beside the damsel, who was awake, and before they went further, opened to him all her mind, beseeching him most earnestly to take her thence, and carry her off. Gianni replied that there was nought that would give him so much pleasure, and that without fail, upon leaving her, he would make all needful arrangements for bringing her away when he next came. Whereupon with exceeding great delight they embraced one another, and plucked that boon than which Love has no greater to bestow ; and having so done divers times, they unwittingly fell asleep in one another's arms.

Now towards daybreak the King, who had been greatly charmed with the damsel at first sight, happened to call her to mind, and feeling himself fit, resolved, notwithstanding the hour, to go lie with her a while ; and so, attended by a few of his servants, he hied him privily to Cuba. Having entered the house, he passed (the door being softly opened) into the room in which he knew the damsel slept. A great blazing torch was borne before him, and so, as he bent his glance on the bed, he espied the damsel and Gianni lying asleep, naked and in one another's arms. Whereat he was seized with a sudden and vehement passion of wrath, insomuch that, albeit he said never a word, he could scarce refrain from slaying both of them there and then with a dagger that he had with him. Then, bethinking him that 'twere the depth of baseness in any man—not to say a king—to slay two naked sleepers, he mastered himself, and determined to do them to death in public and by fire. Wherefore, turning to a single companion that he had with him, he said :—" What thinkest thou of this base woman, in whom I had placed my hope ? " And then he asked whether he knew the gallant, that had presumed to enter his house to do him such outrage and despite. Whereto the other replied that he minded not ever to have seen him. Thereupon the King hied him out of the room in a rage, and bade take the two lovers, naked as they were, and bind them, and, as soon as 'twas broad day, bring them to Palermo, and bind them back to back to a stake in the piazza, there to remain until tierce, that all might see them, after which they were to be burned, as they had deserved. And having so ordered, he went back to Palermo, and shut himself up in his room, very wroth.

No sooner was he gone than there came unto the two lovers folk not a few, who, having awakened them, did forthwith ruthlessly take and bind them : whereat, how they did grieve and tremble for their lives, and weep and bitterly bewail their fate, may readily be understood.

Pursuant to the King's commandment they were brought to Palermo, and bound to a stake in the piazza ; and before their eyes faggots and fire were made ready to burn them at the hour appointed by the King. Great was the concourse of the folk of Palermo, both men and women, that came to see the two lovers, the men all agog to feast their eyes on the damsel, whom they lauded for shapeliness and loveliness, and no less did the women commend the gallant, whom in like manner they crowded to see, for the same qualities. Meanwhile the two hapless lovers, both exceeding shamefast, stood with bent heads bitterly bewailing their evil fortune, and momently expecting their death by the cruel fire. So they awaited the time appointed by the King ; but their offence being bruited abroad, the tidings reached the ears of Ruggieri dell' Oria, a man of peerless worth, and at that time the King's admiral, who, being likewise minded to see them, came to the place where they were bound, and after gazing on the damsel and finding her very fair, turned to look at the gallant, whom with little trouble he recognized, and drawing nearer to him, he asked him if he were Gianni di Procida. Gianni raised his head, and recognizing the admiral, made answer :—" My lord, he, of whom you speak, I was ; but I am now as good as no more." The admiral then asked him what it was that had brought him to such a pass. Whereupon :—" Love and the King's wrath," quoth Gianni. The admiral induced him to be more explicit, and having learned from him exactly how it had come about, was turning away, when Gianni called him back, saying : —" Oh ! my lord, if so it may be, procure me one favour of him by whose behest I thus stand here." " What favour ? " demanded Ruggieri. " I see," returned Gianni, " that die I must, and that right soon. I crave, then, as a favour, that, whereas this damsel and I, that have loved one another more dearly than life, are here set back to back, we may be set face to face, that I may have the consolation of gazing on her face as I depart." Ruggieri laughed as he replied :—" With all my heart. I will so order it that thou shalt see enough of her to tire of her." He then left him and charged the executioners to do nothing more without further order of the King ; and being assured of their obedience, he hied him forthwith to the King, to whom, albeit he found him in a wrathful mood, he spared not to speak his mind, saying :—" Sire, wherein

have they wronged thee, those two young folk, whom thou
hast ordered to be burned down there in the piazza ? " The
King told him. Whereupon Ruggieri continued :—" Their
offence does indeed merit such punishment, but not at thy
hands, and if misdeeds should not go unpunished, services
should not go unrewarded ; nay, may warrant indulgence and
mercy. Knowest thou who they are whom thou wouldst have
burned ? " The King signified that he did not. Whereupon
Ruggieri :—" But I," quoth he, " am minded that thou
shouldst know them, to the end that thou mayst know with
what discretion thou surrenderest thyself to a transport of
rage. The young man is the son of Landolfo di Procida,
brother of Messer Gianni di Procida, to whom thou owest
it that thou art lord and king of this island. The damsel is
a daughter of Marin Bolgaro, whose might alone to-day prevents
Ischia from throwing off thy yoke. Moreover, these young
folk have long been lovers, and 'tis for that the might of Love
constrained them, and not that they would do despite to thy
lordship, that they have committed this offence, if indeed 'tis
meet to call that an offence which young folk do for Love's
sake. Wherefore, then, wouldst thou do them to death, when
thou shouldst rather do them all cheer, and honour them with
lordly gifts ? " The King gave ear to Ruggieri's words, and
being satisfied that he spoke sooth, repented him, not only of
his evil purpose, but of what he had already done, and forthwith gave order to loose the two young folk from the stake,
and bring them before him ; and so 'twas done. And having
fully apprised himself of their case, he saw fit to make them
amends of the wrong he had done them with honours and
largess. Wherefore he caused them to be splendidly arrayed,
and being assured that they were both minded to wed, he
himself gave Gianni his bride, and loading them with rich
presents, sent them well content back to Ischia, where they
were welcomed with all festal cheer, and lived long time thereafter to their mutual solace and delight.

NOVEL VII

Teodoro, being enamoured of Violante, daughter of Messer Amerigo, his lord, gets her with child, and is sentenced to the gallows ; but while he is being scourged thither, he is recognized by his father, and being set at large, takes Violante to wife.

WHILE they doubted whether the two lovers would be burned, the ladies were all fear and suspense ; but when they heard of their deliverance, they all with one accord put on a cheerful countenance, praising God. The story ended, the queen ordained that the next should be told by Lauretta, who blithely thus began :—

Fairest ladies, what time good King Guglielmo ruled Sicily there dwelt on the island a gentleman, Messer Amerigo Abate da Trapani by name, who was well provided, as with other temporal goods, so also with children. For which cause being in need of servants, he took occasion of the appearance in Trapani waters of certain Genoese corsairs from the Levant, who, scouring the coast of Armenia, had captured not a few boys, to purchase of them some of these youngsters, supposing them to be Turks ; among whom, albeit most shewed as mere shepherd boys, there was one, Teodoro by name, whose less rustic mien seemed to betoken gentle blood. Who, though still treated as a slave, was suffered to grow up in the house with Messer Amerigo's children, and, nature getting the better of circumstance, bore himself with such grace and dignity that Messer Amerigo gladly gave him his freedom, and still deeming him to be a Turk, had him baptized and named Pietro, and made him his majordomo, and placed much trust in him. Now among the other children that grew up in Messer Amerigo's house was his fair and dainty daughter, Violante ; and, as her father was in no hurry to give her in marriage, it so befell that she became enamoured of Pietro ; but, for all her love and the great conceit she had of his qualities and conduct, she nevertheless was too shamefast to discover her passion to him. However, Love spared her the pains, for Pietro had cast many a furtive glance in her direction, and had grown so enamoured of her that 'twas never well with him except he saw her ; but great was his fear lest any should detect his passion, for he deemed 'twould be the worse for him. The damsel, who was fain indeed of the sight of him, understood his case ; and to encourage him dissembled not her exceeding great satisfaction. On which footing they remained a great while, neither venturing to say aught to the other, much as both longed to do so. But, while they both burned with a mutual flame, Fortune, as if their entanglement were of her preordaining, found means to banish the fear and hesitation that kept them tongue-tied.

Messer Amerigo possessed, a mile or so from Trapani, a goodly estate, to which he was wont not seldom to resort with his daughter and other ladies by way of recreation ; and on one of these days, while there they tarried with Pietro, whom they had brought with them, suddenly, as will sometimes happen in summer, the sky became overcast with black clouds, inso-much that the lady and her companions, lest the storm should surprise them there, set out on their return to Trapani, making all the haste they might. But Pietro and the girl being young, and sped perchance by Love no less than by fear of the storm, completely outstripped her mother and the other ladies ; and when they were gotten so far ahead as to be well-nigh out of sight of the lady and all the rest, the thunder burst upon them peal upon peal, hard upon which came a fall of hail very thick and close, from which the lady sought shelter in the house of a husbandman. Pietro and the damsel, finding no more con-venient refuge, betook them to an old, and all but ruinous, and now deserted, cottage, which, however, still had a bit of roof left, whereunder they both took their stand in such close quarters, owing to the exiguity of the shelter, that they perforce touched one another. Which contact was the occasion that they gathered somewhat more courage to disclose their love ; and so it was that Pietro began on this wise :—" Now would to God that this hail might never cease, that so I might stay here for ever ! " " And well content were I," returned the damsel. And by and by their hands met, not without a tender pressure, and then they fell to embracing and so to kissing one another, while the hail continued. And not to dwell on every detail, the sky was not clear before they had known the last degree of love's felicity, and had taken thought how they might secretly enjoy one another in the future. The cottage being close to the city gate, they hied them thither, as soon as the storm was overpast, and having there awaited the lady, returned home with her. Nor, using all discretion, did they fail thereafter to meet from time to time in secret, to their no small solace ; and the affair went so far that the damsel conceived,

whereby they were both not a little disconcerted ; insomuch
that the damsel employed many artifices to arrest the course
of nature, but to no effect. Wherefore Pietro, being in fear
of his life, saw nothing for it but flight, and told her so. Whereupon :—" If thou leave me," quoth she, " I shall certainly
kill myself." Much as he loved her, Pietro answered :—" Nay
but, my lady, wherefore wouldst thou have me tarry here ?
Thy pregnancy will discover our offence : thou wilt be readily
forgiven ; but 'twill be my woeful lot to bear the penalty of
thy sin and mine." " Pietro," returned the damsel, " too
well will they wot of my offence, but be sure that, if thou confess
not, none will ever wot of thine." Then quoth he :—" Since
thou givest me this promise, I will stay ; but mind thou
keep it."

The damsel, who had done her best to keep her condition
secret, saw at length by the increase of her bulk that 'twas
impossible : wherefore one day most piteously bewailing herself, she made her avowal to her mother, and besought her
to shield her from the consequences. Distressed beyond
measure, the lady chid her severely, and then asked her how
it had come to pass. The damsel, to screen Pietro, invented
a story by which she put another complexion on the affair.
The lady believed her, and, that her fall might not be discovered,
took her off to one of their estates ; where, the time of her
delivery being come, and she, as women do in such a case,
crying out for pain, it so befell that Messer Amerigo, whom the
lady expected not, as indeed he was scarce ever wont, to come
there, did so, having been out a-hawking, and passing by the
chamber where the damsel lay, marvelled to hear her cries,
and forthwith entered, and asked what it meant. On sight
of whom the lady rose and sorrowfully gave him her daughter's
version of what had befallen her. But he, less credulous than
his wife, averred that it could not be true that she knew not
by whom she was pregnant, and was minded to know the whole
truth : let the damsel confess and she might regain his favour ;
otherwise she must expect no mercy and prepare for death.

The lady did all she could to induce her husband to rest
satisfied with what she had told him ; but all to no purpose.
Mad with rage, he rushed, drawn sword in hand, to his daughter's
bedside (she, pending the parley, having given birth to a boy)
and cried out :—" Declare whose this infant is, or forthwith
thou diest." Overcome by fear of death, the damsel broke
her promise to Pietro, and made a clean breast of all that had

passed between him and her. Whereat the knight, grown fell
with rage, could scarce refrain from slaying her. However,
having given vent to his wrath in such words as it dictated, he
remounted his horse and rode to Trapani, and there before one
Messer Currado, the King's lieutenant, laid information of the
wrong done him by Pietro, in consequence whereof Pietro, who
suspected nothing, was forthwith taken, and being put to the
torture, confessed all. Some days later the lieutenant sentenced
him to be scourged through the city, and then hanged by the
neck ; and Messer Amerigo, being minded that one and the
same hour should rid the earth of the two lovers and their son
(for to have compassed Pietro's death was not enough to appease
his wrath), mingled poison and wine in a goblet, and gave it
to one of his servants with a drawn sword, saying :—" Get
thee with this gear to Violante, and tell her from me to make
instant choice of one of these two deaths, either the poison or
the steel ; else, I will have her burned, as she deserves, in view
of all the citizens ; which done, thou wilt take the boy that she
bore a few days ago, and beat his brains out against the wall,
and cast his body for a prey to the dogs."

Hearing the remorseless doom thus passed by the angry father
upon both his daughter and his grandson, the servant, prompt
to do evil rather than good, hied him thence.

Now, as Pietro in execution of his sentence was being scourged
to the gallows by the serjeants, 'twas so ordered by the leaders
of the band that he passed by an inn, where were three noblemen
of Armenia, sent by the king of that country as ambassadors
to Rome, to treat with the Pope of matters of the highest
importance, touching a crusade that was to be ; who, having
there alighted to rest and recreate them for some days, had
received not a few tokens of honour from the nobles of Trapani,
and most of all from Messer Amerigo. Hearing the tramp of
Pietro's escort, they came to a window to see what was toward ;
and one of them, an aged man, and of great authority, Fineo
by name, looking hard at Pietro, who was stripped from the
waist up, and had his hands bound behind his back, espied
on his breast a great spot of scarlet, not laid on by art, but
wrought in the skin by operation of Nature, being such as the
ladies here call a rose. Which he no sooner saw, than he was
reminded of a son that had been stolen from him by corsairs
on the coast of Lazistan some fifteen years before, nor had he
since been able to hear tidings of him ; and guessing the age
of the poor wretch that was being scourged, he set it down as

about what his son's would be, were he living, and, what with
the mark and the age, he began to suspect that 'twas even his
son, and bethought him that, if so, he would scarce as yet have
forgotten his name or the speech of Armenia. Wherefore, as
he was within earshot he called to him :—" Teodoro ! " At
the word Pietro raised his head : whereupon Fineo, speaking
in Armenian, asked him :—" Whence and whose son art thou ? "
The serjeants, that were leading him, paused in deference
to the great man, and so Pietro answered :—" Of Armenia was
I, son of one Fineo, brought hither by folk I wot not of, when
I was but a little child." Then Fineo, witting that in very
truth 'twas the boy that he had lost, came down with his
companions, weeping ; and, all the serjeants making way, he
ran to him, and embraced him, and doffing a mantle of richest
texture that he wore, he prayed the captain of the band to
be pleased to tarry there until he should receive orders to go
forward, and was answered by the captain that he would
willingly so wait.

Fineo already knew, for 'twas bruited everywhere, the cause
for which Pietro was being led to the gallows ; wherefore he
straightway hied him with his companions and their retinue to
Messer Currado, and said to him :—" Sir, this lad, whom you
are sending to the gallows like a slave, is freeborn, and my
son, and is ready to take to wife her whom, as 'tis said, he has
deflowered ; so please you, therefore, delay the execution until
such time as it may be understood whether she be minded to
have him for husband, lest, should she be so minded, you be
found to have broken the law." Messer Currado marvelled
to hear that Pietro was Fineo's son, and not without shame,
albeit 'twas not his but Fortune's fault, confessed that 'twas
even as Fineo said : and having caused Pietro to be taken home
with all speed, and Messer Amerigo to be brought before him,
told him the whole matter. Messer Amerigo, who supposed
that by this time his daughter and grandson must be dead, was
the saddest man in the world to think that 'twas by his deed,
witting that, were the damsel still alive, all might very easily
be set right : however, he sent post haste to his daughter's
abode, revoking his orders, if they were not yet carried out.
The servant, whom he had earlier despatched, had laid the
sword and poison before the damsel, and, for that she was in
no hurry to make her choice, was giving her foul words, and
endeavouring to constrain her thereto, when the messenger
arrived ; but on hearing the injunction laid upon him by his

lord, he desisted, and went back, and told him how things stood. Whereupon Messer Amerigo, much relieved, hied him to Fineo, and well-nigh weeping, and excusing himself for what had befallen, as best he knew how, craved his pardon, and professed himself well content to give Teodoro, so he were minded to have her, his daughter to wife. Fineo readily accepted his excuses, and made answer :—" 'Tis my will that my son espouse your daughter, and, so he will not, let thy sentence passed upon him be carried out."

So Fineo and Messer Amerigo being agreed, while Teodoro still languished in fear of death, albeit he was glad at heart to have found his father, they questioned him of his will in regard of this matter.

When he heard that, if he would, he might have Violante to wife, Teodoro's delight was such that he seemed to leap from hell to paradise, and said that, if 'twas agreeable to them all, he should deem it the greatest of favours. So they sent to the damsel to learn her pleasure : who, having heard how it had fared, and was now like to fare, with Teodoro, albeit, saddest of women, she looked for nought but death, began at length to give some credence to their words, and to recover heart a little, and answered that, were she to follow the bent of her desire, nought that could happen would delight her more than to be Teodoro's wife ; but nevertheless she would do as her father bade her.

So, all agreeing, the damsel was espoused with all pomp and festal cheer, to the boundless delight of all the citizens, and was comforted, and nurtured her little boy, and in no long time waxed more beautiful than ever before ; and, her confinement being ended, she presented herself before Fineo, who was then about to quit Rome on his homeward journey, and did him such reverence as is due to a father. Fineo, mighty well pleased to have so fair a daughter-in-law, caused celebrate her nuptials most bravely and gaily, and received, and did ever thereafter entreat, her as his daughter.

And so he took her, not many days after the festivities were ended, with his son and little grandson, aboard a galley, and brought them to Lazistan, and there thenceforth the two lovers dwelt with him in easeful and lifelong peace.

NOVEL VIII

*Nastagio degli Onesti, loving a damsel of the Traversari family,
by lavish expenditure gains not her love. At the instance
of his kinsfolk he hies him to Chiassi, where he sees a knight
hunt a damsel and slay her and cause her to be devoured by
two dogs. He bids his kinsfolk and the lady that he loves
to breakfast. During the meal the said damsel is torn in
pieces before the eyes of the lady, who, fearing a like fate,
takes Nastagio to husband.*

LAURETTA was no sooner silent than thus at the queen's behest
began Filomena :—Sweet ladies, as in us pity has ever its meed
of praise, even so Divine justice suffers not our cruelty to escape
severe chastisement : the which that I may shew you, and
thereby dispose you utterly to banish that passion from your
souls, I am minded to tell you a story no less touching than
delightsome.

In Ravenna, that most ancient city of Romagna, there dwelt
of yore noblemen and gentlemen not a few, among whom was a
young man, Nastagio degli Onesti by name, who by the death
of his father and one of his uncles inherited immense wealth.
Being without a wife, Nastagio, as 'tis the way with young
men, became enamoured of a daughter of Messer Paolo Traversaro, a damsel of much higher birth than his, whose love he
hoped to win by gifts and the like modes of courting, which,
albeit they were excellent and fair and commendable, not only
availed him not, but seemed rather to have the contrary effect,
so harsh and ruthless and unrelenting did the beloved damsel
shew herself towards him ; for whether it was her uncommon
beauty or her noble lineage that puffed her up, so haughty and
disdainful was she grown that pleasure she had none either in
him or in aught that pleased him.   The burden of which disdain
Nastagio found so hard to bear, that many a time, when he
had made his moan, he longed to make away with himself.
However he refrained therefrom, and many a time resolved
to give her up altogether, or, if so he might, to hold her in
despite, as she did him : but 'twas all in vain, for it seemed as
if, the more his hope dwindled, the greater grew his love.
And, as thus he continued, loving and spending inordinately,
certain of his kinsfolk and friends, being apprehensive lest he
should waste both himself and his substance, did many a time

counsel and beseech him to depart Ravenna, and go tarry for
a time elsewhere, that so he might at once cool his flame and
reduce his charges. For a long while Nastagio answered their
admonitions with banter ; but as they continued to ply him
with them, he grew weary of saying no so often, and promised
obedience. Whereupon he equipped himself as if for a journey
to France or Spain, or other distant parts, got on horseback
and sallied forth of Ravenna, accompanied by not a few of
his friends, and being come to a place called Chiassi, about
three miles from Ravenna, he halted, and having sent for tents
and pavilions, told his companions that there he meant to
stay, and they might go back to Ravenna. So Nastagio pitched
his camp, and there commenced to live after as fine and lordly
a fashion as did ever any man, bidding divers of his friends
from time to time to breakfast or sup with him, as he had been
wont to do. Now it so befell that about the beginning of May,
the season being very fine, he fell a-brooding on the cruelty of
his mistress, and, that his meditations might be the less dis-
turbed, he bade all his servants leave him, and sauntered slowly,
wrapt in thought, as far as the pinewood. Which he had
threaded for a good half-mile, when, the fifth hour of the day
being well-nigh past, yet he recking neither of food nor of
aught else, 'twas as if he heard a woman wailing exceedingly
and uttering most piercing shrieks : whereat, the train of his
sweet melancholy being broken, he raised his head to see what
was toward, and wondered to find himself in the pinewood ;
and saw, moreover, before him running through a grove, close
set with underwood and brambles, towards the place where
he was, a damsel most comely, stark naked, her hair dishevelled,
and her flesh all torn by the briers and brambles, who wept and
cried piteously for mercy ; and at her flanks he saw two mastiffs,
exceeding great and fierce, that ran hard upon her track, and
not seldom came up with her and bit her cruelly ; and in the
rear he saw, riding a black horse, a knight sadly accoutred, and
very wrathful of mien, carrying a rapier in his hand, and with
despiteful, blood-curdling words threatening her with death.
Whereat he was at once amazed and appalled, and then filled
with compassion for the hapless lady, whereof was bred a desire
to deliver her, if so he might, from such anguish and peril of
death. Wherefore, as he was unarmed, he ran and took in
lieu of a cudgel a branch of a tree, with which he prepared
to encounter the dogs and the knight. Which the knight
observing, called to him before he was come to close quarters,

saying :—" Hold off, Nastagio, leave the dogs and me alone
to deal with this vile woman as she has deserved." And, even
as he spoke, the dogs gripped the damsel so hard on either
flank that they arrested her flight, and the knight, being come
up, dismounted. Whom Nastagio approached, saying :—
" I know not who thou art, that knowest me so well, but thus
much I tell thee : 'tis a gross outrage for an armed knight to
go about to kill a naked woman, and set his dogs upon her
as if she were a wild beast : rest assured that I shall do all I
can to protect her." Whereupon :—" Nastagio," replied the
knight, " of the same city as thou was I, and thou wast yet a
little lad when I, Messer Guido degli Anastagi by name, being
far more enamoured of this damsel than thou art now of her
of the Traversari, was by her haughtiness and cruelty brought
to so woeful a pass that one day in a fit of despair I slew myself
with this rapier which thou seest in my hand ; for which cause
I am condemned to the eternal pains. Nor was it long after
my death that she, who exulted therein over measure, also
died, and for that she repented her not of her cruelty and the
joy she had of my sufferings, for which she took not blame to
herself, but merit, was likewise condemned to the pains of hell.
Nor had she sooner made her descent, than for her pain and
mine 'twas ordained, that she should flee before me, and that
I, who so loved her, should pursue her, not as my beloved lady,
but as my mortal enemy, and so, as often as I come up with
her, I slay her with this same rapier with which I slew myself,
and having ripped her up by the back, I take out that hard
and cold heart, to which neither love nor pity had ever access,
and therewith her other inward parts, as thou shalt forthwith
see, and cast them to these dogs to eat. And in no long time,
as the just and mighty God decrees, she rises even as if she had
not died, and recommences her dolorous flight, I and the dogs
pursuing her. And it so falls out that every Friday about this
hour I here come up with her, and slaughter her as thou shalt
see ; but ween not that we rest on other days ; for there are
other places in which I overtake her, places in which she used,
or devised how she might use, me cruelly ; on which wise,
changed as thou seest from her lover into her foe, I am to pursue
her for years as many as the months during which she shewed
herself harsh to me. Wherefore leave me to execute the
decree of the Divine justice, and presume not to oppose that
which thou mayst not avail to withstand."

Affrighted by the knight's words, insomuch that there was

scarce a hair on his head but stood on end, Nastagio shrank back, still gazing on the hapless damsel, and waited all a-tremble to see what the knight would do. Nor had he long to wait ; for the knight, as soon as he had done speaking, sprang, rapier in hand, like a mad dog upon the damsel, who, kneeling, while the two mastiffs gripped her tightly, cried him mercy ; but the knight, thrusting with all his force, struck her between the breasts, and ran her clean through the body. Thus stricken, the damsel fell forthwith prone on the ground sobbing and shrieking : whereupon the knight drew forth a knife, and having therewith opened her in the back, took out the heart and all the circumjacent parts, and threw them to the two mastiffs, who, being famished, forthwith devoured them. And in no long time the damsel, as if nought thereof had happened, started to her feet, and took to flight towards the sea, pursued, and ever and anon bitten, by the dogs, while the knight, having gotten him to horse again, followed them as before, rapier in hand ; and so fast sped they that they were quickly lost to Nastagio's sight.

Long time he stood musing on what he had seen, divided between pity and terror, and then it occurred to him that, as this passed every Friday, it might avail him not a little. So, having marked the place, he rejoined his servants, and in due time thereafter sent for some of his kinsfolk and friends, and said to them :—" 'Tis now a long while that you urge me to give up loving this lady that is no friend to me, and therewith make an end of my extravagant way of living ; and I am now ready so to do, provided you procure me one favour, to wit, that next Friday Messer Paolo Traversaro, and his wife and daughter, and all the ladies, their kinswomen, and as many other ladies as you may be pleased to bid, come hither to breakfast with me : when you will see for yourselves the reason why I so desire." A small matter this seemed to them ; and so, on their return to Ravenna, they lost no time in conveying Nastagio's message to his intended guests : and, albeit she was hardly persuaded, yet in the end the damsel that Nastagio loved came with the rest.

Nastagio caused a lordly breakfast to be prepared, and had the tables set under the pines about the place where he had witnessed the slaughter of the cruel lady ; and in ranging the ladies and gentlemen at table he so ordered it, that the damsel whom he loved was placed opposite the spot where it should be enacted. The last course was just served, when the despairing cries of the hunted damsel became audible to all, to their no small amazement; and each asking, and none knowing, what it might import, up they all started intent to see what was toward; and perceived the suffering damsel, and the knight and the dogs, who in a trice were in their midst. They hollaed amain to dogs and knight, and not a few advanced to succour the damsel: but the words of the knight, which were such as he had used to Nastagio, caused them to fall back, terror-stricken and lost in amazement. And when the knight proceeded to do as he had done before, all the ladies that were there, many of whom were of kin to the suffering damsel and to the knight, and called to mind his love and death, wept as bitterly as if 'twere their own case.

When 'twas all over, and the lady and the knight had disappeared, the strange scene set those that witnessed it pondering many and divers matters: but among them all none was so appalled as the cruel damsel that Nastagio loved, who, having clearly seen and heard all that had passed, and being ware that it touched her more nearly than any other by reason of the harshness that she had ever shewn to Nastagio, seemed already to be fleeing from her angered lover, and to have the mastiffs on her flanks. And so great was her terror that, lest a like fate should befall her, she converted her aversion into affection, and as soon as occasion served, which was that very night, sent a trusty chambermaid privily to Nastagio with a request that he would be pleased to come to her, for that she was ready in all respects to pleasure him to the full. Nastagio made answer that he was greatly flattered, but that he was minded with her consent to have his pleasure of her in an honourable way, to wit, by marrying her. The damsel, who knew that none but herself was to blame that she was not already Nastagio's wife, made answer that she consented. Wherefore by her own mouth she acquainted her father and mother that she agreed to marry Nastagio; and, they heartily approving her choice, Nastagio wedded her on the ensuing Sunday, and lived happily with her many a year. Nor was it in her instance alone that this terror was productive of good: on the contrary, it so wrought among the ladies of Ravenna that they all became, and have ever since been, much more compliant with men's desires than they had been wont to be.

NOVEL IX

*Federigo degli Alberighi loves and is not loved in return : he
wastes his substance by lavishness until nought is left but a
single falcon, which, his lady being come to see him at his
house, he gives her to eat : she, knowing his case, changes
her mind, takes him to husband and makes him rich.*

So ended Filomena ; and the queen, being ware that besides
herself only Dioneo (by virtue of his privilege) was left to speak,
said with gladsome mien :—'Tis now for me to take up my
parable ; which, dearest ladies, I will do with a story like in
some degree to the foregoing, and that, not only that you may
know how potent are your charms to sway the gentle heart,
but that you may also learn how upon fitting occasions to make
bestowal of your guerdons of your own accord, instead of
always waiting for the guidance of Fortune, which most times,
not wisely, but without rule or measure, scatters her gifts.

You are then to know, that Coppo di Borghese Domenichi, a
man that in our day was, and perchance still is, had in respect
and great reverence in our city, being not only by reason of
his noble lineage, but, and yet more, for manners and merit
most illustrious and worthy of eternal renown, was in his old
age not seldom wont to amuse himself by discoursing of things
past with his neighbours and other folk ; wherein he had not
his match for accuracy and compass of memory and concinnity
of speech. Among other good stories, he would tell, how that
there was of yore in Florence a gallant named Federigo di Messer
Filippo Alberighi, who for feats of arms and courtesy had not
his peer in Tuscany ; who, as is the common lot of gentlemen,
became enamoured of a lady named Monna Giovanna, who in
her day held rank among the fairest and most elegant ladies
of Florence ; to gain whose love he jousted, tilted, gave enter-
tainments, scattered largess, and in short set no bounds to his
expenditure. However the lady, no less virtuous than fair,
cared not a jot for what he did for her sake, nor yet for him.

Spending thus greatly beyond his means, and making nothing,
Federigo could hardly fail to come to lack, and was at length
reduced to such poverty that he had nothing left but a little
estate, on the rents of which he lived very straitly, and a single
falcon, the best in the world. The estate was at Campi, and
thither, deeming it no longer possible for him to live in the city

as he desired, he repaired, more in love than ever before ; and there, in complete seclusion, diverting himself with hawking, he bore his poverty as patiently as he might.

Now, Federigo being thus reduced to extreme poverty, it so happened that one day Monna Giovanna's husband, who was very rich, fell ill, and, seeing that he was nearing his end, made his will, whereby he left his estate to his son, who was now growing up, and in the event of his death without lawful heir named Monna Giovanna, whom he dearly loved, heir in his stead ; and having made these dispositions he died.

Monna Giovanna, being thus left a widow, did as our ladies are wont, and repaired in the summer to one of her estates in the country which lay very near to that of Federigo. And so it befell that the urchin began to make friends with Federigo, and to shew a fondness for hawks and dogs, and having seen Federigo's falcon fly not a few times, took a singular fancy to him, and greatly longed to have him for his own, but still did not dare to ask him of Federigo, knowing that Federigo prized him so much. So the matter stood when by chance the boy fell sick ; whereby the mother was sore distressed, for he was her only son, and she loved him as much as might be, insomuch that all day long she was beside him, and ceased not to comfort him, and again and again asked him if there were aught that he wished for, imploring him to say the word, and, if it might by any means be had, she would assuredly do her utmost to procure it for him. Thus repeatedly exhorted, the boy said :—" Mother mine, do but get me Federigo's falcon, and I doubt not I shall soon be well." Whereupon the lady was silent a while, bethinking her what she should do. She knew that Federigo had long loved her, and had never had so much as a single kind look from her : wherefore she said to herself :— How can I send or go to beg of him this falcon, which by what I hear is the best that ever flew, and moreover is his sole comfort ? And how could I be so unfeeling as to seek to deprive a gentleman of the one solace that is now left him ? And so, albeit she very well knew that she might have the falcon for the asking, she was perplexed, and knew not what to say, and gave her son no answer. At length, however, the love she bore the boy carried the day, and she made up her mind, for his contentment, come what might, not to send, but to go herself and fetch him the falcon. So :—" Be of good cheer, my son," she said, " and doubt not thou wilt soon be well ; for I promise thee that the very first thing that I shall do to-morrow morning

will be to go and fetch thee the falcon." Whereat the child
was so pleased that he began to mend that very day.

On the morrow the lady, as if for pleasure, hied her with
another lady to Federigo's little house, and asked to see him.
'Twas still, as for some days past, no weather for hawking, and
Federigo was in his garden, busy about some small matters
which needed to be set right there. When he heard that Monna
Giovanna was at the door, asking to see him, he was not a little
surprised and pleased, and hied him to her with all speed.
As soon as she saw him, she came forward to meet him with
womanly grace, and having received his respectful salutation,
said to him :—" Good morrow, Federigo," and continued :—
" I am come to requite thee for what thou hast lost by loving
me more than thou shouldst : which compensation is this,
that I and this lady that accompanies me will breakfast with thee
without ceremony this morning." " Madam," Federigo replied
with all humility, " I mind not ever to have lost aught by loving
you, but rather to have been so much profited that, if I ever
deserved well in aught, 'twas to your merit that I owed it, and
to the love that I bore you. And of a surety had I still as
much to spend as I have spent in the past, I should not prize
it so much as this visit you so frankly pay me, come as you are
to one who can afford you but a sorry sort of hospitality." Which
said, with some confusion, he bade her welcome to his house,
and then led her into his garden, where, having none else to
present to her by way of companion, he said :—" Madam, as
there is none other here, this good woman, wife of this husbandman, will bear you company, while I go to have the table set."
Now, albeit his poverty was extreme, yet he had not known as
yet how sore was the need to which his extravagance had reduced
him ; but this morning 'twas brought home to him, for that
he could find nought wherewith to do honour to the lady, for love
of whom he had done the honours of his house to men without
number : wherefore, distressed beyond measure, and inwardly
cursing his evil fortune, he sped hither and thither like one
beside himself, but never a coin found he, nor yet aught to
pledge. Meanwhile it grew late, and sorely he longed that the
lady might not leave his house altogether unhonoured, and yet
to crave help of his own husbandman was more than his pride
could brook. In these desperate straits his glance happened
to fall on his brave falcon on his perch in his little parlour.
And so, as a last resource, he took him, and finding him plump,
deemed that he would make a dish meet for such a lady. Where-

fore, without thinking twice about it, he wrung the bird's neck, and caused his maid forthwith pluck him and set him on a spit, and roast him carefully; and having still some spotless table-linen, he had the table laid therewith, and with a cheerful countenance hied him back to his lady in the garden, and told her that such breakfast as he could give her was ready. So the lady and her companion rose and came to table, and there, with Federigo, who waited on them most faithfully, ate the brave falcon, knowing not what they ate.

When they were risen from table, and had dallied a while in gay converse with him, the lady deemed it time to tell the reason of her visit: wherefore, graciously addressing Federigo, thus began she:—"Federigo, by what thou rememberest of thy past life and my virtue, which, perchance, thou hast deemed harshness and cruelty, I doubt not thou must marvel at my presumption, when thou hearest the main purpose of my visit; but if thou hadst sons, or hadst had them, so that thou mightest know the full force of the love that is borne them, I should make no doubt that thou wouldst hold me in part excused. Nor, having a son, may I, for that thou hast none, claim exemption from the laws to which all other mothers are subject, and, being thus bound to own their sway, I must, though fain were I not, and though 'tis neither meet nor right, crave of thee that which I know thou dost of all things and with justice prize most highly, seeing that this extremity of thy adverse fortune has left thee nought else wherewith to delight, divert and console thee; which gift is no other than thy falcon, on which my boy has so set his heart that, if I bring him it not, I fear lest he grow so much worse of the malady that he has, that thereby it may come to pass that I lose him. And so, not for the love which thou dost bear me, and which may nowise bind thee, but for that nobleness of temper, whereof in courtesy more conspicuously than in aught else thou hast given proof, I implore thee that thou be pleased to give me the bird, that thereby I may say that I have kept my son alive, and thus made him for aye thy debtor."

No sooner had Federigo apprehended what the lady wanted, than, for grief that 'twas not in his power to serve her, because he had given her the falcon to eat, he fell a-weeping in her presence, before he could so much as utter a word. At first the lady supposed that 'twas only because he was loath to part with the brave falcon that he wept, and as good as made up her mind that he would refuse her: however, she awaited with patience Federigo's answer, which was on this wise:—" Madam, since it pleased God that I should set my affections upon you there have been matters not a few, in which to my sorrow I have deemed Fortune adverse to me; but they have all been trifles in comparison of the trick that she now plays me: the which I shall never forgive her, seeing that you are come here to my poor house, where, while I was rich, you deigned not to come, and ask a trifling favour of me, which she has put it out of my power to grant: how 'tis so, I will briefly tell you. When I learned that you, of your grace, were minded to breakfast with me, having respect to your high dignity and desert, I deemed it due and seemly that in your honour I should regale you, to the best of my power, with fare of a more excellent quality than is commonly set before others; and, calling to mind the falcon which you now ask of me, and his excellence, I judged him meet food for you, and so you have had him roasted on the trencher this morning; and well indeed I thought I had bestowed him; but, as now I see that you would fain have had him in another guise, so mortified am I that I am not able to serve you, that I doubt I shall never know peace of mind more." In witness whereof he had the feathers and feet and beak of the bird brought in and laid before her.

The first thing the lady did, when she had heard Federigo's story, and seen the relics of the bird, was to chide him that he had killed so fine a falcon to furnish a woman with a breakfast; after which the magnanimity of her host, which poverty had been and was powerless to impair, elicited no small share of inward commendation. Then, frustrate of her hope of possessing the falcon, and doubting of her son's recovery, she took her leave with the heaviest of hearts, and hied her back to the boy: who, whether for fretting, that he might not have the falcon, or by the unaided energy of his disorder, departed this life not many days after, to the exceeding great grief of his mother. For a while she would do nought but weep and bitterly bewail herself; but being still young, and left very wealthy, she was often urged by her brothers to marry again, and though she would rather have not done so, yet being importuned, and remembering Federigo's high desert, and the magnificent generosity with which he had finally killed his falcon to do her honour, she said to her brothers:—" Gladly, with your consent, would I remain a widow, but if you will not be satisfied except I take a husband, rest assured that none other will I ever take save Federigo degli Alberighi." Whereupon her brothers derided her, saying:—" Foolish woman, what is't thou sayst? How shouldst thou want Federigo, who has not a thing in the world?" To whom she answered:— " My brothers, well wot I that 'tis as you say; but I had rather have a man without wealth than wealth without a man." The brothers, perceiving that her mind was made up, and knowing Federigo for a good man and true, poor though he was, gave her to him with all her wealth. And so Federigo, being mated with such a wife, and one that he had so much loved, and being very wealthy to boot, lived happily, keeping more exact accounts, to the end of his days.

NOVEL X

Pietro di Vinciolo goes from home to sup: his wife brings a boy into the house to bear her company: Pietro returns, and she hides her gallant under a hen-coop: Pietro explains that in the house of Ercolano, with whom he was to have supped, there was discovered a young man bestowed there by Ercolano's wife: the lady thereupon censures Ercolano's wife: but unluckily an ass treads on the fingers of the boy that is hidden under the hen-coop, so that he cries for pain: Pietro runs to the place, sees him, and apprehends the trick played on him by his wife, which nevertheless he finally condones, for that he is not himself free from blame.

WHEN the queen had done speaking, and all had praised God that He had worthily rewarded Federigo, Dioneo, who never waited to be bidden, thus began:—I know not whether I am to term it a vice accidental and superinduced by bad habits in us mortals, or whether it be a fault seated in nature, that we are more prone to laugh at things dishonourable than at good deeds, and that more especially when they concern not ourselves. However, as the sole scope of all my efforts has been and still shall be to dispel your melancholy, and in lieu thereof to minister to you laughter and jollity; therefore, enamoured my damsels, albeit the ensuing story is not altogether free from matter that is scarce seemly, yet, as it may afford you pleasure, I shall not fail to relate it; premonishing you my hearers, that you take it with the like discretion as when, going into your gardens, you stretch forth your delicate hands and cull the roses, leaving the thorns alone: which, being interpreted,

means that you will leave the caitiff husband to abide in sorry
plight with his dishonour, and will gaily laugh at the amorous
wiles of his wife, and commiserate her unfortunate gallant,
when occasion requires.

'Tis no great while since there dwelt at Perugia a rich man
named Pietro di Vinciolo, who rather, perchance, to blind
others and mitigate the evil repute in which he was held by
the citizens of Perugia, than for any desire to wed, took a wife :
and such being his motive, Fortune provided him with just
such a spouse as he merited. For the wife of his choice was a
stout, red-haired young woman, and so hot-blooded that two
husbands would have been more to her mind than one, whereas
one fell to her lot that gave her only a subordinate place in
his regard. Which she perceiving, while she knew herself
to be fair and lusty, and felt herself to be gamesome and fit,
waxed very wroth, and now and again had high words with
her husband, and led but a sorry life with him at most times.
Then, seeing that thereby she was more like to fret herself than
to dispose her husband to conduct less base, she said to herself :
—This poor creature deserts me to go walk in pattens in the
dry ; wherefore it shall go hard but I will bring another aboard
the ship for the wet weather. I married him, and brought him
a great and goodly dowry, knowing that he was a man, and
supposing him to have the desires which men have and ought
to have ; and had I not deemed him to be a man, I should
never have married him. He knew me to be a woman : why
then took he me to wife, if women were not to his mind ? 'Tis
not to be endured. Had I not been minded to live in the world,
I had become a nun ; and being minded there to live, as I
am, if I am to wait until I have pleasure or solace of him, I
shall wait perchance until I am old ; and then, too late, I shall
bethink me to my sorrow that I have wasted my youth ; and
as to the way in which I should seek its proper solace I need no
better teacher and guide than him, who finds his delight where
I should find mine, and finds it to his own condemnation,
whereas in me 'twere commendable. 'Tis but the laws that
I shall set at nought, whereas he sets both them and Nature
herself at nought.

So the good lady reasoned, and peradventure more than once ;
and then, casting about how she might privily compass her
end, she made friends with an old beldam, that shewed as a
veritable Santa Verdiana, foster-mother of vipers, who was
ever to be seen going to pardonings with a parcel of paternosters

in her hand, and talked of nothing but the lives of the holy
Fathers, and the wounds of St. Francis, and was generally
reputed a saint ; to whom in due time she opened her whole
mind. " My daughter," replied the beldam, " God, who knows
all things, knows that thou wilt do very rightly indeed : were
it for no other reason, 'twould be meet for thee and every other
young woman so to do, that the heyday of youth be not wasted ;
for there is no grief like that of knowing that it has been wasted.
And what the devil are we women fit for when we are old—
except to pore over the cinders on the hearth ? The which if
any know, and may attest it, 'tis I, who, now that I am old,
call to mind the time that I let slip from me, not without most
sore and bitter and fruitless regret : and albeit 'twas not all
wasted, for I would not have thee think that I was entirely
without sense, yet I did not make the best use of it : whereof
when I bethink me, and that I am now, even as thou seest
me, such a hag that never a spark of fire may I hope to get
from any, God knows how I rue it. Now with men 'tis otherwise : they are born meet for a thousand uses, not for this
alone ; and the more part of them are of much greater consequence in old age than in youth : but women are fit for nought
but this, and 'tis but for that they bear children that they are
cherished. Whereof, if not otherwise, thou mayst assure thyself, if thou do but consider that we are ever ready for it ; which
is not the case with men ; besides which, one woman will tire
out many men without being herself tired out. Seeing then
that 'tis for this we are born, I tell thee again that thou wilt
do very rightly to give thy husband thy loaf for his cake,
that in thy old age thy soul may have no cause of complaint
against thy flesh. Every one has just as much of this life as
he appropriates : and this is especially true of women, whom
therefore it behoves, much more than men, to seize the moment
as it flies : indeed, as thou mayst see for thyself, when we grow
old neither husband, nor any other man will spare us a glance ;
but, on the contrary, they banish us to the kitchen, there to
tell stories to the cat, and to count the pots and pans ; or,
worse, they make rhymes about us :—' To the damsel dainty
bits ; to the beldam ague-fits ; ' and such-like catches. But
to make no more words about it, I tell thee at once that there
is no person in the world to whom thou couldst open thy mind
with more advantage than to me ; for there is no gentleman so
fine but I dare speak my mind to him, nor any so harsh and
forbidding but I know well how to soften him and fashion him

to my will. Tell me only what thou wouldst have, and leave
the rest to me : but one word more : I pray thee to have me
in kindly remembrance, for that I am poor ; and thou shalt
henceforth go shares with me in all my indulgences and every
paternoster that I say, that God may make thereof light and
tapers for thy dead : " wherewith she ended.

So the lady came to an understanding with the beldam, that,
as soon as she set eyes on a boy that often came along that
street, and of whom the lady gave her a particular description,
she would know what she was to do : and thereupon the lady
gave her a chunk of salt meat, and bade her God-speed. The
beldam before long smuggled into the lady's chamber the boy
of whom she had spoken, and not long after another, such being
the humour of the lady, who, standing in perpetual dread of her
husband, was disposed, in this particular, to make the most
of her opportunities. And one of these days, her husband
being to sup in the evening with a friend named Ercolano,
the lady bade the beldam bring her a boy as pretty and dainty
as was to be found in Perugia ; and so the beldam forthwith
did. But the lady and the boy being set at table to sup, lo,
Pietro's voice was heard at the door, bidding open to him.
Whereupon the lady gave herself up for dead ; but being fain,
if she might, to screen the boy, and knowing not where else
to convey or conceal him, bestowed him under a hen-coop that
stood in a veranda hard by the chamber in which they were
supping, and threw over it a sorry mattress that she had that
day emptied of its straw ; which done she hastened to open
the door to her husband ; saying to him as he entered :—
" You have gulped your supper mighty quickly to-night."
Whereto Pietro replied :—" We have not so much as tasted
it." " How so ? " enquired the lady. " I will tell thee,"
said Pietro. " No sooner were we set at table, Ercolano, his
wife, and I, than we heard a sneeze close to us, to which, though
'twas repeated, we paid no heed ; but as the sneezer continued
to sneeze a third, a fourth, a fifth, and many another time to
boot, we all began to wonder, and Ercolano, who was somewhat
out of humour with his wife, because she had kept us a long
time at the door before she opened it, burst out in a sort of
rage with :—' What means this ? Who is't that thus sneezes ? '
and made off to a stair hard by, beneath which and close to its
foot was a wooden closet, of the sort which, when folk are furnishing their houses, they commonly cause to be placed there, to
stow things in upon occasion. And as it seemed to him that the

sneezing proceeded thence, he undid the wicket, and no sooner had he opened it than out flew never so strong a stench of brimstone ; albeit we had already been saluted by a whiff of it, and complained thereof, but had been put off by the lady with :—
' 'Tis but that a while ago I bleached my veils with brimstone, having sprinkled it on a dish, that they might catch its fumes, which dish I then placed under the stair, so that it still smells a little.'

"However the door being now, as I have said, open, and the smoke somewhat less dense, Ercolano, peering in, espied the fellow that had sneezed, and who still kept sneezing, being thereto constrained by the pungency of the brimstone. And for all he sneezed, yet was he by this time so well-nigh choked with the brimstone that he was like neither to sneeze nor to do aught else again. As soon as he caught sight of him, Ercolano bawled out :—' Now see I, Madam, why it was that a while ago, when we came here, we were kept waiting so long at the gate before 'twas opened ; but woe betide me for the rest of my days, if I pay you not out.' Whereupon the lady, perceiving that her offence was discovered, ventured no excuse, but fled from the table, whither I know not. Ercolano, ignoring his wife's flight, bade the sneezer again and again to come forth ; but he, being by this time fairly spent, budged not an inch for aught that Ercolano said. Wherefore Ercolano caught him by one of his feet, and dragged him forth, and ran off for a knife with intent to kill him ; but I, standing in fear of the Signory on my own account, got up and would not suffer him to kill the fellow or do him any hurt, and for his better protection raised the alarm, whereby some of the neighbours came up and took the lad, more dead than alive, and bore him off, I know not whither. However, our supper being thus rudely interrupted, not only have not gulped it, but I have not so much as tasted it, as I said before."

Her husband's story shewed his wife that there were other ladies as knowing as she, albeit misfortune might sometimes overtake them ; and gladly would she have spoken out in defence of Ercolano's wife, but, thinking that, by censuring another's sin, she would secure more scope for her own, she launched out on this wise :—" Fine doings indeed, a right virtuous and saintly lady she must be : here is the loyalty of an honest woman, and one to whom I had lief have confessed, so spiritual I deemed her ; and the worst of it is that, being no longer young, she sets a rare example to those that are so.

Curses on the hour that she came into the world : curses upon her that she make not away with herself, basest, most faithless of women that she must needs be, the reproach of her sex, the opprobrium of all the ladies of this city, to cast aside all regard for her honour, her marriage vow, her reputation before the world, and, lost to all sense of shame, to scruple not to bring disgrace upon a man so worthy, a citizen so honourable, a husband by whom she was so well treated, ay, and upon herself to boot ! By my hope of salvation no mercy should be shewn to such women ; they should pay the penalty with their lives ; to the fire with them while they yet live, and let them be burned to ashes." Then, calling to mind the lover that she had close at hand in the hen-coop, she fell to coaxing Pietro to get him to bed, for the hour grew late. Pietro, who was more set on eating than sleeping, only asked whether there was aught he might have by way of supper. "Supper, forsooth ! " replied the lady. "Ay, of course 'tis our way to make much of supper when thou art not at home. As if I were Ercolano's wife ! Now, wherefore tarry longer ? Go, get thy night's rest : 'twere far better for thee."

Now so it was that some of Pietro's husbandmen had come to the house that evening with divers things from the farm, and had put up their asses in a stable that adjoined the veranda, but had neglected to water them ; and one of the asses being exceeding thirsty, got his head out of the halter and broke loose from the stable, and went about nosing everything, if haply he might come by water : whereby he came upon the hen-coop, beneath which was the boy ; who, being constrained to stand on all fours, had the fingers of one hand somewhat protruding from under the hen-coop ; and so as luck or rather ill-luck would have it, the ass trod on them ; whereat, being sorely hurt, he set up a great howling, much to the surprise of Pietro, who perceived that 'twas within his house. So forth he came, and hearing the boy still moaning and groaning, for the ass still kept his hoof hard down on the fingers, called out :— "Who is there ? " and ran to the hen-coop and raised it, and espied the fellow, who, besides the pain that the crushing of his fingers by the ass's hoof occasioned him, trembled in every limb for fear that Pietro should do him a mischief. He was one that Pietro had long been after for his foul purposes : so Pietro, recognizing him, asked him :—" What dost thou here ? " The boy making no answer, save to beseech him for the love of God to do him no hurt, Pietro continued :—" Get

up, have no fear that I shall hurt thee ; but tell me :—How,
and for what cause comest thou to be here ? " The boy then
confessed everything. Whereupon Pietro, as elated by the
discovery as his wife was distressed, took him by the hand ;
and led him into the room where the lady in the extremity of
terror awaited him ; and, having seated himself directly in
front of her, said :—" 'Twas but a moment ago that thou didst
curse Ercolano's wife, and averred that she ought to be burned,
and that she was the reproach of your sex : why saidst thou
not, of thyself ?   Or, if thou wast not minded to accuse thyself,
how hadst thou the effrontery to censure her, knowing that
thou hadst done even as she ?   Verily 'twas for no other reason
than that ye are all fashioned thus, and study to cover your
own misdeeds with the delinquencies of others : would that
fire might fall from heaven and burn you all, brood of iniquity
that ye are ! "

The lady, marking that in the first flush of his wrath he had
given her nothing worse than hard words, and discerning, as
she thought, that he was secretly overjoyed to hold so beautiful
a boy by the hand, took heart of grace and said :—" I doubt
not indeed that thou wouldst be well pleased that fire should
fall from heaven and devour us all, seeing that thou art as fond
of us as a dog is of the stick, though by the Holy Rood thou
wilt be disappointed ; but I would fain have a little argument
with thee, to know whereof thou complainest. Well indeed
were it with me, didst thou but place me on an equality with
Ercolano's wife, who is an old sanctimonious hypocrite, and
has of him all that she wants, and is cherished by him as a
wife should be : but that is not my case. For, granted that
thou givest me garments and shoes to my mind, thou knowest
how otherwise ill bested I am, and how long it is since last thou
didst lie with me ; and far liefer had I go barefoot and in rags,
and have thy benevolence abed, than have all that I have, and
be treated as thou dost treat me. Understand me, Pietro, be
reasonable ; consider that I am a woman like other women,
with the like craving ; whereof if thou deny me the gratification, 'tis no blame to me that I seek it elsewhere ; and at least
I do thee so much honour as not forgather with stable-boys or
scurvy knaves."

Pietro perceived that she was like to continue in this vein the
whole night : wherefore, indifferent as he was to her, he said :
—" Now, Madam, no more of this ; in the matter of which thou
speakest I will content thee ; but of thy great courtesy let us

have something to eat by way of supper; for, methinks, the boy, as well as I, has not yet supped." "Ay, true enough," said the lady, " he has not supped; for we were but just sitting down to table to sup, when, beshrew thee, thou madest thy appearance." "Go then," said Pietro, "get us some supper; and by and by I will arrange this affair in such a way that thou shalt have no more cause of complaint." The lady, perceiving that her husband was now tranquil, rose, and soon had the table laid again and spread with the supper which she had ready; and so they made a jolly meal of it, the caitiff husband, the lady and the boy. What after supper Pietro devised for their mutual satisfaction has slipped from my memory. But so much as this I know, that on the morrow as he wended his way to the piazza, the boy would have been puzzled to say, whether of the twain, the wife or the husband, had had the most of his company during the night. But this I would say to you, dear my ladies, that whoso gives you tit, why, just give him tat; and if you cannot do it at once, why, bear it in mind until you can, that even as the ass gives, so he may receive.

Dioneo's story, whereat the ladies laughed the less for shame-fastness rather than for disrelish, being ended, the queen, taking note that the term of her sovereignty was come, rose to her feet, and took off the laurel wreath and set it graciously upon Elisa's head, saying :—" Madam, 'tis now your turn to bear sway." The dignity accepted, Elisa followed in all respects the example of her predecessors : she first conferred with the seneschal, and directed him how meetly to order all things during the time of her sovereignty ; which done to the satisfaction of the company : —" Ofttimes," quoth she, " have we heard how with bright sallies, and ready retorts, and sudden devices, not a few have known how to repugn with apt checks the bites of others, or to avert imminent perils ; and because 'tis an excellent argument, and may be profitable, I ordain that to-morrow, God helping us, the following be the rule of our discourse ; to wit, that it be of such as by some sprightly sally have repulsed an attack, or by some ready retort or device have avoided loss, peril or scorn." The rule being heartily approved by all, the queen rose and dismissed them till supper-time. So the honourable company, seeing the queen risen, rose all likewise, and as their wont was, betook them to their diversions as to each seemed best. But when the cicalas had hushed their chirping, all were mustered again for supper ; and having blithely feasted, they all addressed them to song and dance. And the queen, while Emilia led a dance, called for a song from Dioneo, who at once came out with :—" Monna Aldruda, come perk up thy mood, a piece of glad tidings I bring thee." Whereat all the ladies fell a-laughing, and most of all the queen, who bade him give them no more of that, but sing another. Quoth Dioneo :— " Madam, had I a tabret, I would sing :—' Up with your smock, Monna Lapa!' or :—' Oh! the greensward under the olive!' Or perchance you had liefer I should give you :—' Woe is me, the wave of the sea!' But no tabret have I: wherefore choose which of these others you will have. Perchance you would like :—' Now hie thee to us forth, that so it may be cut, as May the fields about.'" "No," returned the queen, "give us another." "Then," said Dioneo, "I will sing :— ' Monna Simona, embarrel, embarrel. Why, 'tis not the month of October.'" [1] " Now a plague upon thee," said the queen, with a laugh; "give us a proper song, wilt thou? for we will have none of these." "Never fear, Madam," replied Dioneo; "only say which you prefer. I have more than a thousand songs by heart. Perhaps you would like :—' This my little covert, make I ne'er it overt'; or :—' Gently, gently, husband mine'; or :—' A hundred pounds were none too high a price for me a cock to buy.'" The queen now shewed some offence, though the other ladies laughed, and :—" A truce to thy jesting, Dioneo," said she, " and give us a proper song : else thou mayst prove the quality of my ire." Whereupon Dioneo forthwith ceased his fooling, and sang on this wise :—

> So ravishing a light
>> Doth from the fair eyes of my mistress move
>> As keeps me slave to her and thee, O Love.
>
> A beam from those bright orbs did radiate
>> That flame that through mine own eyes to my breast
>> Did whilom entrance gain.
> Thy majesty, O Love, thy might, how great
> They be, 'twas her fair face did manifest :
>> Whereon to brood still fain,
>> I felt thee take and chain
> Each sense, my soul enthralling on such wise
> That she alone henceforth evokes my sighs.
>
> Wherefore, O dear my Lord, myself I own
>> Thy slave, and, all obedience, wait and yearn,
>> Till thy might me console.
> Yet wot I not if it be throughly known
> How noble is the flame wherewith I burn,
>> My loyalty how whole
>> To her that doth control
> Ev'n in such sort my mind that shall I none,
> Nor would I, peace receive, save hers alone.

[1] The song is evidently amœbean.

And so I pray thee, sweet my Lord, that thou
   Give her to feel thy fire, and shew her plain
   How grievous my disease.
   This service deign to render ; for that now
   Thou seest me waste for love, and in the pain
   Dissolve me by degrees :
   And then the apt moment seize
   My cause to plead with her, as is but due
From thee to me, who fain with thee would sue.

When Dioneo's silence shewed that his song was ended, the
queen accorded it no stinted meed of praise ; after which she
caused not a few other songs to be sung. Thus passed some
part of the night ; and then the queen, taking note that its
freshness had vanquished the heat of the day, bade all go rest
them, if they would, till the morning.

Endeth here the fifth day of the Decameron, beginneth the sixth, wherein, under the rule of Elisa, discourse is had of such as by some sprightly sally have repulsed an attack, or by some ready retort or device have avoided loss, peril or scorn.

STILL in mid heaven, the moon had lost her radiance, nor was any part of our world unillumined by the fresh splendour of the dawn, when, the queen being risen and having mustered her company, they hied them, gently sauntering, across the dewy mead some distance from the beautiful hill, conversing now of this, now of the other matter, canvassing the stories, their greater or less degree of beauty, and laughing afresh at divers of their incidents, until, the sun being now in his higher ascendant, they began to feel his heat, and turning back by common consent, retraced their steps to the palace, where, the tables being already set, and fragrant herbs and fair flowers strewn all about, they by the queen's command, before it should grow hotter, addressed themselves to their meal. So, having blithely breakfasted, they first of all sang some dainty and jocund ditties, and then, as they were severally minded, composed them to sleep or sat them down to chess or dice, while Dioneo and Lauretta fell a-singing of Troilus and Cressida.

The hour of session being come, they took their places, at the queen's summons, in their wonted order by the fountain ; but, when the queen was about to call for the first story, that happened which had not happened before ; to wit, there being a great uproar in the kitchen among the maids and men, the sound thereof reached the ears of the queen and all the company. Whereupon the queen called the seneschal and asked him who bawled so loud, and what was the occasion of the uproar. The seneschal made answer that 'twas some contention between Licisca and Tindaro ; but the occasion he knew not, having but just come to quiet them, when he received her summons. The queen then bade him cause Licisca and Tindaro to come thither forthwith : so they came, and the queen enquired of them the cause of the uproar. Tindaro was about to make answer, when Licisca, who was somewhat advanced in years, and disposed to give herself airs, and heated

63

to the strife of words, turned to Tindaro, and scowling upon him said :—" Unmannerly varlet that makest bold to speak before me ; leave me to tell the story." Then, turning to the queen, she said :—" Madam, this fellow would fain instruct me as to Sicofante's wife, and—neither more or less—as if I had not known her well—would have me believe that, the first night that Sicofante lay with her, 'twas by force and not without effusion of blood that Master Yard made his way into Dusky Hill ; which I deny, averring that he met with no resistance, but, on the contrary, with a hearty welcome on the part of the garrison.   And such a numskull is he as fondly to believe that the girls are so simple as to let slip their oppor- tunities, while they wait on the caprice of father or brothers, who six times out of seven delay to marry them for three or four years after they should.   Ay, ay indeed, doubtless they were well advised to tarry so long !   Christ's faith !   I should know the truth of what I swear ; there is never a woman in my neighbourhood whose husband had her virginity ; and well I know how many and what manner of tricks our married dames play their husbands ; and yet this booby would fain teach me to know women as if I were but born yesterday."

While Licisca thus spoke, the ladies laughed till all their teeth were ready to start from their heads.   Six times at least the queen bade her be silent : but all in vain ; she halted not till she had said all that she had a mind to.   When she had done, the queen turned with a smile to Dioneo saying :—" This is a question for thee to deal with, Dioneo ; so hold thyself in readiness to give final judgment upon it, when our stories are ended." " Madam," replied Dioneo forthwith, " I give judgment without more ado :   I say that Licisca is in the right ; I believe that 'tis even as she says, and that Tindaro is a fool."   Whereupon Licisca burst out laughing, and turning to Tindaro :—" Now did I not tell thee so ? " quothed she.   " Begone in God's name :   dost think to know more than I, thou that art but a sucking babe ?   Thank God, I have not lived for nothing, not I."   And had not the queen sternly bade her be silent, and make no more disturbance, unless she had a mind to be whipped, and sent both her and Tindaro back to the kitchen, the whole day would have been spent in nought but listening to her. So Licisca and Tindaro having withdrawn, the queen charged Filomena to tell the first story : and gaily thus Filomena began.

NOVEL I

A knight offers to carry Madonna Oretta a-horseback with a story,
but tells it so ill that she prays him to dismount her.

As stars are set for an ornament in the serene expanse of heaven,
and likewise in springtime flowers and leafy shrubs in the green
meadows, so, damsels, in the hour of rare and excellent discourse, is wit with its bright sallies. Which, being brief, are
much more proper for ladies than for men, seeing that prolixity
of speech, where brevity is possible, is much less allowable to
them. But for whatever cause, be it the sorry quality of our
understanding, or some especial enmity that heaven bears to
our generation, few ladies or none are left to-day that, when
occasion prompts, are able to meet it with apt speech, ay, or
if aught of the kind they hear, can understand it aright : to
our common shame be it spoken ! But as, touching this
matter, enough has already been said by Pampinea,[1] I purpose
not to enlarge thereon ; but, that you may know what excellence
resides in speech apt for the occasion, I am minded to tell you
after how courteous a fashion a lady imposed silence upon a
gentleman.

'Tis no long time since there dwelt in our city a lady, noble,
debonair and of excellent discourse, whom not a few of you
may have seen or heard of, whose name—for such high qualities
merit not oblivion—was Madonna Oretta, her husband being
Messer Geri Spina. Now this lady, happening to be, as we are,
in the country, moving from place to place for pleasure with a
company of ladies and gentlemen, whom she had entertained
the day before at breakfast at her house, and the place of their
next sojourn, whither they were to go afoot, being some considerable distance off, one of the gentlemen of the company
said to her :—" Madonna Oretta, so please you, I will carry
you great part of the way a-horseback with one of the finest
stories in the world." " Indeed, Sir," replied the lady, " I
pray you do so ; and I shall deem it the greatest of favours."
Whereupon the gentleman, who perhaps was no better master
of his weapon than of his story, began a tale, which in itself
was indeed excellent, but which, by repeating the same word
three, four or six times, and now and again harking back, and
saying :—" I said not well " ; and erring not seldom in the

[1] Cf. First Day, Novel X.

names, setting one in place of another, he utterly spoiled; besides which, his mode of delivery accorded very ill with the character of the persons and incidents : insomuch that Madonna Oretta, as she listened, did oft sweat, and was like to faint, as if she were ill and at the point of death. And being at length able to bear no more of it, witting that the gentleman had got into a mess and was not like to get out of it, she said pleasantly to him :—" Sir, this horse of yours trots too hard; I pray you be pleased to set me down." The gentleman, being perchance more quick of apprehension than he was skilful in narration, missed not the meaning of her sally, and took it in all good and gay humour. So, leaving unfinished the tale which he had begun, and so mishandled, he addressed himself to tell her other stories.

NOVEL II

Cisti, a baker, by an apt speech gives Messer Geri Spina to know that he has by inadvertence asked that of him which he should not.

ALL the ladies and the men alike having greatly commended Madonna Oretta's apt saying, the queen bade Pampinea follow suit, and thus she began :—

Fair ladies, I cannot myself determine whether Nature or Fortune be the more at fault, the one in furnishing a noble soul with a vile body, or the other in allotting a base occupation to a body endowed with a noble soul, whereof we may have seen an example, among others, in our fellow-citizen, Cisti; whom, furnished though he was with a most lofty soul, Fortune made a baker. And verily I should curse Nature and Fortune alike, did I not know that Nature is most discreet, and that Fortune, albeit the foolish imagine her blind, has a thousand eyes. For 'tis, I suppose, that, being wise above a little, they do as mortals ofttimes do, who, being uncertain as to their future, provide against contingencies by burying their most precious treasures in the basest places in their houses, as being the least likely to be suspected; whence, in the hour of their greatest need, they bring them forth, the base place having kept them more safe than the dainty chamber would have done. And so these two arbitresses of the world not seldom hide their most precious commodities in the obscurity of the crafts that are reputed most base, that thence being brought to light they may shine with a brighter splendour. Whereof how in a trifling matter Cisti, the baker, gave proof, restoring the eyes of the mind to Messer Geri Spina, whom the story of his wife, Madonna Oretta, has brought to my recollection, I am minded to shew you in a narrative which shall be of the briefest.

I say then that Pope Boniface, with whom Messer Geri Spina stood very high in favour and honour, having sent divers of his courtiers to Florence as ambassadors to treat of certain matters of great moment, and they being lodged in Messer Geri's house, where he treated with them of the said affairs of the Pope, 'twas, for some reason or another, the wont of Messer Geri and the ambassadors of the Pope to pass almost every morning by Santa Maria Ughi, where Cisti, the baker, had his bakehouse, and plied his craft in person. Now, albeit Fortune had allotted him a very humble occupation, she had nevertheless prospered him therein to such a degree that he was grown most wealthy, and without ever aspiring to change it for another, lived in most magnificent style, having among his other good things a cellar of the best wines, white and red, that were to be found in Florence, or the country parts; and marking Messer Geri and the ambassadors of the Pope pass every morning by his door, he bethought him that, as 'twas very hot, 'twould be a very courteous thing to give them to drink of his good wine; but comparing his rank with that of Messer Geri, he deemed it unseemly to presume to invite him, and cast about how he might lead Messer Geri to invite himself. So, wearing always the whitest of doublets and a spotless apron, that denoted rather the miller than the baker, he let bring, every morning about the hour that he expected Messer Geri and the ambassadors to pass by his door, a spick-and-span bucket of fresh and cool spring water, and a small Bolognese flagon of his good white wine, and two beakers that shone like silver, so bright were they: and there down he sat him, as they came by, and after hawking once or twice, fell a-drinking his wine with such gusto that 'twould have raised a thirst in a corpse. Which Messer Geri having observed on two successive mornings, said on the third:—"What is't, Cisti? Is't good?" Whereupon Cisti jumped up, and answered:—"Ay, Sir, good it is; but in what degree I might by no means make you understand, unless you tasted it." Messer Geri, in whom either the heat of the weather, or unwonted fatigue, or, perchance, the gusto with which he had seen Cisti drink, had bred a thirst, turned to the ambassadors

and said with a smile :—" Gentlemen, 'twere well to test the
quality of this worthy man's wine : it may be such that we shall
not repent us." And so in a body they came up to where Cisti
stood ; who, having caused a goodly bench to be brought out
of the bakehouse, bade them be seated, and to their servants,
who were now coming forward to wash the beakers, said :—
" Stand back, comrades, and leave this office to me, for I know
as well how to serve wine as to bake bread ; and expect not to
taste a drop yourselves." Which said, he washed four fine new
beakers with his own hands, and having sent for a small flagon
of his good wine, he heedfully filled the beakers, and presented
them to Messer Geri and his companions ; who deemed the
wine the best that they had drunk for a great while. So Messer
Geri, having praised the wine not a little, came there to drink
every morning with the ambassadors as long as they tarried
with him.

Now when the ambassadors had received their *congé*, and
were about to depart, Messer Geri gave a grand banquet, to
which he bade some of the most honourable of the citizens, and
also Cisti, who could by no means be induced to come. However, Messer Geri bade one of his servants go fetch a flask of
Cisti's wine, and serve half a beaker thereof to each guest at
the first course. The servant, somewhat offended, perhaps,
that he had not been suffered to taste any of the wine, took
with him a large flask, which Cisti no sooner saw, than :—
" Son," quoth he, " Messer Geri does not send thee to me " :
and often as the servant affirmed that he did, he could get no
other answer : wherewith he was fain at last to return to Messer
Geri. " Go, get thee back," said Messer Geri, " and tell him
that I do send thee to him, and if he answers thee so again, ask
him, to whom then I send thee." So the servant came back,
and said :—" Cisti, Messer Geri does, for sure, send me to thee."
" Son," answered Cisti, " Messer Geri does, for sure, not send
thee to me." " To whom then," said the servant, " does he
send me ? " " To Arno," returned Cisti. Which being reported by the servant to Messer Geri, the eyes of his mind were
straightway opened, and :—" Let me see," quoth he to the
servant, " what flask it is thou takest there." And when he
had seen it :—" Cisti says sooth," he added ; and having sharply
chidden him, he caused him take with him a suitable flask, which
when Cisti saw :—" Now know I," quoth he, " that 'tis indeed
Messer Geri that sends thee to me," and blithely filled it. And
having replenished the rundlet that same day with wine of the

same quality, he had it carried with due care to Messer Geri's house, and followed after himself; where finding Messer Geri he said :—" I would not have you think, Sir, that I was appalled by the great flask your servant brought me this morning; 'twas but that I thought you had forgotten that which by my little beakers I gave you to understand, when you were with me of late; to wit, that this is no table wine; and so wished this morning to refresh your memory. Now, however, being minded to keep the wine no longer, I have sent you all I have of it, to be henceforth entirely at your disposal." Messer Geri set great store by Cisti's gift, and thanked him accordingly, and ever made much of him and entreated him as his friend.

NOVEL III

Monna Nonna de' Pulci by a ready retort silences the scarce seemly jesting of the Bishop of Florence.

PAMPINEA'S story ended, and praise not a little bestowed on Cisti alike for his apt speech and for his handsome present, the queen was pleased to call forthwith for a story from Lauretta, who blithely thus began :—

Debonair my ladies, the excellency of wit, and our lack thereof, have been noted with no small truth first by Pampinea and after her by Filomena. To which topic 'twere bootless to return : wherefore to that which has been said touching the nature of wit I purpose but to add one word, to remind you that its bite should be as a sheep's bite and not as a dog's; for if it bite like a dog, 'tis no longer wit but discourtesy. With which maxim the words of Madonna Oretta, and the apt reply of Cisti, accorded excellently. True indeed it is that if 'tis by way of retort, and one that has received a dog's bite gives the biter a like bite in return, it does not seem to be reprehensible, as otherwise it would have been. Wherefore one must consider how and when and on whom and likewise where one exercises one's wit. By ill observing which matters one of our prelates did once upon a time receive no less shrewd a bite than he gave; as I will shew you in a short story.

While Messer Antonio d'Orso, a prelate both worthy and wise, was Bishop of Florence, there came thither a Catalan gentleman, Messer Dego della Ratta by name, being King Ruberto's marshal. Now Dego being very goodly of person and inordinately fond of women, it so befell that of the ladies of Florence she that he regarded with especial favour was the very beautiful niece of a brother of the said bishop. And having learned that her husband, though of good family, was but a caitiff, and avaricious in the last degree, he struck a bargain with him that he should lie one night with the lady for five hundred florins of gold : whereupon he had the same number of popolins [1] of silver, which were then current, gilded, and having lain with the lady, albeit against her will, gave them to her husband. Which coming to be generally known, the caitiff husband was left with the loss and the laugh against him ; and the bishop, like a wise man, feigned to know nought of the affair. And so the bishop and the marshal being much together, it befell that on St. John's day, as they rode side by side down the street whence they start to run the palio,[2] and took note of the ladies, the bishop espied a young gentlewoman, whom this present pestilence has reft from us, Monna Nonna de' Pulci by name, a cousin of Messer Alesso Rinucci, whom you all must know ; whom, for that she was lusty and fair, and of excellent discourse and a good courage, and but just settled with her husband in Porta San Piero, the bishop presented to the marshal ; and then, being close beside her, he laid his hand on the marshal's shoulder and said to her :— " Nonna, what thinkest thou of this gentleman ? That thou mightst make a conquest of him ? " Which words the lady resented as a jibe at her honour, and like to tarnish it in the eyes of those, who were not a few, in whose hearing they were spoken. Wherefore without bestowing a thought upon the vindication of her honour, but being minded to return blow for blow, she retorted hastily :—" Perchance, Sir, he might not make a conquest of me ; but if he did so, I should want good money." The answer stung both the marshal and the bishop to the quick, the one as contriver of the scurvy trick played upon the bishop's brother in regard of his niece, the other as thereby outraged in the person of his brother's niece ; insomuch that they dared not look one another in the face, but took themselves off in shame and silence, and said never a word more to her that day.

In such a case, then, the lady having received a bite, 'twas allowable in her wittily to return it.

---

[1] A coin of the same size and design as the fiorino d'oro, but worth only two soldi.

[2] A sort of horse-race still in vogue at Siena.

NOVEL IV

*Chichibio, cook to Currado Gianfigliazzi, owes his safety to a
ready answer, whereby he converts Currado's wrath into
laughter, and evades the evil fate with which Currado had
threatened him.*

Lauretta being now silent, all lauded Nonna to the skies ;
after which Neifile received the queen's command to follow suit,
and thus began :—

Albeit, loving ladies, ready wit not seldom ministers words
apt and excellent and congruous with the circumstances of the
speakers, 'tis also true that Fortune at times comes to the aid
of the timid, and unexpectedly sets words upon the tongue,
which in a quiet hour the speaker could never have found for
himself : the which 'tis my purpose to shew you by my story.

Currado Gianfigliazzi, as the eyes and ears of each of you
may bear witness, has ever been a noble citizen of our city,
open-handed and magnificent, and one that lived as a gentleman
should with hounds and hawks, in which, to say nothing at
present of more important matters, he found unfailing delight.
Now, having one day hard by Peretola despatched a crane
with one of his falcons, finding it young and plump, he sent it
to his excellent cook, a Venetian, Chichibio by name, bidding
him roast it for supper and make a dainty dish of it. Chichibio,
who looked, as he was, a very green-head, had dressed the crane,
and set it to the fire and was cooking it carefully, when, the
bird being all but roasted, and the fumes of the cooking very
strong, it so chanced that a girl, Brunetta by name, that lived
in the same street, and of whom Chichibio was greatly
enamoured, came into the kitchen, and perceiving the smell
and seeing the bird, began coaxing Chichibio to give her a
thigh. By way of answer Chichibio fell a-singing :—"You get
it not from me, Madam Brunetta, you get it not from me."
Whereat Madam Brunetta was offended, and said to him :—
" By God, if thou givest it me not, thou shalt never have aught
from me to pleasure thee." In short there was not a little
altercation ; and in the end Chichibio, fain not to vex his mistress, cut off one of the crane's thighs, and gave it to her. So
the bird was set before Currado and some strangers that he had
at table with him, and Currado, observing that it had but one
thigh, was surprised, and sent for Chichibio, and demanded of

him what was become of the missing thigh. Whereto the mendacious Venetian answered readily :—" The crane, Sir, has but one thigh and one leg." " What the devil ? " rejoined Currado in a rage : " so the crane has but one thigh and one leg ? thinkst thou I never saw crane before this ? " But Chichibio continued :—" 'Tis even so as I say, Sir ; and, so please you, I will shew you that so it is in the living bird." Currado had too much respect for his guests to pursue the topic ; he only said :—" Since thou promisest to shew me in the living bird what I have never seen or heard tell of, I bid thee do so to-morrow, and I shall be satisfied, but if thou fail, I swear to thee by the body of Christ that I will serve thee so that thou shalt ruefully remember my name for the rest of thy days."

No more was said of the matter that evening, but on the morrow, at daybreak, Currado, who had by no means slept off his wrath, got up still swelling therewith, and ordered his horses, mounted Chichibio on a hackney, and saying to him :— " We shall soon see which of us lied yesternight, thou or I," set off with him for a place where there was much water, beside which there were always cranes to be seen about dawn. Chichibio, observing that Currado's ire was unabated, and knowing not how to bolster up his lie, rode by Currado's side in a state of the utmost trepidation, and would gladly, had he been able, have taken to flight ; but, as he might not, he glanced, now ahead, now aback, now aside, and saw everywhere nought but cranes standing on two feet. However, as they approached the river, the very first thing they saw upon the bank was a round dozen of cranes standing each and all on one foot, as is their wont, when asleep. Which Chichibio presently pointed out to Currado, saying :—" Now may you see well enough, Sir, that 'tis true as I said yesternight, that the crane has but one thigh and one leg ; mark but how they stand over there." Whereupon Currado :—" Wait," quoth he, " and I will shew thee that they have each thighs and legs twain." So, having drawn a little nigher to them, he ejaculated, " Oho ! " Which caused the cranes to bring each the other foot to the ground, and, after hopping a step or two, to take to flight. Currado then turned to Chichibio, saying :—" How now, rogue ? art satisfied that the bird has thighs and legs twain ? " Whereto Chichibio, all but beside himself with fear, made answer :—" Ay, Sir ; but you cried not, oho ! to our crane of yestereve : had you done so, it would have popped its other thigh and foot forth, as these have done." Which answer Currado so much relished, that, all his wrath changed to jollity and laughter :— "Chichibio," quoth he, "thou art right, indeed I ought to have so done."

Thus did Chichibio by his ready and jocund retort arrest impending evil, and make his peace with his master.

NOVEL V

Messer Forese da Rabatta and Master Giotto, the painter, journeying together from Mugello, deride one another's scurvy appearance.

NEIFILE being silent, and the ladies having made very merry over Chichibio's retort, Pamfilo at the queen's command thus spoke :—Dearest ladies, if Fortune, as Pampinea has shewn us, does sometimes hide treasures most rich of native worth in the obscurity of base occupations, so in like manner 'tis not seldom found that Nature has enshrined prodigies of wit in the most ignoble of human forms. Whereof a notable example is afforded by two of our citizens, of whom I purpose for a brief while to discourse. The one, Messer Forese da Rabatta by name, was short and deformed of person and withal flat-cheeked and flat-nosed, insomuch that never a Baroncio [1] had a visage so misshapen but his would have shewed as hideous beside it ; yet so conversant was this man with the laws, that by not a few of those well able to form an opinion he was reputed a veritable storehouse of civil jurisprudence. The other, whose name was Giotto, was of so excellent a wit that, let Nature, mother of all, operant ever by continual revolution of the heavens, fashion what she would, he with his style and pen and pencil would depict its like on such wise that it shewed not as its like, but rather as the thing itself, insomuch that the visual sense of men did often err in regard thereof, mistaking for real that which was but painted. Wherefore, having brought back to light that art which had for many ages lain buried beneath the blunders of those who painted rather to delight the eyes of the ignorant than to satisfy the intelligence of the wise, he may deservedly be called one of the lights that compose the glory

[1] The name of a Florentine family famous for the extraordinary ugliness of its men : whereby it came to pass that any grotesque or extremely ugly man was called a Baroncio. Fanfani, *Vocab. della Lingua Italiana*, 1891.

of Florence, and the more so, the more lowly was the spirit in which he won that glory, who, albeit he was, while he yet lived, the master of others, yet did ever refuse to be called their master. And this title that he rejected adorned him with a lustre the more splendid in proportion to the avidity with which it was usurped by those who were less knowing than he, or were his pupils. But for all the exceeding greatness of his art, yet in no particular had he the advantage of Messer Forese either in form or in feature. But to come to the story:—'Twas in Mugello that Messer Forese, as likewise Giotto, had his country-seat, whence returning from a sojourn that he had made there during the summer vacation of the courts, and being, as it chanced, mounted on a poor jade of a draught horse, he fell in with the said Giotto, who was also on his way back to Florence after a like sojourn on his own estate, and was neither better mounted, nor in any other wise better equipped, than Messer Forese. And so, being both old men, they jogged on together at a slow pace : and being surprised by a sudden shower, such as we frequently see fall in summer, they presently sought shelter in the house of a husbandman that was known to each of them, and was their friend. But after a while, as the rain gave no sign of ceasing, and they had a mind to be at Florence that same day, they borrowed of the husbandman two old cloaks of Romagnole cloth, and two hats much the worse for age (there being no better to be had), and resumed their journey. Whereon they had not proceeded far, when, taking note that they were soaked through and through, and liberally splashed with the mud cast up by their nags' hooves (circumstances which are not of a kind to add to one's dignity), they, after long silence, the sky beginning to brighten a little, began to converse. And Messer Forese, as he rode and hearkened to Giotto, who was an excellent talker, surveyed him sideways, and from head to foot, and all over, and seeing him in all points in so sorry and scurvy a trim, and recking nought of his own appearance, broke into a laugh and said :—" Giotto, would e'er a stranger that met us, and had not seen thee before, believe, thinkst thou, that thou wert, as thou art, the greatest painter in the world." Whereto Giotto answered promptly :—" Methinks, Sir, he might, if, scanning you, he gave you credit for knowing the A B C." Which hearing, Messer Forese recognized his error, and perceived that he had gotten as good as he brought.

NOVEL VI

Michele Scalza proves to certain young men that the Baronci are the best gentlemen in the world and the Maremma, and wins a supper.

The ladies were still laughing over Giotto's ready retort, when the queen charged Fiammetta to follow suit ; wherefore thus Fiammetta began :—Pamfilo's mention of the Baronci, who to you, Damsels, are perchance not so well known as to him, has brought to my mind a story in which 'tis shewn how great is their nobility ; and, for that it involves no deviation from our rule of discourse, I am minded to tell it you.

'Tis no long time since there dwelt in our city a young man, Michele Scalza by name, the pleasantest and merriest fellow in the world, and the best furnished with quaint stories : for which reason the Florentine youth set great store on having him with them when they forgathered in company. Now it so befell that one day, he being with a party of them at Mont' Ughi, they fell a-disputing together on this wise ; to wit, who were the best gentlemen and of the longest descent in Florence. One said, the Uberti, another, the Lamberti, or some other family, according to the predilection of the speaker. Whereat Scalza began to smile, and said :—" Now out upon you, out upon you, blockheads that ye are : ye know not what ye say. The best gentlemen and of longest descent in all the world and the Maremma (let alone Florence) are the Baronci by the common consent of all phisopholers,[1] and all that know them as I do ; and lest you should otherwise conceive me, I say that 'tis of your neighbours the Baronci[2] of Santa Maria Maggiore that I speak." Whereupon the young men, who had looked for somewhat else from him, said derisively :—" Thou dost but jest with us ; as if we did not know the Baronci as well as thou ! " Quoth Scalza :—" By the Gospels I jest not, but speak sooth ; and if there is any of you will wager a supper to be given to the winner and six good fellows whom he shall choose, I will gladly do the like, and—what is more—I will abide by the decision of such one of you as you may choose." Then said one of them whose name was Neri Mannini :—" I am ready to

---

[1] In the Italian *fisofoli :* an evidently intentional distortion.
[2] Villani, *Istorie Fiorentine,* iv. cap. ix., and Dante, *Paradiso,* xvi. 104, spell the name Barucci.

adventure this supper;" and so they agreed together that
Piero di Fiorentino, in whose house they were, should be judge,
and hied them to him followed by all the rest, eager to see
Scalza lose, and triumph in his discomfiture, and told Piero all
that had been said. Piero, who was a young man of sound
sense, heard what Neri had to say; and then turning to Scalza:
—"And how," quoth he, "mayst thou make good what thou
averrest?" "I will demonstrate it," returned Scalza, "by
reasoning so cogent that not only you, but he that denies it
shall acknowledge that I say sooth. You know, and so they
were saying but now, that the longer men's descent, the better
is their gentility, and I say that the Baronci are of longer descent,
and thus better gentlemen than any other men. If, then, I
prove to you that they are of longer descent than any other
men, without a doubt the victory in this dispute will rest with
me. Now you must know that when God made the Baronci,
He was but a novice in His art, of which, when He made the
rest of mankind, He was already master. And to assure
yourself that herein I say sooth, you have but to consider the
Baronci, how they differ from the rest of mankind, who all have
faces well composed and duly proportioned, whereas of the
Baronci you will see one with a face very long and narrow,
another with a face inordinately broad, one with a very long
nose, another with a short one, one with a protruding and upturned chin, and great jaws like an ass's; and again there will
be one that has one eye larger than its fellow, or set on a lower
plane; so that their faces resemble those that children make
when they begin to learn to draw. Whereby, as I said, 'tis
plainly manifest that, when God made them, He was but
novice in His art; and so they are of longer descent than the
rest of mankind, and by consequence better gentlemen." By
which entertaining argument Piero, the judge, and Neri who
had wagered the supper, and all the rest, calling to mind the
Baronci's ugliness, were so tickled, that they fell a-laughing,
and averred that Scalza was in the right, and that he had won
the wager, and that without a doubt the Baronci were the best
gentlemen, and of the longest descent, not merely in Florence,
but in the world and the Maremma to boot. Wherefore 'twas
not without reason that Pamfilo, being minded to declare Messer
Forese's ill-favouredness, said that he would have been hideous
beside a Baroncio.

NOVEL VII

Madonna Filippa, being found by her husband with her lover, is cited before the court, and by a ready and jocund answer acquits herself, and brings about an alteration of the statute.

Fiammetta had been silent some time, but Scalza's novel argument to prove the pre-eminent nobility of the Baronci kept all still laughing, when the queen called for a story from Filostrato, who thus began :—Noble ladies, an excellent thing is apt speech on all occasions, but to be proficient therein I deem then most excellent when the occasion does most imperatively demand it. As was the case with a gentlewoman, of whom I purpose to speak to you, who not only ministered gaiety and merriment to her hearers, but extricated herself, as you shall hear, from the toils of an ignominious death.

There was aforetime in the city of Prato a statute no less censurable than harsh, which, making no distinction between the wife whom her husband took in adultery with her lover, and the woman found pleasuring a stranger for money, condemned both alike to be burned. While this statute was in force, it befell that a gentlewoman, fair and beyond measure enamoured, Madonna Filippa by name, was by her husband, Rinaldo de' Pugliesi, found in her own chamber one night in the arms of Lazzarino de' Guazzagliotri, a handsome young noble of the same city, whom she loved even as herself. Whereat Rinaldo, very wroth, scarce refrained from falling upon them and killing them on the spot ; and indeed, but that he doubted how he should afterwards fare himself, he had given way to the vehemence of his anger, and so done. Nor, though he so far mastered himself, could he forbear recourse to the statute, thereby to compass that which he might not otherwise lawfully compass, to wit, the death of his lady. Wherefore, having all the evidence needful to prove her guilt, he took no further counsel ; but, as soon as 'twas day, he charged the lady and had her summoned. Like most ladies that are veritably enamoured, the lady was of a high courage ; and, though not a few of her friends and kinsfolk sought to dissuade her, she resolved to appear to the summons, having liefer die bravely confessing the truth than basely flee and for defiance of the law live in exile, and shew herself unworthy of such a lover as had had her in his arms that night. And so, attended by many

ladies and gentlemen, who all exhorted her to deny the charge,
she came before the Podestà, and with a composed air and
unfaltering voice asked whereof he would interrogate her.
The Podestà, surveying her, and taking note of her extraordinary
beauty, and exquisite manners, and the high courage that her
words evinced, was touched with compassion for her, fearing
she might make some admission, by reason whereof, to save
his honour, he must needs do her to death. But still, as he
could not refrain from examining her of that which was laid to
her charge, he said :—" Madam, here, as you see, is your
husband, Rinaldo, who prefers a charge against you, alleging
that he has taken you in adultery, and so he demands that,
pursuant to a statute which is in force here, I punish you with
death : but this I may not do, except you confess ; wherefore
be very careful what you answer, and tell me if what your
husband alleges against you be true." The lady, no wise
dismayed, and in a tone not a little jocund, thus made answer :—
" True it is, Sir, that Rinaldo is my husband, and that last
night he found me in the arms of Lazzarino, in whose arms for
the whole-hearted love that I bear him I have ofttimes lain ;
nor shall I ever deny it ; but, as well I wot you know, the laws
ought to be common and enacted with the common consent of
all that they affect ; which conditions are wanting to this law,
inasmuch as it binds only us poor women, in whom to be liberal
is much less reprehensible than it were in men ; and furthermore
the consent of no woman was—I say not had, but—so much
as asked before 'twas made ; for which reasons it justly deserves
to be called a bad law. However, if in scathe of my body and
your own soul, you are minded to put it in force, 'tis your affair ;
but, I pray you, go not on to try this matter in any wise, until
you have granted me this trifling grace, to wit, to ask my husband if I ever gainsaid him, but did not rather accord him,
when and so often as he craved it, complete enjoyment of
myself." Whereto Rinaldo, without awaiting the Podestà's
question, forthwith answered, that assuredly the lady had ever
granted him all that he had asked of her for his gratification.
" Then," promptly continued the lady, " if he has ever had of
me as much as sufficed for his solace, what was I or am I to do
with the surplus ? Am I to cast it to the dogs ? Is it not
much better to bestow it on a gentleman that loves me more
dearly than himself, than to suffer it to come to nought or
worse ? " Which jocund question being heard by well-nigh
all the folk of Prato, who had flocked thither all agog to see a

dame so fair and of such quality on her trial for such an offence, they laughed loud and long, and then all with one accord, and as with one voice, exclaimed that the lady was in the right and said well; nor left they the court until in concert with the Podestà they had so altered the harsh statute as that thenceforth only such women as should wrong their husbands for money should be within its purview.

Wherefore Rinaldo left the court, discomfited of his foolish enterprise; and the lady blithe and free, as if rendered back to life from the burning, went home triumphant.

NOVEL VIII

Fresco admonishes his niece not to look at herself in the glass, if 'tis, as she says, grievous to her to see nasty folk.

'TWAS not at first without some flutterings of shame, evinced by the modest blush mantling on their cheeks, that the ladies heard Filostrato's story; but afterwards, exchanging glances, they could scarce forbear to laugh, and hearkened tittering. However, when he had done, the queen turning to Emilia bade her follow suit. Whereupon Emilia, fetching a deep breath as if she were roused from sleep, thus began:—Loving ladies, brooding thought has kept my spirit for so long time remote from here that perchance I may make a shift to satisfy our queen with a much shorter story than would have been forth-coming but for my absence of mind, wherein I purpose to tell you how a young woman's folly was corrected by her uncle with a pleasant jest, had she but had the sense to apprehend it. My story, then, is of one, Fresco da Celatico by name, that had a niece, Ciesca, as she was playfully called, who, being fair of face and person, albeit she had none of those angelical charms that we ofttimes see, had so superlative a conceit of herself, that she had contracted a habit of disparaging both men and women and all that she saw, entirely regardless of her own defects, though for odiousness, tiresomeness, and petulance she had not her match among women, insomuch that there was nought that could be done to her mind; besides which, such was her pride that had she been of the blood royal of France, 'twould have been inordinate. And when she walked abroad, so fastidious was her humour, she was ever averting her head, as if there was never a soul she saw or met but reeked with a foul smell. Now one day—not to speak of other odious and tiresome ways that she had—it so befell that being come home, where Fresco was, she sat herself down beside him with a most languishing air, and did nought but fume and chafe. Whereupon :—" Ciesca," quoth he, " what means this, that, though 'tis a feast-day, yet thou art come back so soon ? " She, all but dissolved with her vapourish humours, made answer :— " Why, the truth is, that I am come back early because never, I believe, were there such odious and tiresome men and women in this city as there are to-day. I cannot pass a soul in the street that I loathe not like ill-luck ; and I believe there is not a woman in the world that is so distressed by the sight of odious people as I am ; and so I am come home thus soon to avoid the sight of them." Whereupon Fresco, to whom his niece's bad manners were distasteful in the extreme :—" Daughter," quoth he, " if thou loathe odious folk as much as thou sayest, thou wert best, so thou wouldst live happy, never to look at thyself in the glass." But she, empty as a reed, albeit in her own conceit a match for Solomon in wisdom, was as far as any sheep from apprehending the true sense of her uncle's jest ; but answered that on the contrary she was minded to look at herself in the glass like other women. And so she remained, and yet remains, hidebound in her folly.

NOVEL IX

Guido Cavalcanti by a quip meetly rebukes certain Florentine gentlemen who had taken him at a disadvantage.

THE queen, perceiving that Emilia had finished her story, and that none but she, and he who had the privilege of speaking last, now remained to tell, began on this wise :—Albeit, debonair my ladies, you have forestalled me to-day of more than two of the stories, of which I had thought to tell one, yet one is still left me to recount, which carries at the close of it a quip of such a sort, that perhaps we have as yet heard nought so pregnant.

You are to know, then, that in former times there obtained in our city customs excellent and commendable not a few, whereof to-day not one is left to us, thanks to the greed which, growing with the wealth of our folk, has banished them all from among us. One of which customs was that in divers quarters of Florence the gentlemen that there resided would

assemble together in companies of a limited number, taking
care to include therein only such as might conveniently bear
the expenses, and to-day one, another to-morrow, each in his
turn for a day, would entertain the rest of the company ; and
so they would not seldom do honour to gentlemen from distant
parts when they visited the city, and also to their fellow-citizens ;
and in like manner they would meet together at least once a
year all in the same trim, and on the most notable days would
ride together through the city, and now and again they would
tilt together, more especially on the greater feasts, or when the
city was rejoiced by tidings of victory or some other glad
event. Among which companies was one of which Messer
Betto Brunelleschi was the leading spirit, into which Messer
Betto and his comrades had striven hard to bring Guido, son
of Cavalcante de' Cavalcanti, and not without reason, inasmuch
as, besides being one of the best logicians in the world, and an
excellent natural philosopher (qualities of which the company
made no great account), he was without a peer for gallantry
and courtesy and excellence of discourse and aptitude for all
matters which he might set his mind to, and that belonged to
a gentleman ; and therewithal he was very rich, and, when he
deemed any worthy of honour, knew how to bestow it to the
uttermost. But, as Messer Betto had never been able to gain
him over, he and his comrades supposed that 'twas because
Guido, being addicted to speculation, was thereby estranged
from men. And, for that he was somewhat inclined to the
opinion of the Epicureans, the vulgar averred that these specu-
lations of his had no other scope than to prove that God did not
exist. Now one day it so befell that, Guido being come, as
was not seldom his wont, from Or San Michele by the Corso
degli Adimari as far as San Giovanni, around which were then
the great tombs of marble that are to-day in Santa Reparata,
besides other tombs not a few, and Guido being between the
columns of porphyry, that are there, and the tombs and the
door of San Giovanni, which was locked, Messer Betto and his
company came riding on to the piazza of Santa Reparata, and
seeing him among the tombs, said :—" Go we and flout him."
So they set spurs to their horses, and making a mock onset,
were upon him almost before he saw them. Whereupon :—
" Guido," they began, " thou wilt be none of our company ;
but, lo now, when thou hast proved that God does not exist,
what wilt thou have achieved ? " Guido, seeing that he was
surrounded, presently answered :—" Gentlemen, you may say

to me what you please in your own house." Thereupon he laid his hand on one of the great tombs, and being very nimble, vaulted over it, and so evaded them, and went his way, while they remained gazing in one another's faces, and some said that he had taken leave of his wits, and that his answer was but nought, seeing that the ground on which they stood was common to them with the rest of the citizens, and among them Guido himself. But Messer Betto, turning to them:—" Nay but," quoth he, "'tis ye that have taken leave of your wits, if ye have not understood him; for meetly and in few words he has given us never so shrewd a reprimand; seeing that, if you consider it well, these tombs are the houses of the dead, that are laid and tarry therein; which he called our house, to shew us that we, and all other simple, unlettered men, are, in comparison of him and the rest of the learned, in sorrier case than dead men, and so being here, we are in our own house." Then none was there but understood Guido's meaning and was abashed, insomuch that they flouted him no more, and thenceforth reputed Messer Betto a gentleman of a subtle and discerning wit.

NOVEL X

Fra Cipolla promises to shew certain country-folk a feather of the Angel Gabriel, in lieu of which he finds coals, which he avers to be of those with which St. Lawrence was roasted.

ALL the company save Dioneo being delivered of their several stories, he wist that 'twas his turn to speak. Wherefore, without awaiting any very express command, he enjoined silence on those that were commending Guido's pithy quip, and thus began:—Sweet my ladies, albeit 'tis my privilege to speak of what likes me most, I purpose not to-day to deviate from that theme whereon you have all discoursed most appositely; but, following in your footsteps, I am minded to shew you with what adroitness and readiness of resource one of the Friars of St. Antony avoided a pickle that two young men had in readiness for him. Nor, if, in order to do the story full justice, I be somewhat prolix of speech, should it be burdensome to you, if you will but glance at the sun, which is yet in mid-heaven.

Certaldo, as perchance you may have heard, is a town of Val d'Elsa within our country-side, which, small though it is, had in it aforetin e people of rank and wealth. Thither, for that there he found good pasture, 'twas long the wont of one of the Friars of St. Antony to resort once every year, to collect the alms that fools gave them.   Fra Cipolla[1]—so hight the friar— met with a hearty welcome, no less, perchance, by reason of his name than for other cause, the onions produced in that district being famous throughout Tuscany.   He was little of person, red-haired, jolly-visaged, and the very best of good fellows ; and therewithal, though learning he had none, he was so ex- cellent and ready a speaker that whoso knew him not would not only have esteemed him a great rhetorician, but would have pronounced him Tully himself or, perchance, Quintilian ; and in all the country-side there was scarce a soul to whom he was not either gossip or friend or lover.   Being thus wont from time to time to visit Certaldo, the friar came there once upon a time in the month of August, and on a Sunday morning, all the good folk of the neighbouring farms being come to mass in the parish church, he took occasion to come forward and say :— " Ladies and gentlemen, you wot 'tis your custom to send year by year to the poor of Baron Master St. Antony somewhat of your wheat and oats, more or less, according to the ability and the devoutness of each, that blessed St. Antony may save your oxen and asses and pigs and sheep from harm ; and you are also accustomed, and especially those whose names are on the books of our confraternity, to pay your trifling annual dues. To collect which offerings, I am hither sent by my superior, to wit, Master Abbot ; wherefore, with the blessing of God, after none, when you hear the bells ring, you will come out of the church to the place where in the usual way I shall deliver you my sermon, and you will kiss the cross ; and therewithal, knowing, as I do, that you are one and all most devoted to Baron Master St. Antony, I will by way of especial grace shew you a most holy and goodly relic, which I brought myself from the Holy Land overseas, which is none other than one of the feathers of the Angel Gabriel, which he left behind him in the room of the Virgin Mary, when he came to make her the annun- ciation in Nazareth."   And having said thus much, he ceased, and went on with the mass.   Now among the many that were in the church, while Fra Cipolla made this speech, were two very wily young wags, the one Giovanni del Bragoniera by name, the other Biagio Pizzini ; who, albeit they were on the best of terms with Fra Cipolla and much in his company, had a sly laugh together over the relic, and resolved to make game

[1] Onion.

of him and his feather. So, having learned that Fra Cipolla
was to breakfast that morning in the town with one of his friends,
as soon as they knew that he was at table, down they hied
them into the street, and to the inn where the friar lodged,
having complotted that Biagio should keep the friar's servant
in play, while Giovanni made search among the friar's goods
and chattels for this feather, whatever it might be, to carry it
off, that they might see how the friar would afterwards explain
the matter to the people. Now Fra Cipolla had for servant
one Guccio,[1] whom some called by way of addition Balena,[2]
others Imbratta,[3] others again Porco,[4] and who was such a
rascallion that sure it is that Lippo Topo[5] himself never painted
his like. Concerning whom Fra Cipolla would ofttimes make
merry with his familiars, saying :—" My servant has nine
qualities, any one of which in Solomon, Aristotle, or Seneca,
would have been enough to spoil all their virtue, wisdom and
holiness. Consider, then, what sort of a man he must be that
has these nine qualities, and yet never a spark of either virtue
or wisdom or holiness."   And being asked upon divers occasions
what these nine qualities might be, he strung them together in
rhyme, and answered :—" I will tell you. Lazy and uncleanly
and a liar he is, Negligent, disobedient and foul-mouthed, iwis,
And reckless and witless and mannerless : and therewithal he
has some other petty vices, which 'twere best to pass over.
And the most amusing thing about 'him is, that, wherever he
goes, he is for taking a wife and renting a house, and on the
strength of a big, black, greasy beard he deems himself so very
handsome a fellow and seductive, that he takes all the women
that see him to be in love with him, and, if he were left alone,
he would slip his girdle and run after them all.   True it is that
he is of great use to me, for that, be any minded to speak with
me never so secretly, he must still have his share of the audience ;
and, if perchance aught is demanded of me, such is his fear lest
I should be at a loss what answer to make, that he presently
replies, ay or no, as he deems meet."

Now, when he left this knave at the inn, Fra Cipolla had
strictly enjoined him on no account to suffer any one to touch
aught of his, and least of all his wallet, because it contained the
holy things. But Guccio Imbratta, who was fonder of the
kitchen than any nightingale of the green boughs, and most

---

[1] Diminutive of Arriguccio.   [2] Whale.
[3] Filth.   [4] Hog.
[5] The works of this painter seem to be lost.

particularly if he espied there a maid, and in the host's kitchen
had caught sight of a coarse fat woman, short and misshapen,
with a pair of breasts that shewed as two buckets of muck and
a face that might have belonged to one of the Baronci, all
reeking with sweat and grease and smoke, left Fra Cipolla's
room and all his things to take care of themselves, and like a
vulture swooping down upon the carrion, was in the kitchen in
a trice. Where, though 'twas August, he sat him down by the
fire, and fell a-gossiping with Nuta—such was the maid's name—
and told her that he was a gentleman by procuration,[1] and had
more florins than could be reckoned, besides those that he had
to give away, which were rather more than less, and that he
could do and say such things as never were or might be seen or
heard forever, good Lord! and a day. And all heedless of his
cowl, which had as much grease upon it as would have furnished
forth the caldron of Altopascio,[2] and of his rent and patched
doublet, inlaid with filth about the neck and under the armpits,
and so stained that it shewed hues more various than ever did
silk from Tartary or the Indies, and of his shoes that were all
to pieces, and of his hose that were all in tatters, he told her in
a tone that would have become the Sieur de Châtillon, that he
was minded to rehabit her and put her in trim, and raise her
from her abject condition, and place her where, though she
would not have much to call her own, at any rate she would
have hope of better things, with much more to the like effect ;
which professions, though made with every appearance of good
will, proved, like most of his schemes, insubstantial as air, and
came to nothing.

Finding Guccio Porco thus occupied with Nuta, the two
young men gleefully accounted their work half done, and, none
gainsaying them, entered Fra Cipolla's room, which was open,
and lit at once upon the wallet, in which was the feather. The
wallet opened, they found, wrapt up in many folds of taffeta, a
little casket, on opening which they discovered one of the tail-
feathers of a parrot, which they deemed must be that which
the friar had promised to shew the good folk of Certaldo. And
in sooth he might well have so imposed upon them, for in those
days the luxuries of Egypt had scarce been introduced into
Tuscany, though they have since been brought over in prodigious
abundance, to the grave hurt of all Italy. And though some
conversance with them there was, yet in those parts folk knew

1 One of the humorous ineptitudes of which Boccaccio is fond.
2 An abbey near Lucca famous for its doles of broth.

next to nothing of them ; but, adhering to the honest, simple ways of their forefathers, had not seen, nay for the most part had not so much as heard tell of, a parrot.

So the young men, having found the feather, took it out with great glee ; and looking around for something to replace it, they espied in a corner of the room some pieces of coal, wherewith they filled the casket ; which they then closed, and having set the room in order exactly as they had found it, they quitted it unperceived, and hied them merrily off with the feather, and posted themselves where they might hear what Fra Cipolla would say when he found the coals in its stead. Mass said, the simple folk that were in the church went home with the tidings that the feather of the Angel Gabriel was to be seen after none ; and this goodman telling his neighbour, and that goodwife her gossip, by the time every one had breakfasted, the town could scarce hold the multitude of men and women that flocked thither all agog to see this feather.

Fra Cipolla, having made a hearty breakfast and had a little nap, got up shortly after none, and marking the great concourse of country-folk that were come to see the feather, sent word to Guccio Imbratta to go up there with the bells, and bring with him the wallet. Guccio, though 'twas with difficulty that he tore himself away from the kitchen and Nuta, hied him up with the things required ; and though, when he got up, he was winded, for he was corpulent with drinking nought but water, he did Fra Cipolla's bidding by going to the church door and ringing the bells amain. When all the people were gathered about the door, Fra Cipolla, all unwitting that aught of his was missing, began his sermon, and after much said in glorification of himself, caused the confiteor to be recited with great solemnity, and two torches to be lit by way of preliminary to the shewing of the feather of the Angel Gabriel : he then bared his head, carefully unfolded the taffeta, and took out the casket, which, after a few prefatory words in praise and laudation of the Angel Gabriel and his relic, he opened. When he saw that it contained nought but coals, he did not suspect Guccio Balena of playing the trick, for he knew that he was not clever enough, nor did he curse him, that his carelessness had allowed another to play it, but he inly imprecated himself, that he had committed his things to the keeping of one whom he knew to be " negligent and disobedient, reckless and witless." Nevertheless, he changed not colour, but with face and hands upturned to heaven, he said in a voice that all might hear :—" O God, blessed by Thy might

for ever and ever." Then, closing the casket, and turning to
the people :—" Ladies and gentlemen," he said, " you are to
know, that when I was yet a very young man, I was sent by
my superior into those parts where the sun rises, and I was
expressly bidden to search until I should find the Privileges of
Porcellana, which, though they cost nothing to seal, are of
much more use to others than to us. On which errand I set
forth, taking my departure from Venice, and traversing the
Borgo de' Greci,[1] and thence on horseback the realm of Algarve,[2]
and so by Baldacca[3] I came to Parione,[4] whence, somewhat
athirst, I after a while got on to Sardinia.[5] But wherefore go
I about to enumerate all the lands in which I pursued my quest ?
Having passed the straits of San Giorgio, I arrived at Truffia[6]
and Buffia,[7] countries thickly populated and with great nations,
whence I pursued my journey to Menzogna,[8] where I met with
many of our own brethren, and of other religious not a few,
intent one and all on eschewing hardship for the love of God,
making little account of others' toil, so they might ensue their
own advantage, and paying in nought but unminted coin[9]
throughout the length and breadth of the country ; and so I
came to the land of Abruzzi, where the men and women go in
pattens on the mountains, and clothe the hogs with their own
entrails ;[10] and a little further on I found folk that carried
bread in staves and wine in sacks.[11] And leaving them, I arrived
at the mountains of the Bachi,[12] where all the waters run down-
wards. In short I penetrated so far that I came at last to India
Pastinaca,[13] where I swear to you by the habit that I wear, that

1 Perhaps part of the " sesto " of Florence known as the Borgo, as the
tradition of the commentators that the friar's itinerary is wholly Florentine
is not to be lightly set aside.
2 *Il Garbo*, a quarter or street in Florence, doubtless so called because
the wares of Algarve were there sold. *Rer. Ital. Script.* (Muratori : Suppl.
Tartini) ii. 119. Villani, *Istorie Fiorentine*, iv. 12, xii. 18.
3 A famous tavern in Florence. Florio, *Vocab. Ital. e Ingl.*, ed. Tor-
riano, 1659.
4 A " borgo " in Florence. Villani, *Istorie Fiorentine*, iv. 7.
5 A suburb of Florence on the Arno, *ib.* ix. 256.
6 The land of Cajolery.
7 The land of Drollery.
8 The land of Lies.
9 *I.e.* in false promises : suggested by Dante's Pagando di moneta
senza conio. *Parad.* xxix. 126.
10 A reference to sausage-making.
11 *I.e.* cakes fashioned in a hollow ring, and wines in leathern bottles.
12 Grubs.
13 In allusion to the shapeless fish, so called, which was proverbially
taken as a type of the outlandish.

I saw pruning-hooks [1] fly : a thing that none would believe that had not seen it.   Whereof be my witness that I lie not Maso del Saggio, that great merchant, whom I found there cracking nuts, and selling the shells by retail !   However, not being able to find that whereof I was in quest, because from thence one must travel by water, I turned back, and so came at length to the Holy Land, where in summer cold bread costs four deniers, and hot bread is to be had for nothing.   And there I found the venerable father Nonmiblasmetesevoipiace,[2] the most worshipful Patriarch of Jerusalem ; who out of respect for the habit that I have ever worn, to wit, that of Baron Master St. Antony, was pleased to let me see all the holy relics that he had by him, which were so many, that, were I to enumerate them all, I should not come to the end of them in some miles.   However, not to disappoint you, I will tell you a few of them.   In the first place, then, he shewed me the finger of the Holy Spirit, as whole and entire as it ever was, and the tuft of the Seraph that appeared to St. Francis, and one of the nails of the Cherubim, and one of the ribs of the Verbum Caro hie thee to the casement,[3] and some of the vestments of the Holy Catholic Faith, and some of the rays of the star that appeared to the Magi in the East, and a phial of the sweat of St. Michael a-battling with the Devil and the jaws of death of St. Lazarus, and other relics. And for that I gave him a liberal supply of the acclivities [4] of Monte Morello in the vulgar and some chapters of Caprezio, of which he had long been in quest, he was pleased to let me participate in his holy relics, and gave me one of the teeth of the Holy Cross, and in a small phial a bit of the sound of the bells of Solomon's temple, and this feather of the Angel Gabriel, whereof I have told you, and one of the pattens of San Gherardo da Villa Magna, which, not long ago, I gave at Florence to Gherardo di Bonsi, who holds him in prodigious veneration. He also gave me some of the coals with which the most blessed martyr, St. Lawrence, was roasted.   All which things I devoutly brought thence, and have them all safe.   True it is that my superior has not hitherto permitted me to shew them, until he should be certified that they are genuine.   However, now that this is avouched by certain miracles wrought by them, of which

---

[1] A *jeu de mots*, " pennati," pruning-hooks, signifying also *feathered*, though " pennuti " is more common in that sense.

[2] Takemenottotaskanitlikeyou.

[3] *fatti alle finestre*, a subterfuge for *factum est*.

[4] *piagge*, jocularly for *pagine :* doubtless some mighty tome of school divinity is meant.

we have tidings by letter from the Patriarch, he has given me
leave to shew them. But, fearing to trust them to another, I
always carry them with me ; and to tell you the truth I carry
the feather of the Angel Gabriel, lest it should get spoiled, in a
casket, and the coals, with which St. Lawrence was roasted, in
another casket ; which caskets are so like the one to the other,
that not seldom I mistake one for the other, which has befallen
me on this occasion ; for, whereas I thought to have brought
with me the casket wherein is the feather, I have brought instead that which contains the coals. Nor deem I this a mis-
chance ; nay, methinks, 'tis by interposition of God, and that
He Himself put the casket of coals in my hand, for I mind me
that the feast of St. Lawrence falls but two days hence. Wherefore God, being minded that by shewing you the coals, with
which he was roasted, I should rekindle in your souls the devotion
that you ought to feel towards him, guided my hand, not to the
feather which I meant to take, but to the blessed coals that
were extinguished by the humours that exuded from that most
holy body. And so, blessed children, bare your heads and
devoutly draw nigh to see them. But first of all I would have
you know, that whoso has the sign of the cross made upon him
with these coals, may live secure for the whole of the ensuing
year, that fire shall not touch him, that he feel it not."

Having so said, the friar, chanting a hymn in praise of St.
Lawrence, opened the casket, and shewed the coals. Whereon
the foolish crowd gazed a while in awe and reverent wonder, and
then came pressing forward in a mighty throng about Fra
Cipolla with offerings beyond their wont, each and all praying
him to touch them with the coals. Wherefore Fra Cipolla took
the coals in his hand, and set about making on their white
blouses, and on their doublets, and on the veils of the women
crosses as big as might be, averring the while that whatever
the coals might thus lose would be made good to them again in
the casket, as he had often proved. On this wise, to his exceeding great profit, he marked all the folk of Certaldo with the
cross, and, thanks to his ready wit and resource, had his laugh
at those, who by robbing him of the feather thought to make a
laughing-stock of him. They, indeed, being among his hearers,
and marking his novel expedient, and how voluble he was,
and what a long story he made of it, laughed till they thought
their jaws would break ; and, when the congregation was
dispersed, they went up to him, and never so merrily told him
what they had done, and returned him his feather ; which next

year proved no less lucrative to him than that day the coals had been.

Immense was the delight and diversion which this story afforded to all the company alike, and great and general was the laughter over Fra Cipolla, and more especially at his pilgrimage, and the relics, as well those that he had but seen as those that he had brought back with him. Which being ended, the queen, taking note that therewith the close of her sovereignty was come, stood up, took off the crown, and set it on Dioneo's head, saying with a laugh :—" 'Tis time, Dioneo, that thou prove the weight of the burden of having ladies to govern and guide. Be thou king then ; and let thy rule be such that, when 'tis ended, we may have cause to commend it." Dioneo took the crown, and laughingly answered :—" Kings worthier far than I you may well have seen many a time ere now—I speak of the kings in chess ; but let me have of you that obedience which is due to a true king, and of a surety I will give you to taste of that solace, without which perfection of joy there may not be in any festivity. But enough of this : I will govern as best I may." Then, as was the wont, he sent for the seneschal, and gave him particular instruction how to order matters during the term of his sovereignty ; which done, he said :— " Noble ladies, such and so diverse has been our discourse of the ways of men and their various fortunes, that but for the visit that we had a while ago from Madam Licisca, who by what she said has furnished me with matter of discourse for to-morrow, I doubt I had been not a little put to it to find a theme. You heard how she said that there was not a woman in her neighbourhood whose husband had her virginity ; adding that well she knew how many and what manner of tricks they, after marriage, played their husbands. The first count we may well leave to the girls whom it concerns ; the second, methinks, should prove a diverting topic : wherefore I ordain that, taking our cue from Madam Licisca, we discourse to-morrow of the tricks that, either for love or for their deliverance from peril, ladies have heretofore played their husbands, and whether they were by the said husbands detected or no." To discourse of such a topic some of the ladies deemed unmeet for them, and besought the king to find another theme. But the king made answer :—" Ladies, what manner of theme I have prescribed I know as well as you, nor was I to be diverted from prescribing it by that which you now think to declare unto me, for I wot the times are such that, so only men and women have a care to do nought that is unseemly, 'tis allowable to them to discourse of what they please. For in sooth, as you must know, so out of joint are the times that the judges have deserted the judgment-seat, the laws are silent, and ample licence to preserve his life as best he may is accorded to each and all. Wherefore, if you are somewhat less strict of speech than is your wont, not that aught unseemly in act may follow, but that you may afford solace to yourselves and others, I see not how you can be open to reasonable censure on the part of any. Furthermore, nought that has been said from the first day to the present moment has, methinks, in any degree sullied the immaculate honour of your company, nor, God helping us, shall aught ever sully it. Besides, who is there that knows not the quality of your honour? which were proof, I make no doubt, against not only the seductive influence of diverting discourse, but even the terror of death. And, to tell you the truth, whoso wist that you refused to discourse of these light matters for a while, would be apt to suspect that 'twas but for that you had yourselves erred in like sort. And truly a goodly honour would you confer upon me, obedient as I have ever been to you, if after making me your king and your lawgiver, you were to refuse to discourse of the theme which I prescribe. Away, then, with this scruple fitter for low minds than yours, and let each study how she may give us a goodly story, and Fortune prosper her therein."

So spake the king, and the ladies, hearkening, said that, even as he would, so it should be : whereupon he gave all leave to do as they might be severally minded until the supper-hour. The sun was still quite high in the heaven, for they had not enlarged in their discourse : wherefore, Dioneo with the other gallants being set to play at dice, Elisa called the other ladies apart, and said :—" There is a nook hard by this place, where I think none of you has ever been : 'tis called the Ladies' Vale : whither, ever since we have been here, I have desired to take you, but time meet I have not found until to-day, when the sun is still so high : if, then, you are minded to visit it, I have no manner of doubt that, when you are there, you will be very glad you came." The ladies answered that they were ready, and so, saying nought to the young men, they summoned one of their maids, and set forth ; nor had they gone much more than a mile, when they arrived at the Vale of Ladies. They entered it by a very strait gorge, through which there issued a rivulet, clear as crystal, and a sight, than which nought more fair and pleasant, especially at that time when the heat was great, could be imagined, met their eyes. Within the valley, as one of them afterwards told me, was a plain about half-a-mile in circumference, and so exactly circular that it might have been fashioned according to the compass, though it seemed a work of Nature's art, not man's : 'twas girdled about by six hills of no great height, each crowned with a palace that shewed as a goodly little castle. The slopes of the hills were graduated from summit to base after the manner of the successive tiers, ever abridging their circle, that we see in our theatres ; and as many as fronted the southern rays were all planted so close with vines, olives, almond-trees, cherry-trees, fig-trees and other fruit-bearing trees not a few, that there was not a hand's-breadth of vacant space. Those that fronted the north were in like manner covered with copses of oak saplings, ashes and other trees, as green and straight as might be. Besides which, the plain, which was shut in on all sides save that on which the ladies had entered, was full of firs, cypresses, and bay-trees, with here and there a pine, in order and symmetry so meet and excellent as had they been planted by an artist, the best that might be found in that kind ; where-through, even when the sun was in the zenith, scarce a ray of light might reach the ground, which was all one lawn of the finest turf, pranked with the hyacinth and divers other flowers. Add to which—nor was there aught there more delightsome— a rivulet that, issuing from one of the gorges between two of the hills, descended over ledges of living rock, making, as it fell, a murmur most gratifying to the ear, and, seen from a distance, shewed as a spray of finest, powdered quick-silver, and no sooner reached the little plain, than 'twas gathered into a tiny channel, by which it sped with great velocity to the middle of the plain, where it formed a diminutive lake, like the fishponds that townsfolk sometimes make in their gardens, when they have occasion for them. The lake was not so deep but that a man might stand therein with his breast above the water ; and so clear, so pellucid was the water that the bottom, which was of the finest gravel, shewed so distinct, that one, had he wished, who had nought better to do, might have counted the stones. Nor was it only the bottom that was to be seen, but such a multitude of fishes, glancing to and fro, as was at once a delight and a marvel to behold. Bank it had none, but its margin was the lawn, to which it imparted a goodlier freshness. So much of the water as it might not contain was received by another tiny channel, through which, issuing from the vale, it glided swiftly to the plain below.

To which pleasaunce the damsels being come surveyed it with
roving glance, and finding it commendable, and marking the
lake in front of them, did, as 'twas very hot, and they deemed
themselves secure from observation, resolve to take a bath.
So, having bidden their maid wait and keep watch over the access
to the vale, and give them warning, if haply any should approach
it, they all seven undressed and got into the water, which to
the whiteness of their flesh was even such a veil as fine glass is
to the vermeil of the rose. They, being thus in the water, the
clearness of which was thereby in no wise affected, did presently
begin to go hither and thither after the fish, which had much
ado where to bestow themselves so as to escape out of their
hands. In which diversion they spent some time, and caught
a few, and then they hied them out of the water and dressed
them again, and bethinking them that 'twas time to return
to the palace, they began slowly sauntering thither, dilating
much as they went upon the beauty of the place, albeit they
could not extol it more than they had already done. 'Twas
still quite early when they reached the palace, so that they
found the gallants yet at play where they had left them. To
whom quoth Pampinea with a smile :—" We have stolen a
march upon you to-day." " So," replied Dioneo, " 'tis with
you do first and say after ? " " Ay, my lord," returned Pampinea, and told him at large whence they came, and what the
place was like, and how far 'twas off, and what they had done.
What she said of the beauty of the spot begat in the king a
desire to see it : wherefore he straightway ordered supper,
whereof when all had gaily partaken, the three gallants parted
from the ladies and hied them with their servants to the vale,
where none of them had ever been before, and, having marked
all its beauties, extolled it as scarce to be matched in all the
world. Then, as the hour was very late, they did but bathe,
and as soon as they had resumed their clothes, returned to the
ladies, whom they found dancing a carol to an air that
Fiammetta sang, which done, they conversed of the Ladies'
Vale, waxing eloquent in praise thereof : insomuch that the
king called the seneschal, and bade him have some beds made
ready and carried thither on the morrow, that any that were
so minded might there take their siesta. He then had lights
and wine and comfits brought ; and when they had taken a
slight refection, he bade all address them to the dance. So at
his behest Pamfilo led a dance, and then the king, turning with
gracious mien to Elisa :—" Fair damsel," quoth he, " 'twas

thou to-day didst me this honour of the crown; and 'tis my
will that thine to-night be the honour of the song; wherefore
sing us whatsoever thou hast most lief." "That gladly will
I," replied Elisa smiling; and thus with dulcet voice began:—

> If of thy talons, Love, be quit I may,
>   I deem it scarce can be
>   But other fangs I may elude for aye.
>
> Service I took with thee, a tender maid,
>   In thy war thinking perfect peace to find,
>   And all my arms upon the ground I laid,
>   Yielding myself to thee with trustful mind:
>   Thou, harpy-tyrant, whom no faith may bind,
>   Eftsoons didst swoop on me,
>   And with thy cruel claws mad'st me thy prey.
>
> Then thy poor captive, bound with many a chain,
>   Thou tookst, and gav'st to him, whom fate did call
>   Hither my death to be; for that in pain
>   And bitter tears I waste away, his thrall:
>   Nor heave I e'er a sigh, or tear let fall,
>   So harsh a lord is he,
>   That him inclines a jot my grief to allay.
>
> My prayers upon the idle air are spent:
>   He hears not, will not hear; wherefore in vain
>   The more each hour my soul doth her torment;
>   Nor may I die, albeit to die were gain.
>   Ah! Lord, have pity on my bitter pain!
>   Help have I none but thee;
>   Then take and bind and at my feet him lay.
>
> But if thou wilt not, do my soul but loose
>   From hope, that her still binds with triple chain.
>   Sure, O my Lord, this prayer thou'lt not refuse:
>   The which so thou to grant me do but deign,
>   I look my wonted beauty to regain,
>   And banish misery
>   With roses white and red bedecked and gay.

So with a most piteous sigh ended Elisa her song, whereat all
wondered exceedingly, nor might any conjecture wherefore she
so sang. But the king, who was in a jolly humour, sent for
Tindaro, and bade him out with his cornemuse, and caused
them tread many a measure thereto, until, no small part of the
night being thus spent, he gave leave to all to betake them to
rest.

Endeth here the sixth day of the Decameron, beginneth the seventh, in which, under the rule of Dioneo, discourse is had of the tricks which, either for love or for their deliverance from peril, ladies have heretofore played their husbands, and whether they were by the said husbands detected, or no.

FLED was now each star from the eastern sky, save only that which we call Lucifer, which still glowed in the whitening dawn, when uprose the seneschal, and with a goodly baggage-train hied him to the Ladies' Vale, there to make all things ready according to the ordinance and commandment of the king. Nor was it long after his departure that the king rose, being awaked by the stir and bustle that the servants made in lading the horses, and being risen he likewise roused all the ladies and the other gallants; and so, when as yet 'twas scarce clear daybreak, they all took the road; nor seemed it to them that the nightingales and the other birds had ever chanted so blithely as that morning. By which choir they were attended to the Ladies' Vale, where they were greeted by other warblers not a few, that seemed rejoiced at their arrival. Roving about the vale, and surveying its beauties afresh, they rated them higher than on the previous day, as indeed the hour was more apt to shew them forth. Then with good wine and comfits they broke their fast, and, that they might not lag behind the songsters, they fell a-singing, whereto the vale responded, ever echoing their strains; nor did the birds, as minded not to be beaten, fail to swell the chorus with notes of unwonted sweetness. However, breakfast-time came, and then, the tables being laid under a living canopy of trees, and beside other goodly trees that fringed the little lake, they sat them down in order as to the king seemed meet. So they took their meal, glancing from time to time at the lake, where the fish darted to and fro in multitudinous shoals, which afforded not only delight to their eyes but matter for converse. Breakfast ended, and the tables removed, they fell a-singing again more blithely than before. After which, there being set, in divers places about the little vale, beds which the discreet seneschal had duly furnished and equipped within and without with store of French coverlets,

95

and other bedgear, all, that were so minded, had leave of the
king to go to sleep, and those that cared not to sleep might betake
them, as each might choose, to any of their wonted diversions.
But, all at length being risen, and the time for addressing
them to the story-telling being come, the king had carpets
spread on the sward no great way from the place where they
had breakfasted ; and, all having sat them down beside the
lake, he bade Emilia begin ; which, blithe and smiling, Emilia
did on this wise.

NOVEL I

*Gianni Lotteringhi hears a knocking at his door at night : he
awakens his wife, who persuades him that 'tis the bogey,
which they fall to exorcizing with a prayer ; whereupon the
knocking ceases.*

My lord, glad indeed had I been, that, saving your good pleasure,
some other than I had had precedence of discourse upon so
goodly a theme as this of which we are to speak : I doubt I
am but chosen to teach others confidence ; but, such being
your will, I will gladly obey it. And my endeavour shall be,
dearest ladies, to tell you somewhat that may be serviceable
to you in the future : for, if you are, as I am, timorous, and that
most especially of the bogey, which, God wot, I know not what
manner of thing it may be, nor yet have found any that knew,
albeit we are all alike afraid of it, you may learn from this my
story how to put it to flight, should it intrude upon you, with
a holy, salutary and most efficacious orison.

There dwelt of yore at Florence, in the quarter of San
Pancrazio, a master-spinner, Gianni Lotteringhi by name, one
that had prospered in his business, but had little understanding
of aught else ; insomuch that being somewhat of a simpleton,
he had many a time been chosen leader of the band of laud-
singers of Santa Maria Novella, and had charge of their school ;
and not a few like offices had he often served, upon which he
greatly plumed himself. Howbeit, 'twas all for no other
reason than that, being a man of substance, he gave liberal
doles to the friars ; who, for that they got thereof, this one
hose, another a cloak, and a third a hood, would teach him
good orisons, or give him the paternoster in the vernacular, or
the chant of St. Alexis, or the lament of St. Bernard, or the laud

of Lady Matilda, or the like sorry stuff, which he greatly prized,
and guarded with jealous care, deeming them all most conducive
to the salvation of his soul.

Now our simple master-spinner had a most beautiful wife,
and amorous withal, her name Monna Tessa. Daughter she
was of Mannuccio dalla Cuculla, and not a little knowing and
keen-witted ; and being enamoured of Federigo di Neri Pego-
lotti, a handsome and lusty gallant, as he also of her, she, knowing her husband's simplicity, took counsel with her maid, and
arranged that Federigo should come to chat with her at a right
goodly pleasure-house that the said Gianni had at Camerata,
where she was wont to pass the summer, Gianni coming now
and again to sup and sleep, and going back in the morning to
his shop, or, maybe, to his laud-singers.   Federigo, who desired
nothing better, went up there punctually on the appointed
day about vespers, and as the evening passed without Gianni
making his appearance, did most comfortably, and to his no
small satisfaction, sup and sleep with the lady, who lying in
his arms taught him that night some six of her husband's lauds.
But, as neither she nor Federigo was minded that this beginning
should also be the end of their intercourse, and that it might
not be needful for the maid to go each time to make the assignation with him, they came to the following understanding ;
to wit, that as often as he came and went between the house
and an estate that he had a little higher up, he should keep an
eye on a vineyard that was beside the house, where he would
see an ass's head stuck on one of the poles of the vineyard, and
as often as he observed the muzzle turned towards Florence, he
might visit her without any sort of misgiving ; and if he found
not the door open, he was to tap it thrice, and she would open
it ; and when he saw the muzzle of the ass's head turned towards
Fiesole, he was to keep away, for then Gianni would be there.
Following which plan, they forgathered not seldom : but on
one of these evenings, when Federigo was to sup with Monna
Tessa on two fat capons that she had boiled, it so chanced that
Gianni arrived there unexpectedly and very late, much to the
lady's chagrin : so she had a little salt meat boiled apart, on
which she supped with her husband ; and the maid by her
orders carried the two boiled capons laid in a spotless napkin
with plenty of fresh eggs and a bottle of good wine into the
garden, to which there was access otherwise than from the
house, and where she was wont at times to sup with Federigo ;
and there the maid set them down at the foot of a peach-tree,

that grew beside a lawn. But in her vexation she forgot to tell the maid to wait till Federigo should come, and let him know that Gianni was there, and he must take his supper in the garden : and she and Gianni and the maid were scarce gone to bed, when Federigo came and tapped once at the door, which being hard by the bedroom, Gianni heard the tap, as did also the lady, albeit, that Gianni might have no reason to suspect her, she feigned to be asleep. Federigo waited a little, and then gave a second tap ; whereupon, wondering what it might mean, Gianni nudged his wife, saying :—" Tessa, dost hear what I hear ? Methinks some one has tapped at our door." The lady, who had heard the noise much better than he, feigned to wake up, and :—" How ? what sayst thou ? " quoth she. " I say," replied Gianni, " that, meseems, some one has tapped at our door." " Tapped at it ? " quoth the lady. " Alas, my Gianni, wottest thou not what that is ? 'Tis the bogey, which for some nights past has so terrified me as never was, insomuch that I never hear it but I pop my head under the clothes and venture not to put it out again until 'tis broad day." " Come, come, wife," quoth Gianni, " if such it is, be not alarmed ; for before we got into bed I repeated the *Te lucis*, the *Intemerata*, and divers other good orisons, besides which I made the sign of the cross in the name of the Father, Son and Holy Spirit at each corner of the bed ; wherefore we need have no fear that it may avail to hurt us, whatever be its power." The lady, lest Federigo, perchance suspecting a rival, should take offence, resolved to get up, and let him understand that Gianni was there : so she said to her husband :—" Well, well ; so sayst thou ; but I for my part shall never deem myself safe and secure, unless we exorcize it, seeing that thou art here." " Oh ! " said Gianni, " and how does one exorcize it ? " " That," quoth the lady, " I know right well ; for t'other day, when I went to Fiesole for the pardoning, one of those anchoresses, the saintliest creature, my Gianni, God be my witness, knowing how much afraid I am of the bogey, taught me a holy and salutary orison, which she said she had tried many a time before she was turned anchoress, and always with success. God wot, I should never have had courage to try it alone ; but as thou art here, I propose that we go exorcize it together." Gianni made answer that he was quite of the same mind ; so up they got, and stole to the door, on the outside of which Federigo, now suspicious, was still waiting. And as soon as they were there :—" Now," quoth the lady to Gianni,

"Thou wilt spit, when I tell thee." "Good," said Gianni. Whereupon the lady began her orison, saying:—

> " Bogey, bogey that goest by night,
> Tail erect, thou cam'st, tail erect, take thy flight:
> Hie thee to the garden, and the great peach before,
> Grease upon grease, and droppings five score
> Of my hen shalt thou find :
> Set the flask thy lips to,
> Then away like the wind,
> And no scathe unto me or my Gianni do."

And when she had done :—" Now, Gianni," quoth she, " spit " : and Gianni spat.

There was no more room for jealousy in Federigo's mind as he heard all this from without ; nay, for all his disappointment, he was like to burst with suppressed laughter, and when Gianni spat, he muttered under his breath :—" Now out with thy teeth." The lady, having after this fashion thrice exorcized the bogey, went back to bed with her husband. Federigo, disappointed of the supper that he was to have had with her, and apprehending the words of the orison aright, hied him to the garden, and having found the two capons and the wine and the eggs at the foot of the peach-tree, took them home with him, and supped very comfortably. And many a hearty laugh had he and the lady over the exorcism during their subsequent intercourse.

Now, true it is that some say that the lady had in fact turned the ass's head towards Fiesole, but that a husbandman, passing through the vineyard, had given it a blow with his stick, whereby it had swung round, and remained fronting Florence, and so it was that Federigo thought that he was invited, and came to the house, and that the lady's orison was on this wise :—

> " Bogey, a God's name, away thee hie,
> For whoe'er turned the ass's head, 'twas not I :
> Another it was, foul fall his eyne ;
> And here am I with Gianni mine."

Wherefore Federigo was fain to take himself off, having neither slept nor supped.

But a neighbour of mine, a lady well advanced in years, tells me that, by what she heard when she was a girl, both stories are true ; but that the latter concerned not Gianni Lotteringhi but one Gianni di Nello, that lived at Porta San Piero, and was no less a numskull than Gianni Lotteringhi. Wherefore, dear my ladies, you are at liberty to choose which exorcism you prefer, or take both if you like.   They are both of extraordinary and approved virtue in such cases, as you have heard : get them by heart, therefore, and they may yet stand you in good stead.

NOVEL II

Her husband returning home, Peronella bestows her lover in a tun ; which, being sold by her husband, she avers to have been already sold by herself to one that is inside examining it to see if it be sound.   Whereupon the lover jumps out, and causes the husband to scour the tun for him, and afterwards to carry it to his house.

GREAT indeed was the laughter with which Emilia's story was received ; which being ended, and her orison commended by all as good and salutary, the king bade Filostrato follow suit ; and thus Filostrato began :—Dearest my ladies, so many are the tricks that men play you, and most of all your husbands, that, when from time to time it so befalls that some lady plays her husband a trick, the circumstance, whether it come within your own cognizance or be told you by another, should not only give you joy but should incite you to publish it on all hands, that men may be ware, that, knowing as they are, their ladies also, on their part, know somewhat : which cannot but be serviceable to you, for that one does not rashly essay to take another with guile whom one wots not to lack that quality. Can we doubt, then, that, should but the converse that we shall hold to-day touching this matter come to be bruited among men, 'twould serve to put a most notable check upon the tricks they play you, by doing them to wit of the tricks, which you, in like manner, when you are so minded, may play them ? Wherefore 'tis my intention to tell you in what manner a young girl, albeit she was but of low rank, did, on the spur of the moment, beguile her husband to her own deliverance.

'Tis no long time since at Naples a poor man, a mason by craft, took to wife a fair and amorous maiden—Peronella was her name—who eked out by spinning what her husband made by his craft ; and so the pair managed as best they might on very slender means.   And as chance would have it, one of the gallants of the city, taking note of this Peronella one day, and being mightily pleased with her, fell in love with her, and

by this means and that so prevailed that he won her to accord
him her intimacy. Their times of forgathering they concerted
as follows :—to wit, that, her husband being wont to rise betimes of a morning to go to work or seek for work, the gallant
was to be where he might see him go forth, and, the street where
she dwelt, which is called Avorio, being scarce inhabited, was
to come into the house as soon as her husband was well out of
it ; and so times not a few they did. But on one of these
occasions it befell that, the good man being gone forth, and
Giannello Sirignario—such was the gallant's name—being
come into the house, and being with Peronella, after a while,
back came the good man, though 'twas not his wont to return
until the day was done ; and finding the door locked, he knocked,
and after knocking, he fell a-saying to himself :—O God,
praised be Thy name forever ; for that, albeit Thou hast
ordained that I be poor, at least Thou hast accorded me the
consolation of a good and honest girl for wife. Mark what
haste she made to shut the door when I was gone forth, that
none else might enter to give her trouble.

Now Peronella knew by his knock that 'twas her husband ;
wherefore :—" Alas, Giannello mine," quoth she, " I am a dead
woman, for lo, here is my husband, foul fall him ! come back !
What it may import, I know not, for he is never wont to come
back at this hour ; perchance he caught sight of thee as thou
camest in. However, for the love of God, be it as it may, get
thee into this tun that thou seest here, and I will go open to
him, and we shall see what is the occasion of this sudden
return this morning." So Giannello forthwith got into the
tun, and Peronella went to the door, and let in her husband,
and gave him black looks, saying :—" This is indeed a surprise
that thou art back so soon this morning ! By what I see thou
hast a mind to make this a holiday, that thou returnest tools
in hand ; if so, what are we to live on ? whence shall we get
bread to eat ? Thinkest thou I will let thee pawn my gown
and other bits of clothes ? Day and night I do nought else
but spin, insomuch that the flesh is fallen away from my nails,
that at least I may have oil enough to keep our lamp alight.
Husband, husband, there is never a woman in the neighbourhood but marvels and mocks at me, that I am at such labour
and pains ; and thou comest home to me with thy hands hanging idle, when thou shouldst be at work." Which said, she
fell a-weeping and repeating :—" Alas, alas, woe's me, in what
evil hour was I born ? in what luckless moment came I hither,

I, that might have had so goodly a young man, and I would not, to take up with one that bestows never a thought on her whom he has made his wife ? Other women have a good time with their lovers, and never a one have we here but has two or three ; they take their pleasure, and make their husbands believe that the moon is the sun ; and I, alas ! for that I am an honest woman, and have no such casual amours, I suffer, and am hard bested : I know not why I provide not myself with one of these lovers, as others do. Give good heed, husband, to what I say : were I disposed to dishonour thee, I were at no loss to find the man : for here are gallants enough, that love me, and court me, and have sent me many an offer of money—no stint—or dresses or jewels, should I prefer them ; but my pride would never suffer it, because I was not born of a woman of that sort : and now thou comest home to me when thou oughtest to be at work."

Whereto the husband :—" Wife, wife, for God's sake distress not thyself : thou shouldst give me credit for knowing what manner of woman thou art, as indeed I have partly seen this morning. True it is that I went out to work ; but 'tis plain that thou knowest not, as indeed I knew not, that to-day 'tis the feast of San Galeone, and a holiday, and that is why I am come home at this hour ; but nevertheless I have found means to provide us with bread for more than a month ; for I have sold to this gentleman, whom thou seest with me, the tun, thou wottest of, seeing that it has encumbered the house so long, and he will give me five gigliats for it." Quoth then Peronella :—" And all this but adds to my trouble : thou, that art a man, and goest abroad, and shouldst know affairs, hast sold for five gigliats a tun, which I, that am but a woman, and was scarce ever out of doors, have, for that it took up so much room in the house, sold for seven gigliats to a good man, that but now, as thou cam'st back, got therein, to see if 'twere sound." So hearing, the husband was overjoyed, and said to the man that was come to take it away ;—" Good man, I wish thee Godspeed ; for, as thou hearest, my wife has sold the tun for seven gigliats, whereas thou gavest me only five." Whereupon :—" So be it," said the good man, and took himself off. Then said Peronella to her husband :—" Now, as thou art here, come up, and arrange the matter with the good man."

Now Giannello, who, meanwhile, had been all on the alert to discover if there were aught he had to fear or be on his guard

against, no sooner heard Peronella's last words, than he sprang
out of the tun, and feigning to know nought of her husband's
return, began thus :—"Where art thou, good dame ?"
Whereto the husband, coming up, answered :—"Here am I :
what wouldst thou of me ?" Quoth Giannello :—"And who
art thou ? I would speak with the lady with whom I struck
the bargain for this tun." Then said the good man :—
"Have no fear, you can deal with me ; for I am her husband."
Quoth then Giannello :—"The tun seems to me sound enough ;
but I think you must have let the lees remain in it ; for 'tis all
encrusted with I know not what that is so dry, that I cannot
raise it with the nail ; wherefore I am not minded to take it
unless I first see it scoured." Whereupon Peronella :—"To
be sure : that shall not hinder the bargain ; my husband will
scour it clean." And :—"Well and good," said the husband.

So he laid down his tools, stripped himself to his vest, sent for
a light and a rasp, and was in the tun, and scraping away, in
a trice. Whereupon Peronella, as if she were curious to see
what he did, thrust her head into the vent of the tun, which
was of no great size, and therewithal one of her arms up to the
shoulder, and fell a-saying :—"Scrape here, and here, and there
too, and look, there is a bit left here." So, she being in this
posture, directing and admonishing her husband, Giannello,
who had not, that morning, fully satisfied his desire, when the
husband arrived, now seeing that as he would, he might not,
brought his mind to his circumstances, and resolved to take his
pleasure as he might : wherefore he made up to the lady, who
completely blocked the vent of the tun ; and even on such wise
as on the open champaign the wild and lusty horses do amorously
assail the mares of Parthia, he sated his youthful appetite ;
and so it was that almost at the same moment that he did so,
and was off, the tun was scoured, the husband came forth of it,
and Peronella withdrew her head from the vent, and turning to
Giannello, said :—"Take this light, good man, and see if 'tis
scoured to thy mind." Whereupon Giannello, looking into the
tun, said that 'twas in good trim, and that he was well content,
and paid the husband the seven gigliats, and caused him carry
the tun to his house.

NOVEL III

*Fra Rinaldo lies with his gossip : her husband finds him in the
room with her ; and they make him believe that he was curing
his godson of worms by a charm.*

FILOSTRATO knew not how so to veil what he said touching the
mares of Parthia, but that the keen-witted ladies laughed
thereat, making as if 'twas at somewhat else. However, his
story being ended, the king called for one from Elisa, who, all
obedience, thus began :—Debonair my ladies, we heard from
Emilia how the bogey is exorcized, and it brought to my mind
a story of another incantation : 'tis not indeed so good a story
as hers ; but, as no other, germane to our theme, occurs to me
at present, I will relate it.

You are to know, then, that there dwelt aforetime at Siena
a young man, right gallant and of honourable family, his name
Rinaldo ; who, being in the last degree enamoured of one of
his neighbours, a most beautiful gentlewoman and the wife
of a rich man, was not without hopes that, if he could but find
means to speak with her privately, he might have of her all
that he desired ; but seeing no way, and the lady being pregnant,
he cast about how he might become her child's godfather.
Wherefore, having ingratiated himself with her husband, he
broached the matter to him in as graceful a manner as he might ;
and 'twas arranged. So Rinaldo, being now godfather to
Madonna Agnesa's child, and having a more colourable pretext
for speaking to her, took courage, and told her in words that
message of his heart which she had long before read in his eyes ;
but though 'twas not displeasing to the lady to hear, it availed
him but little.

Now not long afterwards it so befell that, whatever may
have been his reason, Rinaldo betook him to friarage ; and
whether it was that he found good pasture therein, or what
not, he persevered in that way of life. And though for a while
after he was turned friar, he laid aside the love he bore his
gossip, and certain other vanities, yet in course of time,
without putting off the habit, he resumed them, and began to
take a pride in his appearance, and to go dressed in fine clothes,
and to be quite the trim gallant, and to compose songs and
sonnets and ballades, and to sing them, and to make a brave
shew in all else that pertained to his new character. But why

enlarge upon our Fra Rinaldo, of whom we speak? what friars
are there that do not the like? Ah! opprobrium of a corrupt
world? Sleek-faced and sanguine, daintily clad, dainty in all
their accessories, they ruffle it shamelessly before the eyes of
all, shewing not as doves but as insolent cocks with raised crest
and swelling bosom, and, what is worse (to say nought of the
vases full of electuaries and unguents, the boxes packed with
divers comfits, the pitchers and phials of artificial waters, and
oils, the flagons brimming with Malmsey and Greek and other
wines of finest quality, with which their cells are so packed
that they shew not as the cells of friars, but rather as apothe-
caries' or perfumers' shops), they blush not to be known to be
gouty, flattering themselves that other folk wot not that long
fasts and many of them, and coarse fare and little of it, and
sober living, make men lean and thin and for the most part
healthy; or if any malady come thereof, at any rate 'tis not
the gout, the wonted remedy for which is chastity and all
beside that belongs to the regimen of a humble friar. They
flatter themselves, too, that others wot not that over and above
the meagre diet, long vigils and orisons and strict discipline
ought to mortify men and make them pale, and that neither
St. Dominic nor St. Francis went clad in stuff dyed in grain or
any other goodly garb, but in coarse woollen habits innocent
of the dyer's art, made to keep out the cold, and not for shew.
To which matters 'twere well God had a care, no less than
to the souls of the simple folk by whom our friars are nourished.

   Fra Rinaldo, then, being come back to his first affections,
took to visiting his gossip very frequently; and gaining confidence, began with more insistence than before to solicit her
to that which he craved of her. So, being much urged, the
good lady, to whom Fra Rinaldo, perhaps, seemed now more
handsome than of yore, had recourse one day, when she felt
herself unusually hard pressed by him, to the common expedient
of all that would fain concede what is asked of them, and said:
—"Oh! but Fra Rinaldo, do friars then do this sort of thing?"
"Madam," replied Fra Rinaldo, "when I divest myself of this
habit, which I shall do easily enough, you will see that I am a
man furnished as other men, and no friar." Whereto with a
truly comical air the lady made answer:—"Alas! woe's me!
you are my child's godfather: how might it be? nay, but
'twere a very great mischief; and many a time I have heard
that 'tis a most heinous sin; and without a doubt, were it
not so, I would do as you wish." "If," said Fra Rinaldo,

" you forego it for such a scruple as this, you are a fool for your pains. I say not that 'tis no sin ; but there is no sin so great but God pardons it, if one repent. Now tell me : whether is more truly father to your son, I that held him at the font, or your husband that begot him ? " " My husband," replied the lady. " Sooth say you," returned the friar, " and does not your husband lie with you ? " " Why, yes," said the lady. " Then," rejoined the friar, " I that am less truly your son's father than your husband, ought also to lie with you, as does your husband." The lady was no logician, and needed little to sway her : she therefore believed or feigned to believe that what the friar said was true. So :—" Who might avail to answer your words of wisdom ? " quoth she ; and presently forgot the godfather in the lover, and complied with his desires. Nor had they begun their course to end it forthwith : but under cover of the friar's sponsorship, which set them more at ease, as it rendered them less open to suspicion, they forgathered again and again.

But on one of these occasions it so befell that Fra Rinaldo, being come to the lady's house, where he espied none else save a very pretty and dainty little maid that waited on the lady, sent his companion away with her into the pigeon-house, there to teach her the paternoster, while he and the lady, holding her little boy by the hand, went into the bedroom, locked themselves in, got them on to a divan that was there, and began to disport them. And while thus they sped the time, it chanced that the father returned, and, before any was ware of him, was at the bedroom door, and knocked, and called the lady by her name. Whereupon :—" 'Tis as much as my life is worth," quoth Madonna Agnesa ; " lo, here is my husband ; and, the occasion of our intimacy cannot but be now apparent to him." " Sooth say you," returned Fra Rinaldo, who was undressed, that is to say, had thrown off his habit and hood, and was in his tunic ; " if I had but my habit and hood on me in any sort, 'twould be another matter ; but if you let him in, and he find me thus, 'twill not be possible to put any face on it." But with an inspiration as happy as sudden :—" Now get them on you," quoth the lady ; " and when you have them on, take your godson in your arms, and give good heed to what I shall say to him, that your words may accord with mine ; and leave the rest to me."

The good man was still knocking, when his wife made answer : —" Coming, coming." And so up she got, and put on a cheerful

countenance and hied her to the door, and opened it and said :
—" Husband mine : well indeed was it for us that in came
Fra Rinaldo, our sponsor ; 'twas God that sent him to us ; for
in sooth, but for that, we had to-day lost our boy." Which
the poor simpleton almost swooned to hear ; and :—" How
so ? " quoth he. " O husband mine," replied the lady, " he
was taken but now, all of a sudden, with a fainting fit, so that
I thought he was dead : and what to do or say I knew not,
had not Fra Rinaldo, our sponsor, come just in the nick of time,
and set him on his shoulder, and said :—' Gossip, 'tis that he
has worms in his body, and getting, as they do, about the
heart, they might only too readily be the death of him ; but
fear not ; I will say a charm that will kill them all ; and
before I take my leave, you will see your boy as whole as
you ever saw him.' And because to say certain of the prayers
thou shouldst have been with us, and the maid knew not where
to find thee, he caused his companion to say them at the top
of the house, and he and I came in here. And for that 'tis
not meet for any but the boy's mother to assist at such a service,
that we might not be troubled with any one else, we locked the
door ; and he yet has him in his arms ; and I doubt not that
he only waits till his companion have said his prayers, and
then the charm will be complete ; for the boy is already quite
himself again."

The good simple soul, taking all this for sooth, and over-
wrought by the love he bore his son, was entirely without
suspicion of the trick his wife was playing him, and heaving a
great sigh, said :—" I will go look for him." " Nay," replied
the wife, " go not : thou wouldst spoil the efficacy of the charm :
wait here ; I will go see if thou mayst safely go ; and will call
thee."

Whereupon Fra Rinaldo, who had heard all that passed,
and was in his canonicals, and quite at his ease, and had the
boy in his arms, having made sure that all was as it should
be, cried out :—" Gossip, do I not hear the father's voice out
there ? " " Ay indeed, Sir," replied the simpleton. " Come
in then," said Fra Rinaldo. So in came the simpleton. Whereupon quoth Fra Rinaldo :—" I restore to you your boy made
whole by the grace of God, whom but now I scarce thought
you would see alive at vespers. You will do well to have his
image fashioned in wax, not less than life-size, and set it for
a thanksgiving to God, before the statue of Master St. Ambrose,
by whose merits you have this favour of God."

The boy, catching sight of his father, ran to him with joyous greetings, as little children are wont ; and the father, taking him in his arms, and weeping as if he were restored to him from the grave, fell by turns a-kissing him and thanking his godfather, that he had cured him. Fra Rinaldo's companion, who had taught the maid not one paternoster only, but per-adventure four or more, and by giving her a little purse of white thread that a nun had given him, had made her his devotee, no sooner heard Fra Rinaldo call the simpleton into his wife's room, than he stealthily got him to a place whence he might see and hear what was going on. Observing that the affair was now excellently arranged, he came down, and entered the chamber, saying :—" Fra Rinaldo, those four prayers that you bade me say, I have said them all." " Then well done, my brother," quoth Fra Rinaldo, " well-breathed must thou be. For my part, I had but said two, when my gossip came in ; but what with thy travail and mine, God of His grace has vouchsafed us the healing of the boy." The simpleton then had good wine and comfits brought in, and did the honours to the godfather and his companion in such sort as their occasions did most demand. He then ushered them forth of the house, commending them to God ; and without delay had the waxen image made, and directed it to be set up with the others in front of the statue of St. Ambrose, not, be it understood, St. Ambrose of Milan.[1]

NOVEL IV

Tofano one night locks his wife out of the house : she, finding that by no entreaties may she prevail upon him to let her in, feigns to throw herself into a well, throwing therein a great stone. Tofano hies him forth of the house, and runs to the spot : she goes into the house, and locks him out, and hurls abuse at him from within.

THE king no sooner wist that Elisa's story was ended, than, turning to Lauretta, he signified his will that she should tell somewhat : wherefore without delay she began :—O Love, how great and signal is thy potency ! how notable thy stratagems, thy devices ! Was there ever, shall there ever be, philosopher

---

[1] The statue would doubtless be that of St. Ambrose of Siena, of the Dominican Order.

or adept competent to inspire, counsel and teach in such sort
as thou by thine unpremeditated art dost tutor those that
follow thy lead ? Verily laggard teachers are they all in comparison of thee, as by the matters heretofore set forth may very
well be understood. To which store I will add, loving ladies,
a stratagem used by a woman of quite ordinary understanding,
and of such a sort that I know not by whom she could have
been taught it save by Love.

Know, then, that there dwelt aforetime at Arezzo a rich
man, Tofano by name, who took to wife Monna Ghita, a lady
exceeding fair, of whom, for what cause he knew not, he presently grew jealous. Whereof the lady being ware, waxed
resentful, and having on divers occasions demanded of him
the reason of his jealousy, and gotten from him nought precise,
but only generalities and trivialities, resolved at last to give
him cause enough to die of that evil which without cause he so
much dreaded. And being ware that a gallant, whom she
deemed well worthy of her, was enamoured of her, she, using
due discretion, came to an understanding with him ; which
being brought to the point that it only remained to give effect
to their words in act, the lady cast about to devise how this
might be. And witting that, among other bad habits that her
husband had, he was too fond of his cups, she would not
only commend indulgence, but cunningly and not seldom
incite him thereto ; insomuch that, well-nigh as often as she
was so minded, she led him to drink to excess ; and when she
saw that he was well drunken, she would put him to bed ; and
so not once only but divers times without any manner of risk
she forgathered with her lover ; nay, presuming upon her
husband's intoxication, she grew so bold that, not content
with bringing her lover into her house, she would at times
go spend a great part of the night with him at his house, which
was not far off.

Now such being the enamoured lady's constant practice, it
so befell that the dishonoured husband took note that, while
she egged him on to drink, she herself drank never a drop ;
whereby he came to suspect the truth, to wit, that the lady
was making him drunk, that afterwards she might take her
pleasure while he slept. And being minded to put his surmise
to the proof, one evening, having drunken nought all day, he
mimicked never so drunken a sot both in speech and in carriage.
The lady, deeming him to be really as he appeared, and that
'twas needless to ply him with liquor, presently put him to

bed. Which done, she, as she at times was wont, hied her forth to her lover's house, where she tarried until midnight. Tofano no sooner perceived that his wife was gone, than up he got, hied him to the door, locked it, and then posted himself at the window to observe her return, and let her know that he was ware of her misconduct. So there he stood until the lady returned, and finding herself locked out, was annoyed beyond measure, and sought to force the door open. Tofano let her try her strength upon it a while, and then :—" Madam," quoth he, " 'tis all to no purpose : thou canst not get in. Go get thee back thither where thou hast tarried all this while, and rest assured that thou shalt never recross this threshold, until I have done thee such honour as is meet for thee in the presence of thy kinsfolk and neighbours." Thereupon the lady fell entreating him to be pleased to open to her for the love of God, for that she was not come whence he supposed, but had only been passing the time with one of her gossips, because the nights were long, and she could not spend the whole time either in sleep or in solitary watching. But her supplications availed her nothing, for the fool was determined that all Arezzo should know their shame, whereof as yet none wist aught. So as 'twas idle to entreat, the lady assumed a menacing tone, saying :—" So thou open not to me, I will make thee the saddest man alive." Whereto Tofano made answer :—" And what then canst thou do ? " The lady, her wits sharpened by Love, rejoined :—" Rather than endure the indignity to which thou wouldst unjustly subject me, I will cast myself into the well hard by here, and when I am found dead there, all the world will believe that 'twas thou that didst it in thy cups, and so thou wilt either have to flee and lose all that thou hast and be outlawed, or forfeit thy head as guilty of my death, as indeed thou wilt be." But, for all she said, Tofano wavered not a jot in his foolish purpose. So at last :—" Lo, now," quoth the lady, " I can no more abide thy surly humour : God forgive thee : I leave thee my distaff here, which be careful to bestow in a safe place." So saying, away she hied her to the well, and, the night being so dark that wayfarers could scarce see one another as they passed, she took up a huge stone that was by the well, and ejaculating, " God forgive me ! " dropped it therein. Tofano, hearing the mighty splash that the stone made as it struck the water, never doubted that she had cast herself in : so, bucket and rope in hand, he flung himself out of the house, and came running to the well to her rescue.

The lady had meanwhile hidden herself hard by the door, and seeing him make for the well, was in the house in a trice, and having locked the door, hied her to the window, and greeted him with :—" 'Tis while thou art drinking, not now, when the night is far spent, that thou shouldst temper thy wine with water." Thus derided, Tofano came back to the door, and finding his ingress barred, began adjuring her to let him in. Whereupon, changing the low tone she had hitherto used for one so shrill that 'twas well-nigh a shriek, she broke out with : —" By the Holy Rood, tedious drunken sot that thou art, thou gettest no admittance here to-night ; thy ways are more than I can endure : 'tis time I let all the world know what manner of man thou art, and at what hour of the night thou comest home." Tofano, on his part, now grew angry, and began loudly to upbraid her ; insomuch that the neighbours, aroused by the noise, got up, men and women alike, and looked out of the windows, and asked what was the matter. Whereupon the lady fell a-weeping and saying :—" 'Tis this wicked man, who comes home drunk at even, or falls asleep in some tavern, and then returns at this hour. Long and to no purpose have I borne with him ; but 'tis now past endurance, and I have done him this indignity of locking him out of the house in the hope that perchance it may cause him to mend his ways."

Tofano, on his part, told, dolt that he was, just what had happened, and was mighty menacing. Whereupon :—" Now mark," quoth the lady to the neighbours, " the sort of man he is ! What would you say if I were, as he is, in the street, and he were in the house, as I am ? God's faith, I doubt you would believe what he said. Hereby you may gauge his sense. He tells you that I have done just what, I doubt not, he has done himself. He thought to terrify me by throwing I know not what into the well, wherein would to God he had thrown himself indeed, and drowned himself, whereby the wine of which he has taken more than enough, had been watered to some purpose ! " The neighbours, men and women alike, now with one accord gave tongue, censuring Tofano, throwing all the blame upon him, and answering what he alleged against the lady with loud recrimination ; and in short the bruit, passing from neighbour to neighbour, reached at last the ears of the lady's kinsfolk ; who hied them to the spot, and being apprised of the affair from this, that and the other of the neighbours, laid hands on Tofano, and beat him till he was black and blue from head to foot. Which done, they entered his house, stripped

it of all that belonged to the lady, and took her home with them,
bidding Tofano look for worse to come. Thus hard bested, and
ruing the plight in which his jealousy had landed him, Tofano,
who loved his wife with all his heart, set some friends to work
to patch matters up, whereby he did in fact induce his lady
to forgive him and live with him again ; albeit he was fain to
promise her never again to be jealous, and to give her leave
to amuse herself to her heart's content, provided she used such
discretion that he should not be ware of it. On such wise, like
the churl and booby that he was, being despoiled, he made
terms. Now long live Love, and perish war, and all that
wage it !

NOVEL V

*A jealous husband disguises himself as a priest, and hears his own
wife's confession : she tells him that she loves a priest, who
comes to her every night. The husband posts himself at the
door to watch for the priest, and meanwhile the lady brings
her lover in by the roof, and tarries with him.*

WHEN Lauretta had done speaking, and all had commended the
lady, for that she had done well, and treated her caitiff husband
as he had deserved, the king, not to lose time, turned to Fiammetta, and graciously bade her take up her parable ; which
she did on this wise :—Most noble ladies, the foregoing story
prompts me likewise to discourse of one of these jealous
husbands, deeming that they are justly requited by their wives,
more especially when they grow jealous without due cause.
And had our legislators taken account of everything, I am of
opinion that they would have visited ladies in such a case with
no other penalty than such as they provide for those that offend
in self-defence, seeing that a jealous husband does cunningly
practise against the life of his lady, and most assiduously
machinate her death. All the week the wife stays at home,
occupied with her domestic duties ; after which, on the day
that is sacred to joy, she, like every one else, craves some solace,
some peace, some recreation, not unreasonably, for she craves
but what the husbandmen take in the fields, the craftsmen in the
city, the magistrates in the courts, nay what God Himself took,
when He rested from all His labours on the seventh day, and
which laws human and Divine, mindful alike to the honour of

God and the common well-being, have ordained, appropriating
certain days to work, and others to repose. To which ordinance
these jealous husbands will in no wise conform ; on the contrary
by then most sedulously secluding their wives, they make those
days which to all other women are gladsome, to them most
grievous and dolorous. And what an affliction it is to the poor
creatures, they alone know, who have proved it ; for which
reason, to sum up, I say that a wife is rather to be commended
than censured, if she take her revenge upon a husband that is
jealous without cause.

Know then that at Rimini there dwelt a merchant, a man of
great substance in lands and goods and money, who, having a
most beautiful woman to wife, waxed inordinately jealous of
her, and that for no better reason than that, loving her greatly,
and esteeming her exceeding fair, and knowing that she did
her utmost endeavour to pleasure him, he must needs suppose
that every man loved her, and esteemed her fair, and that she,
moreover, was as zealous to stand well with every other man
as with himself ; whereby you may see that he was a poor
creature, and of little sense. Being thus so deeply infected
with jealousy, he kept so strict and close watch over her, that
some, maybe, have lain under sentence of death and been less
rigorously confined by their warders. 'Twas not merely that
the lady might not go to a wedding, or a festal gathering, or
even to church, or indeed set foot out of doors in any sort ;
but she dared not so much as shew herself at a window, or
cast a glance outside the house, no matter for what purpose.
Wherefore she led a most woeful life of it, and found it all
the harder to bear because she knew herself to be innocent.
Accordingly, seeing herself evilly entreated by her husband
without good cause, she cast about how for her own consolation
she might devise means to justify his usage of her. And for
that, as she might not shew herself at the window, there could
be no interchange of amorous glances between her and any
man that passed along the street, but she wist that in the
next house there was a goodly and debonair gallant, she bethought her, that, if there were but a hole in the wall that
divided the two houses, she might watch thereat, until she
should have sight of the gallant on such wise that she might
speak to him, and give him her love, if he cared to have it,
and, if so it might be contrived, forgather with him now and
again, and after this fashion relieve the burden of her woeful
life, until such time as the evil spirit should depart from her

husband. So peering about, now here, now there, when her husband was away, she found in a very remote part of the house a place, where, by chance, the wall had a little chink in it. Peering through which, she made out, though not without great difficulty, that on the other side was a room, and said to herself :
—If this were Filippo's room—Filippo was the name of the gallant, her neighbour—I should be already halfway to my goal. So cautiously, through her maid, who was grieved to see her thus languish, she made quest, and discovered that it was indeed the gallant's room, where he slept quite alone. Wherefore she now betook her frequently to the aperture, and whenever she was ware that the gallant was in the room, she would let fall a pebble or the like trifle ; whereby at length she brought the gallant to the other side of the aperture to see what the matter was. Whereupon she softly called him, and he knowing her voice, answered ; and so, having now the opportunity she had sought, she in few words opened to him all her mind. The gallant, being overjoyed, wrought at the aperture on such wise that albeit none might be ware thereof, he enlarged it ; and there many a time they held converse together, and touched hands, though further they might not go by reason of the assiduous watch that the jealous husband kept.

Now towards Christmas the lady told her husband that, if he approved, she would fain go on Christmas morning to church, and confess and communicate, like other Christians. " And what sins," quoth he, " hast thou committed, that wouldst be shriven ? " " How ? " returned the lady ; " dost thou take me for a saint ? For all thou keepest me so close, thou must know very well that I am like all other mortals. However, I am not minded to confess to thee, for that thou art no priest." Her husband, whose suspicions were excited by what she had said, cast about how he might discover these sins of hers, and having bethought him of what seemed an apt expedient, made answer that she had his consent, but he would not have her go to any church but their own chapel, where she might hie her betimes in the morning, and confess either to their own chaplain or some other priest that the chaplain might assign her, but to none other, and presently return to the house. The lady thought she half understood him, but she answered only that she would do as he required. Christmas morning came, and with the dawn the lady rose, dressed herself, and hied her to the church appointed by her husband, who also rose, and hied him to the same church, where he arrived before her ; and having already concerted matters with the priest that was in charge, he forthwith put on one of the priest's robes with a great hood, overshadowing the face, such as we see priests wear, and which he pulled somewhat forward ; and so disguised he seated himself in the choir.

On entering the church the lady asked for the priest, who came, and learning that she was minded to confess, said that he could not hear her himself, but would send her one of his brethren ; so away he hied him and sent her, in an evil hour for him, her husband. For though he wore an air of great solemnity, and 'twas not yet broad day, and he had pulled the hood well over his eyes, yet all did not avail, but that his lady forthwith recognized him, and said to herself :—God be praised ! why, the jealous rogue is turned priest : but leave it to me to give him that whereof he is in quest. So she feigned not to know him, and seated herself at his feet. (I should tell you that he had put some pebbles in his mouth, that his speech, being impeded, might not betray him to his wife, and in all other respects he deemed himself so thoroughly disguised that there was nought whereby she might recognize him.) Now, to come to the confession, the lady, after informing him that she was married, told him among other matters that she was enamoured of a priest, who came every night to lie with her. Which to hear was to her husband as if he were stricken through the heart with a knife ; and had it not been that he was bent on knowing more, he would have forthwith given over the confession, and taken himself off. However he kept his place, and :—" How ? " said he to the lady, " does not your husband lie with you ? " The lady replied in the affirmative. " How, then," quoth the husband, " can the priest also lie with you ? " " Sir," replied she, " what art the priest employs I know not ; but door there is none, however well locked, in the house, that comes not open at his touch ; and he tells me that, being come to the door of my room, before he opens it, he says certain words, whereby my husband forthwith falls asleep ; whereupon he opens the door, and enters the room, and lies with me ; and so 'tis always, without fail." " Then 'tis very wrong, Madam, and you must give it up altogether," said the husband. " That, Sir," returned the lady, " I doubt I can never do ; for I love him too much." " In that case," quoth the husband, " I cannot give you absolution." " The pity of it ! " ejaculated the lady ; " I came not hither to tell you falsehoods : if I could give it up, I would." " Madam," replied the husband, " indeed

I am sorry for you ; for I see that you are in a fair way to lose your soul. However, this I will do for you ; I will make special supplication to God on your behalf ; and perchance you may be profited thereby. And from time to time I will send you one of my young clerks ; and you will tell him whether my prayers have been of any help to you, or no, and if they have been so, I shall know what to do next." "Nay, Sir," quoth the lady, "do not so ; send no man to me at home ; for, should my husband come to know it, he is so jealous that nothing in the world would ever disabuse him of the idea that he came but for an evil purpose, and so I should have no peace with him all the year long." "Madam," returned the husband, "have no fear ; rest assured that I will so order matters that you shall never hear a word about it from him." "If you can make sure of that," quoth the lady, "I have no more to say." And so, her confession ended, and her penance enjoined, she rose, and went to mass, while the luckless husband, fuming and fretting, hasted to divest himself of his priest's trappings, and then went home bent upon devising some means to bring the priest and his wife together, and take his revenge upon them both.

When the lady came home from church she read in her husband's face that she had spoiled his Christmas for him, albeit he dissembled to the uttermost, lest she should discover what he had done, and supposed himself to have learned. His mind was made up to keep watch for the priest that very night by his own front door. So to the lady he said :—"I have to go out to-night to sup and sleep ; so thou wilt take care that the front door, and the mid-stair door, and the bedroom door are well locked ; and for the rest thou mayst go to bed, at thine own time." "Well and good," replied the lady : and as soon as she was able, off she hied her to the aperture, and gave the wonted signal, which Filippo no sooner heard, than he was at the spot. The lady then told him what she had done in the morning, and what her husband had said to her after breakfast, adding :—"Sure I am that he will not stir out of the house, but will keep watch beside the door ; wherefore contrive to come in to-night by the roof, that we may be together." "Madam," replied the gallant, nothing loath, "trust me for that."

Night came, the husband armed, and noiselessly hid himself in a room on the ground floor : the lady locked all the doors, being especially careful to secure the mid-stair door, to bar her husband's ascent ; and in due time the gallant, having found his way cautiously enough over the roof, they got them to bed, and there had solace of one another and a good time ; and at daybreak the gallant hied him back to his house. Meanwhile the husband, rueful and supperless, half dead with cold, kept his armed watch beside his door, momently expecting the priest, for the best part of the night ; but towards daybreak, his powers failing him, he lay down and slept in the ground-floor room. 'Twas hard upon tierce when he awoke, and the front door was then open ; so, making as if he had just come in, he went upstairs and breakfasted. Not long afterwards he sent to his wife a young fellow, disguised as the priest's underling, who asked her if he of whom she wist had been with her again. The lady, who quite understood what that meant, made answer that he had not come that night, and that, if he continued to neglect her so, 'twas possible he might be forgotten, though she had no mind to forget him.

Now, to make a long story short, the husband passed many a night in the same way, hoping to catch the priest as he came in, the lady and her gallant meanwhile having a good time. But at last the husband, being able to stand it no longer, sternly demanded of his wife what she had said to the priest the morning when she was confessed. The lady answered that she was not minded to tell him, for that 'twas not seemly or proper so to do. Whereupon :—" Sinful woman," quoth the husband, " in thy despite I know what thou saidst to him, and know I must and will who this priest is, of whom thou art enamoured, and who by dint of his incantations lies with thee a-nights, or I will sluice thy veins for thee." " 'Tis not true," replied the lady, " that I am enamoured of a priest." " How ? " quoth the husband, " saidst thou not as much to the priest that confessed thee ? " " Thou canst not have had it from him," rejoined the lady. " Wast thou then present thyself ? For sure I never told him so." " Then tell me," quoth the husband, " who this priest is ; and lose no time about it." Whereat the lady began to smile, and :—" I find it not a little diverting," quoth she, " that a wise man should suffer himself to be led by a simple woman as a ram is led by the horns to the shambles ; albeit no wise man art thou : not since that fatal hour when thou gavest harbourage in thy breast, thou wist not why, to the evil spirit of jealousy ; and the more foolish and insensate thou art, the less glory have I. Deemest thou, my husband, that I am as blind of the bodily eye as thou art of the mind's eye ? Nay, but for sure I am not so. I knew at a glance the priest that confessed me, and that 'twas even thyself. But I was minded to give thee that of which thou wast in quest, and I gave it thee. Howbeit, if thou hadst been the wise man thou takest thyself to be, thou wouldst not have chosen such a way as that to worm out thy good lady's secrets, nor wouldst thou have fallen a prey to a baseless suspicion, but wouldst have understood that what she confessed was true, and she all the while guiltless. I told thee that I loved a priest ; and wast not thou, whom I love, though ill enough dost thou deserve it, turned priest ? I told thee that there was no door in my house but would open when he was minded to lie with me : and when thou wouldst fain have access to me, what door was ever closed against thee ? I told thee that the priest lay nightly with me : and what night was there that thou didst not lie with me ? Thou sentest thy young clerk to me : and thou knowest that, as often as thou hadst not been with me, I sent word that the priest had not been with me. Who but thou, that hast suffered jealousy to blind thee, would have been so witless as not to read such a riddle ? But thou must needs mount guard at night beside the door, and think to make me believe that thou hadst gone out to sup and sleep. Consider thy ways, and court not the mockery of those that know them as I do, but turn a man again as thou wast wont to be : and let there be no more of this strict restraint in which thou keepest me ; for I swear to thee by God that, if I were minded to set horns on thy brow, I should not fail so to take my pastime that thou wouldst never find it out, though thou hadst a hundred eyes, as thou hast but two."

Thus admonished, the jealous caitiff, who had flattered himself that he had very cunningly discovered his wife's secret, was ashamed, and made no answer save to commend his wife's wit and honour ; and thus, having cause for jealousy, he discarded it, as he had erstwhile been jealous without cause. And so the adroit lady had, as it were, a charter of indulgence, and needed no more to contrive for her lover to come to her over the roof like a cat, but admitted him by the door, and using due discretion, had many a good time with him, and sped her life gaily.

NOVEL VI

*Madonna Isabella has with her Leonetto, her accepted lover,
when she is surprised by one Messer Lambertuccio, by whom
she is beloved : her husband coming home about the same
time, she sends Messer Lambertuccio forth of the house drawn
sword in hand, and the husband afterwards escorts Leonetto
home.*

Wᴏɴᴅʀᴏᴜs was the delight that all the company had of Fiammetta's story, nor was there any but affirmed that the lady
had done excellent well, and dealt with her insensate husband
as he deserved. However, it being ended, the king bade
Pampinea follow suit ; which she did on this wise :—Not a few
there are that in their simplicity aver that Love deranges the
mind, insomuch that whoso loves becomes as it were witless :
the folly of which opinion, albeit I doubt it not, and deem it
abundantly proven by what has been already said, I purpose
once again to demonstrate.

In our city, rich in all manner of good things, there dwelt a
young gentlewoman, fair exceedingly, and wedded to a most
worthy and excellent gentleman.   And as it not seldom happens
that one cannot keep ever to the same diet, but would fain at
times vary it, so this lady, finding her husband not altogether
to her mind, became enamoured of a gallant, Leonetto by name,
who, though of no high rank, was not a little debonair and
courteous, and he in like manner fell in love with her ; and (as
you know that 'tis seldom that what is mutually desired fails
to come about) 'twas not long before they had fruition of their
love.   Now the lady being, as I said, fair and winsome, it so
befell that a gentleman, Messer Lambertuccio by name, grew
mightily enamoured of her, but so tiresome and odious did she
find him, that for the world she could not bring herself to love
him.   So, growing tired of fruitlessly soliciting her favour by
ambassage, Messer Lambertuccio, who was a powerful signior,
sent her at last another sort of message in which he threatened
to defame her if she complied not with his wishes.   Wherefore
the lady, knowing her man, was terrified, and disposed herself
to pleasure him.

Now it so chanced that Madonna Isabella, for such was the
lady's name, being gone, as is our Florentine custom in the
summer, to spend some time on a very goodly estate that she

had in the contado, one morning finding herself alone, for her
husband had ridden off to tarry some days elsewhere, she sent
for Leonetto to come and keep her company ; and Leonetto
came forthwith in high glee. But while they were together,
Messer Lambertuccio, who, having got wind that the husband
was away, had mounted his horse and ridden thither quite alone,
knocked at the door. Whereupon the lady's maid hied her
forthwith to her mistress, who was alone with Leonetto, and
called her, saying :—" Madam, Messer Lambertuccio is here
below, quite alone." Whereat the lady was vexed beyond
measure ; and being also not a little dismayed, she said to
Leonetto :—" Prithee, let it not irk thee to withdraw behind
the curtain, and there keep close until Messer Lambertuccio be
gone." Leonetto, who stood in no less fear of Messer Lambertuccio than did the lady, got into his hiding place ; and the
lady bade the maid go open to Messer Lambertuccio : she did
so ; and having dismounted and fastened his palfrey to a pin,
he ascended the stairs ; at the head of which the lady received
him with a smile and as gladsome a greeting as she could find
words for, and asked him on what errand he was come. The
gentleman embraced and kissed her, saying :—" My soul, I am
informed that your husband is not here, and therefore I am come
to stay a while with you." Which said, they went into the
room, and locked them in, and Messer Lambertuccio fell a-toying
with her.

Now, while thus he sped the time with her, it befell that the
lady's husband, albeit she nowise expected him, came home,
and, as he drew nigh the palace, was observed by the maid, who
forthwith ran to the lady's chamber, and said :—" Madam, the
master will be here anon ; I doubt he is already in the courtyard." Whereupon, for that she had two men in the house,
and the knight's palfrey, that was in the courtyard, made it
impossible to hide him, the lady gave herself up for dead.
Nevertheless she made up her mind on the spur of the moment,
and springing out of bed :—" Sir," quoth she to Messer Lambertuccio, " if you have any regard for me, and would save my
life, you will do as I bid you : that is to say, you will draw your
blade, and put on a fell and wrathful countenance, and hie you
downstairs, saying :—' By God, he shall not escape me elsewhere.' And if my husband would stop you, or ask you aught,
say nought but what I have told you, and get you on horseback
and tarry with him on no account." " To hear is to obey,"
quoth Messer Lambertuccio, who, with the flush of his recent

exertion and the rage that he felt at the husband's return still
on his face, and drawn sword in hand, did as she bade him.
The lady's husband, being now dismounted in the courtyard,
and not a little surprised to see the palfrey there, was about to
go up the stairs, when he saw Messer Lambertuccio coming down
them, and marvelling both at his words and at his mien :—
" What means this, Sir ? " quoth he.   But Messer Lambertuccio
clapped foot in stirrup, and mounted, saying nought but :—
" Zounds, but I will meet him elsewhere ; " and so he rode off.

The gentleman then ascended the stairs, at the head of which
he found his lady distraught with terror, to whom he said :—
" What manner of thing is this ?   After whom goes Messer
Lambertuccio, so wrathful and menacing ? "   Whereto the lady,
drawing nigher the room, that Leonetto might hear her, made
answer :—" Never, Sir, had I such a fright as this.   There came
running in here a young man, who to me is quite a stranger, and
at his heels Messer Lambertuccio with a drawn sword in his hand ;
and as it happened the young man found the door of this room
open, and trembling in every limb, cried out :—' Madam, your
succour, for God's sake, that I die not in your arms.'   So up I
got, and would have asked him who he was, and how bested,
when up came Messer Lambertuccio, exclaiming :—' Where art
thou, traitor ? '   I planted myself in the doorway, and kept
him from entering, and seeing that I was not minded to give
him admittance, he was courteous enough, after not a little
parley, to take himself off, as you saw."   Whereupon :—
" Wife," quoth the husband, " thou didst very right.   Great
indeed had been the scandal, had some one been slain here,
and 'twas a gross affront on Messer Lambertuccio's part to
pursue a fugitive within the house."   He then asked where the
young man was.   Whereto the lady answered :—" Nay, where
he may be hiding, Sir, I wot not."   So :—" Where art thou ? "
quoth the knight.   " Fear not to shew thyself."   Then forth of
his hiding-place, all of a tremble, for in truth he had been
thoroughly terrified, crept Leonetto, who had heard all that
had passed.   To whom :—" What hast thou to do with Messer
Lambertuccio ? " quoth the knight.   " Nothing in the world,"
replied the young man :   " wherefore, I doubt he must either
be out of his mind, or have mistaken me for another : for no
sooner had he sight of me in the street hard by the palace, than
he laid his hand on his sword, and exclaimed :—' Traitor, thou
art a dead man.'   Whereupon I sought not to know why, but
fled with all speed, and got me here, and so, thanks to God and

this gentlewoman, I escaped his hands." "Now away with thy
fears," quoth the knight; "I will see thee home safe and
sound; and then 'twill be for thee to determine how thou shalt
deal with him." And so, when they had supped, he set him on
horseback, and escorted him to Florence, and left him not until
he was safe in his own house. And the very same evening,
following the lady's instructions, Leonetto spoke privily with
Messer Lambertuccio, and so composed the affair with him, that,
though it occasioned not a little talk, the knight never wist how
he had been tricked by his wife.

NOVEL VII

*Lodovico discovers to Madonna Beatrice the love that he bears her :
she sends Egano, her husband, into a garden disguised as
herself, and lies with Lodovico ; who thereafter, being risen,
hies him to the garden and cudgels Egano.*

THIS device of Madonna Isabella, thus recounted by Pampinea,
was held nothing short of marvellous by all the company.   But,
being bidden by the king to tell the next story, thus spake
Filomena :—Loving ladies, if I mistake not, the device, of which
you shall presently hear from me, will prove to be no less excellent than the last.

You are to know, then, that there dwelt aforetime at Paris a
Florentine gentleman, who, being by reason of poverty turned
merchant, had prospered so well in his affairs that he was
become very wealthy ; and having by his lady an only son,
Lodovico by name, whose nobility disrelished trade, he would
not put him in any shop ; but that he might be with other
gentlemen, he caused him to enter the service of the King of
France, whereby he acquired very fine manners and other
accomplishments. Being in this service, Lodovico was one
day with some other young gallants that talked of the fair
ladies of France, and England, and other parts of the world,
when they were joined by certain knights that were returned
from the Holy Sepulchre ; and hearing their discourse, one of
the knights fell a-saying, that of a surety in the whole world, so
far as he had explored it, there was not any lady, of all that he
had ever seen, that might compare for beauty with Madonna
Beatrice, the wife of Egano de' Galluzzi, of Bologna : wherein
all his companions, who in common with him had seen the lady

at Bologna, concurred. Which report Lodovico, who was as
yet fancy-free, no sooner heard, than he burned with such a
yearning to see the lady that he was able to think of nought
else : insomuch that he made up his mind to betake him to
Bologna to see her, and if she pleased him, to remain there ; to
which end he gave his father to understand that he would fain
visit the Holy Sepulchre, whereto his father after no little
demur consented.

So to Bologna Anichino—for so he now called himself—came ;
and, as Fortune would have it, the very next day, he saw the
lady at a festal gathering, and deemed her vastly more beautiful
than he had expected : wherefore he waxed most ardently
enamoured of her, and resolved never to quit Bologna, until he
had gained her love.   So, casting about how he should proceed,
he could devise no other way but to enter her husband's service,
which was the more easy that he kept not a few retainers : on
this wise Lodovico surmised that, peradventure, he might
compass his end.   He therefore sold his horses and meetly
bestowed his servants, bidding them make as if they knew him
not ; and being pretty familiar with his host, he told him that
he was minded to take service with some worthy lord, if any
such he might find.   " Thou wouldst make," quoth the host,
" the very sort of retainer to suit a gentleman of this city,
Egano by name, who keeps not a few of them, and will have all
of them presentable like thee : I will mention the matter to
him."   And so he accordingly did, and before he took leave of
Egano had placed Anichino with him, to Egano's complete
satisfaction.

Being thus resident with Egano, and having abundant opportunities of seeing the fair lady, Anichino set himself to serve
Egano with no little zeal ; wherein he succeeded so well, that
Egano was more than satisfied, insomuch that by and by there
was nought he could do without his advice, and he entrusted
to him the guidance not only of himself, but of all his affairs.
Now it so befell that one day when Egano was gone a-hawking,
having left Anichino at home, Madonna Beatrice, who as yet
wist not of his love, albeit she had from time to time taken note
of him and his manners, and had not a little approved and
commended them, sat herself down with him to a game of chess,
which, to please her, Anichino most dexterously contrived to
lose, to the lady's prodigious delight.   After a while, the lady's
women, one and all, gave over watching their play, and left
them to it ; whereupon Anichino heaved a mighty sigh.   The

lady, looking hard at him, said :—"What ails thee, Anichino?
Is it, then, such a mortification to thee to be conquered by
me?" "Nay, Madam," replied Anichino, "my sigh was
prompted by a much graver matter." "Then, if thou hast
any regard for me," quoth the lady, "tell me what it is."
Hearing himself thus adjured by "any regard" he had for her
whom he loved more than aught else, Anichino heaved a yet
mightier sigh, which caused the lady to renew her request that
he would be pleased to tell her the occasion of his sighs. Whereupon :—"Madam," said Anichino, "I greatly fear me, that,
were I to tell it you, 'twould but vex you; and, moreover, I
doubt you might repeat it to some one else." "Rest assured,"
returned the lady, "that I shall neither be annoyed, nor, without
thy leave, ever repeat to any other soul aught that thou mayst
say." "Then," said Anichino, "having this pledge from you,
I will tell it you." And, while the tears all but stood in his
eyes, he told her, who he was, the report he had heard of her,
and where and how he had become enamoured of her, and with
what intent he had taken service with her husband: after
which, he humbly besought her, that, if it might be, she would
have pity on him, and gratify this his secret and ardent desire;
and that, if she were not minded so to do, she would suffer him
to retain his place there, and love her. Ah! Bologna! how
sweetly mixed are the elements in thy women! How commendable in such a case are they all! No delight have they in sighs
and tears, but are ever inclinable to prayers, and ready to yield
to the solicitations of Love. Had I but words apt to praise
them as they deserve, my eloquence were inexhaustible.

The gentlewoman's gaze was fixed on Anichino as he spoke;
she made no doubt that all he said was true, and yielding to his
appeal, she entertained his love within her heart in such measure
that she too began to sigh, and after a sigh or two made answer:
—"Sweet my Anichino, be of good cheer; neither presents nor
promises, nor any courting by gentleman, or lord, or whoso else
(for I have been and am still courted by not a few) was ever able
to sway my soul to love any of them: but thou, by the few
words that thou hast said, hast so wrought with me that, brief
though the time has been, I am already in far greater measure
thine than mine. My love I deem thee to have won right
worthily; and so I give it thee, and vow to give thee joyance
thereof before the coming night be past. To which end thou
wilt come to my room about midnight; I will leave the door
open; thou knowest the side of the bed on which I sleep; thou

wilt come there ; should I be asleep, thou hast but to touch me, and I shall awake, and give thee solace of thy long-pent desire. In earnest whereof I will even give thee a kiss." So saying, she threw her arms about his neck, and lovingly kissed him, as Anichino her.

Their colloquy thus ended, Anichino betook him elsewhere about some matters which he had to attend to, looking forward to midnight with boundless exultation. Egano came in from his hawking ; and after supper, being weary, went straight to bed, whither the lady soon followed him, leaving, as she had promised, the door of the chamber open. Thither accordingly, at the appointed hour, came Anichino, and having softly entered the chamber, and closed the door behind him, stole up to where the lady lay, and laying his hand upon her breast, found that she was awake. Now, as soon as she wist that Anichino was come, she took his hand in both her own ; and keeping fast hold of him, she turned about in the bed, until she awoke Egano ; whereupon :—" Husband," quoth she, " I would not say aught of this to thee, yestereve, because I judged thou wast weary ; but tell me, upon thy hope of salvation, Egano, whom deemest thou thy best and most loyal retainer, and the most attached to thee, of all that thou hast in the house ? " " What a question is this, wife ? " returned Egano. " Dost not know him ? Retainer I have none, nor ever had, so trusted, or loved, as Anichino. But wherefore put such a question ? "

Now, when Anichino wist that Egano was awake, and heard them talk of himself, he more than once tried to withdraw his hand, being mightily afraid lest the lady meant to play him false ; but she held it so tightly that he might not get free, while thus she made answer to Egano :—" I will tell thee what he is. I thought that he was all thou sayst, and that none was so loyal to thee as he, but he has undeceived me, for that yesterday, when thou wast out a-hawking, he, being here, chose his time, and had the shamelessness to crave of me compliance with his wanton desires : and I, that I might not need other evidence than that of thine own senses to prove his guilt to thee, I made answer, that I was well content, and that to-night, after midnight, I would get me into the garden, and await him there at the foot of the pine. Now go thither I shall certainly not ; but, if thou wouldst prove the loyalty of thy retainer, thou canst readily do so, if thou but slip on one of my loose robes, and cover thy face with a veil, and go down and attend his coming, for come, I doubt not, he will." Whereto Egano :—" Meet indeed

it is," quoth he, " that I should go see ; " and straightway up
he got, and, as best he might in the dark, he put on one of the
lady's loose robes and veiled his face, and then hied him to the
garden, and sate down at the foot of the pine to await Anichino.
The lady no sooner wist that he was out of the room, than she
rose, and locked the door. Anichino, who had never been so
terrified in all his life, and had struggled with all his might to
disengage his hand from the lady's clasp, and had inwardly
cursed her and his love, and himself for trusting her, a hundred
thousand times, was overjoyed beyond measure at this last
turn that she had given the affair. And so, the lady having
got her to bed again, and he, at her bidding, having stripped
and laid him down beside her, they had solace and joyance of
one another for a good while. Then, the lady, deeming it unmeet for Anichino to tarry longer with her, caused him to get
up and resume his clothes, saying to him :—" Sweet my mouth,
thou wilt take a stout cudgel, and get thee to the garden, and
making as if I were there, and thy suit to me had been but to
try me, thou wilt give Egano a sound rating with thy tongue
and a sound belabouring with thy cudgel, the sequel whereof
will be wondrously gladsome and delightful." Whereupon
Anichino hied him off to the garden, armed with a staff of wild
willow ; and as he drew nigh the pine, Egano saw him, and rose
and came forward to meet him as if he would receive him with
the heartiest of cheer. But :—" Ah ! wicked woman ! " quoth
Anichino ; " so thou art come ! Thou didst verily believe, then,
that I was, that I am, minded thus to wrong my lord ? Foul
fall thee a thousand times ! " And therewith he raised his
cudgel, and began to lay about him. Egano, however, had
heard and seen enough, and without a word took to flight, while
Anichino pursued him, crying out :—" Away with thee ! God
send thee a bad year, lewd woman that thou art ; nor doubt
that Egano shall hear of this to-morrow." Egano, having received sundry round knocks, got him back to his chamber with
what speed he might ; and being asked by the lady, whether
Anichino had come into the garden :—" Would to God he had
not ! " quoth he, " for that, taking me for thee, he has beaten
me black and blue with his cudgel, and rated me like the vilest
woman that ever was : passing strange, indeed, it had seemed
to me that he should have said those words to thee with intent
to dishonour me ; and now 'tis plain that 'twas but that, seeing
thee so blithe and frolicsome, he was minded to prove thee."
Whereto :—" God be praised," returned the lady, " that he

proved me by words, as thee by acts : and I doubt not he may
say that I bear his words with more patience than thou his acts.
But since he is so loyal to thee, we must make much of him and
do him honour."   "Ay, indeed," quoth Egano, "thou sayst
sooth."

Thus was Egano fortified in the belief that never had any
gentleman wife so true, or retainer so loyal, as he ; and many
a hearty laugh had he with Anichino and his lady over this
affair, which to them was the occasion that, with far less let
than might else have been, they were able to have solace and
joyance of one another, so long as it pleased Anichino to tarry
at Bologna.

NOVEL VIII

*A husband grows jealous of his wife, and discovers that she has
warning of her lover's approach by a piece of pack-thread,
which she ties to her great toe a nights. While he is pursuing
her lover, she puts another woman in bed in her place. The
husband, finding her there, beats her, and cuts off her hair.
He then goes and calls his wife's brothers, who, holding his
accusation to be false, give him a rating.*

RARE indeed was deemed by common consent the subtlety
shewn by Madonna Beatrice in the beguilement of her husband,
and all affirmed that the terror of Anichino must have been
prodigious, when, the lady still keeping fast hold of him, he had
heard her say that he had made suit of love to her.   However,
Filomena being silent, the king turned to Neifile, saying :—
" 'Tis now for you to tell."   Whereupon Neifile, while a slight
smile died away upon her lips, thus began :—Fair ladies, to
entertain you with a goodly story, such as those which my
predecessors have delighted you withal, is indeed a heavy burden,
but, God helping me, I trust fairly well to acquit myself thereof.

You are to know, then, that there dwelt aforetime in our city
a most wealthy merchant, Arriguccio Berlinghieri by name, who
foolishly, as we wot by daily experience is the way of merchants,
thinking to compass gentility by matrimony, took to wife a
young gentlewoman, by no means suited to him, whose name
was Monna Sismonda.   Now Monna Sismonda, seeing that her
husband was much abroad, and gave her little of his company,
became enamoured of a young gallant, Ruberto by name, who

had long courted her : and she being grown pretty familiar with him, and using, perchance, too little discretion, for she affected him extremely, it so befell that Arriguccio, whether it was that he detected somewhat, or howsoever, waxed of all men the most jealous, and gave up going abroad, and changed his way of life altogether, and made it his sole care to watch over his wife, insomuch that he never allowed himself a wink of sleep until he had seen her to bed : which occasioned the lady the most grievous dumps, because 'twas on no wise possible for her to be with her Ruberto. So, casting about in many ways how she might contrive to meet him, and being thereto not a little plied by Ruberto himself, she bethought her at last of the following expedient : to wit, her room fronting the street, and Arriguccio, as she had often observed, being very hard put to it to get him to sleep, but thereafter sleeping very soundly, she resolved to arrange with Ruberto that he should come to the front door about midnight, whereupon she would get her down, and open the door, and stay some time with him while her husband was in his deep sleep. And that she might have tidings of his arrival, yet so as that none else might wot aught thereof, she adopted the device of lowering a pack-thread from the bedroom window on such wise that, while with one end it should all but touch the ground, it should traverse the floor of the room, until it reached the bed, and then be brought under the clothes, so that, when she was abed, she might attach it to her great toe. Having so done, she sent word to Ruberto, that when he came, he must be sure to jerk the pack-thread, and, if her husband were asleep, she would loose it, and go open to him ; but, if he were awake, she would hold it taut and draw it to herself, to let him know that he must not expect her. Ruberto fell in with the idea, came there many times, and now forgathered with her and again did not. But at last, they still using this cunning practice, it so befell that one night, while the lady slept, Arriguccio, letting his foot stray more than he was wont about the bed, came upon the pack-thread, and laying his hand upon it, found that it was attached to his lady's great toe, and said to himself :—This must be some trick : and afterwards discovering that the thread passed out of the window, was confirmed in his surmise. Wherefore, he softly severed it from the lady's toe, and affixed it to his own ; and waited, all attention, to learn the result of his experiment. Nor had he long to wait before Ruberto came, and Arriguccio felt him jerk the thread according to his wont : and as Arriguccio had not known how to attach the thread securely, and Ruberto jerked it with some force, it gave way, whereby he understood that he was to wait, and did so. Arriguccio straightway arose, caught up his arms, and hasted to the door to see who might be there, intent to do him a mischief. Now Arriguccio, for all he was a merchant, was a man of spirit, and of thews and sinews ; and being come to the door, he opened it by no means gingerly, as the lady was wont ; whereby Ruberto, who was in waiting, surmised the truth, to wit, that 'twas Arriguccio by whom the door was opened. Wherefore he forthwith took to flight, followed by Arriguccio. But at length, when he had run a long way, as Arriguccio gave not up the pursuit, he being also armed, drew his sword, and faced about ; and so they fell to, Arriguccio attacking, and Ruberto defending himself.

Now when Arriguccio undid the bedroom door, the lady awoke, and finding the pack-thread cut loose from her toe, saw at a glance that her trick was discovered ; and hearing Arriguccio running after Ruberto, she forthwith got up, foreboding what the result was like to be, and called her maid, who was entirely in her confidence : whom she so plied with her obsecrations that at last she got her into bed in her room, beseeching her not to say who she was, but to bear patiently all the blows that Arriguccio might give her ; and she would so reward her that she should have no reason to complain. Then, extinguishing the light that was in the room, forth she hied her, and having found a convenient hiding-place in the house, awaited the turn of events. Now Arriguccio and Ruberto being hotly engaged in the street, the neighbours, roused by the din of the combat, got up and launched their curses upon them. Wherefore Arriguccio, fearing lest he should be recognized, drew off before he had so much as discovered who the young gallant was, or done him any scathe, and in a fell and wrathful mood betook him home. Stumbling into the bedroom, he cried out angrily : —" Where art thou, lewd woman ? Thou hast put out the light, that I may not be able to find thee ; but thou hast miscalculated." And going to the bedside, he laid hold of the maid, taking her to be his wife, and fell a-pummelling and kicking her with all the strength he had in his hands and feet, insomuch that he pounded her face well-nigh to pulp, rating her the while like the vilest woman that ever was ; and last of all he cut off her hair. The maid wept bitterly, as indeed she well might ; and though from time to time she ejaculated an " Alas ! Mercy, for God's sake ! " or " Spare me, spare me ; " yet her voice was so broken by her sobs, and Arriguccio's hearing so dulled by his wrath, that he was not able to discern that 'twas not his wife's voice but that of another woman. So, having soundly thrashed her, and cut off her hair, as we said:—" Wicked woman," quoth he, " I touch thee no more; but I go to find thy brothers, and shall do them to wit of thy good works; and then they may come here, and deal with thee as they may deem their honour demands, and take thee hence, for be sure thou shalt no more abide in this house." With this he was gone, locking the door of the room behind him, and quitted the house alone.

Now no sooner did Monna Sismonda, who had heard all that passed, perceive that her husband was gone, than she opened the door of the bedroom, rekindled the light, and finding her maid all bruises and tears, did what she could to comfort her, and carried her back to her own room, where, causing her to be privily waited on and tended, she helped her so liberally from Arriguccio's own store, that she confessed herself content. The maid thus bestowed in her room, the lady presently hied her back to her own, which she set all in neat and trim order, remaking the bed, so that it might appear as if it had not been slept in, relighting the lamp, and dressing and tiring herself, until she looked as if she had not been abed that night; then, taking with her a lighted lamp and some work, she sat down at the head of the stairs, and began sewing, while she waited to see how the affair would end.

Arriguccio meanwhile had hied him with all speed straight from the house to that of his wife's brothers, where by dint of much knocking he made himself heard, and was admitted. The lady's three brothers, and her mother, being informed that 'twas Arriguccio, got up, and having set lights a-burning, came to him and asked him on what errand he was come there at that hour, and alone. Whereupon Arriguccio, beginning with the discovery of the pack-thread attached to his lady's great toe, gave them the whole narrative of his discoveries and doings down to the very end; and to clinch the whole matter, he put in their hands the locks which he had cut, as he believed, from his wife's head, adding that 'twas now for them to come for her and deal with her on such wise as they might deem their honour required, seeing that he would nevermore have her in his house. Firmly believing what he told them, the lady's brothers were very wroth with her, and having provided themselves with lighted torches, set out with Arriguccio, and hied them to his house with intent to scorn her, while their mother followed,

weeping and beseeching now one, now another, not to credit
these matters so hastily, until they had seen or heard somewhat
more thereof ; for that the husband might have some other
reason to be wroth with her, and having ill-treated her, might
have trumped up this charge by way of exculpation, adding
that, if true, 'twas passing strange, for well she knew her daughter, whom she had brought up from her tenderest years, and
much more to the like effect.

However, being come to Arriguccio's house, they entered, and
were mounting the stairs, when Monna Sismonda, hearing them,
called out :—" Who is there ? "   Whereto one of the brothers
responded :—" Lewd woman, thou shalt soon have cause enough
to know who it is."   " Now Lord love us ! " quoth Monna
Sismonda, " what would he be at ? "   Then, rising, she greeted
them with :—" Welcome, my brothers ; but what seek ye
abroad at this hour, all three of you ? "   They had seen her
sitting and sewing with never a sign of a blow on her face,
whereas Arriguccio had averred that he had pummelled her all
over : wherefore their first impression was one of wonder, and
refraining the vehemence of their wrath, they asked her what
might be the truth of the matter which Arriguccio laid to her
charge, and threatened her with direful consequences, if she
should conceal aught.   Whereto the lady :—" What you would
have me tell you," quoth she, " or what Arriguccio may have
laid to my charge, that know not I."   Arriguccio could but
gaze upon her, as one that had taken leave of his wits, calling
to mind how he had pummelled her about the face times without
number, and scratched it for her, and mishandled her in all
manner of ways, and there he now saw her with no trace of
aught of it all upon her.   However, to make a long story short,
the lady's brothers told her what Arriguccio had told them
touching the pack-thread and the beating and all the rest of it.
Whereupon the lady turned to him with :—" Alas, my husband,
what is this that I hear ?   Why givest thou me, to thy own great
shame, the reputation of a lewd woman, when such I am not,
and thyself the reputation of a wicked and cruel man, which
thou art not ?   Wast thou ever to-night, I say not in my company, but so much as in the house until now ?   Or when didst
thou beat me ?   For my part I mind me not of it."   Arriguccio
began :—" How sayst thou, lewd woman ?   Did we not go to
bed together ?   Did I not come back, after chasing thy lover ?
Did I not give thee bruises not a few, and cut thy hair for
thee ? "   But the lady interrupted him, saying :—" Nay, thou

didst not lie here to-night. But leave we this, of which my true words are my sole witness, and pass we to this of the beating thou sayst thou gavest me, and how thou didst cut my hair. Never a beating had I from thee, and I bid all that are here, and thee among them, look at me, and say if I have any trace of a beating on my person ; nor should I advise thee to dare lay hand upon me ; for, by the Holy Rood, I would spoil thy beauty for thee. Nor didst thou cut my hair, for aught that I saw or felt : however, thou didst it, perchance, on such wise that I was not ware thereof : so let me see whether 'tis cut or no." Then, unveiling herself, she shewed that her hair was uncut and entire. Wherefore her brothers and mother now turned to Arriguccio with :—" What means this, Arriguccio ? This accords not with what thou gavest us to understand thou hadst done ; nor know we how thou wilt prove the residue."

Arriguccio was lost, as it were, in a dream, and yet he would fain have spoken ; but, seeing that what he had thought to prove was otherwise, he essayed no reply. So the lady turning to her brothers :—" I see," quoth she, " what he would have : he will not be satisfied unless I do what I never would otherwise have done, to wit, give you to know what a pitiful caitiff he is ; as now I shall not fail to do. I make no manner of doubt that, as he has said, even so it befell, and so he did. How, you shall hear. This worthy man, to whom, worse luck ! you gave me to wife, a merchant, as he calls himself, and as such would fain have credit, and who ought to be more temperate than a religious, and more continent than a girl, lets scarce an evening pass but he goes a-boozing in the taverns, and consorting with this or the other woman of the town ; and 'tis for me to await his return until midnight or sometimes until matins, even as you now find me. I doubt not that, being thoroughly well drunk, he got him to bed with one of these wantons, and, awaking, found the packthread on her foot, and afterwards did actually perform all these brave exploits of which he speaks, and in the end came back to her, and beat her, and cut her hair off, and being not yet quite recovered from his debauch, believed, and, I doubt not, still believes, that 'twas I that he thus treated ; and if you will but scan his face closely, you will see that he is still half drunk. But, whatever he may have said about me, I would have you account it as nothing more than the disordered speech of a tipsy man ; and forgive him as I do." Whereupon the lady's mother raised no small outcry, saying :—" By the Holy Rood, my daughter, this may not be ! A daughter, such as thou, to be mated with one so unworthy of thee! The pestilent, insensate cur should be slain on the spot! A pretty state of things, indeed! Why, he might have picked thee up from the gutter! Now foul fall him! but thou shalt no more be vexed with the tedious drivel of a petty dealer in ass's dung, some blackguard, belike, that came hither from the country because he was dismissed the service of some petty squire, clad in romagnole, with belfry-breeches, and a pen in his arse, and, for that he has a few pence, must needs have a gentleman's daughter, and a fine lady to wife, and set up a coat of arms, and say :—' I am of the such and such,' and ' my ancestors did thus and thus.' Ah! had my sons but followed my advice! Thy honour were safe in the house of the Counts Guidi, where they might have bestowed thee, though thou hadst but a morsel of bread to thy dowry : but they must needs give thee to this rare treasure, who, though better daughter and more chaste there is none than thou in Florence, has not blushed this very midnight and in our presence to call thee a strumpet, as if we knew thee not. God's faith! so I were hearkened to, he should shrewdly smart for it." Then, turning to her sons, she said :— " My sons, I told you plainly enough that this ought not to be. Now, have you heard how your worthy brother-in-law treats your sister ? Petty twopenny trader that he is : were it for me to act, as it is for you, after what he has said of her and done to her, nought would satisfy or appease me, till I had rid the earth of him. And were I a man, who am but a woman, none other but myself should meddle with the affair. God's curse upon him, the woeful, shameless sot ! " Whereupon the young men, incensed by what they had seen and heard, turned to Arriguccio, and after giving him the soundest rating that ever was bestowed upon caitiff, concluded as follows :—" This once we pardon thee, witting thee to be a drunken knave ; but as thou holdest thy life dear, have a care that henceforth we hear no such tales of thee ; for rest assured that if aught of the kind do reach our ears, we will requite thee for both turns." Which said, they departed. Arriguccio, standing there like one dazed, not witting whether his late doings were actual fact or but a dream, made no more words about the matter, but left his wife in peace. Thus did she by her address not only escape imminent peril, but open a way whereby in time to come she was able to gratify her passion to the full without any farther fear of her husband.

NOVEL IX

Lydia, wife of Nicostratus, loves Pyrrhus, who to assure himself thereof, asks three things of her, all of which she does, and therewithal enjoys him in presence of Nicostratus, and makes Nicostratus believe that what he saw was not real.

So diverting did the ladies find Neifile's story that it kept them still laughing and talking, though the king, having bidden Pamfilo tell his story, had several times enjoined silence upon them. However, as soon as they had done, Pamfilo thus began :—Methinks, worshipful ladies, there is no venture, though fraught with gravest peril, that whoso loves ardently will not make : of which truth, exemplified though it has been in stories not a few, I purpose to afford you yet more signal proof in one which I shall tell you ; wherein you will hear of a lady who in her enterprises owed far more to the favour of Fortune than to the guidance of reason : wherefore I should not advise any of you rashly to follow in her footsteps, seeing that Fortune is not always in a kindly mood, nor are the eyes of all men equally holden.

In Argos, that most ancient city of Achaia, the fame of whose kings of old time is out of all proportion to its size, there dwelt of yore Nicostratus, a nobleman, to whom, when he was already verging on old age, Fortune gave to wife a great lady, Lydia by name, whose courage matched her charms. Nicostratus, as suited with his rank and wealth, kept not a few retainers and hounds and hawks, and was mightily addicted to the chase. Among his dependants was a young man named Pyrrhus, a gallant of no mean accomplishment, and goodly of person and beloved and trusted by Nicostratus above all other. Of whom Lydia grew mighty enamoured, insomuch that neither by day nor by night might her thoughts stray from him : but, whether it was that Pyrrhus wist not her love, or would have none of it, he gave no sign of recognition ; whereby the lady's suffering waxing more than she could bear, she made up her mind to declare her love to him ; and having a chambermaid, Lusca by name, in whom she placed great trust, she called her, and said :—
" Lusca, tokens thou hast had from me of my regard that should ensure thy obedience and loyalty ; wherefore have a care that what I shall now tell thee reach the ears of none but him to whom I shall bid thee impart it. Thou seest, Lusca, that I am

in the prime of my youth and lustihead, and have neither lack nor stint of all such things as folk desire, save only, to be brief, that I have one cause to repine, to wit, that my husband's years so far outnumber my own. Wherefore with that wherein young ladies take most pleasure I am but ill provided, and, as my desire is no less than theirs, 'tis now some while since I determined that, if Fortune has shewn herself so little friendly to me by giving me a husband so advanced in years, at least I will not be mine own enemy by sparing to devise the means whereby my happiness and health may be assured ; and that herein, as in all other matters, my joy may be complete, I have chosen, thereto to minister by his embraces, our Pyrrhus, deeming him more worthy than any other man, and have so set my heart upon him that I am ever ill at ease save when he is present either to my sight or to my mind, insomuch that, unless I forgather with him without delay, I doubt not that 'twill be the death of me. And so, if thou holdest my life dear, thou wilt shew him my love on such wise as thou mayst deem best, and make my suit to him that he be pleased to come to me, when thou shalt go to fetch him." " That gladly will I," replied the chambermaid ; and as soon as she found convenient time and place, she drew Pyrrhus apart, and, as best she knew how, conveyed her lady's message to him. Which Pyrrhus found passing strange to hear, for 'twas in truth a complete surprise to him, and he doubted the lady did but mean to try him. Wherefore he presently, and with some asperity, answered thus :—" Lusca, believe I cannot that this message comes from my lady : have a care, therefore, what thou sayst, and if, perchance, it does come from her, I doubt she does not mean it ; and if, perchance, she does mean it, why, then I am honoured by my lord above what I deserve, and I would not for my life do him such a wrong : so have a care never to speak of such matters to me again." Lusca, nowise disconcerted by his uncompliant tone, rejoined :—" I shall speak to thee, Pyrrhus, of these and all other matters, wherewith I may be commissioned by my lady, as often as she shall bid me, whether it pleases or irks thee ; but thou art a blockhead."

So, somewhat chafed, Lusca bore Pyrrhus' answer back to her lady, who would fain have died, when she heard it, and some days afterwards resumed the topic, saying :—" Thou knowest, Lusca, that 'tis not the first stroke that fells the oak ; wherefore, methinks, thou wert best go back to this strange man, who is minded to evince his loyalty at my expense, and

choosing a convenient time, declare to him all my passion, and
do thy best endeavour that the affair be carried through ; for
if it should thus lapse, 'twould be the death of me ; besides
which, he would think we had but trifled with him, and, whereas
'tis his love we would have, we should earn his hatred." So,
after comforting the lady, the maid hied her in quest of Pyrrhus,
whom she found in a gladsome and propitious mood, and thus
addressed :—" 'Tis not many days, Pyrrhus, since I declared
to thee how ardent is the flame with which thy lady and mine
is consumed for love of thee, and now again I do thee to wit
thereof, and that, if thou shalt not relent of the harshness
that thou didst manifest the other day, thou mayst rest assured
that her life will be short : wherefore I pray thee to be pleased
to give her solace of her desire, and shouldst thou persist in thy
obduracy, I, that gave thee credit for not a little sense, shall
deem thee a great fool. How flattered thou shouldst be to
know thyself beloved above all else by a lady so beauteous and
high-born ! And how indebted shouldst thou feel thyself to
Fortune, seeing that she has in store for thee a boon so great and
so suited to the cravings of thy youth, ay, and so like to be of
service to thee upon occasion of need ! Bethink thee, if there
be any of thine equals whose life is ordered more agreeably than
thine will be if thou but be wise. Which of them wilt thou
find so well furnished with arms and horses, clothes and money
as thou shalt be, if thou but give my lady thy love ? Receive,
then, my words with open mind ; be thyself again ; bethink
thee that 'tis Fortune's way to confront a man but once with
smiling mien and open lap, and, if he then accept not her bounty,
he has but himself to blame, if afterward he find himself in
want, in beggary. Besides which, no such loyalty is demanded
between servants and their masters as between friends and
kinsfolk ; rather 'tis for servants, so far as they may, to behave
towards their masters as their masters behave towards them.
Thinkest thou, that, if thou hadst a fair wife or mother or
daughter or sister that found favour in Nicostratus' eyes, he
would be so scrupulous on the point of loyalty as thou art disposed to be in regard of his lady ? Thou art a fool, if so thou
dost believe. Hold it for certain, that, if blandishments and
supplications did not suffice, he would, whatever thou mightest
think of it, have recourse to force. Observe we, then, towards
them and theirs the same rule which they observe towards us
and ours. Take the boon that Fortune offers thee ; repulse her
not ; rather go thou to meet her, and hail her advance ; for be

sure that, if thou do not so, to say nought of thy lady's health, which will certainly ensue, thou thyself wilt repent thee thereof so often that thou wilt be fain of death."

Since he had last seen Lusca, Pyrrhus had repeatedly pondered what she had said to him, and had made his mind up that, should she come again, he would answer her in another sort, and comply in all respects with the lady's desires, provided he might be assured that she was not merely putting him to the proof ; wherefore he now made answer :—" Lo, now, Lusca, I acknowledge the truth of all that thou sayst ; but, on the other hand, I know that my lord is not a little wise and wary, and, as he has committed all his affairs to my charge, I sorely misdoubt me that 'tis with his approbation, and by his advice, and but to prove me, that Lydia does this : wherefore let her do three things which I shall demand of her for my assurance, and then there is nought that she shall crave of me, but I will certainly render her prompt obedience. Which three things are these :— first, let her in Nicostratus' presence kill his fine sparrow-hawk : then she must send me a lock of Nicostratus' beard, and lastly one of his best teeth." Hard seemed these terms to Lusca, and hard beyond measure to the lady, but Love, that great fautor of enterprise, and master of stratagem, gave her resolution to address herself to their performance : wherefore through the chambermaid she sent him word that what he required of her she would do, and that without either reservation or delay ; and therewithal she told him, that, as he deemed Nicostratus so wise, she would contrive that they should enjoy one another in Nicostratus' presence, and that Nicostratus should believe that 'twas a mere show. Pyrrhus, therefore, anxiously expected what the lady would do. Some days thus passed, and then Nicostratus gave a great breakfast, as was his frequent wont, to certain gentlemen, and when the tables were removed, the lady, robed in green samite, and richly adorned, came forth of her chamber into the hall wherein they sate, and before the eyes of Pyrrhus and all the rest of the company hied her to the perch, on which stood the sparrow-hawk that Nicostratus so much prized, and loosed him, and, as if she were minded to carry him on her hand, took him by the jesses and dashed him against the wall so that he died. Whereupon :—" Alas ! my lady, what hast thou done ? " exclaimed Nicostratus : but she vouchsafed no answer, save that, turning to the gentlemen that had sate at meat with him, she said :—" My lords, ill fitted were I to take vengeance on a king that had done me despite, if I lacked the courage to be avenged on a sparrow-hawk. You are to know that by this bird I have long been cheated of all the time that ought to be devoted by gentlemen to pleasuring their ladies; for with the first streaks of dawn Nicostratus has been up and got him to horse, and hawk on hand hied him to the champaign to see him fly, leaving me, such as you see me, alone and ill content abed. For which cause I have oftentimes been minded to do that which I have now done, and have only refrained therefrom, that, biding my time, I might do it in the presence of men that should judge my cause justly, as I trust you will do." Which hearing, the gentlemen, who deemed her affections no less fixed on Nicostratus than her words imported, broke with one accord into a laugh, and turning to Nicostratus, who was sore displeased, fell a-saying:—"Now well done of the lady to avenge her wrongs by the death of the sparrow-hawk!" and so, the lady being withdrawn to her chamber, they passed the affair off with divers pleasantries, turning the wrath of Nicostratus to laughter.

Pyrrhus, who had witnessed what had passed, said to himself:—Nobly indeed has my lady begun, and on such wise as promises well for the felicity of my love. God grant that she so continue. And even so Lydia did: for not many days after she had killed the sparrow-hawk, she, being with Nicostratus in her chamber, from caressing passed to toying and trifling with him, and he, sportively pulling her by the hair, gave her occasion to fulfil the second of Pyrrhus' demands; which she did by nimbly laying hold of one of the lesser tufts of his beard, and, laughing the while, plucking it so hard that she tore it out of his chin. Which Nicostratus somewhat resenting:—"Now what cause hast thou," quoth she, "to make such a wry face? 'Tis but that I have plucked some half-dozen hairs from thy beard. Thou didst not feel it as much as did I but now thy tugging of my hair." And so they continued jesting and sporting with one another, the lady jealously guarding the tuft that she had torn from the beard, which the very same day she sent to her cherished lover. The third demand caused the lady more thought; but, being amply endowed with wit, and powerfully seconded by Love, she failed not to hit upon an apt expedient.

Nicostratus had in his service two lads, who, being of gentle birth, had been placed with him by their kinsfolk, that they might learn manners, one of whom, when Nicostratus sate at meat, carved before him, while the other gave him to drink.

Both lads Lydia called to her, and gave them to understand that their breath smelt, and admonished them that, when they waited on Nicostratus, they should hold their heads as far back as possible, saying never a word of the matter to any. The lads believing her, did as she bade them. Whereupon she took occasion to say to Nicostratus :—" Hast thou marked what these lads do when they wait upon thee ? " " Troth, that have I," replied Nicostratus ; " indeed I have often had it in mind to ask them why they do so." " Nay," rejoined the lady, " spare thyself the pains ; for I can tell thee the reason, which I have for some time kept close, lest it should vex thee ; but as I now see that others begin to be ware of it, it need no longer be withheld from thee. 'Tis for that thy breath stinks shrewdly that they thus avert their heads from thee : 'twas not wont to be so, nor know I why it should be so ; and 'tis most offensive when thou art in converse with gentlemen ; and therefore 'twould be well to find some way of curing it." " I wonder what it could be," returned Nicostratus ; " is it perchance that I have a decayed tooth in my jaw ? " " That may well be," quoth Lydia : and taking him to a window, she caused him open his mouth, and after regarding it on this side and that :— " Oh ! Nicostratus," quoth she, " how couldst thou have endured it so long ? Thou hast a tooth here, which, by what I see, is not only decayed, but actually rotten throughout ; and beyond all manner of doubt, if thou let it remain long in thy head, 'twill infect its neighbours ; so 'tis my advice that thou out with it before the matter grows worse." " My judgment jumps with thine," quoth Nicostratus ; " wherefore send without delay for a chirurgeon to draw it." " God forbid," returned the lady, " that chirurgeon come hither for such a purpose ; methinks, the case is such that I can very well dispense with him, and draw the tooth myself. Besides which, these chirurgeons do these things in such a cruel way, that I could never endure to see thee or know thee under the hands of any of them : wherefore my mind is quite made up to do it myself, that, at least, if thou shalt suffer too much, I may give it over at once, as a chirurgeon would not do." And so she caused the instruments that are used on such occasions to be brought her, and having dismissed all other attendants save Lusca from the chamber, and locked the door, made Nicostratus lie down on a table, set the pincers in his mouth, and clapped them on one of his teeth, which, while Lusca held him, so that, albeit he roared for pain, he might not move, she wrenched by main

force from his jaw, and keeping it close, took from Lusca's hand
another and horribly decayed tooth, which she shewed him,
suffering and half dead as he was, saying :—" See what thou
hadst in thy jaw ; mark how far gone it is." Believing what
she said, and deeming that, now the tooth was out, his breath
would no more be offensive, and being somewhat eased of the
pain, which had been extreme, and still remained, so that he
murmured not little, by divers comforting applications, he
quitted the chamber : whereupon the lady forthwith sent the
tooth to her lover, who, having now full assurance of her love,
placed himself entirely at her service. But the lady being
minded to make his assurance yet more sure, and deeming each
hour a thousand till she might be with him, now saw fit, for the
more ready performance of the promise she had given him, to
feign sickness ; and Nicostratus, coming to see her one day
after breakfast, attended only by Pyrrhus, she besought him
for her better solacement, to help her down to the garden.
Wherefore Nicostratus on one side, and Pyrrhus on the other,
took her and bore her down to the garden, and set her on a
lawn at the foot of a beautiful pear-tree : and after they had
sate there a while, the lady, who had already given Pyrrhus to
understand what he must do, said to him :—" Pyrrhus, I should
greatly like to have some of those pears ; get thee up the tree,
and shake some of them down." Pyrrhus climbed the tree in a
trice, and began to shake down the pears, and while he did so :—
" Fie ! Sir," quoth he, " what is this you do ? And you,
Madam, have you no shame, that you suffer him to do so in
my presence ? Think you that I am blind ? 'Twas but now
that you were gravely indisposed. Your cure has been speedy
indeed to permit of your so behaving : and as for such a purpose
you have so many goodly chambers, why betake you not yourselves to one of them, if you must needs so disport yourselves ?
'Twould be much more decent than to do so in my presence."
Whereupon the lady, turning to her husband :—" Now what
can Pyrrhus mean ? " said she. " Is he mad ? " " Nay,
Madam," quoth Pyrrhus ; " mad am not I. Think you I see
you not ? " Whereat Nicostratus marvelled not a little ; and :
—" Pyrrhus," quoth he, " I verily believe thou dreamest."
" Nay, my lord," replied Pyrrhus, " not a whit do I dream ;
neither do you ; rather you wag it with such vigour, that, if
this pear-tree did the like, there would be never a pear left on
it." Then the lady :—" What can this mean ? " quoth she :
" can it be that it really seems to him to be as he says ? Upon

my hope of salvation, were I but in my former health, I would
get me up there to judge for myself what these wonders are
which he professes to see." Whereupon, as Pyrrhus in the
pear-tree continued talking in the same strange strain :—" Come
down," quoth Nicostratus ; and when he was down :—" Now
what," said Nicostratus, " is it thou sayst thou seest up there ? "
" I suppose," replied Pyrrhus, " that you take me to be deluded
or dreaming : but as I must needs tell you the truth, I saw you
lying upon your wife, and then, when I came down, I saw you
get up and sit you down here where you now are." " Therein,"
said Nicostratus, " thou wast certainly deluded, for, since thou
clombest the pear-tree, we have not budged a jot, save as thou
seest." Then said Pyrrhus :—" Why make more words about
the matter ? See you I certainly did ; and, seeing you, I saw
you lying upon your own." Nicostratus' wonder now waxed
momently, insomuch that he said :—" I am minded to see if
this pear-tree be enchanted, so that whoso is in it sees marvels ; "
and so he got him up into it. Whereupon the lady and Pyrrhus
fell to disporting them, and Nicostratus, seeing what they were
about, exclaimed :—"Ah ! lewd woman, what is this thou
doest ? And thou, Pyrrhus, in whom I so much trusted ! "
And so saying, he began to climb down. Meanwhile the lady
and Pyrrhus had made answer :—" We are sitting here : " and
seeing him descending, they placed themselves as they had
been when he had left them, whom Nicostratus, being come
down, no sooner saw, than he fell a-rating them. Then quoth
Pyrrhus :—" Verily, Nicostratus, I now acknowledge, that, as
you said a while ago, what I saw when I was in the pear-tree
was but a false show, albeit I had never understood that so it
was but that I now see and know that thou hast also seen a
false show. And that I speak truth, you may sufficiently
assure yourself, if you but reflect whether 'tis likely that your
wife, who for virtue and discretion has not her peer among
women, would, if she were minded so to dishonour you, see fit
to do so before your very eyes. Of myself I say nought, albeit
I had liefer be hewn in pieces than that I should so much as
think of such a thing, much less do it in your presence. Wherefore 'tis evident that 'tis some illusion of sight that is propagated
from the pear-tree ; for nought in the world would have made
me believe that I saw not you lying there in carnal intercourse
with your wife, had I not heard you say that you saw me doing
that which most assuredly, so far from doing, I never so much
as thought of." The lady then started up with a most resentful

mien, and burst out with :—" Foul fall thee, if thou knowest so
little of me as to suppose that, if I were minded to do thee such
foul dishonour as thou sayst thou didst see me do, I would come
hither to do it before thine eyes ! Rest assured that for such a
purpose, were it ever mine, I should deem one of our chambers
more meet, and it should go hard but I would so order the
matter that thou shouldst never know aught of it." Nicostratus,
having heard both, and deeming that what they both averred
must be true, to wit, that they would never have ventured
upon such an act in his presence, passed from chiding to talk of
the singularity of the thing, and how marvellous it was that
the vision should reshape itself for every one that clomb the
tree. The lady, however, made a show of being distressed that
Nicostratus should so have thought of her, and :—" Verily,"
quoth she, " no woman, neither I nor another, shall again suffer
loss of honour by this pear-tree : run, Pyrrhus, and bring hither
an axe, and at one and the same time vindicate thy honour and
mine by felling it, albeit 'twere better far Nicostratus' skull
should feel the weight of the axe, seeing that in utter heedlessness
he so readily suffered the eyes of his mind to be blinded ; for,
albeit this vision was seen by the bodily eye, yet ought the
understanding by no means to have entertained and affirmed
it as real."

So Pyrrhus presently hied him to fetch the axe, and returning
therewith felled the pear ; whereupon the lady, turning towards
Nicostratus :—" Now that this foe of my honour is fallen,"
quoth she, " my wrath is gone from me." Nicostratus then
craving her pardon, she graciously granted it him, bidding him
never again to suffer himself to be betrayed into thinking such
a thing of her, who loved him more dearly than herself. So
the poor duped husband went back with her and her lover to
the palace, where not seldom in time to come Pyrrhus and Lydia
took their pastime together more at ease. God grant us the like.

NOVEL X

Two Sienese love a lady, one of them being her gossip : the gossip dies, having promised his comrade to return to him from the other world ; which he does, and tells him what sort of life is led there.

NONE now was left to tell, save the king, who, as soon as the ladies had ceased mourning over the fall of the pear-tree, that had done no wrong, and were silent, began thus :—Most manifest it is that 'tis the prime duty of a just king to observe the laws that he has made ; and, if he do not so, he is to be esteemed no king, but a slave that has merited punishment, into which fault, and under which condemnation, I, your king, must, as of necessity, fall. For, indeed, when yesterday I made the law which governs our discourse of to-day, I thought not to-day to avail myself of my privilege, but to submit to the law, no less than you, and to discourse of the same topic whereof you all have discoursed ; but not only has the very story been told which I had intended to tell, but therewithal so many things else, and so very much goodlier have been said, that, search my memory as I may, I cannot mind me of aught, nor wot I that touching such a matter there is indeed aught, for me to say, that would be comparable with what has been said ; wherefore, as infringe I must the law that I myself have made, I confess myself worthy of punishment, and instantly declaring my readiness to pay any forfeit that may be demanded of me, am minded to have recourse to my wonted privilege. And such, dearest ladies, is the potency of Elisa's story of the godfather and his gossip, and therewith of the simplicity of the Sienese, that I am prompted thereby to pass from this topic of the beguilement of foolish husbands by their cunning wives to a little story touching these same Sienese, which, albeit there is not a little therein which you were best not to believe, may yet be in some degree entertaining to hear.

Know, then, that at Siena there dwelt in Porta Salaia two young men of the people, named, the one, Tingoccio Mini, the other Meuccio di Tura, who, by what appeared, loved one another not a little, for they were scarce ever out of one another's company ; and being wont, like other folk, to go to church and listen to sermons, they heard from time to time of the glory and the woe, which in the other world are allotted, according to merit, to the souls of the dead. Of which matters craving, but being unable to come by, more certain assurance, they agreed together that, whichever of them should die first, should, if he might, return to the survivor, and certify him of that which he would fain know ; and this agreement they confirmed with an oath. Now, after they had made this engagement, and while they were still constantly together, Tingoccio chanced to become sponsor to one Ambruogio Anselmini, that dwelt in Campo Reggi, who had had a son by his wife, Monna Mita. The lady was exceeding fair, and amorous withal, and Tingoccio being wont sometimes to visit her as his gossip, and to take Meuccio with him, he, notwithstanding his sponsorship, grew enamoured of her, as did also Meuccio, for she pleased him not a little, and he heard her much commended by Tingoccio. Which love each concealed from the other ; but not for the same reason. Tingoccio was averse to discover it to Meuccio, for that he deemed it an ignominious thing to love his gossip, and was ashamed to let any one know it. Meuccio was on his guard for a very different reason, to wit, that he was already ware that the lady was in Tingoccio's good graces. Wherefore he said to himself :—If I avow my love to him, he will be jealous of me, and as, being her gossip, he can speak with her as often as he pleases, he will do all he can to make her hate me, and so I shall never have any favour of her.

Now, the two young men being thus, as I have said, on terms of most familiar friendship, it befell that Tingoccio, being the better able to open his heart to the lady, did so order his demeanour and discourse that he had from her all that he desired. Nor was his friend's success hidden from Meuccio ; though, much as it vexed him, yet still cherishing the hope of eventually attaining his end, and fearing to give Tingoccio occasion to baulk or hamper him in some way, he feigned to know nought of the matter. So Tingoccio, more fortunate than his comrade, and rival in love, did with such assiduity till his gossip's good land that he got thereby a malady, which in the course of some days waxed so grievous that he succumbed thereto, and departed this life. And on the night of the third day after his decease (perchance because earlier he might not) he made his appearance, according to his promise, in Meuccio's chamber, and called Meuccio, who was fast asleep, by his name. Whereupon :—" Who art thou ? " quoth Meuccio, as he awoke. " 'Tis I, Tingoccio," replied he, " come back, in fulfilment of the pledge I gave thee, to give thee tidings of the other world."

For a while Meuccio saw him not without terror : then, his courage reviving :—" Welcome, my brother," quoth he : and proceeded to ask him if he were lost.   " Nought is lost but what is irrecoverable," replied Tingoccio : "how then should I be here, if I were lost ? "   " Nay," quoth then Meuccio ; " I mean it not so : I would know of thee, whether thou art of the number of the souls that are condemned to the penal fire of hell." " Why no," returned Tingoccio, " not just that ; but still for the sins that I did I am in most sore and grievous torment." Meuccio then questioned Tingoccio in detail of the pains there meted out for each of the sins done here ; and Tingoccio enumerated them all.   Whereupon Meuccio asked if there were aught he might do for him here on earth.   Tingoccio answered in the affirmative ; to wit, that he might have masses and prayers said and alms-deeds done for him, for that such things were of great service to the souls there.   " That gladly will I," replied Meuccio ; and then, as Tingoccio was about to take his leave, he bethought him of the gossip, and raising his head a little, he said :—" I mind me, Tingoccio, of the gossip, with whom thou wast wont to lie when thou wast here.   Now what is thy punishment for that ? "   " My brother," returned Tingoccio, " as soon as I got down there, I met one that seemed to know all my sins by heart, who bade me betake me to a place, where, while in direst torment I bewept my sins, I found comrades not a few condemned to the same pains ; and so, standing there among them, and calling to mind what I had done with the gossip, and foreboding in requital thereof a much greater torment than had yet been allotted me, albeit I was in a great and most vehement flame, I quaked for fear in every part of me.   Which one that was beside me observing :—' What,' quoth he, ' hast thou done more than the rest of us that are here, that thou quakest thus as thou standest in the fire ? ' ' My friend,' quoth I, ' I am in mortal fear of the doom that I expect for a great sin that I once committed.'   He then asked what sin it might be.   ' 'Twas on this wise,' replied I : ' I lay with my gossip, and that so much that I died thereof.'   Whereat, he did but laugh, saying :—' Go to, fool, make thy mind easy ; for here there is no account taken of gossips.'   Which completely revived my drooping spirits."

'Twas now near daybreak : wherefore :—" Adieu ! Meuccio," quoth his friend : " for longer tarry with thee I may not ; " and so he vanished.   As for Meuccio, having learned that no account was taken of gossips in the other world, he began to

laugh at his own folly in that he had already spared divers such ;
and so, being quit of his ignorance, he in that respect in course
of time waxed wise. Which matters had Fra Rinaldo but
known, he would not have needed to go about syllogizing in
order to bring his fair gossip to pleasure him.

The sun was westering, and a light breeze blew, when the
king, his story ended, and none else being left to speak, arose,
and taking off the crown, set it on Lauretta's head, saying :—
" Madam, I crown you with yourself [1] queen of our company :
'tis now for you, as our sovereign lady, to make such ordinances
as you shall deem meet for our common solace and delectation ; "
and having so said, he sat him down again. Queen Lauretta
sent for the seneschal, and bade him have a care that the tables
should be set in the pleasant vale somewhat earlier than had
been their wont, that their return to the palace might be more
leisurely ; after which she gave him to know what else he had
to do during her sovereignty. Then turning to the company :—
" Yesterday," quoth she, " Dioneo would have it that to-day
we should discourse of the tricks that wives play their husbands ;
and but that I am minded not to shew as of the breed of yelping
curs, that are ever prompt to retaliate, I would ordain that to-
morrow we discourse of the tricks that husbands play their wives.
However, in lieu thereof, I will have every one take thought to
tell of those tricks that, daily, woman plays man, or man woman,
or one man another ; wherein, I doubt not, there will be matter
of discourse no less agreeable than has been that of to-day."
So saying, she rose and dismissed the company until supper-
time. So the ladies and the men being risen, some bared their
feet and betook them to the clear water, there to disport them,
while others took their pleasure upon the green lawn amid the
trees that there grew goodly and straight. For no brief while
Dioneo and Fiammetta sang in concert of Arcite and Palamon.
And so, each and all taking their several pastimes, they sped the
hours with exceeding great delight until supper-time. Which
being come, they sat them down at table beside the little lake,
and there, while a thousand songsters charmed their ears, and
a gentle breeze, that blew from the environing hills, fanned
them, and never a fly annoyed them, reposefully and joyously
they supped. The tables removed, they roved a while about
the pleasant vale, and then, the sun being still high, for 'twas
but half vespers, the queen gave the word, and they wended
their way back to their wonted abode, and going slowly, and

1 A play upon *laurea* (laurel wreath) and Lauretta.

beguiling the way with quips and quirks without number upon
divers matters, nor those alone of which they had that day discoursed, they arrived, hard upon nightfall, at the goodly palace.
There, the short walk's fatigue dispelled by wines most cool and
comfits, they presently gathered for the dance about the fair
fountain, and now they footed it to the strains of Tindaro's
cornemuse, and now to other music. Which done, the queen
bade Filomena give them a song ; and thus Filomena sang :—

> Ah ! woe is me, my soul !
> > Ah ! shall I ever thither fare again
> > Whence I was parted to my grievous dole ?
>
> Full sure I know not ; but within my breast
> > Throbs ever the same fire
> > Of yearning there where erst I was to be.
> > O thou in whom is all my weal, my rest,
> > Lord of my heart's desire,
> > Ah ! tell me thou ! for none to ask save thee
> > Neither dare I, nor see.
> > Ah ! dear my Lord, this wasted heart disdain
> > Thou wilt not, but with hope at length console.
>
> Kindled the flame I know not what delight,
> > Which me doth so devour,
> > That day and night alike I find no ease ;
> > For whether it was by hearing, touch, or sight,
> > Unwonted was the power,
> > And fresh the fire that me each way did seize ;
> > Wherein without release
> > I languish still, and of thee, Lord, am fain,
> > For thou alone canst comfort and make whole.
>
> Ah ! tell me if it shall be, and how soon,
> > That I again thee meet
> > Where those death-dealing eyes I kissed.   Thou, chief
> > Weal of my soul, my very soul, this boon
> > Deny not ; say that fleet
> > Thou hiest hither : comfort thus my grief.
> > Ah ! let the time be brief
> > Till thou art here, and then long time remain ;
> > For I, Love-stricken, crave but Love's control.
>
> Let me but once again mine own thee call,
> > No more so indiscreet
> > As erst, I'll be, to let thee from me part :
> > Nay, I'll still hold thee, let what may befall,
> > And of thy mouth so sweet
> > Such solace take as may content my heart :
> > So this be all my art,
> > Thee to entice, me with thine arms to enchain :
> > Whereon but musing inly chants my soul.

This song set all the company conjecturing what new and
delightsome love might now hold Filomena in its sway ; and as

its words imported that she had had more joyance thereof than sight alone might yield, some that were there grew envious of her excess of happiness.   However, the song being ended, the queen, bethinking her that the morrow was Friday, thus graciously addressed them all :—" Ye wot, noble ladies, and ye also, my gallants, that to-morrow is the day that is sacred to the passion of our Lord, which, if ye remember, we kept devoutly when Neifile was queen, intermitting delectable discourse, as we did also on the ensuing Saturday.   Wherefore, being minded to follow Neifile's excellent example, I deem that now, as then, 'twere a seemly thing to surcease from this our pastime of story-telling for those two days, and compose our minds to meditation on what was at that season accomplished for the weal of our souls."   All the company having approved their queen's devout speech, she, as the night was now far spent, dismissed them ; and so they all betook them to slumber.

Endeth here the seventh day of the Decameron, beginneth the eighth, in which, under the rule of Lauretta, discourse is had of those tricks that, daily, woman plays man, or man woman, or one man another.

THE summits of the loftiest mountains were already illumined by the rays of the rising sun, the shades of night were fled, and all things plainly visible, when the queen and her company arose, and hied them first to the dewy mead, where for a while they walked: then, about half tierce, they wended their way to a little church that was hard by, where they heard Divine service; after which, they returned to the palace, and having breakfasted with gay and gladsome cheer, and sung and danced a while, were dismissed by the queen, to rest them as to each might seem good. But when the sun was past the meridian, the queen mustered them again for their wonted pastime; and, all being seated by the fair fountain, thus, at her command, Neifile began.

NOVEL I

Gulfardo borrows moneys of Guasparruolo, which he has agreed to give Guasparruolo's wife, that he may lie with her. He gives them to her, and in her presence tells Guasparruolo that he has done so, and she acknowledges that 'tis true.

SITH God has ordained that 'tis for me to take the lead to-day with my story, well pleased am I. And for that, loving ladies, much has been said touching the tricks that women play men, I am minded to tell you of one that a man played a woman, not because I would censure what the man did, or say that 'twas not merited by the woman, but rather to commend the man and censure the woman, and to shew that men may beguile those that think to beguile them, as well as be beguiled by those they think to beguile; for peradventure what I am about to relate should in strictness of speech not be termed beguilement, but rather retaliation; for, as it behoves woman to be most strictly virtuous, and to guard her chastity as her very life, nor on any account to allow herself to sully it, which notwith-standing, 'tis not possible by reason of our frailty that there should be as perfect an observance of this law as were meet, I affirm, that she that allows herself to infringe it for money merits the fire ; whereas she that so offends under the prepotent stress of Love will receive pardon from any judge that knows how to temper justice with mercy : witness what but the other day we heard from Filostrato touching Madonna Filippa at Prato.[1]

Know, then, that there was once at Milan a German mer-cenary, Gulfardo by name, a doughty man, and very loyal to those with whom he took service ; a quality most uncommon in Germans.   And as he was wont to be most faithful in repaying whatever moneys he borrowed, he would have had no difficulty in finding a merchant to advance him any amount of money at a low rate of interest.   Now, tarrying thus at Milan, Gulfardo fixed his affection on a very fine woman, named Madonna Ambruogia, the wife of a wealthy merchant, one Guasparruolo Cagastraccio, with whom he was well acquainted and on friendly terms : which amour he managed with such discretion that neither the husband nor any one else wist aught of it.   So one day he sent her a message, beseeching her of her courtesy to gratify his passion, and assuring her that he on his part was ready to obey her every behest.

The lady made a great many words about the affair, the upshot of which was that she would do as Gulfardo desired upon the following terms : to wit, that, in the first place, he should never discover the matter to a soul, and, secondly, that, as for some purpose or another she required two hundred florins of gold, he out of his abundance should supply her necessity ; these condi-tions being satisfied she would be ever at his service.   Offended by such base sordidness in one whom he had supposed to be an honourable woman, Gulfardo passed from ardent love to some-thing very like hatred, and cast about how he might flout her. So he sent her word that he would right gladly pleasure her in this and in any other matter that might be in his power ; let her but say when he was to come to see her, and he would bring the moneys with him, and none should know of the matter except a comrade of his, in whom he placed much trust, and who was privy to all that he did.   The lady, if she should not rather be called the punk, gleefully made answer that in the course of a few days her husband, Guasparruolo, was to go to

[1] Cf. Sixth Day, Novel VII.

Genoa on business, and that, when he was gone, she would let
Gulfardo know, and appoint a time for him to visit her. Gulfardo thereupon chose a convenient time, and hied him to Guasparruolo, to whom :—" I am come," quoth he, " about a little
matter of business which I have on hand, for which I require
two hundred florins of gold, and I should be glad if thou wouldst
lend them me at the rate of interest which thou art wont to
charge me." " That gladly will I," replied Guasparruolo, and
told out the money at once. A few days later Guasparruolo
being gone to Genoa, as the lady had said, she sent word to
Gulfardo that he should bring her the two hundred florins of
gold. So Gulfardo hied him with his comrade to the lady's
house, where he found her expecting him, and lost no time in
handing her the two hundred florins of gold in his comrade's
presence, saying :—" You will keep the money, Madam, and
give it to your husband when he returns." Witting not why
Gulfardo so said, but thinking that 'twas but to conceal from
his comrade that it was given by way of price, the lady made
answer :—" That will I gladly ; but I must first see whether
the amount is right ; " whereupon she told the florins out upon
a table, and when she found that the two hundred were there,
she put them away in high glee, and turning to Gulfardo, took
him into her chamber, where, not on that night only but on
many another night, while her husband was away, he had of
her all that he craved. On Guasparruolo's return Gulfardo
presently paid him a visit, having first made sure that the lady
would be with him, and so in her presence :—" Guasparruolo,"
quoth he, " I had after all no occasion for the money, to wit, the
two hundred florins of gold that thou didst lend me the other
day, being unable to carry through the transaction for which
I borrowed them, and so I took an early opportunity of bringing
them to thy wife, and gave them to her : thou wilt therefore
cancel the account." Whereupon Guasparruolo turned to the
lady, and asked her if she had had them. She, not daring to
deny the fact in presence of the witness, answered :—" Why,
yes, I had them, and quite forgot to tell thee." " Good," quoth
then Guasparruolo, " we are quits, Gulfardo ; make thy mind
easy ; I will see that thy account is set right." Gulfardo then
withdrew, leaving the flouted lady to hand over her ill-gotten
gains to her husband ; and so the astute lover had his pleasure
of his greedy mistress for nothing.

NOVEL II

The priest of Varlungo lies with Monna Belcolore : he leaves with
her his cloak by way of pledge, and receives from her a mortar.
He returns the mortar, and demands of her the cloak that he
had left in pledge, which the good lady returns him with a gibe.

LADIES and men alike commended Gulfardo for the check that
he gave to the greed of the Milanese lady ; but before they had
done, the queen turned to Pamfilo, and with a smile bade him
follow suit : wherefore thus Pamfilo began :—Fair my ladies, it
occurs to me to tell you a short story, which reflects no credit
on those by whom we are continually wronged without being
able to retaliate, to wit, the priests, who have instituted a
crusade against our wives, and deem that, when they have
made conquest of one of them, they have done a work every
whit as worthy of recompense by remission of sin and punishment as if they had brought the Soldan in chains to Avignon :
in which respect 'tis not possible for the hapless laity to be
even with them : howbeit they are as hot to make reprisals on
the priests' mothers, sisters, mistresses, and daughters as the
priests to attack their wives. Wherefore I am minded to give
you, as I may do in few words, the history of a rustic amour,
the conclusion whereof was not a little laughable, nor barren
of moral, for you may also gather therefrom, that 'tis not always
well to believe everything that a priest says.

I say then, that at Varlungo, a village hard by here, as all
of you, my ladies, should wot either of your own knowledge or
by report, there dwelt a worthy priest, and doughty of body
in the service of the ladies : who, albeit he was none too quick
at his book, had no lack of precious and blessed solecisms to
edify his flock withal of a Sunday under the elm. And when
the men were out of doors, he would visit their wives as never
a priest had done before him, bringing them feast-day gowns
and holy water, and now and again a bit of candle, and giving
them his blessing. Now it so befell that among those of his
fair parishioners whom he most affected the first place was at
length taken by one Monna Belcolore, the wife of a husbandman that called himself Bentivegna del Mazzo. And in good
sooth she was a winsome and lusty country lass, brown as a
berry and buxom enough, and fitter than e'er another for his
mill. Moreover she had not her match in playing the tabret

and singing :—The borage is full sappy,[1] and in leading a brawl
or a breakdown, no matter who might be next her, with a fair
and dainty kerchief in her hand. Which spells so wrought
upon Master Priest, that for love of her he grew distracted, and
did nought all day long but loiter about the village on the chance
of catching sight of her. And if of a Sunday morning he espied
her in church, he strove might and main to acquit himself of his
Kyrie and Sanctus in the style of a great singer, albeit his performance was liker to the braying of an ass : whereas, if he saw
her not, he scarce exerted himself at all. However, he managed
with such discretion that neither Bentivegna del Mazzo nor
any of the neighbours wist aught of his love. And hoping
thereby to ingratiate himself with Monna Belcolore, he from
time to time would send her presents, now a clove of fresh garlic,
the best in all the country-side, from his own garden, which he
tilled with his own hands, and anon a basket of beans or a
bunch of chives or shallots ; and, when he thought it might
serve his turn, he would give her a sly glance, and follow it up
with a little amorous mocking and mowing, which she, with
rustic awkwardness, feigned not to understand, and ever maintained her reserve, so that Master Priest made no headway.

Now it so befell that one day, when the priest at high noon
was aimlessly gadding about the village, he encountered Bentivegna del Mazzo at the tail of a well laden ass, and greeted
him, asking him whither he was going. " I'faith, Sir," quoth
Bentivegna, " for sure 'tis to town I go, having an affair or two
to attend to there ; and I am taking these things to Ser Buonac-
corri da Ginestreto, to get him to stand by me in I wot not what
matter, whereof the justice o' th' coram has by his provoker
served me with a pertrumpery summons to appear before him."
Whereupon :—" 'Tis well, my son," quoth the priest, overjoyed,
" my blessing go with thee : good luck to thee and a speedy
return ; and harkye, shouldst thou see Lapuccio or Naldino,

---

1 For this folk-song see *Cantilene e Ballate, Strambotti e Madrigali*, ed.
Carducci (1871), p. 60. The fragment there printed may be freely rendered
as follows :—

> The borage is full sappy,
>   And clusters red we see,
> And my love would make me happy;
>   So that maiden gave to me.
>
> Ill set I find this dance,
>   And better might it be :
> So, comrade mine, advance,
>   And, changing place with me,
> Stand thou thy love beside.

do not forget to tell them to send me those thongs for my flails."
" It shall be done," quoth Bentivegna, and jogged on towards
Florence, while the priest, thinking that now was his time to
hie him to Belcolore and try his fortune, put his best leg
forward, and stayed not till he was at the house, which
entering, he said :—" God be gracious to us ! Who is within ? "
Belcolore, who was up in the loft, made answer :—" Welcome,
Sir ; but what dost thou, gadding about in the heat ? "
" Why, as I hope for God's blessing," quoth he, " I am just
come to stay with thee a while, having met thy husband on
his way to town." Whereupon down came Belcolore, took
a seat, and began sifting cabbage-seed that her husband had
lately threshed. By and by the priest began :—" So, Belcolore,
wilt thou keep me ever a-dying thus ? " Whereat Belcolore
tittered, and said :—" Why, what is't I do to you ? " " Truly,
nothing at all," replied the priest : " but thou sufferest me
not to do to thee that which I had lief, and which God commands." " Now away with you ! " returned Belcolore, " do
priests do that sort of thing ? " " Indeed we do," quoth the
priest, " and to better purpose than others : why not ? I tell
you our grinding is far better ; and wouldst thou know why ?
'tis because 'tis intermittent. And in truth 'twill be well worth
thy while to keep thine own counsel, and let me do it." " Worth
my while ! " ejaculated Belcolore. " How may that be ?
There is never a one of you but would overreach the very Devil."
" 'Tis not for me to say," returned the priest ; " say but what
thou wouldst have : shall it be a pair of dainty shoes ? Or
wouldst thou prefer a fillet ? Or perchance a gay riband ?
What's thy will ? " " Marry, no lack have I," quoth Belcolore,
" of such things as these. But, if you wish me so well, why do
me not a service ? and I would then be at your command."
" Name but the service," returned the priest, " and gladly will
I do it." Quoth then Belcolore :—" On Saturday I have to
go to Florence to deliver some wool that I have spun, and to
get my spinning-wheel put in order : lend me but five pounds—
I know you have them—and I will redeem my perse petticoat
from the pawnshop, and also the girdle that I wear on saints'
days, and that I had when I was married—you see that without
them I cannot go to church or anywhere else, and then I will
do just as you wish thenceforth and forever." Whereupon :—
" So God give me a good year," quoth he, " as I have not the
money with me : but never fear that I will see that thou hast
it before Saturday with all the pleasure in life." " Ay, ay,"

rejoined Belcolore, "you all make great promises, but then you never keep them. Think you to serve me as you served Biliuzza, whom you left in the lurch at last ? God's faith, you do not so. To think that she turned woman of the world just for that ! If you have not the money with you, why, go and get it." "Prithee," returned the priest, "send me not home just now. For, seest thou, 'tis the very nick of time with me, and the coast is clear, and perchance it might not be so on my return, and in short I know not when it would be likely to go so well as now." Whereto she did but rejoin :—"Good ; if you are minded to go, get you gone ; if not, stay where you are." The priest, therefore, seeing that she was not disposed to give him what he wanted, as he was fain, to wit, on his own terms, but was bent upon having a *quid pro quo*, changed his tone ; and :—"Lo, now," quoth he, "thou doubtest I will not bring thee the money ; so to set thy mind at rest, I will leave thee this cloak—thou seest 'tis good sky-blue silk—in pledge." So raising her head and glancing at the cloak :—"And what may the cloak be worth ?" quoth Belcolore. "Worth !" ejaculated the priest : "I would have thee know that 'tis all Douai, not to say Trouai, make : nay, there are some of our folk here that say 'tis Quadrouai ; and 'tis not a fortnight since I bought it of Lotto, the second-hand dealer, for seven good pounds, and then had it five good soldi under value, by what I hear from Buglietto, who, thou knowest, is an excellent judge of these articles." "Oh ! say you so ?" exclaimed Belcolore. "So help me God, I should not have thought it ; however, let me look at it." So Master Priest, being ready for action, doffed the cloak and handed it to her. And she, having put it in a safe place, said to him :—"Now, Sir, we will away to the hut ; there is never a soul goes there ;" and so they did. And there Master Priest, giving her many a mighty buss and straining her to his sacred person, solaced himself with her no little while.

Which done, he hied him away in his cassock, as if he were come from officiating at a wedding ; but, when he was back in his holy quarters, he bethought him that not all the candles that he received by way of offering in the course of an entire year would amount to the half of five pounds, and saw that he had made a bad bargain, and repented him that he had left the cloak in pledge, and cast about how he might recover it without paying anything. And as he did not lack cunning, he hit upon an excellent expedient, by which he compassed his end. So on the morrow, being a saint's day, he sent a neigh-

bour's lad to Monna Belcolore with a request that she would
be so good as to lend him her stone mortar, for that Binguccio
dal Poggio and Nuto Buglietti were to breakfast with him
that morning, and he therefore wished to make a sauce. Belcolore having sent the mortar, the priest, about breakfast time,
reckoning that Bentivegna del Mazzo and Belcolore would be at
their meal, called his clerk, and said to him :—" Take the mortar
back to Belcolore, and say :—' My master thanks you very
kindly, and bids you return the cloak that the lad left with you
in pledge.' " The clerk took the mortar to Belcolore's house,
where, finding her at table with Bentivegna, he set the mortar
down and delivered the priest's message. Whereto Belcolore
would fain have demurred ; but Bentivegna gave her a threatening glance, saying :—" So, then, thou takest a pledge from
Master Priest ? By Christ, I vow, I have half a mind to give
thee a great clout o' the chin. Go, give it back at once, a
murrain on thee ! And look to it that whatever he may have
a mind to, were it our very ass, he be never denied." So, with
a very bad grace, Belcolore got up, and went to the wardrobe,
and took out the cloak, and gave it to the clerk, saying :—
" Tell thy master from me :—Would to God he may never ply
pestle in my mortar again, such honour has he done me for
this turn ! " So the clerk returned with the cloak, and delivered
the message to Master Priest ; who, laughing, made answer :
—" Tell her, when thou next seest her, that, so she lend us not
the mortar, I will not lend her the pestle : be it tit for tat."

Bentivegna made no account of his wife's words, deeming
that 'twas but his chiding that had provoked them. But
Belcolore was not a little displeased with Master Priest, and had
never a word to say to him till the vintage ; after which, what
with the salutary fear in which she stood of the mouth of Lucifer
the Great, to which he threatened to consign her, and the
must and roast chestnuts that he sent her, she made it up with
him, and many a jolly time they had together. And though
she got not the five pounds from him, he put a new skin on her
tabret, and fitted it with a little bell, wherewith she was satisfied.

NOVEL III

Calandrino, Bruno and Buffalmacco go in quest of the heliotrope beside the Mugnone. Thinking to have found it, Calandrino gets him home laden with stones. His wife chides him: whereat he waxes wroth, beats her, and tells his comrades what they know better than he.

ENDED Pamfilo's story, which moved the ladies to inextinguishable laughter, the queen bade Elisa follow suit : whereupon, laughing, she thus began :—I know not, debonair my ladies, whether with my little story, which is no less true than entertaining, I shall give you occasion to laugh as much as Pamfilo has done with his, but I will do my best.

In our city, where there has never been lack of odd humours and queer folk, there dwelt, no long time ago, a painter named Calandrino, a simple soul, of uncouth manners, that spent most of his time with two other painters, the one Bruno, the other Buffalmacco, by name, pleasant fellows enough, but not without their full share of sound and shrewd sense, and who kept with Calandrino for that they not seldom found his singular ways and his simplicity very diverting. There was also at the same time at Florence one Maso del Saggio, a fellow marvellously entertaining by his cleverness, dexterity and unfailing resource ; who having heard somewhat touching Calandrino's simplicity, resolved to make fun of him by playing him a trick, and inducing him to believe some prodigy. And happening one day to come upon Calandrino in the church of San Giovanni, where he sate intently regarding the paintings and intaglios of the tabernacle above the altar, which had then but lately been set there, he deemed time and place convenient for the execution of his design ; which he accordingly imparted to one of his comrades : whereupon the two men drew nigh the place where Calandrino sate alone, and feigning not to see him fell a-talking of the virtues of divers stones, of which Maso spoke as aptly and pertinently as if he had been a great and learned lapidary. Calandrino heard what passed between them, and witting that 'twas no secret, after a while got up, and joined them, to Maso's no small delight. He therefore continued his discourse, and being asked by Calandrino, where these stones of such rare virtues were to be found, made answer :—" Chiefly in Berlinzone, in the land of the Basques. The district is called Bengodi, and there they bind the vines with sausages, and a denier will buy a goose and a gosling into the bargain ; and on a mountain, all of grated Parmesan cheese, dwell folk that do nought else but make macaroni and raviuoli,[1] and boil them in capon's broth, and then throw them down to be scrambled for ; and hard by flows a rivulet of Vernaccia, the best that ever was drunk, and never a drop of water therein." "Ah ! 'tis a sweet country !" quoth Calandrino ; " but tell me, what becomes of the capons that they boil ? " " They are all eaten by the Basques," replied Maso. Then :—" Wast thou ever there ? " quoth Calandrino. Whereupon :—" Was I ever there, sayst thou ? " replied Maso. " Why, if I have been there once, I have been there a thousand times." " And how many miles is't from here ? " quoth Calandrino. " Oh ! " returned Maso, " more than thou couldst number in a night without slumber." " Farther off, then, than the Abruzzi ? " said Calandrino. " Why, yes, 'tis a bit farther," replied Maso.

Now Calandrino, like the simple soul that he was, marking the composed and grave countenance with which Maso spoke, could not have believed him more thoroughly if he had uttered the most patent truth, and thus taking his words for gospel :— " 'Tis a trifle too far for my purse," quoth he ; " were it nigher, I warrant thee, I would go with thee thither one while, just to see the macaroni come tumbling down, and take my fill thereof. But tell me, so good luck befall thee, are none of these stones, that have these rare virtues, to be found in these regions ? " " Ay," replied Maso, " two sorts of stone are found there, both of virtues extraordinary. The one sort are the sandstones of Settignano and Montisci, which being made into millstones, by virtue thereof flour is made ; wherefore 'tis a common saying in those countries that blessings come from God and millstones from Montisci : but, for that these sandstones are in great plenty, they are held cheap by us, just as by them are emeralds, whereof they have mountains, bigger than Monte Morello, that shine at midnight, a God's name ! And know this, that whoso should make a goodly pair of millstones, and connect them with a ring before ever a hole was drilled in them, and take them to the Soldan, should get all he would have thereby. The other sort of stone is the heliotrope, as we lapidaries call it, a stone of very great virtue, inasmuch as whoso carries it on his person is seen, so long as he keep it, by never another soul, where he is not." " These be virtues great indeed," quoth Calandrino ;

[1] A sort of rissole.

"but where is this second stone to be found?" Whereto
Maso made answer that there were usually some to be found
in the Mugnone. "And what are its size and colour?" quoth
Calandrino. "The size varies," replied Maso, "for some are
bigger and some smaller than others; but all are of the same
colour, being nearly black." All these matters duly marked and
fixed in his memory, Calandrino made as if he had other things
to attend to, and took his leave of Maso with the intention of
going in quest of the stone, but not until he had let his
especial friends, Bruno and Buffalmacco, know of his project.
So, that no time might be lost, but, postponing everything
else, they might begin the quest at once, he set about looking
for them, and spent the whole morning in the search. At
length, when 'twas already past none, he called to mind that
they would be at work in the Faentine women's convent, and
though 'twas excessively hot, he let nothing stand in his way,
but at a pace that was more like a run than a walk, hied him
thither; and so soon as he had made them ware of his presence,
thus he spoke :—" Comrades, so you are but minded to hearken
to me, 'tis in our power to become the richest men in Florence;
for I am informed by one that may be trusted that there is a
kind of stone in the Mugnone which renders whoso carries it
invisible to every other soul in the world. Wherefore, methinks, we were wise to let none have the start of us, but go
search for this stone without any delay. We shall find it without a doubt, for I know what 'tis like, and when we have found
it, we have but to put it in the purse, and get us to the money-
changers, whose counters, as you know, are always laden with
groats and florins, and help ourselves to as many as we have
a mind to. No one will see us, and so, hey presto! we shall be
rich folk in the twinkling of an eye, and have no more need to
go besmearing the walls all day long like so many snails."
Whereat Bruno and Buffalmacco began only to laugh, and
exchanging glances, made as if they marvelled exceedingly,
and expressed approval of Calandrino's project. Then Buffalmacco asked, what might be the name of the stone. Calandrino,
like the numskull that he was, had already forgotten the name:
so he made answer :—" Why need we concern ourselves with
the name, since we know the stone's virtue? methinks, we
were best to go look for it, and waste no more time."
"Well, well," said Bruno, "but what are the size and shape
of the stone?" "They are of all sizes and shapes," said
Calandrino, "but they are all pretty nearly black; wherefore,

methinks, we were best to collect all the black stones that we
see until we hit upon it : and so, let us be off, and lose no more
time." " Nay, but," said Bruno, " wait a bit." And turning
to Buffalmacco :—" Methinks," quoth he, " that Calandrino
says well : but I doubt this is not the time for such work, seeing
that the sun is high, and his rays so flood the Mugnone as to
dry all the stones ; insomuch that stones will now shew as white
that in the morning, before the sun had dried them, would shew
as black : besides which, to-day being a working-day, there will
be for one cause or another folk not a few about the Mugnone,
who, seeing us, might guess what we were come for, and peradventure do the like themselves ; whereby it might well be
that they found the stone, and we might miss the trot by
trying after the amble. Wherefore, so you agree, methinks
we were best to go about it in the morning, when we shall
be better able to distinguish the black stones from the white,
and on a holiday, when there will be none to see us."

Buffalmacco's advice being approved by Bruno, Calandrino
chimed in ; and so 'twas arranged that they should all three
go in quest of the stone on the following Sunday. So Calandrino, having besought his companions above all things
to let never a soul in the world hear aught of the matter, for
that it had been imparted to him in strict confidence, and
having told them what he had heard touching the land of
Bengodi, the truth of which he firmed with oaths, took leave
of them ; and they concerted their plan, while Calandrino
impatiently expected the Sunday morning. Whereon, about
dawn, he arose, and called them ; and forth they issued by the
Porta a San Gallo, and hied them to the Mugnone, and following
its course, began their quest of the stone, Calandrino, as was
natural, leading the way, and jumping lightly from rock to
rock, and wherever he espied a black stone, stooping down,
picking it up and putting it in the fold of his tunic, while his
comrades followed, picking up a stone here and a stone there.
Thus it was that Calandrino had not gone far, before, finding
that there was no more room in his tunic, he lifted the skirts
of his gown, which was not cut after the fashion of Hainault,
and gathering them under his leathern girdle and making
them fast on every side, thus furnished himself with a fresh and
capacious lap, which, however, taking no long time to fill, he
made another lap out of his cloak, which in like manner he soon
filled with stones. Wherefore, Bruno and Buffalmacco
seeing that Calandrino was well laden, and that 'twas nigh upon

breakfast-time, and the moment for action come :—" Where is Calandrino ? " quoth Bruno to Buffalmacco. Whereto Buffalmacco, who had Calandrino full in view, having first turned about and looked here, there and everywhere, made answer :—" That wot not I ; but not so long ago he was just in front of us." " Not so long ago, forsooth," returned Bruno ; " 'tis my firm belief that at this very moment he is at breakfast at home, having left to us this wild-goose chase of black stones in the Mugnone." " Marry," quoth Buffalmacco, " he did but serve us right so to trick us and leave, seeing that we were so silly as to believe him. Why, who could have thought that any but we would have been so foolish as to believe that a stone of such rare virtue was to be found in the Mugnone ? " Calandrino, hearing their colloquy, forthwith imagined that he had the stone in his hand, and by its virtue, though present, was invisible to them ; and overjoyed by such good fortune, would not say a word to undeceive them, but determined to hie him home, and accordingly faced about, and put himself in motion. Whereupon :—" Ay ! " quoth Buffalmacco to Bruno, " what are we about that we go not back too ? " " Go we then," said Bruno ; " but by God I swear that Calandrino shall never play me another such trick ; and as to this, were I nigh him, as I have been all the morning, I would teach him to remember it for a month or so, such a reminder would I give him in the heel with this stone." And even as he spoke he threw back his arm, and launched the stone against Calandrino's heel. Galled by the blow, Calandrino gave a great hop and a slight gasp but said nothing, and halted not. Then, picking out one of the stones that he had collected :—" Bruno," quoth Buffalmacco, " see what a goodly stone I have here, would it might but catch Calandrino in the back ; " and forthwith he discharged it with main force upon the said back. And in short, suiting action to word, now in this way, now in that, they stoned him all the way up the Mugnone as far as the Porta a San Gallo. There they threw away the stones they had picked up, and tarried a while with the customs' officers, who, being primed by them, had let Calandrino pass unchallenged, while their laughter knew no bounds.

So Calandrino, halting nowhere, betook him to his house, which was hard by the corner of the Macina. And so well did Fortune prosper the trick, that all the way by the stream and across the city there was never a soul that said a word to Calandrino, and indeed he encountered but few, for most folk

were at breakfast. But no sooner was Calandrino thus gotten
home with his stones, than it so happened that his good lady,
Monna Tessa, shewed her fair face at the stair's head, and
catching sight of him, and being somewhat annoyed by his
long delay, chid him, saying:—"What the Devil brings thee
here so late? Must breakfast wait thee until all other folk
have had it?" Calandrino caught the words, and angered
and mortified to find that he was not invisible, broke out with:
—"Alas! curst woman! so 'twas thou! Thou hast undone
me: but, God's faith, I will pay thee out." Whereupon he
was upstairs in a trice, and having discharged his great load of
stones in a parlour, rushed with fell intent upon his wife, and
laid hold of her by the hair, and threw her down at his feet,
and beat and kicked her in every part of her person with all the
force he had in his arms and legs, insomuch that he left never
a hair of her head or bone of her body unscathed, and 'twas
all in vain that she laid her palms together and crossed her
fingers and cried for mercy.

Now Buffalmacco and Bruno, after making merry a while
with the warders of the gate, had set off again at a leisurely
pace, keeping some distance behind Calandrino. Arrived at
his door, they heard the noise of the sound thrashing that he
was giving his wife; and making as if they were but that very
instant come upon the scene, they called him. Calandrino,
flushed, all of a sweat, and out of breath, shewed himself at
the window and bade them come up. They, putting on a somewhat angry air, did so; and espied Calandrino sitting in the
parlour, amid the stones which lay all about, untrussed, and
puffing with the air of a man spent with exertion, while his
lady lay in one of the corners, weeping bitterly, her hair all
dishevelled, her clothes torn to shreds, and her face livid,
bruised and battered. So after surveying the room a while:—
"What means this, Calandrino?" quoth they. "Art thou
minded to build thee a wall, that we see so many stones about?"
And then, as they received no answer, they continued:—"And
how's this? How come Monna Tessa in this plight? 'Twould
seem thou hast given her a beating! What unheard-of doings
are these?" What with the weight of the stones that he
had carried, and the fury with which he had beaten his wife,
and the mortification that he felt at the miscarriage of his
enterprise, Calandrino was too spent to utter a word by way of
reply. Wherefore in a menacing tone Buffalmacco began,
again:—"However out of sorts thou mayst have been, Calan-

drino, thou shouldst not have played us so scurvy a trick of
thou hast. To take us with thee to the Mugnone in quest as
this stone of rare virtue, and then, without so much as saying
either God-speed or Devil-speed, to be off, and leave us there
like a couple of gowks ! We take it not a little unkindly : and
rest assured that thou shalt never so fool us again." Whereto
with an effort Calandrino replied :—" Comrades, be not wroth
with me : 'tis not as you think. I, luckless wight ! found the
stone : listen, and you will no longer doubt that I say sooth.
When you began saying one to the other :—' Where is Calandrino ? ' I was within ten paces of you, and marking that you
came by without seeing me, I went before, and so, keeping ever
a little ahead of you, I came hither." And then he told them
the whole story of what they had said and done from beginning
to end, and shewed them his back and heel, how they had been
mauled by the stones ; after which :—" And I tell you," he
went on, " that, laden though I was with all these stones,
that you see here, never a word was said to me by the warders
of the gate as I passed in, though you know how vexatious and
grievous these warders are wont to make themselves in their
determination to see everything : and moreover I met by the
way several of my gossips and friends that are ever wont to greet
me, and ask me to drink, and never a word said any of them
to me, no, nor half a word either ; but they passed me by as
men that saw me not. But at last, being come home, I was
met and seen by this devil of a woman, curses upon her, for-
asmuch as all things, as you know, lose their virtue in the
presence of a woman ; whereby I from being the most lucky
am become the most luckless man in Florence : and therefore
I thrashed her as long as I could stir a hand, nor know I where
fore I forbear to sluice her veins for her, cursed be the hour that
first I saw her, cursed be the hour that I brought her into the
house ! " And so, kindling with fresh wrath, he was about
to start up and give her another thrashing ; when Buffalmacco
and Bruno, who had listened to his story with an air of great
surprise, and affirmed its truth again and again, while they all
but burst with suppressed laughter, seeing him now frantic
to renew his assault upon his wife, got up and withstood and
held him back, averring that the lady was in no wise to blame
for what had happened, but only he, who, witting that things
lost their virtue in the presence of women, had not bidden her
keep aloof from him that day ; which precaution God had not
suffered him to take. either because the luck was not to be his,

or because he was minded to cheat his comrades, to whom he should have shewn the stone as soon as he found it. And so, with many words they hardly prevailed upon him to forgive his injured wife, and leaving him to rue the ill-luck that had filled his house with stones, went their way.

NOVEL IV

The Rector of Fiesole loves a widow lady, by whom he is not loved, and thinking to lie with her, lies with her maid, with whom the lady's brothers cause him to be found by his Bishop.

ELISA being come to the end of her story, which in the telling had yielded no small delight to all the company, the queen, turning to Emilia, signified her will, that her story should ensue at once upon that of Elisa. And thus with alacrity Emilia began :—Noble ladies, how we are teased and tormented by these priests and friars, and indeed by clergy of all sorts, I mind me to have been set forth in more than one of the stories that have been told ; but as 'twere not possible to say so much thereof but that more would yet remain to say, I purpose to supplement them with the story of a rector, who, in defiance of all the world, was bent upon having the favour of a gentlewoman, whether she would or no. Which gentlewoman, being discreet above a little, treated him as he deserved.

Fiesole, whose hill is here within sight, is, as each of you knows, a city of immense antiquity, and was aforetime great, though now 'tis fallen into complete decay ; which notwithstanding, it always was, and still is the see of a bishop. Now there was once a gentlewoman, Monna Piccarda by name, a widow, that had an estate at Fiesole, hard by the cathedral, on which, for that she was not in the easiest circumstances, she lived most part of the year, and with her her two brothers, very worthy and courteous young men, both of them. And the lady being wont frequently to resort to the cathedral, and being still quite young and fair and debonair withal, it so befell that the rector grew in the last degree enamoured of her, and waxed at length so bold, that he himself avowed his passion to the lady, praying her to entertain his love, and requite it in like measure. The rector was advanced in years, but otherwise the veriest springald, being bold and of a high spirit, of a boundless conceit of himself, and of mien and manners most affected and in the worst taste, and withal so tiresome and insufferable that he was on bad terms with everybody, and, if with one person more than another, with this lady, who not only cared not a jot for him, but had liefer have had a headache than his company. Wherefore the lady discreetly made answer:—"I may well prize your love, Sir, and love you I should and will right gladly; but such love as yours and mine may never admit of aught that is not honourable. You are my spiritual father and a priest, and now verging towards old age, circumstances which should ensure your honour and chastity; and I, on my part, am no longer a girl, such as these love affairs might beseem, but a widow, and well you wot how it behoves widows to be chaste. Wherefore I pray you to have me excused; for, after the sort you crave, you shall never have my love, nor would I in such sort be loved by you." With this answer the rector was for the nonce fain to be content; but he was not the man to be dismayed and routed by a first repulse; and with his wonted temerity and effrontery he plied her again and again with letters and ambassages, and also by word of mouth, when he espied her entering the church. Wherefore the lady finding this persecution more grievous and harassing than she could well bear, cast about how she might be quit thereof in such fashion as he deserved, seeing that he left her no choice; howbeit she would do nought in the matter until she had conferred with her brothers. She therefore told them how the rector pursued her, and how she meant to foil him; and, with their full concurrence, some few days afterwards she went, as she was wont, to church. The rector no sooner saw her, than he approached and accosted her, as he was wont, in a tone of easy familiarity. The lady greeted him, as he came up, with a glance of gladsome recognition; and when he had treated her to not a little of his wonted eloquence, she drew him aside, and heaving a great sigh, said:—" I have oftentimes heard it said, Sir, that there is no castle so strong, but that, if the siege be continued day by day, it will sooner or later be taken; which I now plainly perceive is my own case. For so fairly have you hemmed me in with this, that, and the other pretty speech or the like blandishments, that you have constrained me to make nought of my former resolve, and, seeing that I find such favour with you, to surrender myself unto you." Whereto, overjoyed, the rector made answer:—" Madam, I am greatly honoured; and, sooth to say, I marvelled not a little how you should hold out so long, seeing that I have never had the like experience with any other

woman, insomuch that I have at times said :—' Were women of
silver, they would not be worth a denier, for there is none but
would give under the hammer.' But no more of this : when and
where may we come together ? " " Sweet my lord," replied
the lady, " for the when, 'tis just as we may think best, for I
have no husband to whom to render account of my nights, but
the where passes my wit to conjecture." " How so ? " quoth
the rector. " Why not in your own house ? " " Sir," replied
the lady, " you know that I have two brothers, both young
men, who day and night bring their comrades into the house,
which is none too large : for which reason it might not be done
there, unless we were minded to make ourselves, as it were,
dumb and blind, uttering never a word, not so much as a mono-
syllable, and abiding in the dark : in such sort indeed it might
be, because they do not intrude upon my chamber ; but theirs
is so near to mine that the very least whisper could not but be
heard." " Nay but, Madam," returned the rector, " let not
this stand in our way for a night or two, until I may bethink
me where else we might be more at our ease." " Be that as
you will, Sir," quoth the lady, " I do but entreat that the affair
be kept close, so that never a word of it get wind." " Have
no fear on that score, Madam," replied the priest ; " and if so
it may be, let us forgather to-night." " With pleasure," returned
the lady ; and having appointed him how and when to come,
she left him and went home.

Now the lady had a maid, that was none too young, and had
a countenance the ugliest and most misshapen that ever was
seen ; for indeed she was flat-nosed, wry-mouthed, and thick-
lipped, with huge, ill-set teeth, eyes that squinted and were
ever bleared, and a complexion betwixt green and yellow, that
shewed as if she had spent the summer not at Fiesole but at
Sinigaglia : besides which she was hipshot and somewhat
halting on the right side. Her name was Ciuta, but, for that
she was such a scurvy bitch to look upon, she was called by all
folk Ciutazza.[1] And being thus misshapen of body, she was
also not without her share of guile. So the lady called her
and said : —" Ciutazza, so thou wilt do me a service to-night,
I will give thee a fine new shift." At the mention of the shift
Ciutazza made answer :—" So you give me a shift, Madam, I
will throw myself into the very fire." " Good," said the lady ;
" then I would have thee lie to-night in my bed with a man,
whom thou wilt caress ; but look thou say never a word, that

[1] An augmentative form, with a suggestion of *cagnazza*, bitch-like.

my brothers, who, as thou knowest, sleep in the next room,
hear thee not; and afterwards I will give thee the shift."
"Sleep with a man!" quoth Ciutazza: "why, if need be, I
will sleep with six." So in the evening Master Rector came,
as he had been bidden; and the two young men, as the lady
had arranged, being in their room, and making themselves
very audible, he stole noiselessly, and in the dark, into the
lady's room, and got him on to the bed, which Ciutazza, well
advised by the lady how to behave, mounted from the other
side. Whereupon Master Rector, thinking to have the lady by
his side, took Ciutazza in his arms, and fell a-kissing her, saying
never a word the while, and Ciutazza did the like; and so he
enjoyed her, plucking the boon which he had so long desired.

The rector and Ciutazza thus closeted, the lady charged her
brothers to execute the rest of her plan. They accordingly
stole quietly out of their room, and hied them to the piazza,
where Fortune proved propitious beyond what they had craved
of her; for, it being a very hot night, the bishop had been seeking them, purposing to go home with them, and solace himself
with their society, and quench his thirst. With which desire
he acquainted them, as soon as he espied them coming into
the piazza; and so they escorted him to their house, and there
in the cool of their little courtyard, which was bright with many
a lamp, he took, to his no small comfort, a draught of their good
wine. Which done:—"Sir," said the young men, "since of
your great courtesy you have deigned to visit our poor house,
to which we were but now about to invite you, we should be
gratified if you would be pleased to give a look at somewhat,
a mere trifle though it be, which we have here to shew you."
The bishop replied that he would do so with pleasure. Whereupon one of the young men took a lighted torch and led the
way, the bishop and the rest following, to the chamber where
Master Rector lay with Ciutazza.

Now the rector, being in hot haste, had ridden hard, insomuch that he was already gotten above three miles on his way
when they arrived; and so, being somewhat tired, he was resting,
but, hot though the night was, he still held Ciutazza in his
arms. In which posture he was shewn to the bishop, when,
preceded by the young man bearing the light, and followed by
the others, he entered the chamber. And being roused, and
observing the light and the folk that stood about him, Master
Rector was mighty ashamed and affrighted, and popped his head
under the clothes. But the bishop, reprimanding him severely,

constrained him to thrust his head out again, and take a view of
his bed-fellow. Thus made aware of the trick which the lady
had played him, the rector was now, both on that score and by
reason of his signal disgrace, the saddest man that ever was ;
and his discomfiture was complete, when, having donned his
clothes, he was committed by the bishop's command to close
custody and sent to prison, there to expiate his offence by a
rigorous penance.

The bishop was then fain to know how it had come about
that he had forgathered there with Ciutazza. Whereupon the
young men related the whole story ; which ended, the bishop
commended both the lady and the young men not a little, for
that they had taken condign vengeance upon him without im-
bruing their hands in the blood of a priest. The bishop caused
him to bewail his transgression forty days ; but what with his
love, and the scornful requital which it had received, he bewailed
it more than forty and nine days, not to mention that for a
great while he could not shew himself in the street but the boys
would point the finger at him and say :—" There goes he that
lay with Ciutazza." Which was such an affliction to him that
he was like to go mad. On this wise the worthy lady rid
herself of the rector's vexatious importunity, and Ciutazza
had a jolly night and earned her shift.

NOVEL V

*Three young men pull down the breeches of a judge from the
Marches, while he is administering justice on the bench.*

So ended Emilia her story ; and when all had commended
the widow lady :—" 'Tis now thy turn to speak," quoth the
queen, fixing her gaze upon Filostrato, who answered that he
was ready, and forthwith thus began :—Sweet my ladies, by
what I remember of that young man, to wit, Maso del Saggio,
whom Elisa named a while ago, I am prompted to lay aside a
story that I had meant to tell you, and to tell you another,
touching him and some of his comrades, which, notwithstanding
there are in it certain words (albeit 'tis not unseemly) which
your modesty forbears to use, is yet so laughable that I shall
relate it.

As you all may well have heard, there come not seldom to
our city magistrates from the Marches, who for the most part
are men of a mean spirit, and in circumstances so reduced and

beggarly, that their whole life seems to be but a petty-foggery ;
and by reason of this their inbred sordidness and avarice they
bring with them judges and notaries that have rather the air
of men taken from the plough or the last than trained in the
schools of law.[1] Now one of these Marchers, being come hither
as Podestà, brought with him judges not a few, and among
them one that called himself Messer Niccola da San Lepidio,
and looked liker to a locksmith than aught else. However,
this fellow was assigned with the rest of the judges to hear
criminal causes. And as folk will often go to the court, though
they have no concern whatever there, it so befell that Maso del
Saggio went thither one morning in quest of one of his friends,
and there chancing to set eyes on this Messer Niccola, where he
sate, deemed him a fowl of no common feather, and surveyed
him from head to foot, observing that the vair which
he wore on his head was all begrimed, that he carried an ink-
horn at his girdle, that his gown was longer than his robe, and
many another detail quite foreign to the appearance of a man
of birth and breeding, of which that which he deemed most
notable was a pair of breeches, which, as he saw (for the judge's
outer garments being none too ample were open in front, as he
sate), reached half-way down his legs. By which sight his mind
was presently diverted from the friend whom he came there to
seek ; and forth he hied him in quest of other two of his comrades, the one Ribi, the other Matteuzzo by name, fellows both
of them not a whit less jolly than Maso himself ; and having
found them, he said to them :—" An you love me, come with
me to the court, and I will shew you the queerest scarecrow that
ever you saw." So the two men hied them with him to the
court ; and there he pointed out to them the judge and his
breeches. What they saw from a distance served to set them
laughing : then drawing nearer to the daïs on which Master
Judge was seated, they observed that 'twas easy enough to get
under the daïs, and moreover that the plank, on which the
judge's feet rested, was broken, so that there was plenty of room
for the passage of a hand and arm. Whereupon quoth Maso to
his comrades :—" 'Twere a very easy matter to pull these
breeches right down : wherefore I propose that we do so."
Each of the men had marked how it might be done ; and so,
having concerted both what they should do and what they
should say, they came to the court again next morning ; and,

[1] It was owing to their internal dissensions that the Florentines were
from time to time fain to introduce these stranger Podestàs.

the court being crowded, Matteuzzo, observed by never a soul, slipped beneath the daïs, and posted himself right under the spot where the judge's feet rested, while the other two men took their stand on either side of the judge, each laying hold of the hem of his robe. Then :—" Sir, sir, I pray you for God's sake," began Maso, " that, before the pilfering rascal that is there beside you can make off, you constrain him to give me back a pair of jack boots that he has stolen from me, which theft he still denies, though 'tis not a month since I saw him getting them resoled." Meanwhile Ribi, at the top of his voice, shouted :—" Believe him not, Sir, the scurvy knave ! 'Tis but that he knows that I am come to demand restitution of a valise that he has stolen from me that he now for the first time trumps up this story about a pair of jack boots that I have had in my house down to the last day or two ; and if you doubt what I say, I can bring as witness Trecca, my neighbour, and Grassa, the tripe-woman, and one that goes about gathering the sweepings of Santa Maria a Verzaia, who saw him when he was on his way back from the farm." But shout as he might, Maso was still even with him, nor for all that did Ribi bate a jot of his clamour. And while the judge stood, bending now towards the one, now towards the other, the better to hear them, Matteuzzo seized his opportunity, and thrusting his hand through the hole in the plank caught hold of the judge's breeches, and tugged at them amain. Whereby down they came straight-way, for the judge was a lean man, and shrunk in the buttocks. The judge, being aware of the accident, but knowing not how it had come about, would have gathered his outer garments together in front, so as to cover the defect, but Maso on the one side, and Ribi on the other, held him fast, shouting amain and in chorus :—" You do me a grievous wrong, Sir, thus to deny me justice, nay, even a hearing, and to think of quitting the court : there needs no writ in this city for such a trifling matter as this." And thus they held him by the clothes and in parley, until all that were in the court perceived that he had lost his breeches. However, after a while, Matteuzzo dropped the breeches, and slipped off, and out of the court, without being observed, and Ribi, deeming that the joke had gone far enough, exclaimed :—" By God, I vow, I will appeal to the Syndics ; " while Maso, on the other side, let go the robe, saying :—" Nay, but for my part, I will come here again and again and again, until I find you less embarrassed than you seem to be to-day.' And so the one this way, the other that way, they made off with all speed. Whereupon Master Judge, dis-breeched before all the world, was as one that awakens from sleep, albeit he was ware of his forlorn condition, and asked whither the parties in the case touching the jack boots and the valise were gone. However, as they were not to be found, he fell a-swearing by the bowels of God, that 'twas meet and proper that he should know and wit, whether 'twas the custom at Florence to disbreech judges sitting in the seat of justice.

When the affair reached the ears of the Podestà, he made no little stir about it ; but, being informed by some of his friends, that 'twould not have happened, but that the Florentines were minded to shew him, that, in place of the judges he should have brought with him, he had brought but gowks, to save expense, he deemed it best to say no more about it, and so for that while the matter went no further.

NOVEL VI

Bruno and Buffalmacco steal a pig from Calandrino, and induce him to essay its recovery by means of pills of ginger and vernaccia. Of the said pills they give him two, one after the other, made of dog-ginger compounded with aloes ; and it then appearing as if he had had the pig himself, they constrain him to buy them off, if he would not have them tell his wife.

FILOSTRATO's story, which elicited not a little laughter, was no sooner ended, than the queen bade Filomena follow suit. Wherefore thus Filomena began :—As, gracious ladies, 'twas the name of Maso del Saggio that prompted Filostrato to tell the story that you have but now heard, even so 'tis with me in regard of Calandrino and his comrades, of whom I am minded to tell you another story, which you will, I think, find enter-taining. Who Calandrino, Bruno and Buffalmacco were, I need not explain ; you know them well enough from the former story ; and therefore I will tarry no longer than to say that Calandrino had a little estate not far from Florence, which his wife had brought him by way of dowry, and which yielded them yearly, among other matters, a pig ; and 'twas his custom every year in the month of December to resort to the farm with his wife, there to see to the killing and salting of the said pig. Now, one of these years it so happened that his wife being unwell, Calandrino went thither alone to kill the pig. And

Bruno and Buffalmacco learning that he was gone to the farm, and that his wife was not with him, betook them to the house of a priest that was their especial friend and a neighbour of Calandrino, there to tarry a while. Upon their arrival Calandrino, who had that very morning killed the pig, met them with the priest, and accosted them, saying:—" A hearty welcome to you. I should like you to see what an excellent manager I am ; " and so he took them into his house, and shewed them the pig. They observed that 'twas a very fine pig ; and learned from Calandrino that he was minded to salt it for household consumption. " Then thou art but a fool," quoth Bruno. " Sell it, man, and let us have a jolly time with the money ; and tell thy wife that 'twas stolen." " Not I," replied Calandrino : " she would never believe me, and would drive me out of the house. Urge me no further, for I will never do it." The others said a great deal more, but to no purpose ; and Calandrino bade them to supper, but so coldly that they declined, and left him.

Presently :—" Should we not steal this pig from him to-night ? " quoth Bruno to Buffalmacco. " Could we so ? " returned Buffalmacco. " How ? " " Why as to that," rejoined Bruno, " I have already marked how it may be done, if he bestow not the pig elsewhere." " So be it, then," said Buffalmacco : " we will steal it ; and then, perchance, our good host, Master Priest, will join us in doing honour to such good cheer ? " " That right gladly will I," quoth the priest. Whereupon :—" Some address, though," quoth Bruno, " will be needful : thou knowest, Buffalmacco, what a niggardly fellow Calandrino is, and how greedily he drinks at other folk's expense. Go we, therefore, and take him to the tavern, and there let the priest make as if, to do us honour, he would pay the whole score, and suffer Calandrino to pay never a soldo, and he will grow tipsy, and then we shall speed excellent well, because he is alone in the house."

As Bruno proposed, so they did : and Calandrino, finding that the priest would not suffer him to pay, drank amain, and took a great deal more aboard than he had need of ; and the night being far spent when he left the tavern, he dispensed with supper, and went home, and thinking to have shut the door, got him to bed, leaving it open. Buffalmacco and Bruno went to sup with the priest ; and after supper, taking with them certain implements with which to enter Calandrino's house, where Bruno thought it most feasible, they stealthily approached it ; but finding the door open, they entered, and took down the pig, and carried it away to the priest's house, and having there bestowed it safely, went to bed. In the morning when Calandrino, his head at length quit of the fumes of the wine, got up, and came downstairs and found that his pig was nowhere to be seen, and that the door was open, he asked this, that, and the other man, whether they wist who had taken the pig away, and getting no answer, he began to make a great outcry : —"Alas, alas ! luckless man that I am, that my pig should have been stolen from me !" Meanwhile Bruno and Buffalmacco, being also risen, made up to him, to hear what he would say touching the pig. Whom he no sooner saw, than well-nigh weeping he called them, saying :—"Alas ! my friends ! my pig is stolen from me." Bruno stepped up to him and said in a low tone :—"'Tis passing strange if thou art in the right for once." "Alas !" returned Calandrino, "what I say is but too true." "Why, then, out with it, man," quoth Bruno, "cry aloud, that all folk may know that 'tis so." Calandrino then raised his voice and said :—"By the body o' God I say of a truth that my pig has been stolen from me." "So !" quoth Bruno, "but publish it, man, publish it ; lift up thy voice, make thyself well heard, that all may believe thy report." "Thou art enough to make me give my soul to the Enemy," replied Calandrino. "I say—dost not believe me ?—that hang me by the neck if the pig is not stolen from me !" "Nay, but," quoth Bruno, "how can it be ? I saw it here but yesterday. Dost think to make me believe that it has taken to itself wings and flown away ?" "All the same 'tis as I tell thee," returned Calandrino. "Is it possible ?" quoth Bruno. "Ay indeed," replied Calandrino ; "'tis even so : and I am undone, and know not how to go home. Never will my wife believe me ; or if she do so, I shall know no peace this year." "Upon my hope of salvation," quoth Bruno, "'tis indeed a bad business, if so it really is. But thou knowest, Calandrino, that 'twas but yesterday I counselled thee to make believe that 'twas so. I should be sorry to think thou didst befool thy wife and us at the same time." "Ah !" vociferated Calandrino, "wilt thou drive me to despair and provoke me to blaspheme God and the saints and all the company of heaven ? I tell thee that the pig has been stolen from me in the night." Whereupon :—"If so it be," quoth Buffalmacco, "we must find a way, if we can, to recover it." "Find a way ?" said Calandrino : "how can we compass that ?" "Why," replied Buffalmacco, "'tis

certain that no one has come from India to steal thy pig : it
must have been one of thy neighbours, and if thou couldst
bring them together, I warrant thee, I know how to make the
assay with bread and cheese, and we will find out in a trice who
has had the pig." "Ay," struck in Bruno, "make thy assay
with bread and cheese in the presence of these gentry hereabout,
one of whom I am sure has had the pig ! why, the thing would
be seen through : and they would not come." "What shall
we do, then ? " said Buffalmacco. Whereto Bruno made
answer :—" It must be done with good pills of ginger and good
vernaccia ; and they must be bidden come drink with us. They
will suspect nothing, and will come ; and pills of ginger can be
blessed just as well as bread and cheese." "Beyond a doubt,
thou art right," quoth Buffalmacco ; "and thou, Calandrino,
what sayst thou ? Shall we do as Bruno says ? " "Nay, I
entreat you, for the love of God," quoth Calandrino, "do even
so : for if I knew but who had had the pig, I should feel myself
half consoled for my loss." "Go to, now," quoth Bruno, "I
am willing to do thy errand to Florence for these commodities,
if thou givest me the money."

Calandrino had some forty soldi upon him, which he gave
to Bruno, who thereupon hied him to Florence to a friend of his
that was an apothecary, and bought a pound of good pills of
ginger, two of which, being of dog-ginger, he caused to be compounded with fresh hepatic aloes, and then to be coated with
sugar like the others ; and lest they should be lost, or any of the
others mistaken for them, he had a slight mark set upon them
by which he might readily recognize them. He also bought a
flask of good vernaccia, and, thus laden, returned to the farm,
and said to Calandrino :—" To-morrow morning thou wilt bid
those whom thou suspectest come hither to drink with thee :
as 'twill be a saint's day, they will all come readily enough ;
and to-night I and Buffalmacco will say the incantation over
the pills, which in the morning I will bring to thee here, and for
our friendship's sake will administer them myself, and do
and say all that needs to be said and done." So Calandrino did
as Bruno advised ; and on the morrow a goodly company, as
well of young men from Florence, that happened to be in the
village, as of husbandmen, being assembled in front of the church
around the elm, Bruno and Buffalmacco came, bearing a box
containing the ginger, and the flask of wine, and ranged the folk
in a circle. Whereupon :—" Gentlemen," said Bruno, "'tis
meet I tell you the reason why you are gathered here, that if

aught unpleasant to you should befall, you may have no ground for complaint against me. Calandrino here was the night before last robbed of a fine pig, and cannot discover who has had it ; and, for that it must have been stolen by some one of us here, he would have each of you take and eat one of these pills and drink of this vernaccia. Wherefore I forthwith do you to wit, that whoso has had the pig will not be able to swallow the pill, but will find it more bitter than poison, and will spit it out ; and so, rather than he should suffer this shame in presence of so many, 'twere perhaps best that he that has had the pig should confess the fact to the priest, and I will wash my hands of the affair."

All professed themselves ready enough to eat the pills ; and so, having set them in a row with Calandrino among them, Bruno, beginning at one end, proceeded to give each a pill, and when he came to Calandrino he chose one of the pills of dog-ginger and put it in his hand. Calandrino thrust it forthwith between his teeth and began to chew it ; but no sooner was his tongue acquainted with the aloes, than, finding the bitterness intolerable, he spat it out. Now, the eyes of all the company being fixed on one another to see who should spit out his pill, Bruno, who, not having finished the distribution, feigned to be concerned with nought else, heard some one in his rear say : —" Ha ! Calandrino, what means this ? " and at once turning round, and marking that Calandrino had spit out his pill :— " Wait a while," quoth he, " perchance 'twas somewhat else that caused thee to spit : take another ; " and thereupon whipping out the other pill of dog-ginger, he set it between Calandrino's teeth, and finished the distribution. Bitter as Calandrino had found the former pill, he found this tenfold more so ; but being ashamed to spit it out, he kept it a while in his mouth and chewed it, and, as he did so, tears stood in his eyes that shewed as large as filberts, and at length, being unable to bear it any longer, he spat it out, as he had its predecessor. Which being observed by Buffalmacco and Bruno, who were then administering the wine, and by all the company, 'twas averred by common consent that Calandrino had committed the theft himself ; for which cause certain of them took him severely to task.

However, the company being dispersed, and Bruno and Buffalmacco left alone with Calandrino, Buffalmacco began on this wise :—" I never doubted but that thou hadst had it thyself, and wast minded to make us believe that it had been stolen

from thee, that we might not have of thee so much as a single
drink out of the price which thou gottest for it." Calandrino,
with the bitterness of the aloes still on his tongue, fell a-swearing
that he had not had it. Whereupon :—" Nay, but, comrade,"
quoth Buffalmacco, " upon thy honour, what did it fetch ?
Six florins ? " Whereto, Calandrino being now on the verge of
desperation, Bruno added :—" Now be reasonable, Calandrino ;
among the company that ate and drank with us there was one
that told me that thou hadst up there a girl that thou didst
keep for thy pleasure, giving her what by hook or by crook thou
couldst get together, and that he held it for certain that thou
hadst sent her this pig. And thou art grown expert in this sort
of cozenage. Thou tookest us one while adown the Mugnone
a-gathering black stones, and having thus started us on a wild-
goose chase, thou madest off ; and then wouldst fain have us
believe that thou hadst found the stone : and now, in like
manner, thou thinkest by thine oaths to persuade us that this
pig which thou hast given away or sold, has been stolen from
thee. But we know thy tricks of old ; never another couldst
thou play us ; and, to be round with thee, this spell has cost us
some trouble : wherefore we mean that thou shalt give us two
pair of capons, or we will let Monna Tessa know all." Seeing
that he was not believed, and deeming his mortification ample
without the addition of his wife's resentment, Calandrino gave
them the two pair of capons, with which, when the pig was
salted, they returned to Florence, leaving Calandrino with the
loss and the laugh against him.

NOVEL VII

*A scholar loves a widow lady, who, being enamoured of another,
    causes him to spend a winter's night awaiting her in the snow.
    He afterwards by a stratagem causes her to stand for a whole
    day in July, naked upon a tower, exposed to the flies, the gad-
    flies, and the sun.*

OVER the woes of poor Calandrino the ladies laughed not a little,
and had laughed yet more, but that it irked them that those
that had robbed him of the pig should also take from him the
capons. However, the story being ended, the queen bade
Pampinea give them hers : and thus forthwith Pampinea
began :—Dearest ladies, it happens oftentimes that the artful

scorner meets his match; wherefore 'tis only little wits that
delight to scorn. In a series of stories we have heard tell of
tricks played without aught in the way of reprisals following:
by mine I purpose in some degree to excite your compassion
for a gentlewoman of our city (albeit the retribution that came
upon her was but just) whose flout was returned in the like sort,
and to such effect that she well-nigh died thereof. The which
to hear will not be unprofitable to you, for thereby you will learn
to be more careful how you flout others, and therein you will do
very wisely.

'Tis not many years since there dwelt at Florence a lady
young and fair, and of a high spirit, as also of right gentle lineage,
and tolerably well endowed with temporal goods. Now Elena
—such was the lady's name—being left a widow, was minded
never to marry again, being enamoured of a handsome young
gallant of her own choosing, with whom she, recking nought
of any other lover, did, by the help of a maid in whom she placed
much trust, not seldom speed the time gaily and with marvellous
delight. Meanwhile it so befell that a young nobleman of our
city, Rinieri by name, who had spent much time in study at
Paris, not that he might thereafter sell his knowledge by retail,
but that he might learn the reasons and causes of things, which
accomplishment shews to most excellent advantage in a gentleman, returned to Florence, and there lived as a citizen in no
small honour with his fellows, both by reason of his rank and of
his learning. But as it is often the case that those who are
most versed in deep matters are the soonest mastered by Love,
so was it with Rinieri. For at a festal gathering, to which one
day he went, there appeared before his eyes this Elena, of whom
we spoke, clad in black, as is the wont of our Florentine widows,
and shewing to his mind so much fairer and more debonair than
any other woman that he had ever seen, that happy indeed he
deemed the man might call himself, to whom God in His goodness
should grant the right to hold her naked in his arms. So now
and again he eyed her stealthily, and knowing that boons goodly
and precious are not to be gotten without trouble, he made up
his mind to study and labour with all assiduity how best to please
her, that so he might win her love, and thereby the enjoyment
of her.

The young gentlewoman was not used to keep her eyes bent
ever towards the infernal regions; but, rating herself at no less,
if not more, than her deserts, she was dexterous to move them
to and fro and thus busily scanning her company, soon detected

the men who regarded her with pleasure. By which means
having discovered Rinieri's passion, she inly laughed, and said:
—'Twill turn out that 'twas not for nothing that I came here
to-day, for, if I mistake not, I have caught a gander by the
bill. So she gave him an occasional sidelong glance, and sought
as best she might to make him believe that she was not indifferent
to him, deeming that the more men she might captivate by
her charms, the higher those charms would be rated, and most
especially by him whom she had made lord of them and her
love. The erudite scholar bade adieu to philosophical meditation, for the lady entirely engrossed his mind; and, having discovered her house, he, thinking to please her, found divers
pretexts for frequently passing by it. Whereon the lady, her
vanity flattered for the reason aforesaid, plumed herself not a
little, and shewed herself pleased to see him. Thus encouraged,
the scholar found means to make friends with her maid, to
whom he discovered his love, praying her to do her endeavour
with her mistress, that he might have her favour. The maid
was profuse of promises, and gave her mistress his message,
which she no sooner heard, than she was convulsed with laughter,
and replied:—" He brought sense enough hither from Paris:
knowest thou where he has since been to lose it? Go to, now;
let us give him that which he seeks. Tell him, when he next
speaks to you of the matter, that I love him vastly more than
he loves me, but that I must have regard to my reputation, so
that I may be able to hold my head up among other ladies;
which, if he is really the wise man they say, will cause him to
affect me much more." Ah! poor woman! poor woman! she
little knew, my ladies, how rash it is to try conclusions with
scholars.

The maid found the scholar, and did her mistress's errand.
The scholar, overjoyed, proceeded to urge his suit with more
ardour, to indite letters, and send presents. The lady received
all that he sent her, but vouchsafed no answers save such as were
couched in general terms: and on this wise she kept him dangling
a long while. At last, having disclosed the whole affair to her
lover, who evinced some resentment and jealousy, she, to con-
vince him that his suspicions were groundless, and for that she
was much importuned by the scholar, sent word to him by her
maid, that never since he had assured her of his love, had
occasion served her to do him pleasure, but that next Christmas-
tide she hoped to be with him; wherefore, if he were minded
to await her in the courtyard of her house on the night of the

day next following the feast, she would meet him there as soon
as she could. Elated as ne'er another, the scholar hied him at
the appointed time to the lady's house, and being ushered into
a courtyard by the maid, who forthwith turned the key upon
him, addressed himself there to await the lady's coming.

Now the lady's lover, by her appointment, was with her that
evening; and when they had gaily supped, she told him
what she had in hand that night, adding:—" And so thou wilt
be able to gauge the love which I have borne and bear this
scholar, whom thou hast foolishly regarded as a rival." The
lover heard the lady's words with no small delight, and waited
in eager expectancy to see her make them good. The scholar,
hanging about there in the courtyard, began to find it somewhat
chillier than he would have liked, for it had snowed hard all
day long, so that the snow lay everywhere thick on the ground;
however, he bore it patiently, expecting to be recompensed by
and by. After a while the lady said to her lover:—" Go we
to the chamber and take a peep through a lattice at him of
whom thou art turned jealous, and mark what he does, and
how he will answer the maid, whom I have bidden go speak
with him." So the pair hied them to a lattice, wherethrough
they could see without being seen, and heard the maid call from
another lattice to the scholar, saying:—" Rinieri, my lady is
distressed as never woman was, for that one of her brothers is
come here to-night, and after talking a long while with her, must
needs sup with her, and is not yet gone, but, I think, he will
soon be off; and that is the reason why she has not been able
to come to thee, but she will come soon now. She trusts it
does not irk thee to wait so long." Whereto the scholar, supposing that 'twas true, made answer:—" Tell my lady to give
herself no anxiety on my account, until she can conveniently
come to me, but to do so as soon as she may." Whereupon the
maid withdrew from the window, and went to bed; while the
lady said to her lover:—" Now, what sayst thou? Thinkst
thou that, if I had that regard for him, which thou fearest, I
would suffer him to tarry below there to get frozen? " Which
said, the lady and her now partly reassured lover got them to
bed, where for a great while they disported them right gamesomely, laughing together and making merry over the luckless
scholar.

The scholar, meanwhile, paced up and down the courtyard to
keep himself warm, nor indeed had he where to sit, or take
shelter: in this plight he bestowed many a curse upon the lady's

brother for his long tarrying, and never a sound did he hear but he thought that 'twas the lady opening the door. But vain indeed were his hopes : the lady, having solaced herself with her lover until hard upon midnight, then said to him :—" How ratest thou our scholar, my soul ? whether is the greater his wit, or the love I bear him, thinkst thou ? Will the cold, that, of my ordaining, he now suffers, banish from thy breast the suspicion which my light words the other day implanted there ? " " Ay, indeed, heart of my body ! " replied the lover, " well wot I now that even as thou art to me, my weal, my consolation, my bliss, so am I to thee." " So : " quoth the lady, " then I must have full a thousand kisses from thee, to prove that thou sayst sooth." The lover's answer was to strain her to his heart, and give her not merely a thousand but a hundred thousand kisses. In such converse they dallied a while longer, and then : —" Get we up, now," quoth the lady, " that we may go see if 'tis quite spent, that fire, with which, as he wrote to me daily, this new lover of mine used to burn." So up they got and hied them to the lattice which they had used before, and peering out into the courtyard, saw the scholar dancing a hornpipe to the music that his own teeth made, a-chattering for extremity of cold ; nor had they ever seen it footed so nimbly and at such a pace. Whereupon :—" How sayst thou, sweet my hope ? " quoth the lady. " Know I not how to make men dance without the aid of either trumpet or cornemuse ? " " Indeed thou dost, my heart's delight," replied the lover. Quoth then the lady :— " I have a mind that we go down to the door. Thou wilt keep quiet, and I will speak to him, and we shall hear what he says, which, peradventure, we shall find no less diverting than the sight of him."

So they stole softly out of the chamber and down to the door, which leaving fast closed, the lady set her lips to a little hole that was there, and with a low voice called the scholar, who, hearing her call him, praised God, making too sure that he was to be admitted, and being come to the door, said :—" Here am I, Madam ; open for God's sake ; let me in, for I die of cold." " Oh ! ay," replied the lady, " I know thou hast a chill, and of course, there being a little snow about, 'tis mighty cold ; but well I wot the nights are colder far at Paris. I cannot let thee in as yet, because my accursed brother, that came to sup here this evening, is still with me ; but he will soon take himself off, and then I will let thee in without a moment's delay. I have but now with no small difficulty given him the slip, to come and

give thee heart that the waiting irk thee not." "Nay but,
Madam," replied the scholar, "for the love of God, I entreat
you, let me in, that I may have a roof over my head, because for
some time past there has been never so thick a fall of snow, and
'tis yet snowing ; and then I will wait as long as you please."
"Alas ! sweet my love," quoth the lady, "that I may not, for
this door makes such a din, when one opens it, that my brother
would be sure to hear, were I to let thee in ; but I will go tell
him to get him gone, and so come back and admit thee." "Go
at once, then," returned the scholar, "and prithee, see that a
good fire be kindled, that, when I get in, I may warm myself,
for I am now so chilled through and through that I have scarce
any feeling left." "That can scarce be," rejoined the lady,
"if it be true, what thou hast so protested in thy letters, that
thou art all afire for love of me : 'tis plain to me now that thou
didst but mock me. I now take my leave of thee : wait and
be of good cheer."

So the lady and her lover, who, to his immense delight, had
heard all that passed, betook them to bed ; however, little sleep
had they that night, but spent the best part of it in disporting
themselves and making merry over the unfortunate scholar,
who, his teeth now chattering to such a tune that he seemed to
have been metamorphosed into a stork, perceived that he had
been befooled, and after making divers fruitless attempts to
open the door and seeking means of egress to no better purpose,
paced to and fro like a lion, cursing the villainous weather, the
long night, his simplicity, and the perversity of the lady,
against whom (the vehemence of his wrath suddenly converting
the love he had so long borne her to bitter and remorseless
enmity) he now plotted within himself divers and grand schemes
of revenge, on which he was far more bent than ever he had been
on forgathering with her.

Slowly the night wore away, and with the first streaks of
dawn the maid, by her mistress's direction, came down, opened
the door of the courtyard, and putting on a compassionate air,
greeted Rinieri with :—" Foul fall him that came here yestereve ;
he has afflicted us with his presence all night long, and has kept
thee a-freezing out here : but harkye, take it not amiss ; that
which might not be to-night shall be another time : well wot
I that nought could have befallen that my lady could so ill
brook." For all his wrath, the scholar, witting, like the wise
man he was, that menaces serve but to put the menaced on his
guard, kept pent within his breast that which unbridled resent-

ment would have uttered, and said quietly, and without betraying the least trace of anger:—" In truth 'twas the worst night
I ever spent, but I understood quite well that the lady was in
no wise to blame, for that she herself, being moved to pity of
me, came down here to make her excuses, and to comfort me;
and, as thou sayst, what has not been to-night will be another
time: wherefore commend me to her, and so, adieu!" Then,
well-nigh paralysed for cold, he got him, as best he might, home,
where, weary and fit to die for drowsiness, he threw himself on
his bed, and fell into a deep sleep, from which he awoke to find
that he had all but lost the use of his arms and legs. He therefore sent for some physicians, and having told them what a chill
he had gotten, caused them have a care to his health. But,
though they treated him with active and most drastic remedies,
it cost them some time and no little trouble to restore to the
cramped muscles their wonted pliancy, and, indeed, but for his
youth and the milder weather that was at hand, 'twould have
gone very hard with him.

However, recover he did his health and lustihood, and nursing
his enmity, feigned to be vastly more enamoured of his widow
than ever before. And so it was that after a while Fortune
furnished him with an opportunity of satisfying his resentment,
for the gallant of whom the widow was enamoured, utterly
regardless of the love she bore him, grew enamoured of another
lady, and was minded no more to pleasure the widow in aught
either by word or by deed; wherefore she now pined in tears
and bitterness of spirit. However, her maid, who commiserated
her not a little, and knew not how to dispel the dumps that the
loss of her lover had caused her, espying the scholar pass along
the street, as he had been wont, conceived the silly idea that
the lady's lover might be induced to return to his old love by
some practice of a necromantic order, wherein she doubted not
that the scholar must be a thorough adept; which idea she
imparted to her mistress. The lady, being none too well
furnished with sense, never thinking that, if the scholar had
been an adept in necromancy, he would have made use of it in
his own behoof, gave heed to what her maid said, and forthwith
bade her learn of the scholar whether he would place his skill at
her service, and assure him that, if he so did, she, in guerdon
thereof, would do his pleasure. The maid did her mistress's
errand well and faithfully. The scholar no sooner heard the
message, than he said to himself:—Praised be Thy name, O
God, that the time is now come, when with Thy help I may be

avenged upon this wicked woman of the wrong she did me in requital of the great love I bore her. Then, turning to the maid, he said:—" Tell my lady to set her mind at ease touching this matter; for that, were her lover in India, I would forthwith bring him hither to crave her pardon of that wherein he has offended her. As to the course she should take in the matter, I tarry but her pleasure to make it known to her, when and where she may think fit: tell her so, and bid her from me to be of good cheer." The maid carried his answer to her mistress, and arranged that they should meet in the church of Santa Lucia of Prato. Thither accordingly they came, the lady and the scholar, and conversed apart, and the lady, quite oblivious of the ill-usage by which she had well-nigh done him to death, opened all her mind to him, and besought him, if he had any regard to her welfare, to aid her to the attainment of her desire. " Madam," replied the scholar, " true it is that among other lore that I acquired at Paris was this of necromancy, whereof, indeed, I know all that may be known; but, as 'tis in the last degree displeasing to God, I had sworn never to practise it either for my own or for any other's behoof. 'Tis also true that the love I bear you is such that I know not how to refuse you aught that you would have me do for you; and so, were this single essay enough to consign me to hell, I would adventure it to pleasure you. But I mind me that 'tis a matter scarce so easy of performance as, perchance, you suppose, most especially when a woman would fain recover the love of a man, or a man that of a woman, for then it must be done by the postulant in proper person, and at night, and in lonely places, and un-attended, so that it needs a stout heart; nor know I whether you are disposed to comply with these conditions." The lady, too enamoured to be discreet, made answer:—" So shrewdly does Love goad me, that there is nought I would not do to bring him back to me who wrongfully has deserted me; but tell me, prithee, wherein it is that I have need of this stout heart." " Madam," returned the despiteful scholar, " 'twill be my part to fashion in tin an image of him you would fain lure back to you: and when I have sent you the image, 'twill be for you, when the moon is well on the wane, to dip yourself, being stark naked, and the image, seven times in a flowing stream, and this you must do quite alone about the hour of first sleep, and afterwards, still naked, you must get you upon some tree or some deserted house, and facing the North, with the image in your hand, say certain words that I shall give you in writing seven times; which, when you have done, there will come to you two damsels, the fairest you ever saw, who will greet you graciously, and ask of you what you would fain have; to whom you will disclose frankly and fully all that you crave; and see to it that you make no mistake in the name; and when you have said all, they will depart, and you may then descend and return to the spot where you left your clothes, and resume them, and go home. And rest assured, that before the ensuing midnight your lover will come to you in tears, and crave your pardon and mercy, and that thenceforth he will never again desert you for any other woman."

The lady gave entire credence to the scholar's words, and deeming her lover as good as in her arms again, recovered half her wonted spirits: wherefore :—" Make no doubt," quoth she, " that I shall do as thou biddest; and indeed I am most favoured by circumstance; for in upper Val d'Arno I have an estate adjoining the river, and 'tis now July, so that to bathe will be delightful. Ay, and now I mind me that at no great distance from the river there is a little tower, which is deserted, save that now and again the shepherds will get them up by the chestnut-wood ladder to the roof, thence to look out for their strayed sheep; 'tis a place lonely indeed, and quite out of ken; and when I have clomb it, as climb it I will, I doubt not 'twill be the best place in all the world to give effect to your instructions."

Well pleased to be certified of the lady's intention, the scholar, to whom her estate and the tower were very well known, made answer :—" I was never in those parts, Madam, and therefore know neither your estate nor the tower, but, if 'tis as you say, 'twill certainly be the best place in the world for your purpose. So, when time shall serve, I will send you the image and the orison. But I pray you, when you shall have your heart's desire, and know that I have done you good service, do not forget me, but keep your promise to me." " That will I without fail," quoth the lady; and so she bade him farewell, and went home. The scholar, gleefully anticipating the success of his enterprise, fashioned an image, and inscribed it with certain magical signs, and wrote some gibberish by way of orison, which in due time he sent to the lady, bidding her the very next night do as he had prescribed: and thereupon he hied him privily with one of his servants to the house of a friend hard by the tower, there to carry his purpose into effect. The lady, on her part, set out with her maid, and betook her to her estate, and,

night being come, sent the maid to bed, as if she were minded to
go to rest herself; and about the hour of first sleep stole out
of the house and down to the tower, beside the Arno; and
when, having carefully looked about her, she was satisfied that
never a soul was to be seen or heard, she took off her clothes and
hid them under a bush; then, with the image in her hand, she
dipped herself seven times in the river; which done, she hied
her with the image to the tower. The scholar, having at nightfall couched himself with his servant among the willows and
other trees that fringed the bank, marked all that she did, and
how, as she passed by him, the whiteness of her flesh dispelled
the shades of night, and scanning attentively her bosom and
every other part of her body, and finding them very fair, felt,
as he bethought him what would shortly befall them, some pity
of her; while, on the other hand, he was suddenly assailed by
the solicitations of the flesh which caused that to stand which
had been inert, and prompted him to sally forth of his ambush
and take her by force, and have his pleasure of her. And, what
with his compassion and passion, he was like to be worsted;
but then, as he bethought him who he was, and what a grievous
wrong had been done him, and for what cause, and by whom,
his wrath, thus rekindled, got the better of the other affections,
so that he swerved not from his resolve, but suffered her to go
her way.

The lady ascended the tower, and standing with her face to
the North, began to recite the scholar's orison, while he, having
stolen into the tower but a little behind her, cautiously shifted
the ladder that led up to the roof on which the lady stood, and
waited to observe what she would say and do. Seven times the
lady said the orison, and then awaited the appearance of the
two damsels; and so long had she to wait—not to mention that
the night was a good deal cooler than she would have liked—
that she saw day break; whereupon, disconcerted that it had
not fallen out as the scholar had promised, she said to herself :—
I misdoubt me he was minded to give me such a night as I gave
him; but if such was his intent, he is but maladroit in his
revenge, for this night is not as long by a third as his was,
besides which, the cold is of another quality. And that day
might not overtake her there, she began to think of descending,
but, finding that the ladder was removed, she felt as if the
world had come to nought beneath her feet, her senses reeled,
and she fell in a swoon upon the floor of the roof. When she
came to herself, she burst into tears and piteous lamentations,

and witting now very well that 'twas the doing of the scholar, she began to repent her that she had first offended him, and then trusted him unduly, having such good cause to reckon upon his enmity ; in which frame she abode long time. Then, searching if haply she might find some means of descent, and finding none, she fell a-weeping again, and bitterly to herself she said :—Alas for thee, wretched woman ! what will thy brothers, thy kinsmen, thy neighbours, nay, what will all Florence say of thee, when 'tis known that thou hast been found here naked ? Thy honour, hitherto unsuspect, will be known to have been but a shew, and shouldst thou seek thy defence in lying excuses, if any such may be fashioned, the accursed scholar, who knows all thy doings, will not suffer it. Ah ! poor wretch ! that at one and the same time hast lost thy too dearly cherished gallant and thine own honour ! And therewith she was taken with such a transport of grief, that she was like to cast herself from the tower to the ground. Then, bethinking her that if she might espy some lad making towards the tower with his sheep, she might send him for her maid, for the sun was now risen, she approached one of the parapets of the tower, and looked out, and so it befell that the scholar, awakening from a slumber, in which he had lain a while at the foot of a bush, espied her, and she him. Whereupon :—" Good-day, Madam," quoth he : " are the damsels yet come ? " The lady saw and heard him not without bursting afresh into a flood of tears, and besought him to come into the tower, that she might speak with him : a request which the scholar very courteously granted. The lady then threw herself prone on the floor of the roof ; and, only her head being visible through the aperture, thus through her sobs she spoke :—" Verily, Rinieri, if I gave thee a bad night, thou art well avenged on me, for, though it be July, meseemed I was sore a-cold last night, standing here with never a thread upon me, and, besides, I have so bitterly bewept both the trick I played thee and my own folly in trusting thee, that I marvel that I have still eyes in my head. Wherefore I implore thee, not for love of me, whom thou hast no cause to love, but for the respect thou hast for thyself as a gentleman, that thou let that which thou hast already done suffice thee to avenge the wrong I did thee, and bring me my clothes, that I may be able to get me down from here, and spare to take from me that which, however thou mightst here-after wish, thou couldst not restore to me, to wit, my honour ; whereas, if I deprived thee of that one night with me, 'tis in my power to give thee many another night in recompense thereof, and thou hast but to choose thine own times. Let this, then, suffice, and like a worthy gentleman be satisfied to have taken thy revenge, and to have let me know it : put not forth thy might against a woman : 'tis no glory to the eagle to have vanquished a dove ; wherefore for God's and thine own honour's sake have mercy on me."

The scholar, albeit his haughty spirit still brooded on her evil entreatment of him, yet saw her not weep and supplicate without a certain compunction mingling with his exultation ; but vengeance he had desired above all things, to have wreaked it was indeed sweet, and albeit his humanity prompted him to have compassion on the hapless woman, yet it availed not to subdue the fierceness of his resentment ; wherefore thus he made answer :—" Madam Elena, had my prayers (albeit art I had none to mingle with them tears and honeyed words as thou dost with thine) inclined thee that night, when I stood perishing with cold amid the snow that filled thy courtyard, to accord me the very least shelter, 'twere but a light matter for me to hearken now to thine ; but, if thou art now so much more careful of thy honour than thou wast wont to be, and it irks thee to tarry there naked, address thy prayers to him in whose arms it irked thee not naked to pass that night thou mindest thee of, albeit thou wist that I with hasty foot was beating time upon the snow in thy courtyard to the accompaniment of chattering teeth : 'tis he that thou shouldst call to succour thee, to fetch thy clothes, to adjust the ladder for thy descent ; 'tis he in whom thou shouldst labour to inspire this tenderness thou now shewest for thy honour, that honour which for his sake thou hast not scrupled to jeopardize both now and on a thousand other occasions. Why, then, call'st thou not him to come to thy succour ? To whom pertains it rather than to him ? Thou art his. And of whom will he have a care, whom will he succour, if not thee ? Thou askedst him that night, when thou wast wantoning with him, whether seemed to him the greater, my folly or the love thou didst bear him : call him now, foolish woman, and see if the love thou bearest him, and thy wit and his, may avail to deliver thee from my folly. 'Tis now no longer in thy power to shew me courtesy of that which I no more desire, nor yet to refuse it, did I desire it. Reserve thy nights for thy lover, if so be thou go hence alive. Be they all thine and his. One of them was more than I cared for ; 'tis enough for me to have been flouted once. Ay, and by thy cunning of speech thou strivest might and main to conciliate my good-will, calling me worthy gentleman, by which insinuation thou wouldst fain induce me magnanimously to desist from further chastisement of thy baseness. But thy cajoleries shall not now cloud the eyes of my mind, as did once thy false promises. I know myself, and better now for thy one night's instruction than for all the time I spent at Paris. But, granted that I were disposed to be magnanimous, thou art not of those to whom 'tis meet to shew magnanimity. A wild beast such as thou, having merited vengeance, can claim no relief from suffering save death, though in the case of a human being 'twould suffice to temper vengeance with mercy, as thou saidst. Wherefore I, albeit no eagle, witting thee to be no dove, but a venomous serpent, mankind's most ancient enemy, am minded, bating no jot of malice or of might, to harry thee to the bitter end : natheless this which I do is not properly to be called vengeance but rather just retribution ; seeing that vengeance should be in excess of the offence, and this my chastisement of thee will fall short of it ; for, were I minded to be avenged on thee, considering what account thou madest of my heart and soul, 'twould not suffice me to take thy life, no, nor the lives of a hundred others such as thee ; for I should but slay a vile and base and wicked woman. And what the Devil art thou more than any other pitiful baggage, that I should spare thy little store of beauty, which a few years will ruin, covering thy face with wrinkles ? And yet 'twas not for want of will that thou didst fail to do to death a worthy gentleman, as thou but now didst call me, of whom in a single day of his life the world may well have more profit than of a hundred thousand like thee while the world shall last. Wherefore by this rude discipline I will teach thee what it is to flout men of spirit, and more especially what it is to flout scholars, that if thou escape with thy life thou mayst have good cause ever hereafter to shun such folly. But if thou art so fain to make the descent, why cast not thyself down, whereby, God helping, thou wouldst at once break thy neck, be quit of the torment thou endurest, and make me the happiest man alive ? I have no more to say to thee. 'Twas my art and craft thus caused thee climb ; be it thine to find the way down : thou hadst cunning enough, when thou wast minded to flout me."

While the scholar thus spoke, the hapless lady wept incessantly, and before he had done, to aggravate her misery, the sun was high in the heaven. However, when he was silent, thus she made answer :—" Ah ! ruthless man, if that accursed night has so rankled with thee, and thou deemest my fault so grave that neither my youth and beauty, nor my bitter tears, nor yet my humble supplications may move thee to pity, let this at least move thee, and abate somewhat of thy remorseless severity, that 'twas my act alone, in that of late I trusted thee, and discovered to thee all my secret, that did open the way to compass thy end, and make me cognizant of my guilt, seeing that, had I not confided in thee, on no wise mightst thou have been avenged on me ; which thou wouldst seem so ardently to have desired. Turn thee, then, turn thee, I pray thee, from thy wrath, and pardon me. So thou wilt pardon me, and get me down hence, right gladly will I give up for ever my faithless gallant, and thou shalt be my sole lover and lord, albeit thou sayst hard things of my beauty, slight and shortlived as thou wouldst have it to be, which, however it may compare with others, is, I wot, to be prized, if for no other reason, yet for this, that 'tis the admiration and solace and delight of young men, and thou art not yet old. And albeit I have been harshly treated by thee, yet believe I cannot that thou wouldst have me do myself so shamefully to death as to cast me down, like some abandoned wretch, before thine eyes, in which, unless thou wast then, as thou hast since shewn thyself, a liar, I found such favour. Ah ! have pity on me for God's and mercy's sake ! The sun waxes exceeding hot, and having suffered not a little by the cold of last night, I now begin to be sorely afflicted by the heat."

" Madam," rejoined the scholar, who held her in parley with no small delight, " 'twas not for any love that thou didst bear me that thou trustedst me, but that thou mightst recover that which thou hadst lost, for which cause thou meritest but the greater punishment ; and foolish indeed art thou if thou supposest that such was the sole means available for my revenge. I had a thousand others, and, while I feigned to love thee, I had laid a thousand gins for thy feet, into one or other of which in no long time, though this had not occurred, thou must needs have fallen, and that too to thy more grievous suffering and shame ; nor was it to spare thee, but that I might be the sooner rejoiced by thy discomfiture that I took my present course. And though all other means had failed me, I had still the pen, with which I would have written of thee such matters and in such a sort, that when thou wist them, as thou shouldst have done, thou wouldst have regretted a thousand times that thou hadst ever been born. The might of the pen is greater far than they suppose, who have not proved it by experience. By God I swear, so may He, who has prospered me thus far in this my revenge, prosper me to the end! that I would have written of thee things that would have so shamed thee in thine own—not to speak of others'—sight that thou hadst put out thine eyes that thou mightst no more see thyself; wherefore chide not the sea, for that it has sent forth a tiny rivulet. For thy love, or whether thou be mine or no, nought care I. Be thou still his, whose thou hast been, if thou canst. Hate him as I once did, I now love him, by reason of his present entreatment of thee. Ye go getting you enamoured, ye women, and nought will satisfy you but young gallants, because ye mark that their flesh is ruddier, and their beards are blacker, than other folk's, and that they carry themselves well, and foot it featly in the dance, and joust; but those that are now more mature were even as they, and possess a knowledge which they have yet to acquire. And therewithal ye deem that they ride better, and cover more miles in a day, than men of riper age. Now that they dust the pelisse with more vigour I certainly allow, but their seniors, being more experienced, know better the places where the fleas lurk; and spare and dainty diet is preferable to abundance without savour: moreover hard trotting will gall and jade even the youngest, whereas an easy pace, though it bring one somewhat later to the inn, at any rate brings one thither fresh. Ye discern not, witless creatures that ye are, how much of evil this little shew of bravery serves to hide. Your young gallant is never content with one woman, but lusts after as many as he sets eyes on; nor is there any but he deems himself worthy of her: wherefore 'tis not possible that their love should be lasting, as thou hast but now proved and mayst only too truly witness. Moreover to be worshipped, to be caressed by their ladies they deem but their due; nor is there aught whereon they plume and boast them so proudly as their conquests: which impertinence has caused not a few women to surrender to the friars, who keep their own counsel. Peradventure thou wilt say that never a soul save thy maid and I wist aught of thy loves; but, if so, thou hast been misinformed, and if thou so believest, thou dost misbelieve. Scarce aught else is talked of either in his quarter or in thine; but most often 'tis those most concerned whose ears such matters reach last. Moreover, they rob you, these young gallants, whereas the others make you presents. So, then, having made a bad choice, be thou still his to whom thou hast given thyself, and leave me, whom thou didst flout, to another, for I have found a lady of much greater charms than thine, and that has understood me better than thou didst. And that thou mayst get thee to the other world better certified of the desire of my eyes than thou wouldst seem to be here by my words, delay no more, but cast thyself down, whereby thy soul, taken forthwith, as I doubt not she will be, into the embrace of the Devil, may see whether thy headlong fall afflicts mine eyes, or no. But, for that I doubt thou meanest not thus to gladden me, I bid thee, if thou findest the sun begin to scorch thee, remember the cold thou didst cause me to endure, wherewith, by admixture, thou mayst readily temper the sun's heat."

The hapless lady, seeing that the scholar's words were ever to the same ruthless effect, burst afresh into tears, and said:—" Lo, now, since nought that pertains to me may move thee, be thou at least moved by the love thou bearest this lady of whom thou speakest, who, thou sayst, is wiser than I, and loves thee, and for love of her pardon me, and fetch me my clothes, that I may resume them, and get me down hence." Whereat the scholar fell a-laughing, and seeing that 'twas not a little past tierce, made answer:—" Lo, now, I know not how to deny thee, adjuring me as thou dost by such a lady: tell me, then, where thy clothes are, and I will go fetch them, and bring thee down." The lady, believing him, was somewhat comforted, and told him where she had laid her clothes. The scholar then quitted the tower, bidding his servant on no account to stir from his post, but to keep close by, and, as best he might, bar the tower against all comers until his return: which said, he betook him to the house of his friend, where he breakfasted much at his ease, and thereafter went to sleep. Left alone upon the tower, the lady, somewhat cheered by her fond hope, but still exceeding sorrowful, drew nigh to a part of the wall where there was a little shade, and there sate down to wait. And now lost in most melancholy brooding, now dissolved in tears, now plunged in despair of ever seeing the scholar return with her clothes, but never more than a brief while in any one mood, spent with grief and the night's vigil, she by and by fell asleep. The sun was now in the zenith, and smote with extreme fervour full and unmitigated upon her tender and delicate frame, and upon her bare head, insomuch that his rays did not only scorch but bit by bit excoriate every part of her flesh that was exposed to them, and so shrewdly burn her that, albeit she was in a deep sleep, the pain awoke her. And as by reason thereof she writhed a little, she felt the scorched skin part in sunder and shed itself, as will happen when one tugs at a parchment that has been singed by the fire, while her head ached so sore that it seemed like to split, and no wonder. Nor might she find place either to lie or to stand on the floor of the roof, but ever went to and fro, weeping. Besides which there stirred not the least breath of wind, and flies and gadflies did swarm in prodigious quantity, which, settling upon her excoriate flesh, stung her so shrewdly that 'twas as if she received so many stabs with a javelin, and she was ever restlessly feeling her sores with her hands, and cursing herself, her life, her lover, and the scholar.

Thus by the exorbitant heat of the sun, by the flies and gad-flies, harassed, goaded, and lacerated, tormented also by hunger, and yet more by thirst, and thereto by a thousand distressful thoughts, she planted herself erect on her feet, and looked about her, if haply she might see or hear any one, with intent, come what might, to call to him and crave his succour. But even this hostile Fortune had disallowed her. The husbandmen were all gone from the fields by reason of the heat, and indeed there had come none to work that day in the neighbourhood of the tower, for that all were employed in threshing their corn beside their cottages : wherefore she heard but the cicalas, while Arno, tantalizing her with the sight of his waters, increased rather than diminished her thirst. Ay, and in like manner, wherever she espied a copse, or a patch of shade, or a house, 'twas a torment to her, for the longing she had for it. What more is to be said of this hapless woman ? Only this : that what with the heat of the sun above and the floor beneath her, and the scarification of her flesh in every part by the flies and gadflies, that flesh, which in the night had dispelled the gloom by its whiteness, was now become red as madder, and so besprent with clots of blood, that whoso had seen her would have deemed her the most hideous object in the world.

Thus resourceless and hopeless, she passed the long hours, expecting death rather than aught else, until half none was come and gone ; when, his siesta ended, the scholar bethought him of his lady, and being minded to see how she fared, hied him back to the tower, and sent his servant away to break his fast. As soon as the lady espied him, she came, spent and crushed by her sore affliction, to the aperture, and thus ad-dressed him :—" Rinieri, the cup of thy vengeance is full to overflowing : for if I gave thee a night of freezing in my courtyard, thou hast given me upon this tower a day of scorching, nay, of burning, and therewithal of perishing of hunger and thirst : wherefore, by God I entreat thee to come up hither, and as my heart fails me to take my life, take it thou, for 'tis death I desire of all things, such and so grievous is my suffering. But if this grace thou wilt not grant, at least bring me a cup of water wherewith to lave my mouth, for which my tears do not suffice, so parched and torrid is it within." Well wist the scholar by her voice how spent she was ; he also saw a part of her body burned through and through by the sun ; whereby, and by reason of the lowliness of her entreaties, he felt some little pity for her ; but all the same he made answer :—" Nay, wicked woman, 'tis not by my hands thou shalt die ; thou canst die by thine own whenever thou art so minded ; and to temper thy heat thou shalt have just as much water from me as I had fire from thee to mitigate my cold. I only regret that for the cure of my chill the physicians were fain to use foul-smelling muck, whereas thy burns can be treated with fragrant rose-water ; and that, whereas I was like to lose my muscles and the use of my limbs, thou, for all thy excoriation by the heat, wilt yet be fair again, like a snake that has sloughed off the old skin." " Alas ! woe's me ! " replied the lady, " for charms acquired at such a cost, God grant them to those that hate me. But thou, most fell of all wild beasts, how hast thou borne thus to torture me ? What more had I to expect of thee or any other, had I done all thy kith and kin to death with direst torments ? Verily, I know not what more cruel suffering thou couldst have inflicted on a traitor that had put a whole city to the slaughter than this which thou hast allotted to me, to be thus roasted, and devoured of the flies, and therewithal to refuse me even a cup of water, though the very murderers condemned to death by the law, as they go to execution, not seldom are allowed wine to drink, so they but ask it. Lo now, I see that thou art inexorable in thy ruthlessness, and on no wise to be moved by my suffering : wherefore with resignation I will compose me to await death, that God may have mercy on my soul. And may this that thou doest escape not the searching glance of His just eyes." Which said, she dragged herself, sore suffering, toward the middle of the floor, despairing of ever escaping from her fiery torment, besides which, not once only, but a thousand times she thought to choke for thirst, and ever she wept bitterly and bewailed her evil fate. But at length the day wore to vespers, and the scholar, being sated with his re-

venge, caused his servant to take her clothes and wrap them in
his cloak, and hied him with the servant to the hapless lady's
house, where, finding her maid sitting disconsolate and woebegone and resourceless at the door:—" Good woman," quoth
he, " what has befallen thy mistress? " Whereto:—" Sir,
I know not," replied the maid. " I looked to find her this
morning abed, for methought she went to bed last night, but
neither there nor anywhere else could I find her, nor know I
what is become of her; wherefore exceeding great is my distress; but have you, Sir, nought to say of the matter? "
" Only this," returned the scholar, " that I would I had had
thee with her there where I have had her, that I might have
requited thee of thy offence, even as I had requited her of hers.
But be assured that thou shalt not escape my hands, until thou
hast from me such wage of thy labour that thou shalt never
flout man more, but thou shalt mind thee of me." Then, turning to his servant, he said:—" Give her these clothes, and tell
her that she may go bring her mistress away, if she will." The
servant did his bidding; and the maid, what with the message
and her recognition of the clothes, was mightily afraid, lest they
had slain the lady, and scarce suppressing a shriek, took the
clothes, and, bursting into tears, set off, as soon as the scholar
was gone, at a run for the tower.

Now one of the lady's husbandmen had had the misfortune to
lose two of his hogs that day, and, seeking them, came to the
tower not long after the scholar had gone thence, and peering
about in all quarters, if haply he might have sight of his hogs,
heard the woeful lamentation that the hapless lady made, and
got him up into the tower, and called out as loud as he might:—

" Who wails up there? " The lady recognized her husbandman's voice, and called him by name, saying:—" Prithee, go
fetch my maid, and cause her come up hither to me." The
husbandman, knowing her by her voice, replied:—" Alas!
Madam, who set you there? Your maid has been seeking you
all day long: but who would ever have supposed that you were
there? " Whereupon he took the props of the ladder, and set
them in position, and proceeded to secure the rounds to them
with withies. Thus engaged he was found by the maid, who,
as she entered the tower, beat her face and breast, and unable
longer to keep silence, cried out:—" Alas, sweet my lady,
where are you? " Whereto the lady made answer as loud as
she might:—" O my sister, here above am I, weep not, but
fetch me my clothes forthwith." Wellnigh restored to heart, to

hear her mistress's voice, the maid, assisted by the husbandman, ascended the ladder, which he had now all but set in order, and gaining the roof, and seeing her lady lie there naked, spent and fordone, and liker to a half-burned stump than to a human being, she planted her nails in her face and fell a-weeping over her, as if she were a corpse. However, the lady bade her for God's sake be silent, and help her to dress, and having learned from her that none knew where she had been, save those that had brought her her clothes and the husbandman that was there present, was somewhat consoled, and besought her for God's sake to say nought of the matter to any. Thus long time they conversed, and then the husbandman took the lady on his shoulders, for walk she could not, and bore her safely out of the tower. The unfortunate maid, following after with somewhat less caution, slipped, and falling from the ladder to the ground, broke her thigh, and roared for pain like any lion. So the husbandman set the lady down upon a grassy mead, while he went to see what had befallen the maid, whom, finding her thigh broken, he brought, and laid beside the lady : who, seeing her woes completed by this last misfortune, and that she of whom, most of all, she had expected succour, was lamed of a thigh, was distressed beyond measure, and wept again so piteously that not only was the husbandman powerless to comfort her, but was himself fain to weep. However, as the sun was now low, that they might not be there surprised by night, he, with the disconsolate lady's approval, hied him home, and called to his aid two of his brothers and his wife, who returned with him, bearing a plank, whereon they laid the maid, and so they carried her to the lady's house. There, by dint of cold water and words of cheer, they restored some heart to the lady, whom the husbandman then took upon his shoulders, and bore to her chamber. The husbandman's wife fed her with sops of bread, and then undressed her, and put her to bed. They also provided the means to carry her and the maid to Florence ; and so 'twas done. There the lady, who was very fertile in artifices, invented an entirely fictitious story of what had happened as well in regard of her maid as of herself, whereby she persuaded both her brothers and her sisters and every one else, that 'twas all due to the enchantments of evil spirits. The physicians lost no time, and, albeit the lady's suffering and mortification were extreme, for she left more than one skin sticking to the sheets, they cured her of a high fever, and certain attendant maladies ; as also the maid of her fractured thigh.

The end of all which was that the lady forgot her lover, and
having learned discretion, was thenceforth careful neither to
love nor to flout ; and the scholar, learning that the maid had
broken her thigh, deemed his vengeance complete, and was
satisfied to say never a word more of the affair. Such then
were the consequences of her flouts to this foolish young woman,
who deemed that she might trifle with a scholar with the like
impunity as with others, not duly understanding that they—
I say not all, but the more part—know where the Devil keeps
his tail.[1] Wherefore, my ladies, have a care how you flout
men, and more especially scholars.

NOVEL VIII

*Two men keep with one another : the one lies with the other's wife :
the other, being ware thereof, manages with the aid of his wife
to have the one locked in a chest, upon which he then lies with
the wife of him that is locked therein.*

GRIEVOUS and distressful was it to the ladies to hear how it
fared with Elena ; but as they accounted the retribution in a
measure righteous, they were satisfied to expend upon her but
a moderate degree of compassion, albeit they censured the
scholar as severe, intemperately relentless, and indeed ruthless,
in his vengeance. However, Pampinea having brought the
story to a close, the queen bade Fiammetta follow suit ; and
prompt to obey, Fiammetta thus spoke :—Debonair my ladies,
as, methinks, your feelings must have been somewhat harrowed
by the severity of the resentful scholar, I deem it meet to soothe
your vexed spirits with something of a more cheerful order.
Wherefore I am minded to tell you a little story of a young
man who bore an affront in a milder temper, and avenged
himself with more moderation. Whereby you may understand
that one should be satisfied if the ass and the wall are quits,
nor by indulging a vindictive spirit to excess turn the requital
of a wrong into an occasion of wrong-doing. You are to know,
then, that at Siena, as I have heard tell, there dwelt two young
men of good substance, and, for plebeians, of good family, the
one Spinelloccio Tanena, the other Zeppa di Mino, by name ;
who, their houses being contiguous in the Camollia,[2] kept ever

---

[1] *I.e.* are a match for the Devil himself in cunning.
[2] A suburb of Siena.

together, and, by what appeared, loved each other as brothers,
or even more so, and had each a very fine woman to wife. Now
it so befell that Spinelloccio, being much in Zeppa's house, as
well when Zeppa was not, as when he was there, grew so familiar
with Zeppa's wife that he sometimes lay with her ; and on this
wise they continued to forgather a great while before any one
was ware of it. However, one of these days Zeppa being at
home, though the lady wist it not, Spinelloccio came in quest
of him ; and, the lady sending word that he was not at home,
he forthwith went upstairs and found the lady in the saloon,
and seeing none else there, kissed her, as did she him.

Zeppa saw all that passed, but said nothing and kept close,
being minded to see how the game would end, and soon saw his
wife and Spinelloccio, still in one another's arms, hie them to her
chamber and lock themselves in : whereat he was mightily
incensed. But, witting that to make a noise, or do aught else
overt, would not lessen but rather increase his dishonour, he
cast about how he might be avenged on such wise that, without
the affair getting wind, he might content his soul ; and, having
after long pondering, hit, as he thought, upon the expedient,
he budged not from his retreat, until Spinelloccio had parted
from the lady. Whereupon he hied him into the chamber, and
there finding the lady with her head-gear, which Spinelloccio in
toying with her had disarranged, scarce yet readjusted :—
" Madam, what dost thou ? " quoth he. Whereto :—" Why,
dost not see ? " returned the lady. " Troth do I," rejoined he,
" and somewhat else have I seen that I would I had not."
And so he questioned her of what had passed, and she, being
mightily afraid, did after long parley confess that which she
might not plausibly deny, to wit, her intimacy with Spinelloccio,
and fell a-beseeching him with tears to pardon her. " Lo, now,
wife," quoth Zeppa, " thou hast done wrong, and, so thou
wouldst have me pardon thee, have a care to do exactly as I
shall bid thee ; to wit, on this wise : thou must tell Spinelloccio
to find some occasion to part from me to-morrow morning about
tierce, and come hither to thee ; and while he is here I will come
back, and when thou hearest me coming, thou wilt get him into
this chest, and lock him in there ; which when thou hast done,
I will tell thee what else thou hast to do, which thou mayst do
without the least misgiving, for I promise thee I will do him
no harm." The lady, to content him, promised to do as he bade,
and she kept her word.

The morrow came, and Zeppa and Spinelloccio being together

about tierce, Spinelloccio, having promised the lady to come to see her at that hour, said to Zeppa :—" I must go breakfast with a friend, whom I had lief not keep in waiting; therefore, adieu !" "Nay, but," quoth Zeppa, "'tis not yet breakfast-time." "No matter," returned Spinelloccio, "I have business on which I must speak with him; so I must be in good time." Whereupon Spinelloccio took his leave of Zeppa, and having reached Zeppa's house by a slightly circuitous route, and finding his wife there was taken by her into the chamber, where they had not been long together when Zeppa returned. Hearing him come, the lady, feigning no small alarm, bundled Spinelloccio into the chest, as her husband had bidden her, and having locked him in, left him there. As Zeppa came upstairs :— "Wife," quoth he, "is it breakfast time ?" "Ay, husband, 'tis so," replied the lady. Whereupon :—" Spinelloccio is gone to breakfast with a friend to-day," quoth Zeppa, "leaving his wife at home : get thee to the window, and call her, and bid her come and breakfast with us." The lady, whose fear for herself made her mighty obedient, did as her husband bade her ; and after much pressing Spinelloccio's wife came to breakfast with them, though she was given to understand that her husband would not be of the company. So, she being come, Zeppa received her most affectionately, and taking her familiarly by the hand, bade his wife, in an undertone, get her to the kitchen ; he then led Spinelloccio's wife into the chamber, and locked the door. Hearing the key turn in the lock :—" Alas !" quoth the lady, "what means this, Zeppa ? Is't for this you have brought me here ? Is this the love you bear Spinelloccio ? Is this your loyalty to him as your friend and comrade ?" By the time she had done speaking, Zeppa, still keeping fast hold of her, was beside the chest, in which her husband was locked. Wherefore :—" Madam," quoth he, "spare me thy reproaches, until thou hast heard what I have to say to thee. I have loved, I yet love, Spinelloccio as a brother ; and yesterday, though he knew it not, I discovered that the trust I reposed in him has for its guerdon that he lies with my wife, as with thee. Now, for that I love him, I purpose not to be avenged upon him save in the sort in which he offended. He has had my wife, and I intend to have thee. So thou wilt not grant me what I crave of thee, be sure I shall not fail to take it ; and having no mind to let this affront pass unavenged, will make such play with him that neither thou nor he shall ever be happy again." The lady hearkening, and by dint of his repeated asseverations com-

ing at length to believe him :—" Zeppa mine," quoth she, " as
this thy vengeance is to light upon me, well content am I ; so
only thou let not this which we are to do embroil me with thy
wife, with whom, notwithstanding the evil turn she has done
me, I am minded to remain at peace." " Have no fear on
that score," replied Zeppa ; " nay, I will give thee into the
bargain a jewel so rare and fair that thou hast not the like."
Which said, he took her in his arms and fell a-kissing her, and
having laid her on the chest, in which her husband was safe
under lock and key, did there disport himself with her to his
heart's content, as she with him.

Spinelloccio in the chest heard all that Zeppa had said, and
how he was answered by the lady, and the Trevisan dance that
afterwards went on over his head ; whereat his mortification
was such that for a great while he scarce hoped to live through
it ; and, but for the fear he had of Zeppa, he would have given
his wife a sound rating, close prisoner though he was. But, as
he bethought him that 'twas he that had given the first affront,
and that Zeppa had good cause for acting as he did, and that
he had dealt with him considerately and as a good fellow should,
he resolved that if it were agreeable to Zeppa, they should be
faster friends than ever before. However, Zeppa, having had
his pleasure with the lady, got down from the chest, and being
reminded by the lady of his promise of the jewel, opened the
door of the chamber and brought his wife in. Quoth she with
a laugh :—" Madam, you have given me tit for tat," and never
a word more. Whereupon :—" Open the chest," quoth Zeppa ;
and she obeying, he shewed the lady her Spinelloccio lying
therein. 'Twould be hard to say whether of the twain was the
more shame-stricken, Spinelloccio to be confronted with Zeppa,
knowing that Zeppa wist what he had done, or the lady to meet
her husband's eyes, knowing that he had heard what went on
above his head. " Lo, here is the jewel I give thee," quoth
Zeppa to her, pointing to Spinelloccio, who, as he came forth
of the chest, blurted out :—" Zeppa, we are quits, and so
'twere best, as thou saidst a while ago to my wife, that we still
be friends as we were wont, and as we had nought separate,
save our wives, that henceforth we have them also in common."
" Content," quoth Zeppa ; and so in perfect peace and accord
they all four breakfasted together. And thenceforth each of
the ladies had two husbands, and each of the husbands two
wives ; nor was there ever the least dispute or contention
between them on that score.

NOVEL IX

*Bruno and Buffalmacco prevail upon Master Simone, a physician,
to betake him by night to a certain place, there to be enrolled in
a company that go the course. Buffalmacco throws him into
a foul ditch, and there they leave him.*

WHEN the ladies had made merry a while over the partnership
in wives established by the two Sienese, the queen, who now,
unless she were minded to infringe Dioneo's privilege, alone
remained to tell, began on this wise :—Fairly earned indeed,
loving ladies, was the flout that Spinelloccio got from Zeppa.
Wherefore my judgment jumps with that which Pampinea
expressed a while ago, to wit, that he is not severely to be censured who bestows a flout on one that provokes it or deserves
it ; and as Spinelloccio deserved it, so 'tis my purpose to tell
you of one that provoked it, for I deem that those from whom
he received it, were rather to be commended than condemned.
The man that got it was a physician, who, albeit he was but a
blockhead, returned from Bologna to Florence in mantle and
hood of vair.

'Tis matter of daily experience that our citizens come back
to us from Bologna, this man a judge, that a physician, and the
other a notary, flaunting it in ample flowing robes, and adorned
with the scarlet and the vair and other array most goodly to
see ; and how far their doings correspond with this fair seeming,
is also matter of daily experience. Among whom 'tis not long
since Master Simone da Villa, one whose patrimony was more
ample than his knowledge, came back wearing the scarlet and a
broad stripe [1] on the shoulder, and a doctor, as he called himself,
and took a house in the street that we now call Via del Cocomero.
Now this Master Simone, being thus, as we said, come back,
had this among other singular habits, that he could never see a
soul pass along the street, but he must needs ask any that was
by, who that man was ; and he was as observant of all the
doings of men, and as sedulous to store his memory with such
matters, as if they were to serve him to compound the drugs
that he was to give his patients. Now, of all that he saw, those

---

[1] The distinguishing mark of a doctor in those days. Fanfani, *Vocab.
della Lingua Italiana*, 1891, " Batolo."

that he eyed most observantly were two painters, of whom here to-day mention has twice been made, Bruno, to wit, and Buffalmacco, who were ever together, and were his neighbours.   And as it struck him that they daffed the world aside and lived more lightheartedly than any others that he knew, as indeed they did, he enquired of not a few folk as to their rank.   And learning on all hands that they were poor men and painters, he could not conceive it possible that they should live thus contentedly in poverty, but made his mind up that, being, as he was informed, clever fellows, they must have some secret source from which they drew immense gains ; for which reason he grew all agog to get on friendly terms with them, or any rate with one of them, and did succeed in making friends with Bruno.

Bruno, who had not needed to be much with him in order to discover that this physician was but a dolt, had never such a jolly time in palming off his strange stories upon him, while the physician, on his part, was marvellously delighted with Bruno ; to whom, having bidden him to breakfast, and thinking that for that reason he might talk familiarly with him, he expressed the amazement with which he regarded both him and Buffalmacco, for that, being but poor men, they lived so lightheartedly, and asked him to tell him how they managed.   At which fresh proof of the doctor's simplicity and fatuity Bruno was inclined to laugh ; but, bethinking him that 'twere best to answer him according to his folly, he said :—" Master, there are not many persons to whom I would disclose our manner of life, but, as you are my friend, and I know you will not let it go further, I do not mind telling you.   The fact is that my comrade and I live not only as lightheartedly and jovially as you see, but much more so ; and yet neither our art, nor any property that we possess, yields us enough to keep us in water : not that I would have you suppose that we go a-thieving : no, 'tis that we go the course, and thereby without the least harm done to a soul we get all that we need, nay, all that we desire ; and thus it is that we live so lightheartedly as you see."   Which explanation the doctor believing none the less readily that he knew not what it meant, was lost in wonder, and forthwith burned with a most vehement desire to know what going the course might be, and was instant with Bruno to expound it, assuring him that he would never tell a soul.   " Alas ! Master," said Bruno, " what is this you ask of me ?   'Tis a mighty great secret you would have me impart to you : 'twould be enough to undo me, to send me packing out of the world, nay, into the very jaws of

Lucifer of San Gallo,[1] if it came to be known. But such is the respect in which I hold your quiditative pumpionship of Legnaia, and the trust I repose in you, that I am not able to deny you aught you ask of me; and so I will tell it you, on condition that you swear by the cross at Montesone that you will keep your promise, and never repeat it to a soul."

The Master gave the required assurance. Whereupon:— " You are then to know," quoth Bruno, " sweet my Master, that 'tis not long since there was in this city a great master in necromancy, hight Michael Scott, for that he was of Scotland, and great indeed was the honour in which he was held by not a few gentlemen, most of whom are now dead; and when the time came that he just needs depart from Florence, he at their instant entreaty left behind two pupils, adepts both, whom he bade hold themselves ever ready to pleasure those gentlemen who had done him honour. And very handsomely they did serve the said gentlemen in certain of their love affairs and other little matters; and finding the city and the manners of the citizens agreeable to them, they made up their minds to stay here always, and grew friendly and very intimate with some of the citizens, making no distinction between gentle and simple, rich or poor, so only they were such as were conformable to their ways. And to gratify these their friends they formed a company of perhaps twenty-five men, to meet together at least twice a month in a place appointed by them; where, when they are met, each utters his desire, and forthwith that same night they accomplish it. Now Buffalmacco and I, being extraordinarily great and close friends with these two adepts, were by them enrolled in this company, and are still members of it. And I assure you that, as often as we are assembled together, the adornments of the saloon in which we eat are a marvel to see, ay, and the tables laid as for kings, and the multitudes of stately and handsome servants, as well women as men, at the beck and call of every member of the company, and the basins, and the ewers, the flasks and the cups, and all else that is there for our service in eating and drinking, of nought but gold and silver, and therewithal the abundance and variety of the viands, suited to the taste of each, that are set before us, each in due course, these too be marvels. 'Twere vain for me to seek to describe to you the sweet concord that is there of innumerable instruments of music, and the tuneful songs that salute our ears; nor might I hope to tell you how much wax is burned at

----

[1] Perhaps an allusion to some frightful picture.

these banquets, or compute the quantity of the comfits that are eaten, or the value of the wines that are drunk. Nor, my pumpkin o' wit, would I have you suppose that, when we are there, we wear our common clothes, such as you now see me wear ; nay, there is none there so humble but he shews as an emperor, so sumptuous are our garments, so splendid our trappings. But among all the delights of the place none may compare with the fair ladies, who, so one do but wish, are brought thither from every part of the world. Why, you might see there My Lady of the Barbanichs, the Queen of the Basques, the Consort of the Soldan, the Empress of Osbech, the Ciancianfera of Nornieca, the Semistante of Berlinzone, and the Scalpedra of Narsia. But why seek to enumerate them all ? They include all the queens in the world, ay, even to the Schinchimurra of Prester John, who has the horns sprouting out of her nether end : so there's for you. Now when these ladies have done with the wine and the comfits, they tread a measure or two, each with the man at whose behest she is come, and then all go with their gallants to their chambers. And know that each of these chambers shews us a very Paradise, so fair is it, ay, and no less fragrant than the cases of aromatics in your shop when you are pounding the cumin : and therein are beds that you would find more goodly than that of the Doge of Venice, and 'tis in them we take our rest ; and how busily they ply the treadle, and how lustily they tug at the frame to make the stuff close and compact, I leave you to imagine. However, among the luckiest of all I reckon Buffalmacco and myself ; for that Buffalmacco for the most part fetches him the Queen of France, and I do the like with the Queen of England, who are just the finest women in the world, and we have known how to carry it with them so that we are the very eyes of their heads. So I leave it to your own judgment to determine whether we have not good cause to live and bear ourselves with a lighter heart than others, seeing that we are beloved of two such great queens, to say nothing of the thousand or two thousand florins that we have of them whenever we are so minded. Now this in the vulgar we call going the course, because, as the corsairs prey upon all the world, so do we ; albeit with this difference, that, whereas they never restore their spoil, we do so as soon as we have done with it. So now, my worthy Master, you understand what we mean by going the course ; but how close it behoves you to keep such a secret, you may see for yourself ; so I spare you any further exhortations."

The Master, whose skill did not reach, perhaps, beyond the treatment of children for the scurf, took all that Bruno said for gospel, and burned with so vehement a desire to be admitted into this company, that he could not have longed for the *summum bonum* itself with more ardour. So, after telling Bruno that indeed 'twas no wonder they bore them light-heartedly, he could scarce refrain from asking him there and then to have him enrolled, albeit he deemed it more prudent to defer his suit, until by lavishing honour upon him he had gained a right to urge it with more confidence. He therefore made more and more of him, had him to breakfast and sup with him, and treated him with extraordinary respect. In short, such and so constant was their intercourse that it seemed as though the Master wist not how to live without Bruno. As it went so well with him, Bruno, to mark his sense of the honour done him by the doctor, painted in his saloon a picture symbolical of Lent, and an Agnus Dei at the entrance of his chamber, and an alembic over his front door, that those who would fain consult him might know him from other physicians, besides a battle of rats and mice in his little gallery, which the doctor thought an extremely fine piece. And from time to time, when he had not supped with the Master, he would say to him :—" Last night I was with the company, and being a little tired of the Queen of England, I fetched me the Gumedra of the great Can of Tarisi." "Gumedra," quoth the Master ; "what is she ? I know not the meaning of these words." "Thereat, Master," replied Bruno, "I marvel not ; for I have heard tell that neither Porcograsso nor Vannacena say aught thereof." "Thou wouldst say Ippocrasso and Avicenna," returned the Master. "I'faith I know not," quoth Bruno. "I as ill know the meaning of your words as you of mine. But Gumedra in the speech of the great Can signifies the same as Empress in ours. Ah ! a fine woman you would find her, and plenty of her ! I warrant she would make you forget your drugs and prescriptions and plasters." And so, Bruno from time to time whetting the Master's appetite, and the Master at length thinking that by his honourable entreatment of him he had fairly made a conquest of Bruno, it befell that one evening, while he held the light for Bruno, who was at work on the battle of rats and mice, he determined to discover to him his desire ; and as they were alone, thus he spoke :—" God knows, Bruno, that there lives not the man, for whom I would do as much as for thee : why, if thou wast to bid me go all the way from here to

Peretola,[1] I almost think I would do so; wherefore I trust thou wilt not deem it strange if I talk to thee as an intimate friend and in confidence. Thou knowest 'tis not long since thou didst enlarge with me on thy gay company and their doings, which has engendered in me such a desire as never was to know more thereof. Nor without reason, as thou wilt discover, should I ever become a member of the said company, for I straightway give thee leave to make game of me, should I not then fetch me the fairest maid thou hast seen this many a day, whom I saw last year at Cacavincigli, and to whom I am entirely devoted; and by the body of Christ I offered her ten Bolognese groats, that she should pleasure me, and she would not. Wherefore I do most earnestly entreat thee to instruct me what I must do to fit myself for membership in the company; and never doubt that in me you will have a true and loyal comrade, and one that will do you honour. And above all thou seest how goodly I am of my person, and how well furnished with legs, and of face as fresh as a rose; and therewithal I am a doctor of medicine, and I scarce think you have any such among you; and not a little excellent lore I have, and many a good song by heart, of which I will sing thee one;" and forthwith he fell a-singing.

Bruno had such a mind to laugh, that he could scarce contain himself; but still he kept a grave countenance; and, when the Master had ended his song, and said:—" How likes it thee? " he answered:—" Verily, no lyre of straw could vie with you, so artargutically [2] you refine your strain." " I warrant thee," returned the Master, " thou hadst never believed it, hadst thou not heard me." " Ay, indeed, sooth sayst thou," quoth Bruno. " And I have other songs to boot," said the Master; " but enough of this at present. Thou must know that I, such as thou seest me, am a gentleman's son, albeit my father lived in the contado; and on my mother's side I come of the Vallecchio family. And as thou mayst have observed I have quite the finest library and wardrobe of all the physicians in Florence. God's faith! I have a robe that cost, all told, close upon a hundred pounds in bagattines [3] more than ten years ago. Wherefore I make most instant suit to thee that thou get me enrolled, which if thou do, God's faith! be thou never so ill,

---

[1] About four miles from Florence.
[2] In the Italian " artagoticamente," a word of Boccaccio's own minting.
[3] A Venetian coin of extremely low value, being reckoned as ¼ of the Florentine quattrino.

thou shalt pay me not a stiver for my tendance of thee."
Whereupon Bruno, repeating to himself, as he had done many a
time before, that the doctor was a very numskull :—" Master,"
quoth he, " shew a little more light here, and have patience until
I have put the finishing touches to the tails of these rats, and
then I will answer you." So he finished the tails, and then,
putting on an air as if he were not a little embarrassed by the
request :—" Master mine," quoth he, " I should have great
things to expect from you ; that I know : but yet what you ask
of me, albeit to your great mind it seems but a little thing, is a
weighty matter indeed for me ; nor know I a soul in the world,
to whom, though well able, I would grant such a request, save
to you alone ; and this I say not for friendship's sake alone,
albeit I love you as I ought, but for that your discourse is so
fraught with wisdom, that 'tis enough to make a beguine start
out of her boots, much more, then, to incline me to change my
purpose ; and the more I have of your company, the wiser I
repute you. Whereto I may add, that, if for no other cause,
I should still be well disposed towards you for the love I see
you bear to that fair piece of flesh of which you spoke but now.
But this I must tell you : 'tis not in my power to do as you
would have me in this matter ; but, though I cannot myself
do the needful in your behalf, if you will pledge your faith,
whole and solid as may be, to keep my secret, I will shew you
how to go about it for yourself, and I make no doubt that,
having this fine library and the other matters you spoke of a
while ago, you will compass your end." Quoth then the
Master :—" Nay, but speak freely ; I see thou dost yet scarce
know me, and how well I can keep a secret. There were few
things that Messer Guasparruolo da Saliceto did, when he was
Podestà of Forlinpopoli, that he did not confide to me, so safe
he knew they would be in my keeping : and wouldst thou be
satisfied that I say sooth ? I assure you I was the first man
whom he told that he was about to marry Bergamina : so there's
for thee." " Well and good," said Bruno, " if such as he
confided in you, well indeed may I do the like. Know, then,
that you will have to proceed on this wise :—Our company
is governed by a captain and a council of two, who are
changed every six months : and on the calends without fail
Buffalmacco will be captain, and I councillor : 'tis so fixed :
and the captain has not a little power to promote the admission and enrolment of whomsoever he will : wherefore,
methinks, you would do well to make friends with Buffal-

macco and honourably entreat him : he is one that, marking your great wisdom, will take a mighty liking to you forthwith ; and when you have just a little dazzled him with your wisdom and these fine things of yours, you may make your request to him ; and he will not know how to say no—I have already talked with him of you, and he is as well disposed to you as may be—and having so done you will leave the rest to me."　Whereupon :—"Thy words are to me for an exceeding great joy," quoth the Master : "and if he be one that loves to converse with sages, he has but to exchange a word or two with me, and I will answer for it that he will be ever coming to see me ; for so fraught with wisdom am I, that I could furnish a whole city therewith, and still remain a great sage."

Having thus set matters in train, Bruno related the whole affair, point by point, to Buffalmacco, to whom it seemed a thousand years till he should be able to give Master Noodle that of which he was in quest.　The doctor, now all agog to go the course, lost no time, and found no difficulty, in making friends with Buffalmacco, and fell to entertaining him, and Bruno likewise, at breakfast and supper in most magnificent style ; while they fooled him to the top of his bent, for, being gentlemen that appreciated excellent wines and fat capons, besides other good cheer in plenty, they were inclined to be very neighbourly, and needed no second bidding, but, always letting him understand that there was none other whose company they relished so much, kept ever with him.

However, in due time the Master asked of Buffalmacco that which he had before asked of Bruno.　Whereat Buffalmacco feigned to be not a little agitated, and turning angrily to Bruno, made a great pother about his ears, saying :—"By the Most High God of Pasignano I vow I can scarce forbear to give thee that over the head that should make thy nose fall about thy heels, traitor that thou art, for 'tis thou alone that canst have discovered these secrets to the Master."　Whereupon the Master interposed with no little vigour, averring with oaths that 'twas from another source that he had gotten his knowledge ; and Buffalmacco at length allowed himself to be pacified by the sage's words.　So turning to him :—"Master," quoth he, "'tis evident indeed that you have been at Bologna, and have come back hither with a mouth that blabs not, and that 'twas on no pippin, as many a dolt does, but on the good long pumpkin that you learned your A B C ; and, if I mistake not, you were

baptized on a Sunday;[1] and though Bruno has told me that
'twas medicine you studied there, 'tis my opinion that you there
studied the art of catching men, of which, what with your wisdom and your startling revelations, you are the greatest master
that ever I knew." He would have said more, but the doctor,
turning to Bruno, broke in with:—" Ah ! what it is to consort
and converse with the wise ! Who but this worthy man would
thus have read my mind through and through ? Less quick
by far to rate me at my true worth wast thou. But what said
I when thou toldst me that Buffalmacco delighted to converse
with sages ? Confess now ; have I not kept my word ? "
" Verily," quoth Bruno, " you have more than kept it." Then,
addressing Buffalmacco :—" Ah ! " cried the Master, " what
hadst thou said, hadst thou seen me at Bologna, where there
was none, great or small, doctor or scholar, but was devoted to
me, so well wist I how to entertain them with my words of
wisdom. Nay more ; let me tell thee that there was never a
word I spoke but set every one a-laughing, so great was the
pleasure it gave them. And at my departure they all deplored
it most bitterly, and would have had me remain, and by way
of inducement went so far as to propose that I should be sole
lecturer to all the students in medicine that were there ; which
offer I declined, for that I was minded to return hither, having
vast estates here, that have ever belonged to my family ; which,
accordingly, I did." Quoth then Bruno to Buffalmacco :—
" How shews it, now, man ? Thou didst not believe me when
I told thee what he was. By the Gospels there is never a physician in this city that has the lore of ass's urine by heart as he
has : verily, thou wouldst not find his like between here and the
gates of Paris. Now see if thou canst help doing as he would
have thee." " 'Tis even as Bruno says," observed the doctor,
" but I am not understood here. You Florentines are somewhat
slow of wit. Would you could see me in my proper element,
among a company of doctors ! " Whereupon :—" Of a truth,
Master," quoth Buffalmacco, " your lore far exceeds any I
should ever have imputed to you ; wherefore, addressing you
as 'tis meet to address a man of your wisdom, I give you dis-
jointedly to understand that without fail I will procure your
enrolment in our company."

After this promise the honours lavished by the doctor upon
the two men grew and multiplied ; in return for which they

---

[1] *I.e.* without salt, that Florentine symbol of wit, not being so readily
procurable on a holiday as on working-days.

diverted themselves by setting him a-prancing upon every wild-
est chimera in the world ; and promised, among other matters,
to give him by way of mistress, the Countess of Civillari,[1] whom
they averred to be the goodliest creature to be found in all the
Netherlands of the human race ; and the doctor asking who
this Countess might be :—" Mature my gherkin," quoth Buffalmacco, " she is indeed a very great lady, and few houses are
there in the world in which she has not some jurisdiction ; nay,
the very Friars Minors, to say nought of other folk, pay her
tribute to the sound of the kettle-drum. And I may tell you
that, when she goes abroad, she makes her presence very
sensibly felt, albeit for the most part she keeps herself close :
however, 'tis no great while since she passed by your door one
night on her way to the Arno to bathe her feet and get a breath
of air ; but most of her time she abides at Laterina.[2] Serjeants
has she not a few that go their rounds at short intervals, bearing,
one and all, the rod and the bucket in token of her sovereignty,
and barons in plenty in all parts, as Tamagnino della Porta,[3]
Don Meta,[4] Manico di Scopa,[5] Squacchera,[6] and others, with
whom I doubt not you are intimately acquainted, though you
may not just now bear them in mind. Such, then, is the great
lady, in whose soft arms we, if we delude not ourselves, will
certainly place you, in which case you may well dispense with
her of Cacavincigli."

The doctor, who had been born and bred at Bologna, and
understood not their words, found the lady quite to his mind ;
and shortly afterwards the painters brought him tidings of his
election into the company. Then came the day of the nocturnal
gathering, and the doctor had the two men to breakfast ; and
when they had breakfasted, he asked them after what manner
he was to join the company. Whereupon :—" Lo, now, Master,"
quoth Buffalmacco, " you have need of a stout heart ; otherwise
you may meet with some let, to our most grievous hurt ; and
for what cause you have need of this stout heart, you shall hear.
You must contrive to be to-night about the hour of first sleep
on one of the raised tombs that have been lately placed outside
of Santa Maria Novella ; and mind that you wear one of your
best gowns, that your first appearance may impress the com-

---

[1] A public sink at Florence.
[2] In the contado of Arezzo : the *équivoque* is tolerably obvious.
[3] Slang for an ill-kept jakes.
[4] Also slang : signifying a pyramidal pile of ordure.
[5] Broom-handle.
[6] The meaning of this term may perhaps be divined from the sound.

pany with a proper sense of your dignity, and also because, as
we are informed, for we were not present at the time, the
Countess, by reason that you are a gentleman, is minded to
make you a Knight of the Bath at her own charges. So you
will wait there, until one, whom we shall send, come for you:
who, that you may know exactly what you have to expect, will
be a beast black and horned, of no great size; and he will go
snorting and bounding amain about the piazza in front of you,
with intent to terrify you; but, when he perceives that you are
not afraid, he will draw nigh you quietly, and when he is close
by you, then get you down from the tomb, fearing nothing;
and, minding you neither of God nor of the saints, mount him,
and when you are well set on his back, then fold your arms upon
your breast, as in submission, and touch him no more. Then,
going gently, he will bear you to us; but once mind you of
God, or the saints, or give way to fear, and I warn you, he
might give you a fall, or dash you against something that you
would find scarce pleasant; wherefore, if your heart misgives
you, you were best not to come, for you would assuredly do
yourself a mischief, and us no good at all." Quoth then the
doctor:—" You know me not as yet; 'tis perchance because I
wear the gloves and the long robe that you misdoubt me. Ah!
did you but know what feats I have done in times past at
Bologna, when I used to go after the women with my comrades,
you would be lost in amazement. God's faith! on one of those
nights there was one of them, a poor sickly creature she was
too, and stood not a cubit in height, who would not come
with us; so first I treated her to many a good cuff, and then
I took her up by main force, and carried her well-nigh as far as
a cross-bow will send a bolt, and so caused her, willy-nilly,
come with us. And on another occasion I mind me that, having
none other with me but my servant, a little after the hour of
Ave Maria, I passed beside the cemetery of the Friars Minors,
and, though that very day a woman had been there interred,
I had no fear at all. So on this score you may make your minds
easy; for indeed I am a man of exceeding great courage and
prowess. And to appear before you with due dignity, I will
don my scarlet gown, in which I took my doctor's degree, and
it remains to be seen if the company will not give me a hearty
welcome, and make me captain out of hand. Let me once be
there, and you will see how things will go; else how is it that
this countess, that has not yet seen me, is already so enamoured
of me that she is minded to make me a Knight of the Bath?

And whether I shall find knighthood agreeable, or know how to
support the dignity well or ill, leave that to me." Whereupon :—" Well said, excellent well said," quoth Buffalmacco:
" but look to it you disappoint us not, either by not coming or
by not being found, when we send for you ; and this I say,
because 'tis cold weather, and you medical gentlemen take great
care of your health." " God forbid," replied the doctor, " I
am none of your chilly folk ; I fear not the cold : 'tis seldom
indeed, when I leave my bed a nights, to answer the call of
nature, as one must at times, that I do more than throw a pelisse
over my doublet ; so rest assured that I shall be there."

So they parted ; and towards nightfall the Master found a
pretext for leaving his wife, and privily got out his fine gown,
which in due time he donned, and so hied him to the tombs,
and having perched himself on one of them, huddled himself
together, for 'twas mighty cold, to await the coming of the
beast. Meanwhile Buffalmacco, who was a tall man and strong,
provided himself with one of those dominos that were wont
to be worn in certain revels which are now gone out of fashion ;
and enveloped in a black pelisse turned inside out, shewed like
a bear, save that the domino had the face of a devil, and was
furnished with horns : in which guise, Bruno following close
behind to see the sport, he hied him to the piazza of Santa
Maria Novella. And no sooner wist he that the Master was on
the tomb, than he fell a-careering in a most wild and furious
manner to and fro the piazza, and snorting and bellowing and
gibbering like one demented, insomuch that, as soon as the
Master was ware of him, each several hair on his head stood
on end, and he fell a-trembling in every limb, being in sooth
more timid than a woman, and wished himself safe at home :
but as there he was, he strove might and main to keep his spirits
up, so overmastering was his desire to see the marvels of which
Bruno and Buffalmacco had told him. However, after a while
Buffalmacco allowed his fury to abate, and came quietly up
to the tomb on which the Master was, and stood still. The
Master, still all of a tremble with fear, could not at first make
up his mind, whether to get on the beast's back, or no ; but at
length, doubting it might be the worse for him if he did not
mount the beast, he overcame the one dread by the aid of the
other, got down from the tomb, saying under his breath :—
" God help me ! " and seated himself very comfortably on the
beast's back ; and then, still quaking in every limb, he folded
his arms as he had been bidden.

Buffalmacco now started, going on all-fours, at a very slow
pace, in the direction of Santa Maria della Scala, and so brought
the Master within a short distance of the Convent of the Ladies
of Ripoli. Now, in that quarter there were divers trenches,
into which the husbandmen of those parts were wont to discharge the Countess of Civillari, that she might afterwards
serve them to manure their land. Of one of which trenches, as
he came by, Buffalmacco skirted the edge, and seizing his opportunity, raised a hand, and caught the doctor by one of his feet,
and threw him off his back and head-foremost right into the
trench, and then, making a terrific noise and frantic gestures
as before, went bounding off by Santa Maria della Scala towards
the field of Ognissanti, where he found Bruno, who had betaken
him thither that he might laugh at his ease ; and there the two
men in high glee took their stand to observe from a distance
how the bemired doctor would behave. Finding himself in so
loathsome a place, the Master struggled might and main to
raise himself and get out ; and though again and again he
slipped back, and swallowed some drams of the ordure, yet,
bemired from head to foot, woebegone and crestfallen, he did
at last get out, leaving his hood behind him. Then, removing
as much of the filth as he might with his hands, knowing not
what else to do, he got him home, where, by dint of much knocking, he at last gained admittance ; and scarce was the door
closed behind the malodorous Master, when Bruno and Buffalmacco were at it, all agog to hear after what manner he would
be received by his wife. They were rewarded by hearing her
give him the soundest rating that ever bad husband got.
" Ah ! " quoth she, " fine doings, these ! Thou hast been with
some other woman, and wast minded to make a brave shew in
thy scarlet gown. So I was not enough for thee ! not enough
for thee forsooth, I that might content a crowd ! Would they
had choked thee with the filth in which they have soused thee ;
'twas thy fit resting-place. Now, to think that a physician of
repute, and a married man, should go by night after strange
women ! " Thus, and with much more to the like effect,
while the doctor was busy washing himself, she ceased not to
torment him until midnight.

On the morrow, Bruno and Buffalmacco, having painted their
bodies all over with livid patches to give them the appearance
of having been thrashed, came to the doctor's house, and finding
that he was already risen, went in, being saluted on all hands by
a foul smell, for time had not yet served thoroughly to cleanse

the house. The doctor, being informed that they were come to see him, advanced to meet them, and bade them good morning. Whereto Bruno and Buffalmacco, having prepared their answer, replied :—" No good morning shall you have from us : rather we pray God to give you bad years enough to make an end of you, seeing that there lives no more arrant and faithless traitor. 'Tis no fault of yours, if we, that did our best to honour and pleasure you, have not come by a dog's death ; your faithlessness has cost us to-night as many sound blows as would more than suffice to keep an ass a-trotting all the way from here to Rome ; besides which, we have been in peril of expulsion from the company in which we arranged for your enrolment. If you doubt our words, look but at our bodies, what a state they are in." And so, baring their breasts they gave him a glimpse of the patches they had painted there, and forthwith covered them up again. The doctor would have made them his excuses, and recounted his misfortunes, and how he had been thrown into the trench. But Buffalmacco broke in with :—" Would he had thrown you from the bridge into the Arno ! Why must you needs mind you of God and the saints ? Did we not forewarn you ? " " God's faith," returned the doctor, " that did I not." " How ? " quoth Buffalmacco, " you did not ? You do so above a little ; for he that we sent for you told us that you trembled like an aspen, and knew not where you were. You have played us a sorry trick ; but never another shall do so ; and as for you, we will give you such requital thereof as you deserve." The doctor now began to crave their pardon, and to implore them for God's sake not to expose him to shame, and used all the eloquence at his command to make his peace with them. And if he had honourably entreated them before, he thenceforth, for fear they should publish his disgrace, did so much more abundantly, and courted them both by entertaining them at his table and in other ways. And so you have heard how wisdom is imparted to those that get it not at Bologna.

NOVEL X

A Sicilian woman cunningly conveys from a merchant that which he has brought to Palermo ; he, making a shew of being come back thither with far greater store of goods than before, borrows money of her, and leaves her in lieu thereof water and tow.

How much in divers passages the queen's story moved the ladies to laughter, it boots not to ask : none was there in whose eyes the tears stood not full a dozen times for excess of merriment. However, it being ended, and Dioneo witting that 'twas now his turn, thus spake he :—Gracious ladies, 'tis patent to all that wiles are diverting in the degree of the wiliness of him that is by them beguiled. Wherefore, albeit stories most goodly have been told by you all, I purpose to relate one which should afford you more pleasure than any that has been told, seeing that she that was beguiled was far more cunning in beguiling others than any of the beguiled of whom you have spoken.

There was, and perhaps still is, a custom in all maritime countries that have ports, that all merchants arriving there with merchandise, should, on discharging, bring all their goods into a warehouse, called in many places " dogana," and maintained by the state, or the lord of the land ; where those that are assigned to that office allot to each merchant, on receipt of an invoice of all his goods and the value thereof, a room in which he stores his goods under lock and key ; whereupon the said officers of the dogana enter all the merchant's goods to his credit in the book of the dogana, and afterwards make him pay duty thereon, or on such part as he withdraws from the warehouse. By which book of the dogana the brokers not seldom find out the sorts and quantities of the merchandise that is there, and also who are the owners thereof, with whom, as occasion serves, they afterwards treat of exchanges, barters, sales and other modes of disposing of the goods. Which custom obtained, as in many other places, so also at Palermo in Sicily, where in like manner there were and are not a few women, fair as fair can be, but foes to virtue, who by whoso knows them not would be reputed great and most virtuous ladies. And being given not merely to fleece but utterly to flay men, they no sooner espy a foreign merchant in the city, than they find out from the book of the dogana how much he has there and what he is good for : and then by caressing and amorous

looks and gestures, and words of honeyed sweetness, they strive
to entice and allure the merchant to their love, and not seldom
have they succeeded, and wrested from him great part or the
whole of his merchandise; and of some they have gotten goods
and ship and flesh and bones, so delightsomely have they known
how to ply the shears.

Now 'tis not long since one of our young Florentines, Niccolò
da Cignano by name, albeit he was called Salabaetto, arrived
there, being sent by his masters with all the woollen stuffs that
he had not been able to dispose of at Salerno fair, which might
perhaps be worth five hundred florins of gold; and having given
the invoice to the officers of the dogana and stored the goods,
Salabaetto was in no hurry to get them out of bond, but took a
stroll or two about the city for his diversion. And as he was
fresh-complexioned and fair and not a little debonair, it so befell
that one of these ladies that plied the shears, and called herself
Jancofiore, began to ogle him. Whereof he taking note, and
deeming that she was a great lady, supposed that she was
taken by his good looks, and cast about how he might manage
this amour with all due discretion; wherefore, saying nought
to a soul, he began to pass to and fro before her house. Which
she observing, occupied herself for a few days in inflaming his
passion, and then affecting to be dying of love for him, sent
privily to him a woman that she had in her service, and who was
an adept in the arts of the procuress. She, after not a little
palaver, told him, while the tears all but stood in her eyes,
that for his handsome person and winsome air her mistress was
so enamoured of him, that she found no peace by day or by night;
and therefore, if 'twere agreeable to him, there was nought she
desired so much as to meet him privily at a bagnio: whereupon
she drew a ring from her purse, and gave it him by way of token
from her mistress. Overjoyed as ne'er another to hear such
good news, Salabaetto took the ring, and, after drawing it
across his eyes and kissing it, put it on his finger, and told the
good woman that, if Madonna Jancofiore loved him, she was
well requited, for that he loved her more dearly than himself,
and that he was ready to meet her wherever and whenever she
might see fit. With which answer the procuress hied her back
to her mistress, and shortly afterwards Salabaetto was informed
that he was to meet the lady at a certain bagnio at vespers of
the ensuing day.

So, saying nought to a soul of the matter, he hied him punctually at the appointed hour to the bagnio, and found that it

had been taken by the lady ; nor had he long to wait before
two female slaves made their appearance, bearing on their heads,
the one a great and goodly mattress of wadding, and the other
a huge and well-filled basket ; and having laid the mattress on
a bedstead in one of the rooms of the bagnio, they covered it
with a pair of sheets of the finest fabric, bordered with silk, and
a quilt of the whitest Cyprus buckram, with two daintily-
embroidered pillows. The slaves then undressed and got into
the bath, which they thoroughly washed and scrubbed : whither
soon afterwards the lady, attended by other two female slaves,
came, and made haste to greet Salabaetto with the heartiest
of cheer ; and when, after heaving many a mighty sigh, she had
embraced and kissed him :—" I know not," quoth she, " who
but thou could have brought me to this, such a fire hast thou
kindled in my soul, little dog of a Tuscan ! " Whereupon she
was pleased that they should undress, and get into the bath,
and two of the slaves with them ; which, accordingly, they did ;
and she herself, suffering none other to lay a hand upon him,
did with wondrous care wash Salabaetto from head to foot
with soap perfumed with musk and cloves ; after which she let
the slaves wash and shampoo herself. The slaves then brought
two spotless sheets of finest texture, which emitted such a scent
of roses, that 'twas as if there was nought there but roses, in
one of which having wrapped Salabaetto, and in the other the
lady, they bore them both to bed, where, the sheets in which
they were enfolded being withdrawn by the slaves as soon as
they had done sweating, they remained stark naked in the
others. The slaves then took from the basket cruets of silver
most goodly, and full, this of rose-water, that of water of orange-
blossom, a third of water of jasmine-blossom, and a fourth of
nanfa [1] water, wherewith they sprinkled them : after which,
boxes of comfits and the finest wines being brought forth, they
regaled them a while. To Salabaetto 'twas as if he were in
Paradise ; a thousand times he scanned the lady, who was
indeed most beautiful ; and he counted each hour as a hundred
years until the slaves should get them gone, and he find himself
in the lady's arms.

At length, by the lady's command, the slaves departed,
leaving a lighted torch in the room, and then the lady and
Salabaetto embraced, and to Salabaetto's prodigious delight, for

---

[1] Neither the *Vocab. degli Accad. della Crusca* nor the *Ricchezze* attempts
to define the precise nature of this scent, which Fanfani identifies with
that of the orange-blossom.

it seemed to him that she was all but dissolved for love of him, tarried there a good while. However, the time came when the lady must needs rise : so she called the slaves, with whose help they dressed, regaled them again for a while with wine and comfits, and washed their faces and hands with the odoriferous waters. Then as they were going, quoth the lady to Salabaetto : —" If it be agreeable to thee, I should deem it a very great favour if thou wouldst come to-night to sup and sleep with me." Salabaetto, who, captivated by her beauty and her studied graciousness, never doubted but he was dear to her as her very heart, made answer :—" Madam, there is nought you can desire but is in the last degree agreeable to me ; wherefore to-night and ever 'tis my purpose to do whatsoever you may be pleased to command." So home the lady hied her, and having caused a brave shew to be made in her chamber with her dresses and other paraphernalia, and a grand supper to be prepared, awaited Salabaetto ; who, being come there as soon as 'twas dark, had of her a gladsome welcome, and was regaled with an excellent and well-served supper. After which, they repaired to the chamber, where he was saluted by a wondrous sweet odour of aloe-wood, and observed that the bed was profusely furnished with birds,[1] after the fashion of Cyprus, and that not a few fine dresses were hanging upon the pegs. Which circumstances did, one and all, beget in him the belief that this must be a great and wealthy lady ; and, though he had heard a hint or two to the contrary touching her life, he would by no means credit them ; nor, supposing that she had perchance taken another with guile, would he believe that the same thing might befall him. So to his exceeding great solace, he lay with her that night, and ever grew more afire for her. On the morrow, as she was invest-ing him with a fair and dainty girdle of silver, with a goodly purse attached :—" Sweet my Salabaetto," quoth she, " prithee forget me not ; even as my person, so is all that I have at thy pleasure, and all that I can at thy command."

Salabaetto then embraced and kissed her, and so bade her adieu, and betook him to the place where the merchants were wont to congregate. And so it befell that he, continuing to consort with her from time to time, and being never a denier the poorer thereby, disposed of his merchandise for ready money and at no small profit ; whereof not by him but by another the lady was forthwith advised. And Salabaetto being come to see her one evening, she greeted him gaily and gamesomely, and fell

1 *I.e.* with a sort of musical boxes in the shape of birds.

a-kissing and hugging him, and made as if she were so afire for love of him that she was like to die thereof in his arms; and offered to give him two most goodly silver cups that she had, which Salabaetto would not accept, having already had from her (taking one time with another) fully thirty florins of gold, while he had not been able to induce her to touch so much as a groat of his money. But when by this shew of passion and generosity she had thoroughly kindled his flame, in came, as she had arranged, one of her slaves, and spoke to her; whereupon out of the room she went, and after a while came back in tears, and threw herself prone on the bed, and set up the most dolorous lamentation that ever woman made. Whereat Salabaetto wondering, took her in his arms, and mingled his tears with hers, and said:—"Alas! heart of my body! what ails thee thus of a sudden? Wherefore art thou so distressed? Ah! tell me the reason, my soul." The lady allowed him to run on in this strain for a good while, and then:—"Alas! sweet my lord," quoth she, "I know not either what to do or what to say. I have but now received a letter from Messina, in which my brother bids me sell, if need be, all that I have here, and send him without fail within eight days a thousand florins of gold: otherwise he will forfeit his head. I know not how to come by them so soon: had I but fifteen days, I would make a shift to raise them in a quarter where I might raise a much larger sum, or I would sell one of our estates; but, as this may not be, would I had been dead or e'er this bad news had reached me!" Which said, affecting to be utterly broken-hearted, she ceased not to weep.

Salabaetto, the ardour of whose passion had in great measure deprived him of the sagacity which the circumstances demanded, supposed that the tears were genuine enough, and the words even more so. Wherefore:—"Madam," quoth he, "I could not furnish you with a thousand, but if five hundred florins of gold would suffice, they are at your service, if you think you could repay them within fifteen days; and you may deem yourself in luck's way, for 'twas only yesterday that I sold my woollens, which had I not done, I could not have lent you a groat." "Alas!" returned the lady, "then thou hast been in straits for money? Oh! why didst thou not apply to me? Though I have not a thousand at my command, I could have given thee quite a hundred, nay indeed two hundred florins. By what thou hast said thou hast made me hesitate to accept the service that thou proposest to render me." Which words fairly delivered Salabaetto into the lady's hands, insomuch that :—" Madam," quoth he, " I would not have you decline my help for such a scruple ; for had my need been as great as yours, I should certainly have applied to you." Quoth then the lady :—" Ah ! Salabaetto mine, well I wot that the love thou bearest me is a true and perfect love, seeing that, without waiting to be asked, thou dost so handsomely come to my aid with so large a sum of money. And albeit I was thine without this token of thy love, yet, assuredly, it has made me thine in an even greater degree ; nor shall I ever forget that 'tis to thee I owe my brother's life. But God knows I take thy money from thee reluctantly, seeing that thou art a merchant, and 'tis by means of money that merchants conduct all their affairs ; but, as necessity constrains me, and I have good hope of speedily repaying thee, I will even take it, and by way of security, if I should find no readier method, I will pawn all that I have here." Which said, she burst into tears, and fell upon Salabaetto, pressing her cheek upon his.

Salabaetto tried to comfort her ; and having spent the night with her, on the morrow, being minded to shew himself her most devoted servant, brought her, without awaiting any reminder, five hundred fine florins of gold : which she, laughing at heart while the tears streamed from her eyes, took, Salabaetto trusting her mere promise of repayment. Now that the lady had gotten the money, the complexion of affairs began to alter ; and whereas Salabaetto had been wont to have free access to her, whenever he was so minded, now for one reason or another he was denied admittance six times out of seven ; nor did she greet him with the same smile, or shower on him the same caresses, or do him the same cheer as of yore. So a month, two months, passed beyond the time when he was to have been repaid his money ; and when he demanded it, he was put off with words. Whereby Salabaetto, being now ware of the cheat which his slender wit had suffered the evil-disposed woman to put upon him, and also that, having neither writing nor witness against her, he was entirely at her mercy in regard of his claim, and being, moreover, ashamed to lodge any complaint with any one, as well because he had been forewarned of her character, as because he dreaded the ridicule to which his folly justly exposed him, was chagrined beyond measure, and inly bewailed his simplicity. And his masters having written to him, bidding him change the money and remit it to them, he, being apprehensive that, making default as he must, he should, if he remained

there, be detected, resolved to depart ; and having taken ship, he repaired, not, as he should have done, to Pisa, but to Naples ; where at that time resided our gossip, Pietro dello Canigiano, treasurer of the Empress of Constantinople, a man of great sagacity and acuteness, and a very great friend of Salabaetto and his kinsfolk ; to whom trusting in his great discretion, Salabaetto after a while discovered his distress, telling him what he had done, and the sorry plight in which by consequence he stood, and craving his aid and counsel, that he might the more readily find means of livelihood there, for that he was minded never to go back to Florence. Impatient to hear of such folly :—
" 'Twas ill done of thee," quoth Canigiano, " thou hast mis- behaved thyself, wronged thy masters, and squandered an exorbitant sum in lewdness ; however, 'tis done, and we must consider of the remedy." And indeed, like the shrewd man that he was, he had already bethought him what was best to be done ; and forthwith he imparted it to Salabaetto. Which expedient Salabaetto approving, resolved to make the adven- ture ; and having still a little money, and being furnished with a loan by Canigiano, he provided himself with not a few bales well and closely corded, and bought some twenty oil-casks, which he filled, and having put all on shipboard, returned to Palermo. There he gave the invoice of the bales, as also of the oil-casks, to the officers of the dogana, and having them all entered to his credit, laid them up in the store-rooms, saying that he purposed to leave them there until the arrival of other merchandise that he expected.

Which Jancofiore learning, and being informed that the merchandise, that he had brought with him, was worth fully two thousand florins of gold, or even more, besides that which he expected, which was valued at more than three thousand florins of gold, bethought her that she had not aimed high enough, and that 'twere well to refund him the five hundred, if so she might make the greater part of the five thousand florins her own. Wherefore she sent for him, and Salabaetto, having learned his lesson of cunning, waited on her. Feigning to know nought of the cargo he had brought with him, she received him with marvellous cheer, and began :—" Lo, now, if thou wast angry with me because I did not repay thee thy money in due time : " but Salabaetto interrupted her, saying with a laugh :—
" Madam, 'tis true I was a little vexed, seeing that I would have plucked out my heart to pleasure you ; but listen, and you shall learn the quality of my displeasure. Such and so

great is the love I bear you, that I have sold the best part of all that I possess, whereby I have already in this port merchandise to the value of more than two thousand florins, and expect from the Levant other goods to the value of above three thousand florins, and mean to set up a warehouse in this city, and live here, to be ever near you, for that I deem myself more blessed in your love than any other lover that lives." Whereupon :—
" Harkye, Salabaetto," quoth the lady, " whatever advantages thee is mighty grateful to me, seeing that I love thee more than my very life, and right glad am I that thou art come back with intent to stay, for I hope to have many a good time with thee ; but something I must say to thee by way of excuse, for that, whilst thou wast thinking of taking thy departure, there were times when thou wast disappointed of seeing me, and others when thou hadst not as gladsome a welcome as thou wast wont to have, and therewithal I kept not the time promised for the repayment of thy money. Thou must know that I was then in exceeding great trouble and tribulation, and whoso is thus bested, love he another never so much, cannot greet him with as gladsome a mien, or be as attentive to him, as he had lief ; and thou must further know that 'tis by no means an easy matter for a lady to come by a thousand florins of gold : why, 'tis every day a fresh lie, and never a promise kept ; and so we in our turn must needs lie to others ; and 'twas for this cause, and not for any fault of mine, that I did not repay thee thy money ; however, I had it but a little while after thy departure, and had I known whither to send it, be sure I would have remitted it to thee ; but, as that I wist not, I have kept it safe for thee." She then produced a purse, in which were the very same coins that he had brought her, and placed it in his hand, saying :—" Count and see if there are five hundred there." 'Twas the happiest moment Salabaetto had yet known, as, having told them out, and found the sum exact, he made answer :—" Madam, I know that you say sooth, and what you have done abundantly proves it ; wherefore, and for the love I bear you, I warrant you there is no sum you might ask of me on any occasion of need, with which, if 'twere in my power, I would not accommodate you ; whereof, when I am settled here, you will be able to assure yourself."

Having thus in words reinstated himself as her lover, he proceeded to treat her as his mistress, whereto she responded, doing all that was in her power to pleasure and honour him, and feigning to be in the last degree enamoured of him. But

Salabaetto, being minded to requite her guile with his own, went to her one evening, being bidden to sup and sleep with her, with an aspect so melancholy and dolorous, that he shewed as he had lief give up the ghost. Jancofiore, as she embraced and kissed him, demanded of him the occasion of his melancholy. Whereto he, having let her be instant with him a good while, made answer :—" I am undone, for that the ship, having aboard her the goods that I expected, has been taken by the corsairs of Monaco, and held to ransom in ten thousand florins of gold, of which it falls to me to pay one thousand, and I have not a denier, for the five hundred thou repaidst me I sent forthwith to Naples to buy stuffs for this market, and were I to sell the merchandise I have here, as 'tis not now the right time to sell, I should scarce get half the value ; nor am I as yet so well known here as to come by any to help me at this juncture, and so what to do or what to say I know not ; but this I know that, if I send not the money without delay, my merchandise will be taken to Monaco, and I shall never touch aught of it again." Whereat the lady was mightily annoyed, being apprehensive of losing all, and bethought her how she might prevent the goods going to Monaco : wherefore :—" God knows," quoth she, " that for the love I bear thee I am not a little sorry for thee : but what boots it idly to distress oneself ? Had I the money, God knows I would lend it thee forthwith, but I have it not. One, indeed, there is that accommodated me a day or two ago with five hundred florins that I stood in need of, but he requires a heavy usance, not less than thirty on the hundred, and if thou shouldst have recourse to him, good security must be forthcoming. Now for my part I am ready, so I may serve thee, to pledge all these dresses, and my person to boot, for as much as he will lend thee thereon ; but how wilt thou secure the balance ? "

Salabaetto divined the motive that prompted her thus to accommodate him, and that she was to lend the money herself ; which suiting his purpose well, he first of all thanked her, and then said that, being constrained by necessity, he would not stand out against exorbitant terms, adding that, as to the balance, he would secure it upon the merchandise that he had at the dogana by causing it to be entered in the name of the lender ; but that he must keep the key of the store-rooms, as well that he might be able to shew the goods, if requested, as to make sure that none of them should be tampered with or changed or exchanged. The lady said that this was reasonable, and that 'twas excellent security. So, betimes on the morrow, the lady sent for a broker, in whom she reposed much trust, and having talked the matter over with him, gave him a thousand florins of gold, which the broker took to Salabaetto, and thereupon had all that Salabaetto had at the dogana entered in his name ; they then had the script and counterscript made out, and, the arrangement thus concluded, went about their respective affairs. Salabaetto lost no time in getting aboard a bark with his five hundred florins of gold, and being come to Naples, sent thence a remittance which fully discharged his obligation to his masters that had entrusted him with the stuffs : he also paid all that he owed to Pietro dello Canigiano and all his other creditors, and made not a little merry with Canigiano over the trick he had played the Sicilian lady. He then departed from Naples, and being minded to have done with mercantile affairs, betook him to Ferrara.

Jancofiore, surprised at first by Salabaetto's disappearance from Palermo, waxed after a while suspicious ; and, when she had waited fully two months, seeing that he did not return, she caused the broker to break open the store-rooms. And trying first of all the casks, she found them full of sea-water, save that in each there was perhaps a hog's-head of oil floating on the surface. Then undoing the bales, she found them all, save two that contained stuffs, full of tow, and in short their whole contents put together were not worth more than two hundred florins. Wherefore Jancofiore, knowing herself to have been outdone, regretted long and bitterly the five hundred florins of gold that she had refunded, and still more the thousand that she had lent, repeating many a time to herself :—Who with a Tuscan has to do, Had need of eyesight quick and true. Thus, left with the loss and the laugh against her, she discovered that there were others as knowing as she.

No sooner was Dioneo's story ended, than Lauretta, witting that therewith the end of her sovereignty was come, bestowed her meed of praise on Pietro Canigiano for his good counsel, and also on Salabaetto for the equal sagacity which he displayed in carrying it out, and then, taking off the laurel wreath, set it on the head of Emilia, saying graciously :—" I know not, Madam, how debonair a queen you may prove, but at least we shall have in you a fair one. Be it your care, then, that you exercise your authority in a manner answerable to your charms." Which said, she resumed her seat.

Not so much to receive the crown, as to be thus commended

to her face and before the company for that which ladies are wont to covet the most, Emilia was a little shamefast; a tint like that of the newly-blown rose overspread her face, and a while she stood silent with downcast eyes: then, as the blush faded away, she raised them; and having given her seneschal her commands touching all matters pertaining to the company, thus she spake:—" Sweet my ladies, 'tis matter of common experience that, when the oxen have swunken a part of the day, under the coercive yoke, they are relieved thereof and loosed, and suffered to go seek their pasture at their own sweet will in the woods; nor can we fail to observe that gardens luxuriant with diversity of leafage are not less, but far more fair to see, than woods wherein is nought but oaks. Wherefore I deem that, as for so many days our discourse has been confined within the bounds of certain laws, 'twill be not only meet but profitable for us, being in need of relaxation, to roam a while, and so recruit our strength to undergo the yoke once more. And therefore I am minded that to-morrow the sweet tenor of your discourse be not confined to any particular theme, but that you be at liberty to discourse on such wise as to each may seem best; for well assured am I that thus to speak of divers matters will be no less pleasurable than to limit ourselves to one topic; and by reason of this enlargement my successor in the sovereignty will find you more vigorous, and be therefore all the more forward to reimpose upon you the wonted restraint of our laws." Having so said, she dismissed all the company until supper-time.

All approved the wisdom of what the queen had said; and being risen betook them to their several diversions, the ladies to weave garlands and otherwise disport them, the young men to play and sing; and so they whiled away the hours until supper-time; which being come, they gathered about the fair fountain, and took their meal with gay and festal cheer. Supper ended, they addressed them to their wonted pastime of song and dance. At the close of which the queen, notwithstanding the songs which divers of the company had already gladly accorded them, called for another from Pamfilo, who without the least demur thus sang:—

So great, O Love, the bliss
  Through thee I prove, so jocund my estate,
  That in thy flame to burn I bless my fate!

Such plenitude of joy my heart doth know
  Of that high joy and rare,

Wherewith thou hast me blest,
As, bounds disdaining, still doth overflow,
And by my radiant air
My blitheness manifest ;
For by thee thus possessed
With love, where meeter 'twere to venerate,
I still consume within thy flame elate.

Well wot I, Love, no song may e'er reveal,
Nor any sign declare
What in my heart is pent :
Nay, might they so, that were I best conceal,
Whereof were others ware,
'Twould serve but to torment
Me, whose is such content,
That weak were words and all inadequate
A title of my bliss to adumbrate.

Who would have dreamed that e'er in mine embrace
Her I should clip and fold
Whom there I still do feel,
Or as 'gainst her face e'er to lay my face
Attain such grace untold,
And unimagined weal ?
Wherefore my bliss I seal
Of mine own heart within the circuit strait,
And still in thy sweet flame luxuriate.

So ended Pamfilo his song : whereto all the company responded in full chorus ; nor was there any but gave to its words an inordinate degree of attention, endeavouring by conjecture to penetrate that which he intimated that 'twas meet he should keep secret. Divers were the interpretations hazarded, but all were wide of the mark. At length, however, the queen, seeing that ladies and men alike were fain of rest, bade all betake them to bed.

Endeth here the eighth day of the Decameron, beginneth the ninth, in which, under the rule of Emilia, discourse is had, at the discretion of each, of such matters as most commend themselves to each in turn.

THE luminary, before whose splendour the night takes wing, had already changed the eighth heaven [1] from azure to the lighter blue,[2] and in the meads the flowerets were beginning to lift their heads, when Emilia, being risen, roused her fair gossips, and, likewise, the young men. And so the queen leading the way at an easy pace, and the rest of the company following, they hied them to a copse at no great distance from the palace. Where, being entered, they saw the goats and stags and other wild creatures, as if witting that in this time of pestilence they had nought to fear from the hunter, stand awaiting them with no more sign of fear than if they had been tamed: and so, making now towards this, now towards the other of them as if to touch them, they diverted themselves for a while by making them skip and run. But, as soon as the sun was in the ascendant, by common consent they turned back, and whoso met them, garlanded as they were with oak-leaves, and carrying store of fragrant herbs or flowers in their hands might well have said:—" Either shall death not vanquish these, or they will meet it with a light heart." So, slowly wended they their way, now singing, now bandying quips and merry jests, to the palace, where they found all things in order meet, and their servants in blithe and merry cheer. A while they rested, nor went they to table until six ditties, each gayer than that which went before, has been sung by the young men and the ladies; which done, they washed their hands, and all by the queen's command were ranged by the seneschal at the table; and, the viands being served, they cheerily took their meal: wherefrom being risen, they trod some measures to the accompaniment of music; and then, by the queen's command, whoso would betook him to rest. However, the accustomed hour being come, they all

---

[1] *I.e.* in the Ptolemaic system, the region of the fixed stars.
[2] *Cilestro:* a word for which we have no exact equivalent, the dominant note of the Italian sky, when the sun is well up, being its intense luminosity.

gathered at the wonted spot for their discoursing, and the queen, bending her regard upon Filomena, bade her make a beginning of the day's story-telling, which she with a smile did on this wise :—

NOVEL I

Madonna Francesca, having two lovers, the one Rinuccio, the other Alessandro, by name, and loving neither of them, induces the one to simulate a corpse in a tomb, and the other to enter the tomb to fetch him out : whereby, neither satisfying her demands, she artfully rids herself of both.

MADAM, since so it pleases you, well pleased am I that in this vast, this boundless field of discourse, which you, our Lady Bountiful, have furnished us withal, 'tis mine to run the first course ; wherein if I do well, I doubt not that those, who shall follow me, will do not only well but better. Such, sweet my ladies, has been the tenor of our discourse, that times not a few the might of Love, how great and singular it is, has been set forth : but yet I doubt the topic is not exhausted, nor would it be so, though we should continue to speak of nought else for the space of a full year. And as Love not only leads lovers to debate with themselves whether they were not best to die, but also draws them into the houses of the dead in quest of the dead, I am minded in this regard to tell you a story, wherein you will not only discern the power of Love, but will also learn how the ready wit of a worthy lady enabled her to disembarrass herself of two lovers, whose love was displeasing to her.

Know, then, that there dwelt aforetime in the city of Pistoia a most beauteous widow lady, of whom it so befell that two of our citizens, the one Rinuccio Palermini, the other Alessandro Chiarmontesi, by name, tarrying at Pistoia, for that they were banished from Florence, became, neither witting how it stood with the other, in the last degree enamoured. Wherefore each used all his arts to win the love of Madonna Francesca de' Lazzari—such was the lady's name—and she, being thus continually plied with ambassages and entreaties on the part of both, and having indiscreetly lent ear to them from time to time, found it no easy matter discreetly to extricate herself, when she was minded to be rid of their pestering, until it occurred to her to adopt the following expedient, to wit, to require of

each a service, such as, though not impracticable, she deemed
none would actually perform, to the end that, they making
default, she might have a decent and colourable pretext for
refusing any longer to receive their ambassages. Which
expedient was on this wise. One day there died in Pistoia, and
was buried in a tomb outside the church of the Friars Minors,
a man, who, though his forbears had been gentlefolk, was
reputed the very worst man, not in Pistoia only, but in all the
world, and therewithal he was of form and feature so pre-
ternaturally hideous that whoso knew him not could scarce
see him for the first time without a shudder. Now, the lady
pondering her design on the day of this man's death, it occurred
to her that he might in a measure subserve its accomplishment: wherefore she said to her maid:—" Thou knowest to
what worry and annoyance I am daily put by the ambassages
of these two Florentines, Rinuccio and Alessandro. Now I
am not disposed to gratify either of them with my love, and
therefore, to shake them off, I am minded, as they make such
great protestations, to put them to the proof by requiring of
each something which I am sure he will not perform, and thus
to rid myself of their pestering: so list what I mean to do. Thou
knowest that this morning there was interred in the ground
of the Friars Minors this Scannadio (such was the name of the
bad man of whom we spoke but now) whose aspect, while he
yet lived, appalled even the bravest among us. Thou wilt
therefore go privily to Alessandro, and say to him:—' Madonna
Francesca sends thee word by me that the time is now come when
thou mayst win that which thou hast so much desired, to wit,
her love and joyance thereof, if thou be so minded, on the
following terms. For a reason, which thou shalt learn hereafter, one of her kinsmen is to bring home to her to-night the
corpse of Scannadio, who was buried this morning; and she,
standing in mortal dread of this dead man, would fain not see
him; wherefore she prays thee to do her a great service, and
be so good as to get thee this evening at the hour of first sleep
to the tomb wherein Scannadio is buried, and go in, and having
wrapped thyself in his grave-clothes, lie there, as thou wert
Scannadio himself, until one come for thee, when thou must
say never a word, but let him carry thee forth, and bear thee to
Madonna Francesca's house, where she will give thee welcome,
and let thee stay with her, until thou art minded to depart, and,
for the rest, thou wilt leave it to her.' And if he says that he
will gladly do so, well and good; if not, then thou wilt tell him

from me, never more to shew himself where I am, and, as he
values his life, to have a care to send me no more ambassages.
Which done, thou wilt go to Rinuccio Palermini, and wilt say
to him :—' Madonna Francesca lets thee know that she is ready
in all respects to comply with thy wishes, so thou wilt do her
a great service, which is on this wise : to-night, about midnight,
thou must go to the tomb wherein was this morning interred
Scannadio, and saying never a word, whatever thou mayst hear
or otherwise be ware of, bear him gently forth to Madonna
Francesca's house, where thou shalt learn wherefore she requires
this of thee, and shalt have thy solace of her ; and if thou art
not minded to obey her in this, see that thou never more send
her ambassage.' "

The maid did her mistress's errand, omitting nothing, to both
the men, and received from each the same answer, to wit that
to pleasure the lady, he would adventure a journey to hell, to
say nothing of entering a tomb. With which answer the maid
returned to the lady, who waited to see if they would be such fools
as to make it good. Night came, and at the hour of first sleep
Alessandro Chiarmontesi, stripped to his doublet, quitted his
house, and bent his steps towards Scannadio's tomb, with intent
there to take the dead man's place. As he walked, there came
upon him a great fear, and he fell a-saying to himself :—Ah !
what a fool am I ! Whither go I ? How know I that her
kinsmen, having detected my love, and surmising that which
is not, have not put her upon requiring this of me, in order
that they may slay me in the tomb ? In which event I alone
should be the loser, for nought would ever be heard of it, so
that they would escape scot-free. Or how know I but that 'tis
some machination of one of my ill-wishers, whom perchance she
loves, and is therefore minded to abet ? And again quoth he to
himself :—But allowing that 'tis neither the one nor the other,
and that her kinsmen are really to carry me to her house, I
scarce believe that 'tis either that they would fain embrace
Scannadio's corpse themselves, or let her do so : rather it must
be that they have a mind to perpetrate some outrage upon it,
for that, perchance, he once did them an evil turn. She bids
me say never a word, no matter what I may hear or be otherwise ware of. Suppose they were to pluck out my eyes, or my
teeth, or cut off my hands, or treat me to some other horse-play
of the like sort, how then ? how could I keep quiet ? And if
I open my mouth, they will either recognize me, and perchance
do me a mischief, or, if they spare me, I shall have been at pains

for nought, for they will not leave me with the lady, and she will say that I disobeyed her command, and I shall never have aught of her favours.

As thus he communed with himself, he was on the point of turning back; but his overmastering love plied him with opposing arguments of such force that he kept on his way, and reached the tomb; which having opened, he entered, and after stripping Scannadio, and wrapping himself in the grave-clothes, closed it, and laid himself down in Scannadio's place. He then fell a-thinking of the dead man, and his manner of life, and the things which he had heard tell of as happening by night, and in other less appalling places than the houses of the dead; whereby all the hairs of his head stood on end, and he momently expected Scannadio to rise and cut his throat. However, the ardour of his love so fortified him that he overcame these and all other timorous apprehensions, and lay as if he were dead, awaiting what should betide him.

Towards midnight Rinuccio, bent likewise upon fulfilling his lady's behest, sallied forth of his house, revolving as he went divers forebodings of possible contingencies, as that, having Scannadio's corpse upon his shoulders, he might fall into the hands of the Signory, and be condemned to the fire as a wizard, or that, should the affair get wind, it might embroil him with his kinsfolk, or the like, which gave him pause. But then with a revulsion of feeling :—Shall I, quoth he to himself, deny this lady, whom I so much have loved and love, the very first thing that she asks of me? And that too when I am thereby to win her favour? No, though 'twere as much as my life is worth, far be it from me to fail of keeping my word. So on he fared, and arrived at the tomb, which he had no difficulty in opening, and being entered, laid hold of Alessandro, who, though in mortal fear, had given no sign of life, by the feet, and dragged him forth, and having hoisted him on to his shoulders, bent his steps towards the lady's house. And as he went, being none too careful of Alessandro, he swung him from time to time against one or other of the angles of certain benches that were by the wayside; and indeed the night was so dark and murky that he could not see where he was going. And when he was all but on the threshold of the lady's house (she standing within at a window with her maid, to mark if Rinuccio would bring Alessandro, and being already provided with an excuse for sending them both away), it so befell that the patrol of the Signory, who were posted in the street in dead silence, being on the look-out for a certain bandit, hearing the tramp of Rinuccio's feet, suddenly shewed a light, the better to know what was toward, and whither to go, and advancing targes and lances, cried out:—" Who goes there? " Whereupon Rinuccio, having little leisure for deliberation, let Alessandro fall, and took to flight as fast as his legs might carry him. Alessandro, albeit encumbered by the grave-clothes, which were very long, also jumped up and made off. By the light shewn by the patrol the lady had very plainly perceived Rinuccio, with Alessandro on his back, as also that Alessandro had the grave-clothes upon him; and much did she marvel at the daring of both, but, for all that, she laughed heartily to see Rinuccio drop Alessandro, and Alessandro run away Overjoyed at the turn the affair had taken, and praising God that He had rid her of their harass, she withdrew from the window, and betook her to her chamber, averring to her maid that for certain they must both be mightily in love with her, seeing that 'twas plain they had both done her bidding.

Crestfallen and cursing his evil fortune, Rinuccio nevertheless went not home, but, as soon as the street was clear of the patrol, came back to the spot where he had dropped Alessandro, and stooped down and began feeling about, if haply he might find him, and so do his devoir to the lady; but, as he found him not, he supposed the patrol must have borne him thence, and so at last home he went; as did also Alessandro, knowing not what else to do, and deploring his mishap. On the morrow, Scannadio's tomb being found open and empty, for Alessandro had thrown the corpse into the vault below, all Pistoia debated of the matter with no small diversity of opinion, the fools believing that Scannadio had been carried off by devils. Neither of the lovers, however, forbore to make suit to the lady for her favour and love, telling her what they had done, and what had happened, and praying her to have them excused that they had not perfectly carried out her instructions. But she, feigning to believe neither of them, disposed of each with the same curt answer, to wit, that, as he had not done her bidding, she would never do aught for him.

NOVEL II

*An abbess rises in haste and in the dark, with intent to surprise
an accused nun abed with her lover : thinking to put on her
veil, she puts on instead the breeches of a priest that she has
with her : the nun, espying her headgear, and doing her to
wit thereof, is acquitted, and thenceforth finds it easier to forgather with her lover.*

So ended Filomena ; and when all had commended the address
shewn by the lady in ridding herself of the two lovers that she
affected not, and contrariwise had censured the hardihood of
the two lovers as not love but madness, the queen turned to
Elisa, and with a charming air :—" Now, Elisa, follow," quoth
she : whereupon Elisa began on this wise :—Dearest ladies,
'twas cleverly done of Madonna Francesca, to disembarrass
herself in the way we have heard : but I have to tell of a young
nun, who by a happy retort, and the favour of Fortune, delivered
herself from imminent peril. And as you know that there are
not a few most foolish folk, who, notwithstanding their folly,
take upon themselves the governance and correction of others ;
so you may learn from my story that Fortune at times justly
puts them to shame ; which befell the abbess, who was the
superior of the nun of whom I am about to speak.

You are to know, then, that in a convent in Lombardy of
very great repute for strict and holy living there was, among
other ladies that there wore the veil, a young woman of noble
family, and extraordinary beauty. Now Isabetta—for such
was her name—having speech one day of one of her kinsmen at
the grate, became enamoured of a fine young gallant that was
with him ; who, seeing her to be very fair, and reading her
passion in her eyes, was kindled with a like flame for her :
which mutual and unsolaced love they bore a great while not
without great suffering to both. But at length, both being
intent thereon, the gallant discovered a way by which he might
with all secrecy visit his nun ; and she approving, he paid her
not one visit only, but many, to their no small mutual solace.
But, while thus they continued their intercourse, it so befell
that one night one of the sisters observed him take his leave
of Isabetta and depart, albeit neither he nor she was ware that
they had thus been discovered. The sister imparted what she
had seen to several others. At first they were minded to

denounce her to the abbess, one Madonna Usimbalda, who was
reputed by the nuns, and indeed by all that knew her, to be
a good and holy woman ; but on second thoughts they deemed
it expedient, that there might be no room for denial, to cause
the abbess to take her and the gallant in the act. So they held
their peace, and arranged between them to keep her in watch
and close espial, that they might catch her unawares. Of
which practice Isabetta recking, witting nought, it so befell
that one night, when she had her lover to see her, the sisters that
were on the watch were soon ware of it, and at what they deemed
the nick of time parted into two companies, of which one
mounted guard at the threshold of Isabetta's cell, while the
other hasted to the abbess's chamber, and knocking at the
door, roused her, and as soon as they heard her voice, said :—
" Up, Madam, without delay: we have discovered that Isabetta
has a young man with her in her cell."

Now that night the abbess had with her a priest whom she
used not seldom to have conveyed to her in a chest ; and the
report of the sisters making her apprehensive lest for excess of
zeal and hurry they should force the door open, she rose in a
trice ; and huddling on her clothes as best she might in the
dark, instead of the veil that they wear, which they call the
psalter, she caught up the priest's breeches, and having clapped
them on her head, hied her forth, and locked the door behind
her, saying :—" Where is this woman accursed of God ? "   And
so, guided by the sisters, all so agog to catch Isabetta a-sinning
that they perceived not what manner of headgear the abbess
wore, she made her way to the cell, and with their aid broke open
the door ; and entering they found the two lovers abed in one
another's arms ; who, as it were, thunderstruck to be thus
surprised, lay there, witting not what to do. The sisters took
the young nun forthwith, and by command of the abbess brought
her to the chapter-house. The gallant, left behind in the cell,
put on his clothes and waited to see how the affair would end,
being minded to make as many nuns as he might come at pay
dearly for any despite that might be done his mistress, and to
bring her off with him. The abbess, seated in the chapter-
house with all her nuns about her, and all eyes bent upon the
culprit, began giving her the severest reprimand that ever
woman got, for that by her disgraceful and abominable conduct
should it get wind, she had sullied the fair fame of the convent ;
whereto she added menaces most dire. Shamefast and timorous,
the culprit essayed no defence, and her silence begat pity of her

in the rest; but, while the abbess waxed more and more voluble, it chanced that the girl raised her head and espied the abbess's headgear, and the points that hung down on this side and that. The significance whereof being by no means lost upon her, she quite plucked up heart, and:—" Madam," quoth she, " so help you God, tie up your coif, and then you may say what you will to me." Whereto the abbess, not understanding her, replied:—" What coif, lewd woman? So thou hast the effrontery to jest! Think'st thou that what thou hast done is a matter meet for jests?" Whereupon:—" Madam," quoth the girl again, " I pray you, tie up your coif, and then you may say to me whatever you please." Which occasioned not a few of the nuns to look up at the abbess's head, and the abbess herself to raise her hands thereto, and so she and they at one and the same time apprehended Isabetta's meaning. Wherefore the abbess, finding herself detected by all in the same sin, and that no disguise was possible, changed her tone, and held quite another sort of language than before, the upshot of which was that 'twas impossible to withstand the assaults of the flesh, and that, accordingly, observing due secrecy as theretofore, all might give themselves a good time, as they had opportunity. So, having dismissed Isabetta to rejoin her lover in her cell, she herself returned to lie with her priest. And many a time thereafter, in spite of the envious, Isabetta had her gallant to see her, the others, that lacked lovers, doing in secret the best they might to push their fortunes.

NOVEL III

Master Simone, at the instance of Bruno and Buffalmacco and Nello, makes Calandrino believe that he is with child. Calandrino, accordingly, gives them capons and money for medicines, and is cured without being delivered.

WHEN Elisa had ended her story, and all had given thanks to God that He had vouchsafed the young nun a happy escape from the fangs of her envious companions, the queen bade Filostrato follow suit; and without expecting a second command, this Filostrato began:—Fairest my ladies, the uncouth judge from the Marches, of whom I told you yesterday, took from the tip of my tongue a story of Calandrino, which I was on the point of narrating : and as nought can be said of him without mightily enhancing our jollity, albeit not a little has already been said touching him and his comrades, I will now give you the story which I had meant yesterday to give you. Who they were, this Calandrino and the others that I am to tell of in this story, has already been sufficiently explained ; wherefore, without more ado, I say that one of Calandrino's aunts having died, leaving him two hundred pounds in petty cash, Calandrino gave out that he was minded to purchase an estate, and, as if he had had ten thousand florins of gold to invest, engaged every broker in Florence to treat for him, the negotiation always falling through, as soon as the price was named. Bruno and Buffalmacco, knowing what was afoot, told him again and again that he had better give himself a jolly time with them than go about buying earth as if he must needs make pellets ;[1] but so far were they from effecting their purpose, that they could not even prevail upon him to give them a single meal. Whereat as one day they grumbled, being joined by a comrade of theirs, one Nello, also a painter, they all three took counsel how they might wet their whistle at Calandrino's expense ; and, their plan being soon concerted, the next morning Calandrino was scarce gone out, when Nello met him, saying : —" Good day, Calandrino : " whereto Calandrino replied :— " God give thee a good day and a good year." Nello then drew back a little, and looked him steadily in the face, until :—" What seest thou to stare at ? " quoth Calandrino. " Hadst thou no pain in the night ? " returned Nello ; " thou seemest not thyself to me." Which Calandrino no sooner heard, than he began to be disquieted, and :—" Alas ! How sayst thou ? " quoth he. " What tak'st thou to be the matter with me ? " " Why, as to that I have nothing to say," returned Nello ; " but thou seemest to be quite changed : perchance 'tis not what I suppose ; " and with that he left him.

Calandrino, anxious, though he could not in the least have said why, went on ; and soon Buffalmacco, who was not far off, and had observed him part from Nello, made up to him, and greeted him, asking him if he was not in pain. " I cannot say," replied Calandrino ; " 'twas but now that Nello told me that I looked quite changed : can it be that there is aught the matter with me ? " " Aught ? " quoth Buffalmacco, " ay, indeed, there might be a trifle the matter with thee. Thou look'st to be half dead, man." Calandrino now began to think he must

---

[1] *I.e.* bolts of clay for the cross-bow.

have a fever. And then up came Bruno; and the first thing he said was:—"Why, Calandrino, how ill thou look'st! thy appearance is that of a corpse. How dost thou feel?" To be thus accosted by all three left no doubt in Calandrino's mind that he was ill, and so:—"What shall I do?" quoth he, in a great fright. "My advice," replied Bruno, "is that thou go home and get thee to bed and cover thee well up, and send thy water to Master Simone, who, as thou knowest, is such a friend of ours. He will tell thee at once what thou must do; and we will come to see thee, and will do aught that may be needful." And Nello then joining them, they all three went home with Calandrino, who, now quite spent, went straight to his room, and said to his wife:—"Come now, wrap me well up; I feel very ill." And so he laid himself on the bed, and sent a maid with his water to Master Simone, who had then his shop in the Mercato Vecchio, at the sign of the pumpkin. Whereupon quoth Bruno to his comrades:—"You will stay here with him, and I will go hear what the doctor has to say, and if need be, will bring him hither." "Prithee, do so, my friend," quoth Calandrino, "and bring me word how it is with me, for I feel as how I cannot say in my inside." So Bruno hied him to Master Simone, and before the maid arrived with the water, told him what was afoot. The Master, thus primed, inspected the water, and then said to the maid:—"Go tell Calandrino to keep himself very warm, and I will come at once, and let him know what is the matter with him and what he must do." With which message the maid was scarce returned when the Master and Bruno arrived, and the Master, having seated himself beside Calandrino, felt his pulse, and by and by, in the presence of his wife, said:—"Harkye, Calandrino, I speak to thee as a friend, and I tell thee that what is amiss with thee is just that thou art with child." Whereupon Calandrino cried out querulously:—"Woe's me! 'Tis thy doing, Tessa, for that thou must needs be uppermost: I told thee plainly what would come of it." Whereat the lady, being not a little modest, coloured from brow to neck, and with downcast eyes, withdrew from the room, saying never a word by way of answer. Calandrino ran on in the same plaintive strain:—"Alas! woe's me! What shall I do? How shall I be delivered of this child? What passage can it find? Ah! I see only too plainly that the lasciviousness of this wife of mine has been the death of me: God make her as wretched as I would fain be happy! Were I as well as I am not, I would get me up and thrash her, till

I left not a whole bone in her body, albeit it does but serve
me right for letting her get the upper place ; but if I do win
through this, she shall never have it again ; verily she might
pine to death for it, but she should not have it."

Which to hear, Bruno and Buffalmacco and Nello were like to
burst with suppressed laughter and Master Scimmione [1] laughed
so frantically, that all his teeth were ready to start from his
jaws. However, at length, in answer to Calandrino's appeals
and entreaties for counsel and succour :—" Calandrino," quoth
the Master, " thou mayst dismiss thy fears, for, God be praised,
we were apprised of thy state in such good time that with but
little trouble, in the course of a few days, I shall set thee right ;
but 'twill cost a little." " Woe's me," returned Calandrino,
" be it so, Master, for the love of God : I have here two hundred
pounds, with which I had thoughts of buying an estate : take
them all, all, if you must have all, so only I may escape being
delivered, for I know not how I should manage it, seeing that
women, albeit 'tis much easier for them, do make such a noise
in the hour of their labour, that I misdoubt me, if I suffered so,
I should die before I was delivered." " Disquiet not thyself,"
said the doctor : " I will have a potion distilled for thee ; of
rare virtue it is, and not a little palatable, and in the course of
three days 'twill purge thee of all, and leave thee in better fettle
than a fish ; but thou wilt do well to be careful thereafter, and
commit no such indiscretions again. Now to make this potion
we must have three pair of good fat capons, and, for divers other
ingredients, thou wilt give one of thy friends here five pounds
in small change to purchase them, and thou wilt have everything
sent to my shop, and so, please God, I will send thee this distilled
potion to-morrow morning, and thou wilt take a good beaker-
ful each time." Whereupon :—" Be it as you bid, Master mine,"
quoth Calandrino, and handing Bruno five pounds, and money
enough to purchase three pair of capons, he begged him, if it
were not too much trouble, to do him the service to buy these
things for him. So away went the doctor, and made a little
decoction by way of draught, and sent it him. Bruno bought
the capons and all else that was needed to furnish forth the feast,
with which he and his comrades and the doctor regaled them.
Calandrino drank of the decoction for three mornings, after
which he had a visit from his friends and the doctor, who felt
his pulse, and then :—" Beyond a doubt, Calandrino," quoth
he, " thou art cured, and so thou hast no more occasion to

1 *I.e.* great ape : with a play on Simone.

keep indoors, but needst have no fear to do whatever thou hast
a mind to." Much relieved, Calandrino got up, and resumed his
accustomed way of life, and, wherever he found any one to talk
to, was loud in praise of Master Simone for the excellent manner
in which he had cured him, causing him in three days without
the least suffering to be quit of his pregnancy. And Bruno
and Buffalmacco and Nello were not a little pleased with themselves that they had so cleverly got the better of Calandrino's
niggardliness, albeit Monna Tessa, who was not deceived, murmured not a little against her husband.

NOVEL IV

*Cecco, son of Messer Fortarrigo, loses his all at play at Buon-
convento, besides the money of Cecco, son of Messer Angiulieri ;
whom, running after him in his shirt and crying out that he
has robbed him, he causes to be taken by peasants : he then
puts on his clothes, mounts his palfrey, and leaves him to
follow in his shirt.*

ALL the company laughed beyond measure to hear what Calandrino said touching his wife : but, when Filostrato had done,
Neifile, being bidden by the queen, thus began :—Noble ladies,
were it not more difficult for men to evince their good sense and
virtue than their folly and their vice, many would labour in
vain to set bounds to their flow of words : whereof you have had
a most conspicuous example in poor blundering Calandrino, who,
for the better cure of that with which in his simplicity he supposed
himself to be afflicted, had no sort of need to discover in public
his wife's secret pleasures. Which affair has brought to my
mind one that fell out contrariwise, inasmuch as the guile of one
discomfited the good sense of another to the grievous loss and
shame of the discomfited : the manner whereof I am minded
to relate to you.

'Tis not many years since there were in Siena two young men,
both of age and both alike named Cecco, the one being son of
Messer Angiulieri, the other of Messer Fortarrigo. Who, albeit
in many other respects their dispositions accorded ill, agreed
so well in one, to wit, that they both hated their fathers, that
they became friends, and kept much together. Now Angiulieri,
being a pretty fellow, and well-mannered, could not brook

to live at Siena on the allowance made him by his father, and learning that there was come into the March of Ancona, as legate of the Pope, a cardinal, to whom he was much bounden, resolved to resort to him there, thinking thereby to improve his circumstances. So, having acquainted his father with his purpose, he prevailed upon him to give him there and then all that he would have given him during the next six months, that he might have the wherewith to furnish himself with apparel and a good mount, so as to travel in a becoming manner. And as he was looking out for some one to attend him as his servant, Fortarrigo, hearing of it, came presently to him and besought him with all earnestness to take him with him as his groom, or servant, or what he would, and he would be satisfied with his keep, without any salary whatsoever. Whereto Angiulieri made answer that he was not disposed to take him, not but that he well knew that he was competent for any service that might be required of him, but because he was given to play, and therewithal would at times get drunk. Fortarrigo assured him with many an oath that he would be on his guard to commit neither fault, and added thereto such instant entreaties, that Angiulieri was, as it were, vanquished, and consented. So one morning they took the road for Buonconvento, being minded there to breakfast. Now when Angiulieri had breakfasted, as 'twas a very hot day, he had a bed made in the inn, and having undressed with Fortarrigo's help, he composed himself to sleep, telling Fortarrigo to call him on the stroke of none. Angiulieri thus sleeping, Fortarrigo repaired to the tavern, where, having slaked his thirst, he sate down to a game with some that were there, who speedily won from him all his money, and thereafter in like manner all the clothes he had on his back: wherefore he, being anxious to retrieve his losses, went, stripped as he was to his shirt, to the room where lay Angiulieri; and seeing that he was sound asleep, he took from his purse all the money that he had, and so went back to the gaming-table, and staked it, and lost it all, as he had his own.

By and by Angiulieri awoke, and got up, and dressed, and called for Fortarrigo; and as Fortarrigo answered not, he supposed that he must have had too much to drink, and be sleeping it off somewhere, as was his wont. He accordingly determined to leave him alone; and doubting not to find a better servant at Corsignano, he let saddle his palfrey and attach the valise; but when, being about to depart, he would have paid the host, never a coin could he come by. Whereat there was

no small stir, so that all the inn was in an uproar, Angiulieri
averring that he had been robbed in the house, and threatening
to have them all arrested and taken to Siena ; when, lo, who
should make his appearance but Fortarrigo in his shirt, intent now
to steal the clothes, as he had stolen the moneys, of Angiulieri.
And marking that Angiulieri was accoutred for the road :—
"How is this, Angiulieri ? " quoth he.   "Are we to start so
soon ?   Nay, but wait a little.   One will be here presently that
has my doublet in pawn for thirty-eight soldi ; I doubt not he
will return it me for thirty-five soldi, if I pay money down."
And while they were yet talking, in came one that made it plain
to Angiulieri that 'twas Fortarrigo that had robbed him of his
money, for he told him the amount that Fortarrigo had lost.
Whereat Angiulieri, in a towering passion, rated Fortarrigo
right soundly, and, but that he stood more in fear of man than
of God, would have suited action to word ; and so, threatening
to have him hanged by the neck and proclaimed an outlaw at
the gallows-tree of Siena, he mounted his horse.

Fortarrigo, making as if 'twas not to him, but to another,
that Angiulieri thus spoke, made answer :—"Come now,
Angiulieri, we were best have done with all this idle talk, and
consider the matter of substance : we can redeem for thirty-
five soldi, if we pay forthwith, but if we wait till to-morrow, we
shall not get off with less than thirty-eight, the full amount of
the loan ; and 'tis because I staked by his advice that he will
make me this allowance.   Now why should not we save these
three soldi ? "   Whereat Angiulieri waxed well-nigh desperate,
more particularly that he marked that the bystanders were
scanning him suspiciously, as if, so far from understanding that
Fortarrigo had staked and lost his, Angiulieri's money, they
gave him credit for still being in funds : so he cried out :—
"What have I to do with thy doublet ?   'Tis high time thou
wast hanged by the neck, that, not content with robbing me
and gambling away my money, thou must needs also keep me
in parley here and make mock of me, when I would fain be gone."
Fortarrigo, however, still persisted in making believe that
Angiulieri did not mean this for him, and only said :—"Nay,
but why wilt not thou save me these three soldi ?   Think'st
thou I can be of no more use to thee ?   Prithee, an thou lov'st
me, do me this turn.   Wherefore in such a hurry ?   We have
time enough to get to Torrenieri this evening.   Come now, out
with thy purse.   Thou knowest I might search Siena through,
and not find a doublet that would suit me so well as this:

and for all I let him have it for thirty-eight soldi, 'tis worth forty or more ; so thou wilt wrong me twice over." Vexed beyond measure that, after robbing him, Fortarrigo should now keep him clavering about the matter, Angiulieri made no answer, but turned his horse's head, and took the road for Torrenieri. But Fortarrigo with cunning malice trotted after him in his shirt, and 'twas still his doublet that he would have of him : and when they had thus ridden two good miles, and Angiulieri was forcing the pace to get out of earshot of his pestering, Fortarrigo espied some husbandmen in a field beside the road a little ahead of Angiulieri, and fell a-shouting to them amain :—" Take thief ! take thief ! " Whereupon they came up with their spades and their mattocks, and barred Angiulieri's way, supposing that he must have robbed the man that came shouting after him in his shirt, and stopped him and apprehended him ; and little indeed did it avail him to tell them who he was, and how the matter stood. For up came Fortarrigo with a wrathful air, and :—" I know not," quoth he, " why I spare to kill thee on the spot, traitor, thief that thou art, thus to despoil me and give me the slip ! " And then, turning to the peasants :—" You see, gentlemen," quoth he, " in what a trim he left me in the inn, after gambling away all that he had with him and on him. Well indeed may I say that under God 'tis to you I owe it that I have thus come by my own again : for which cause I shall ever be beholden to you." Angiulieri also had his say ; but his words passed unheeded. Fortarrigo with the help of the peasants compelled him to dismount ; and having stripped him, donned his clothes, mounted his horse, and leaving him barefoot and in his shirt, rode back to Siena, giving out on all hands that he had won the palfrey and the clothes from Angiulieri. So Angiulieri, having thought to present himself to the cardinal in the March a wealthy man, returned to Buonconvento poor and in his shirt ; and being ashamed for the time to shew himself in Siena, pledged the nag that Fortarrigo had ridden for a suit of clothes, and betook him to his kinsfolk at Corsignano, where he tarried, until he received a fresh supply of money from his father. Thus, then, Fortarrigo's guile disconcerted Angiulieri's judicious purpose, albeit when time and occasion served, it was not left unrequited.

NOVEL V

Calandrino being enamoured of a damsel, Bruno gives him a scroll, averring that, if he but touch her therewith, she will go with him: he is found with her by his wife, who subjects him to a most severe and vexatious examination.

So, at no great length, ended Neifile her story, which the company allowed to pass with none too much laughter or remark: whereupon the queen, turning to Fiammetta, bade her follow suit.   Fiammetta, with mien most gladsome, made an answer that she willingly obeyed, and thus began:—As I doubt not, ye know, ladies most debonair, be the topic of discourse never so well worn, it will still continue to please, if the speaker knows how to make due choice of time and occasion meet.   Wherefore, considering the reason for which we are here (how that 'tis to make merry and speed the time gaily, and that merely) I deem that there is nought that may afford us mirth and solace but here may find time and occasion meet, and, after serving a thousand turns of discourse, should still prove not unpleasing for another thousand.   Wherefore, notwithstanding that of Calandrino and his doings not a little has from time to time been said among us, yet, considering that, as a while ago Filostrato observed, there is nought that concerns him that is not entertaining, I will make bold to add to the preceding stories another, which I might well, had I been minded to deviate from the truth, have disguised, and so recounted it to you, under other names; but as whoso in telling a story diverges from the truth does thereby in no small measure diminish the delight of his hearers, I purpose for the reason aforesaid to give you the narrative in proper form.

Niccolò Cornacchini, one of our citizens, and a man of wealth, had among other estates a fine one at Camerata, on which he had a grand house built, and engaged Bruno and Buffalmacco to paint it throughout; in which task, for that 'twas by no means light, they associated with them Nello and Calandrino, and so set to work.   There were a few rooms in the house provided with beds and other furniture, and an old female servant lived there as caretaker, but otherwise the house was unoccupied, for which cause Niccolò's son, Filippo, being a young man and a bachelor, was wont sometimes to bring thither a woman for his pleasure, and after keeping her there for a few days to escort her thence

again. Now on one of these occasions it befell that he brought
thither one Niccolosa, whom a vile fellow, named Mangione,
kept in a house at Camaldoli as a common prostitute. And a
fine piece of flesh she was, and wore fine clothes, and, for one
of her sort, knew how to comport herself becomingly and talk
agreeably.

Now one day at high noon forth tripped the damsel from her
chamber in a white gown, her locks braided about her head, to
wash her hands and face at a well that was in the courtyard of
the house, and, while she was so engaged, it befell that Calandrino
came there for water, and greeted her familiarly. Having
returned his salutation, she, rather because Calandrino struck
her as something out of the common, than for any other interest
she felt in him, regarded him attentively. Calandrino did the
like by her, and being smitten by her beauty, found reasons
enough why he should not go back to his comrades with the
water ; but, as he knew not who she was, he made not bold to
address her. She, upon whom his gaze was not lost, being
minded to amuse herself at his expense, let her glance from time
to time rest upon him, while she heaved a slight sigh or two.
Whereby Calandrino was forthwith captivated, and tarried in the
courtyard, until Filippo called her back into the chamber.
Returned to his work, Calandrino sighed like a furnace : which
Bruno, who was ever regardful of his doings for the diversion
they afforded him, failed not to mark, and by and by :—" What
the Devil is amiss with thee, comrade Calandrino ? " quoth he.
" Thou dost nought but puff and blow." " Comrade," replied
Calandrino, " I should be in luck, had I but one to help me."
" How so ? " quoth Bruno. " Why," returned Calandrino,
" 'tis not to go farther, but there is a damsel below, fairer than
a lamia, and so mightily in love with me that 'twould astonish
thee. I observed it but now, when I went to fetch the water."
" Nay, but, Calandrino, make sure she be not Filippo's wife,"
quoth Bruno. " I doubt 'tis even so," replied Calandrino,
" for he called her and she joined him in the chamber ; but what
signifies it ? I would circumvent Christ Himself in such case,
not to say Filippo. Of a truth, comrade, I tell thee she pleases
me I could not say how." " Comrade," returned Bruno, " I
will find out for thee who she is, and if she be Filippo's wife, two
words from me will make it all straight for thee, for she is much
my friend. But how shall we prevent Buffalmacco knowing
it ? I can never have a word with her, but he is with me."
" As to Buffalmacco," replied Calandrino, " I care not if he do

know it ; but let us make sure that it come not to Nello's ears,
for he is of kin to Monna Tessa, and would spoil it all." Whereto :—" Thou art in the right," returned Bruno.

Now Bruno knew what the damsel was, for he had seen her
arrive, and moreover Filippo had told him. So, Calandrino
having given over working for a while, and betaken him to
her, Bruno acquainted Nello and Buffalmacco with the whole
story ; and thereupon they privily concerted how to entreat
him in regard of this love affair. Wherefore, upon his return,
quoth Bruno softly :—" Didst see her ? " " Ay, woe's me ! "
replied Calandrino : " she has stricken me to the death."
Quoth Bruno :—" I will go see if she be the lady I take her to
be, and if I find that 'tis so, leave the rest to me." Whereupon
down went Bruno, and found Filippo and the damsel, and fully
apprised them what sort of fellow Calandrino was, and what he
had told them, and concerted with them what each should do
and say, that they might have a merry time together over
Calandrino's love affair. He then rejoined Calandrino, saying :
—" 'Tis the very same ; and therefore the affair needs very
delicate handling, for, if Filippo were but ware thereof, not all
Arno's waters would suffice to cleanse us. However, what
should I say to her from thee, if by chance I should get speech
of her ? " " I'faith," replied Calandrino, " why, first, first
of all, thou wilt tell her that I wish her a thousand bushels of
the good seed of generation, and then that I am her servant,
and if she is fain of—aught—thou tak'st me ? " " Ay," quoth
Bruno, " leave it to me."

Supper-time came ; and, the day's work done, they went
down into the courtyard, Filippo and Niccolosa being there,
and there they tarried a while to advance Calandrino's suit.
Calandrino's gaze was soon riveted on Niccolosa, and such and
so strange and startling were the gestures that he made that
they would have given sight to the blind. She on her part
used all her arts to inflame his passion, primed as she had been
by Bruno, and diverted beyond measure as she was by Calandrino's antics, while Filippo, Buffalmacco and the rest feigned
to be occupied in converse, and to see nought of what passed.
However, after a while, to Calandrino's extreme disgust, they
took their leave ; and as they bent their steps towards Florence :
—" I warrant thee," quoth Bruno to Calandrino, " she wastes
away for thee like ice in the sunlight ; by the body o' God, if
thou wert to bring thy rebeck, and sing her one or two of thy
love-songs, she'd throw herself out of window to be with thee."

Quoth Calandrino :—" Think'st thou, comrade, think'st thou, 'twere well I brought it ? " " Ay, indeed," returned Bruno. Whereupon :—" Ah ! comrade," quoth Calandrino, " so thou wouldst not believe me when I told thee to-day ? Of a truth I perceive there's ne'er another knows so well what he would be at as I. Who but I would have known how so soon to win the love of a lady like that ? Lucky indeed might they deem themselves, if they did it, those young gallants that go about, day and night, up and down, a-strumming on the one-stringed viol, and would not know how to gather a handful of nuts once in a millennium. Mayst thou be by to see when I bring her the rebeck ! thou wilt see fine sport. List well what I say : I am not so old as I look ; and she knows it right well : ay, and anyhow I will soon let her know it, when I come to grapple her. By the very body of Christ I will have such sport with her, that she will follow me as any love-sick maid follows her swain." " Oh ! " quoth Bruno, " I doubt not thou wilt make her thy prey : and I seem to see thee bite her dainty vermeil mouth and her cheeks, that shew as twin roses, with thy teeth, that are as so many lute-pegs, and afterwards devour her bodily." So encouraged, Calandrino fancied himself already in action, and went about singing and capering in such high glee that 'twas as if he would burst his skin. And so next day he brought the rebeck, and to the no small amusement of all the company sang several songs to her. And, in short, by frequently seeing her, he waxed so mad with passion that he gave over working ; and a thousand times a day he would run now to the window, now to the door, and anon to the courtyard on the chance of catching sight of her ; nor did she, astutely following Bruno's instructions, fail to afford him abundance of opportunity. Bruno played the go-between, bearing him her answers to all his messages, and sometimes bringing him messages from her. When she was not at home, which was most frequently the case, he would send him letters from her, in which she gave great encouragement to his hopes, at the same time giving him to understand that she was at the house of her kinsfolk, where as yet he might not visit her.

On this wise Bruno and Buffalmacco so managed the affair as to divert themselves inordinately, causing him to send her, as at her request, now an ivory comb, now a purse, now a little knife, and other such dainty trifles ; in return for which they brought him, now and again, a counterfeit ring of no value, with which Calandrino was marvellously pleased. And Calan-

drino, to stimulate their zeal in his interest, would entertain
them hospitably at table, and otherwise flatter them. Now,
when they had thus kept him in play for two good months, and
the affair was just where it had been, Calandrino, seeing that the
work was coming to an end, and bethinking him that, if it did
so before he had brought his love affair to a successful issue,
he must give up all hopes of ever so doing, began to be very
instant and importunate with Bruno. So, in the presence of
the damsel, and by preconcert with her and Filippo, quoth
Bruno to Calandrino :—" Harkye, comrade, this lady has vowed
to me a thousand times that she will do as thou wouldst have
her, and as, for all that, she does nought to pleasure thee, I am
of opinion that she leads thee by the nose : wherefore, as she
keeps not her promises, we will make her do so, willy-nilly, if
thou art so minded." " Nay, but, for the love of God, so be
it," replied Calandrino, " and that speedily." " Darest thou
touch her, then, with a scroll that I shall give thee ? " quoth
Bruno. " I dare," replied Calandrino. " Fetch me, then,"
quoth Bruno, " a bit of the skin of an unborn lamb, a live bat,
three grains of incense, and a blessed candle ; and leave the
rest to me." To catch the bat taxed all Calandrino's art and
craft for the whole of the evening ; but having at length taken
him, he brought him with the other matters to Bruno : who,
having withdrawn into a room by himself, wrote on the skin
some cabalistic jargon, and handed it to him, saying :—" Know,
Calandrino, that, if thou touch her with this scroll, she will
follow thee forthwith, and do whatever thou shalt wish. Wherefore, should Filippo go abroad to-day, get thee somehow up to
her, and touch her ; and then go into the barn that is hereby
—'tis the best place we have, for never a soul goes there—
and thou wilt see that she will come there too. When she is
there, thou wottest well what to do." Calandrino, overjoyed
as ne'er another, took the scroll, saying only :—" Comrade,
leave that to me."

Now Nello, whom Calandrino mistrusted, entered with no
less zest than the others into the affair, and was their confederate
for Calandrino's discomfiture ; accordingly by Bruno's direction
he hied to Florence, and finding Monna Tessa :—" Thou hast
scarce forgotten, Tessa," quoth he, " what a beating Calandrino
gave thee, without the least cause, that day when he came home
with the stones from Mugnone ; for which I would have thee
be avenged, and, so thou wilt not, call me no more kinsman or
friend. He is fallen in love with a lady up there, who is aban-

doned enough to go closeting herself not seldom with him, and
'tis but a short while since they made assignation to forgather
forthwith: so I would have thee go there, and surprise him in
the act, and give him a sound trouncing." Which when the
lady heard, she deemed it no laughing matter; but started
up and broke out with:—" Alas, the arrant knave! is't thus
he treats me? By the Holy Rood, never fear but I will pay
him out! " And wrapping herself in her cloak, and taking a
young woman with her for companion, she sped more at a
run than at a walk, escorted by Nello, up to Camerata. Bruno,
espying her from afar, said to Filippo:—" Lo, here comes our
friend." Whereupon Filippo went to the place where Calandrino and the others were at work, and said:—" My masters,
I must needs go at once to Florence; slacken not on that
account." And so off he went, and hid himself where, un-
observed, he might see what Calandrino would do. Calandrino
waited only until he saw that Filippo was at some distance,
and then he went down into the courtyard, where he found
Niccolosa alone, and fell a-talking with her. She, knowing
well what she had to do, drew close to him, and shewed him a
little more familiarity than she was wont: whereupon Calandrino touched her with the scroll, and having so done, saying
never a word, bent his steps towards the barn, whither Niccolosa
followed him, and being entered, shut the door, and forthwith
embraced him, threw him down on the straw that lay there,
and got astride of him, and holding him fast by the arms about
the shoulders, suffered him not to approach his face to hers,
but gazing upon him, as if he were the delight of her heart:—
" O Calandrino, sweet my Calandrino," quoth she, " heart of
my body, my very soul, my bliss, my consolation, ah! how long
have I yearned to hold thee in my arms and have thee all my
own! Thy endearing ways have utterly disarmed me; thou
hast made prize of my heart with thy rebeck. Do I indeed
hold thee in mine embrace? " Calandrino, scarce able to move,
murmured:—" Ah! sweet my soul, suffer me to kiss thee."
Whereto:—" Nay, but thou art too hasty," replied Niccolosa.
" Let me first feast mine eyes on thee; let me but sate them with
this sweet face of thine."

Meanwhile Bruno and Buffalmacco had joined Filippo, so
that what passed was seen and heard by all three. And while
Calandrino was thus intent to kiss Nissolosa, lo, up came Nello
with Monna Tessa. " By God, I swear they are both there,"
ejaculated Nello, as they entered the doorway; but the lady,

now fairly furious, laid hold of him and thrust him aside, and rushing in, espied Niccolosa astride of Calandrino. Niccolosa no sooner caught sight of the lady, than up she jumped, and in a trice was beside Filippo. Monna Tessa fell upon Calandrino, who was still on the floor, planted her nails in his face, and scratched it all over : she then seized him by the hair and haling him to and fro about the barn :—" Foul, pestilent cur," quoth she, " is this the way thou treatest me ? Thou old fool ! A murrain on the love I have borne thee ! Hast thou not enough to do at home, that thou must needs go falling in love with strange women ? And a fine lover thou wouldst make ! Dost not know thyself, knave ? Dost not know thyself, wretch ? Thou, from whose whole body 'twere not possible to wring enough sap for a sauce ! God's faith, 'twas not Tessa that got thee with child : God's curse on her, whoever she was : verily she must be a poor creature to be enamoured of a jewel of thy rare quality." At sight of his wife, Calandrino, suspended, as it were, between life and death, ventured no defence ; but, his face torn to shreds, his hair and clothes all disordered, fumbled about for his capuche, which having found, up he got, and humbly besought his wife not to publish the matter, unless she were minded that he should be cut to pieces, for that she that was with him was the wife of the master of the house. " Then God give her a bad year," replied the lady. Whereupon Bruno and Buffalmacco, who by this time had laughed their fill with Filippo and Niccolosa, came up as if attracted by the noise ; and after not a little ado pacified the lady, and counselled Calandrino to go back to Florence, and stay there, lest Filippo should get wind of the affair, and do him a mischief. So Calandrino, crestfallen and woebegone, got him back to Florence with his face torn to shreds ; where, daring not to shew himself at Camerata again, he endured day and night the grievous torment of his wife's vituperation. Such was the issue, to which, after ministering not a little mirth to his comrades, as also to Niccolosa and Filippo, this ardent lover brought his amour.

NOVEL VI

Two young men lodge at an inn, of whom the one lies with the host's daughter, his wife by inadvertence lying with the other. He that lay with the daughter afterwards gets into her father's bed and tells him all, taking him to be his comrade. They bandy words: whereupon the good woman, apprehending the circumstances, gets her to bed with her daughter, and by divers apt words re-establishes perfect accord.

CALANDRINO as on former occasions, so also on this, moved the company to laughter. However, when the ladies had done talking of his doings, the queen called for a story from Pamfilo, who thus spoke :—Worshipful ladies, this Niccolosa, that Calandrino loved, has brought to my mind a story of another Niccolosa ; which I am minded to tell you, because 'twill shew you how a good woman by her quick apprehension avoided a great scandal.

In the plain of Mugnone there was not long ago a good man that furnished travellers with meat and drink for money, and, for that he was in poor circumstances, and had but a little house, gave not lodging to every comer, but only to a few that he knew, and if they were hard bested. Now the good man had to wife a very fine woman, and by her had two children, to wit, a pretty and winsome girl of some fifteen or sixteen summers, as yet unmarried, and a little boy, not yet one year old, whom the mother suckled at her own breast. The girl had found favour in the eyes of a goodly and mannerly young gentleman of our city, who was not seldom in those parts, and loved her to the point of passion. And she, being mightily flattered to be loved by such a gallant, studied how to comport herself so debonairly as to retain his regard, and while she did so, grew likewise enamoured of him ; and divers times, by consent of both, their love had had its fruition, but that Pinuccio —such was the gallant's name—shrank from the disgrace that 'twould bring upon the girl and himself alike. But, as his passion daily waxed apace, Pinuccio, yearning to find himself abed with her, bethought him that he were best contrive to lodge with her father, deeming, from what he knew of her father's economy, that, if he did so, he might effect his purpose, and never a soul be the wiser : which idea no sooner struck him, than he set about carrying it into effect.

So, late one evening Pinuccio and a trusty comrade, Adriano by name, to whom he had confided his love, hired two nags, and having set upon them two valises, filled with straw or such-like stuff, sallied forth of Florence, and rode by a circuitous route to the plain of Mugnone, which they reached after night-fall; and having fetched a compass, so that it might seem as if they were coming from Romagna, they rode up to the good man's house, and knocked at the door. The good man, know-ing them both very well, opened to them forthwith: where-upon:—" Thou must even put us up to-night," quoth Pinuccio; " we thought to get into Florence, but, for all the speed we could make, we are but arrived here, as thou seest, at this hour." " Pinuccio," replied the host, " thou well knowest that I can but make a sorry shift to lodge gentlemen like you; but yet, as night has overtaken you here, and time serves not to betake you elsewhere, I will gladly give you such accommoda-tion as I may." The two gallants then dismounted and entered the inn, and having first looked to their horses, brought out some supper that they had carried with them, and supped with the host.

Now the host had but one little bedroom, in which were three beds, set, as conveniently as he could contrive, two on one side of the room, and the third on the opposite side, but, for all that, there was scarce room enough to pass through. The host had the least discomfortable of the three beds made up for the two friends; and having quartered them there, some little while afterwards, both being awake, but feigning to be asleep, he caused his daughter to get into one of the other two beds, while he and his wife took their places in the third, the good woman setting the cradle, in which was her little boy, beside the bed. Such, then, being the partition made of the beds, Pinuccio, who had taken exact note thereof, waited only until he deemed all but himself to be asleep, and then got softly up and stole to the bed in which lay his beloved, and laid himself beside her; and she according him albeit a timorous yet a gladsome welcome, he stayed there, taking with her that solace of which both were most fain.

Pinuccio being thus with the girl, it chanced that certain things, being overset by a cat, fell with a noise that aroused the good woman, who, fearing that it might be a matter of more consequence, got up as best she might in the dark, and betook her to the place whence the noise seemed to proceed. At the same time Adriano, not by reason of the noise, which he heeded not, but perchance to answer the call of nature, also got up, and questing about for a convenient place, came upon the cradle beside the good woman's bed ; and not being able otherwise to go by, took it up, and set it beside his own bed, and when he had accomplished his purpose, went back, and giving never a thought to the cradle got him to bed. The good woman searched until she found that the accident was no such matter as she had supposed ; so without troubling to strike a light to investigate it further, she reproved the cat, and returned to the room, and groped her way straight to the bed in which her husband lay asleep ; but not finding the cradle there, quoth she to herself :—Alas ! blunderer that I am, what was I about ? God's faith ! I was going straight to the guest's bed ; and proceeding a little further, she found the cradle, and laid herself down by Adriano in the bed that was beside it, taking Adriano for her husband ; and Adriano, who was still awake, received her with all due benignity, and tackled her more than once to her no small delight.

Meanwhile Pinuccio fearing lest sleep should overtake him while he was yet with his mistress, and having satisfied his desire, got up and left her, to return to his bed ; but when he got there, coming upon the cradle, he supposed that 'twas the host's bed ; and so going a little further, he laid him down beside the host, who thereupon awoke. Supposing that he had Adriano beside him :—" I warrant thee," quoth Pinuccio to the host, " there was never so sweet a piece of flesh as Niccolosa : by the body of God, such delight have I had of her as never had man of woman ; and, mark me, since I left thee, I have gotten me up to the farm some six times." Which tidings the host being none too well pleased to learn, said first of all to himself :—What the Devil does this fellow here ? Then, his resentment getting the better of his prudence :— " 'Tis a gross affront thou hast put upon me, Pinuccio," quoth he ; " nor know I what occasion thou hast to do me such a wrong ; but by the body of God I will pay thee out." Pinuccio, who was not the most discreet of gallants, albeit he was now apprised of his error, instead of doing his best to repair it, retorted :—" And how wilt thou pay me out ? What canst thou do ? " " Hark what high words our guests are at together ! " quoth meanwhile the host's wife to Adriano, deeming that she spoke to her husband. " Let them be," replied Adriano with a laugh : " God give them a bad year : they drank too much yestereve." The good woman had already

half recognized her husband's angry tones, and now that she
heard Adriano's voice, she at once knew where she was and
with whom. Accordingly, being a discreet woman, she started
up, and saying never a word, took her child's cradle, and, though
there was not a ray of light in the room, bore it, divining rather
than feeling her way, to the side of the bed in which her daughter
slept ; and then, as if aroused by the noise made by her husband,
she called him, and asked what he and Pinuccio were bandying
words about. "Hearest thou not," replied the husband,
"what he says he has this very night done to Niccolosa ?"
"Tush ! he lies in the throat," returned the good woman :
"he has not lain with Niccolosa ; for what time he might have
done so, I laid me beside her myself, and I have been wide
awake ever since ; and thou art a fool to believe him. You
men take so many cups before going to bed that then you dream,
and walk in your sleep, and imagine wonders. 'Tis a great
pity you do not break your necks. What does Pinuccio there ?
Why keeps he not in his own bed ?"

Whereupon Adriano, in his turn, seeing how adroitly the
good woman cloaked her own and her daughter's shame :—
"Pinuccio," quoth he, "I have told thee a hundred times,
that thou shouldst not walk about at night ; for this thy bad
habit of getting up in thy dreams and relating thy dreams for
truth will get thee into a scrape some time or another : come
back, and God send thee a bad night." Hearing Adriano thus
confirm what his wife had said, the host began to think that
Pinuccio must be really dreaming ; so he took him by the
shoulder, and fell a-shaking him, and calling him by his name,
saying :—" Pinuccio, wake up, and go back to thy bed."
Pinuccio, taking his cue from what he had heard, began as a
dreamer would be like to do, to talk wanderingly ; whereat
the host laughed amain. Then, feigning to be aroused by the
shaking, Pinuccio uttered Adriano's name, saying :—" Is't
already day, that thou callest me ?" "Ay, 'tis so," quoth
Adriano : "come hither." Whereupon Pinuccio, making as
if he were mighty drowsy, got him up from beside the host,
and back to bed with Adriano. On the morrow, when they
were risen, the host fell a-laughing and making merry touching
Pinuccio and his dreams. And so the jest passed from mouth
to mouth, while the gallants' horses were groomed and saddled,
and their valises adjusted : which done, they drank with the
host, mounted and rode to Florence, no less pleased with the
manner than with the matter of the night's adventure. Nor,

afterwards, did Pinuccio fail to find other means of meeting
Niccolosa, who assured her mother that he had unquestionably
dreamed. For which cause the good woman, calling to mind
Adriano's embrace, accounted herself the only one that had
watched.

NOVEL VII

*Talano di Molese dreams that a wolf tears and rends all the neck
and face of his wife: he gives her warning thereof, which
she heeds not, and the dream comes true.*

When Pamfilo had brought his story to a close, and all had commended the good woman's quick perception, the queen bade
Pampinea tell hers; and thus Pampinea began:—A while
ago, debonair my ladies, we held discourse of the truths that
dreams shew forth, which not a few of us deride; for which
cause, albeit the topic has been handled before, I shall not
spare to tell you that which not long ago befell a neighbour
of mine, for that she disbelieved a dream that her husband
had.

I wot not if you knew Talano di Molese, a man right worthy
to be had in honour; who, having married a young wife—
Margarita by name—fair as e'er another, but without her match
for whimsical, fractious, and perverse humours, insomuch that
there was nought she would do at the instance of another,
either for his or her own good, found her behaviour most
grievous to bear, but was fain to endure what he might not
cure. Now it so befell that Talano and Margarita being
together at an estate that Talano had in the contado, he,
sleeping, saw in a dream a very beautiful wood that was on the
estate at no great distance from the house, and his lady there
walking. And as she went, there leapt forth upon her a huge
and fierce wolf that griped her by the throat, and bore her
down to the ground, and (she shrieking the while for succour)
would have carried her off by main force; but she got quit
of his jaws, albeit her neck and face shewed as quite disfigured.
On the morrow, as soon as he was risen, Talano said to his
wife:—" Albeit for thy perversity I have not yet known a single
good day with thee, yet I should be sorry, wife, that harm

should befall thee ; and therefore, if thou take my advice, thou wilt not stir out of doors to-day." "Wherefore?" quoth the lady ; and thereupon he recounted to her all his dream.

The lady shook her head, saying :—"Who means ill, dreams ill. Thou makest as if thou wast mighty tender of me, but thou bodest of me in thy dream that which thou wouldst fain see betide me. I warrant thee that to-day and all days I will have a care to avoid this or any other calamity that might gladden thy heart." Whereupon :—"Well wist I," replied Talano, " that thou wouldst so say, for such is ever the requital of those that comb scurfy heads ; but whatever thou mayst be pleased to believe, I for my part speak to thee for thy good, and again I advise thee to keep indoors to-day, or at least not to walk in the wood." "Good," returned the lady, " I will look to it," and then she began communing with herself on this wise :—Didst mark how artfully he thinks to have scared me from going into the wood to-day ? Doubtless 'tis that he has an assignation there with some light o' love, with whom he had rather I did not find him. Ah ! he would sup well with the blind, and what a fool were I to believe him ! But I warrant he will be disappointed, and needs must I, though I stay there all day long, see what commerce it is that he will adventure in to-day.

Having so said she quitted the house on one side, while her husband did so on the other ; and forthwith, shunning observation as best she might, she hied her to the wood, and hid her where 'twas most dense, and there waited on the alert, and glancing, now this way and now that, to see if any were coming. And while thus she stood, nor ever a thought of a wolf crossed her mind, lo, forth of a close covert hard by came a wolf of monstrous size and appalling aspect, and scarce had she time to say, God help me ! before he sprang upon her and griped her by the throat so tightly that she might not utter a cry, but, passive as any lambkin, was borne off by him, and had certainly been strangled, had he not encountered some shepherds, who with shouts compelled him to let her go. The shepherds recognized the poor hapless woman, and bore her home, where the physicians by dint of long and careful treatment cured her ; howbeit the whole of her throat and part of her face remained so disfigured that, fair as she had been before, she was ever thereafter most foul and hideous to look upon. Wherefore, being ashamed to shew her face, she did many a time bitterly deplore her perversity, in that, when it would have cost her nothing, she would nevertheless pay no heed to the true dream of her husband.

NOVEL VIII

Biondello gulls Ciacco in the matter of a breakfast: for which prank Ciacco is cunningly avenged on Biondello, causing him to be shamefully beaten.

ALL the company by common consent pronounced it no dream but a vision that Talano had had in his sleep, so exactly, no circumstance lacking, had it fallen out according as he had seen it. However, as soon as all had done speaking, the queen bade Lauretta follow suit; which Lauretta did on this wise:—As, most discreet my ladies, those that have preceded me to-day have almost all taken their cue from somewhat that has been said before, so, prompted by the stern vengeance taken by the scholar in Pampinea's narrative of yesterday, I am minded to tell you of a vengeance that was indeed less savage, but for all that grievous enough to him on whom it was wreaked.

Wherefore I say that there was once at Florence one that all folk called Ciacco, a man second to none that ever lived for inordinate gluttony, who, lacking the means to support the expenditure which his gluttony demanded, and being, for the rest, well-mannered and well furnished with excellent and merry jests, did, without turning exactly court jester, cultivate a somewhat biting wit, and loved to frequent the houses of the rich, and such as kept good tables; whither, bidden or unbidden, he not seldom resorted for breakfast or supper. There was also in those days at Florence one that was called Biondello, a man very short of stature, and not a little debonair, more trim than any fly, with his blond locks surmounted by a coif, and never a hair out of place; and he and Ciacco were two of a trade.

Now one morning in Lent Biondello, being in the fish-market purchasing two mighty fat lampreys for Messer Vieri de' Cerchi, was observed thus engaged by Ciacco, who came up to him, and:—"What means this?" quoth he. "Why," replied Biondello, " 'tis that yestereve Messer Corso Donati had three lampreys much finer than these and a sturgeon sent to his house, but as they did not suffice for a breakfast that he is to give certain gentlemen, he has commissioned me to buy him

these two beside. Wilt thou not be there?" "Ay, marry,
that will I," returned Ciacco. And in what he deemed due
time he hied him to Messer Corso Donati's house, where he
found him with some of his neighbours not yet gone to breakfast. And being asked by Messer Corso with what intent he
was come, he answered :—"I am come, Sir, to breakfast with
you and your company." "And welcome art thou," returned
Messer Corso, "go we then to breakfast, for 'tis now the time."
So to table they went, where nought was set before them but
pease and the inward part of the tunny salted, and afterwards
the common fish of the Arno fried. Wherefore Ciacco, not a
little wroth at the trick that he perceived Biondello had played
him, resolved to pay him out. And not many days after Biondello, who had meanwhile had many a laugh with his friends
over Ciacco's discomfiture, met him, and after greeting him,
asked him with a laugh what Messer Corso's lampreys had been
like. "That question," replied Ciacco, "thou wilt be able to
answer much better than I before eight days are gone by."
And parting from Biondello upon the word, he went forthwith
and hired a cozening rogue, and having thrust a glass bottle
into his hand, brought him within sight of the Loggia de'
Cavicciuli ; and there, pointing to a knight, one Messer Filippo
Argenti, a tall man and stout, and of a high courage,
and haughty, choleric and cross-grained as ne'er another, he
said to him :—"Thou wilt go, flask in hand, to Messer Filippo,
and wilt say to him :—'I am sent to you, Sir, by Biondello,
who entreats you to be pleased to colour this flask for him with
some of your good red wine, for that he is minded to have a
good time with his catamites.' And of all things have a care
that he lay not hands upon thee, for he would make thee rue
the day, and would spoil my sport." "Have I aught else to
say ?" enquired the rogue. "Nothing more," returned Ciacco :
"and now get thee gone, and when thou hast delivered the
message, bring me back the flask, and I will pay thee."

So away went the rogue, and did the errand to Messer Filippo,
who forthwith, being a hasty man, jumped to the conclusion
that Biondello, whom he knew, was making mock of him, and
while an angry flush overspread his face :—"'Colour the flask,
forsooth !'" quoth he, "and 'Catamites !' God send thee and
him a bad year !" and therewith up he started, and reached
forward to lay hold of the rogue, who, being on the alert, gave
him the slip and was off, and reported Messer Filippo's answer
to Ciacco, who had observed what had passed. Having paid

the rogue, Ciacco rested not until he had found Biondello, to whom :—"Wast thou but now," quoth he, "at the Loggia de' Cavicciuli ? " "Indeed no," replied Biondello : "wherefore such a question ? " "Because," returned Ciacco, "I may tell thee that thou art sought for by Messer Filippo, for what cause I know not." "Good," quoth Biondello, "I will go thither and speak with him." So away went Biondello, and Ciacco followed him to see what course the affair would take.

Now having failed to catch the rogue, Messer Filippo was still very wroth, and inly fumed and fretted, being unable to make out aught from what the rogue had said save that Biondello was set on by some one or another to flout him. And while thus he vexed his spirit, up came Biondello ; whom he no sooner espied than he made for him, and dealt him a mighty blow in the face, and tore his hair and coif, and cast his capuche on the ground, and to his " Alas, Sir, what means this ? " still beating him amain :—" Traitor," cried he ; " I will give thee to know what it means to send me such a message. 'Colour the flask,' forsooth, and 'Catamites !' Dost take me for a stripling, to be befooled by thee ? " And therewith he pummelled Biondello's face all over with a pair of fists that were liker to iron than aught else, until it was but a mass of bruises ; he also tore and dishevelled all his hair, tumbled him in the mud, rent all his clothes upon his back, and that without allowing him breathing-space to ask why he thus used him, or so much as utter a word. " Colour me the flask !" and " Catamites !" rang in his ears ; but what the words signified he knew not. In the end very badly beaten, and in very sorry and ragged trim, many folk having gathered around them, they, albeit not without the utmost difficulty, rescued him from Messer Filippo's hands, and told him why Messer Filippo had thus used him, censuring him for sending him such a message, and adding that thenceforth he would know Messer Filippo better, and that he was not a man to be trifled with. Biondello told them in tearful exculpation that he had never sent for wine to Messer Filippo : then, when they had put him in a little better trim, crestfallen and woebegone, he went home imputing his misadventure to Ciacco. And when, many days afterwards, the marks of his ill-usage being gone from his face, he began to go abroad again, it chanced that Ciacco met him, and with a laugh :—" Biondello," quoth he, " how didst thou relish Messer Filippo's wine ? " " Why, as to that," replied Biondello, " would thou hadst relished the lampreys of Messer Corso as much ! " " So !" returned Ciacco, "such meat as thou then gavest me, thou mayst henceforth give me, as often as thou art so minded ; and I will give thee even such drink as I have given thee." So Biondello, witting that against Ciacco his might was not equal to his spite, prayed God for his peace, and was careful never to flout him again.

NOVEL IX

Two young men ask counsel of Solomon ; the one, how he is to make himself beloved, the other, how he is to reduce an unruly wife to order. The King bids the one to love, and the other to go to the Bridge of Geese.

NONE now remained to tell save the queen, unless she were minded to infringe Dioneo's privilege. Wherefore, when the ladies had laughed their fill over the misfortunes of Biondello, thus gaily the queen began :—Observe we, lovesome ladies, the order of things with a sound mind, and we shall readily perceive that we women are one and all subjected by Nature and custom and law unto man, by him to be ruled and governed at his discretion ; wherefore she, that would fain enjoy quietude and solace and comfort with the man to whom she belongs, ought not only to be chaste but lowly, patient and obedient : the which is the discreet wife's chief and most precious possession. And if the laws, which in all matters have regard unto the common weal, and use and wont or custom (call it what you will), a power very great and to be had in awe, should not suffice to school us thereto ; yet abundantly clear is the witness of Nature, which has fashioned our frames delicate and sensitive, and our spirits timorous and fearful, and has decreed that our bodily strength shall be slight, our voices tunable, and our movements graceful ; which qualities do all avouch that we have need of others' governance. And whoso has need of succour and governance ought in all reason to be obedient and submissive and reverent towards his governor. And whom have we to govern and succour us save men ? 'Tis then our bounden duty to give men all honour and submit ourselves unto them : from which rule if any deviate, I deem her most deserving not only of grave censure but of severe chastisement. Which reflections, albeit they are not new to me, I am now led to make by what but a little while ago Pampinea told us touching the perverse wife of Talano, on whom God bestowed that chastisement which the husband had omitted; and accordingly it jumps with my judgment that all such women as deviate from the graciousness, kindliness and compliancy, which Nature and custom and law prescribe, merit, as I said, stern and severe chastisement. Wherefore, as a salutary medicine for the healing of those of us who may be afflicted with this disease, I am minded to relate to you that which was once delivered by Solomon by way of counsel in such a case. Which let none that stands not in need of such physic deem to be meant for her, albeit a proverb is current among men; to wit:—

> Good steed, bad steed, alike need the rowel's prick,
> Good wife, bad wife, alike demand the stick.

Which whoso should construe as a merry conceit would find you all ready enough to acknowledge its truth. But even in its moral significance I say that it ought to command assent. For women are all by nature apt to be swayed and to fall; and therefore, for the correction of the wrong-doing of such as transgress the bounds assigned to them, there is need of the stick punitive; and also for the maintenance of virtue in others, that they transgress not these appointed bounds, there is need of the stick auxiliary and deterrent. However, to cut short this preachment, and to come to that which I purpose to tell you, I say:—

That the bruit of the incomparable renown of the prodigious wisdom of Solomon, as also of the exceeding great liberality with which he accorded proof thereof to all that craved such assurance, being gone forth over well-nigh all the earth, many from divers parts were wont to resort to him for counsel in matters of most pressing and arduous importance; among whom was a young man, Melisso by name, a very wealthy nobleman, who was, as had been his fathers before him, of Lazistan, and there dwelt. And as Melisso fared toward Jerusalem, on his departure from Antioch he fell in with another young man, Giosefo by name, who was going the same way, and with whom, after the manner of travellers, he entered into converse. Melisso, having learned from Giosefo, who and whence he was, asked him whither he went, and on what errand: whereupon Giosefo made an answer that he was going to seek counsel of Solomon, how he should deal with his wife, who had not her match among women for unruliness and perversity, insomuch that neither entreaties nor blandishments nor aught else availed

him to bring her to a better frame. And thereupon he in like
manner asked Melisso whence he was, and whither he was bound,
and on what errand: whereto:—" Of Lazistan, I," replied
Melisso, " and like thyself in evil plight; for albeit I am wealthy
and spend my substance freely in hospitably entertaining and
honourably entreating my fellow-citizens, yet for all that,
passing strange though it be to think upon, I find never a soul
to love me; and therefore I am bound to the self-same place
as thou, to be advised how it may come to pass that I be
beloved."

So the two men fared on together, and being arrived at
Jerusalem, were, by the good offices of one of Solomon's barons,
ushered into his presence, and Melisso having briefly laid his
case before the King, was answered in one word:—" Love."
Which said, Melisso was forthwith dismissed, and Giosefo
discovered the reason of his coming. To whom Solomon made
no answer but:—" Get thee to the Bridge of Geese." Whereupon Giosefo was likewise promptly ushered out of the King's
presence, and finding Melisso awaiting him, told him what
manner of answer he had gotten. Which utterances of the King
the two men pondered, but finding therein nought that was
helpful or relevant to their need, they doubted the King had
but mocked them, and set forth upon their homeward journey.

Now when they had been some days on the road, they came
to a river, which was spanned by a fine bridge, and a great
caravan of sumpter mules and horses being about to cross,
they must needs tarry, until the caravan had passed by. The
more part of which had done so, when it chanced that a mule
turned sulky, as we know they will not seldom do, and stood
stock still; wherefore a muleteer took a stick and fell a-beating
the mule therewith, albeit at first with no great vigour, to urge
the mule forward. The mule, however, swerving, now to this,
now to the other side of the bridge, and sometimes facing about,
utterly refused to go forward. Whereat the muleteer, wroth
beyond measure, fell a-belabouring him with the stick now on
the head, now on the flanks, and anon on the croup, never so
lustily, but all to no purpose. Which caused Melisso and
Giosefo ofttimes to say to him:—" How now, caitiff? What
is this thou doest? Wouldst kill the beast? Why not try
if thou canst not manage him kindly and gently? He would
start sooner so than for this cudgelling of thine." To whom:
—" You know your horses," replied the muleteer, " and I
know my mule: leave me to deal with him." Which said, he

resumed his cudgelling of the mule, and laid about him on this side and on that to such purpose that he started him; and so the honours of the day rested with the muleteer. Now, as the two young men were leaving the bridge behind them, Giosefo asked a good man that sate at its head what the bridge was called, and was answered:—"Sir, 'tis called the Bridge of Geese." Which Giosefo no sooner heard than he called to mind Solomon's words, and turning to Melisso:—"Now, comrade, I warrant thee I may yet find Solomon's counsel sound and good, for that I knew not how to beat my wife is abundantly clear to me; and this muleteer has shewn me what I have to do."

Now some days afterwards they arrived at Antioch, where Giosefo prevailed upon Melisso to tarry with him and rest a day or two; and meeting with but a sorry welcome on the part of his wife, he told her to take her orders as to supper from Melisso, who, seeing that such was Giosefo's will, briefly gave her his instructions; which the lady, as had been her wont, not only did not obey, but contravened in almost every particular. Which Giosefo marking:—"Wast thou not told," quoth he angrily, "after what fashion thou wast to order the supper?" Whereto:—"So!" replied the lady haughtily: "what means this? If thou hast a mind to sup, why take not thy supper? No matter what I was told, 'tis thus I saw fit to order it. If it like thee, so be it: if not, 'tis thine affair." Melisso heard the lady with surprise and inward disapprobation: Giosefo retorted:—"Ay, wife, thou art still as thou wast used to be; but I will make thee mend thy manners." Then, turning to Melisso:—"Friend," quoth he, "thou wilt soon prove the worth of Solomon's counsel: but, prithee, let it not irk thee to look on, and deem that what I shall do is but done in sport; and if thou shouldst be disposed to stand in my way, bear in mind how we were answered by the muleteer, when we pitied his mule." "I am in thy house," replied Melisso, "and thy pleasure is to me law."

Thereupon Giosefo took a stout cudgel cut from an oak sapling, and hied him into the room whither the lady had withdrawn from the table in high dudgeon, seized her by the hair, threw her on to the floor at his feet, and fell a-beating her amain with the cudgel. The lady at first uttered a shriek or two, from which she passed to threats; but seeing that, for all that, Giosefo slackened not, by the time she was thoroughly well thrashed, she began to cry him mercy, imploring him not to kill her, and adding that henceforth his will should be to her for law. But still Giosefo gave not over, but with ever fresh fury dealt her mighty swingeing blows, now about the ribs, now on the haunches, now over the shoulders ; nor had he done with the fair lady, until, in short, he had left never a bone or other part of her person whole, and he was fairly spent. Then, returning to Melisso :—" To-morrow," quoth he, " we shall see whether ' Get thee to the Bridge of Geese ' will prove to have been sound advice or no." And so, having rested a while, and then washed his hands, he supped with Melisso. With great pain the poor lady got upon her feet and laid herself on her bed, and having there taken such rest as she might, rose betimes on the morrow, and craved to know of Giosefo what he was minded to have to breakfast. Giosefo, laughing with Melisso over the message, gave her his directions, and when in due time they came to breakfast, they found everything excellently ordered according as it had been commanded : for which cause the counsel, which they had at first failed to understand, now received their highest commendation.

Some few days later Melisso, having taken leave of Giosefo, went home, and told a wise man the counsel he had gotten from Solomon. Whereupon :—" And no truer or sounder advice could he have given thee," quoth the sage : " thou knowest that thou lovest never a soul, and that the honours thou payest and the services thou renderest to others are not prompted by love of them, but by love of display. Love, then, as Solomon bade thee, and thou shalt be loved." On such wise was the unruly chastised ; and the young man, learning to love, was beloved.

NOVEL X

*Dom Gianni at the instance of his gossip Pietro uses an enchant-
    ment to transform Pietro's wife into a mare ; but, when he
    comes to attach the tail, Gossip Pietro, by saying that he will
    have none of the tail, makes the enchantment of no effect.*

THE queen's story evoked some murmurs from the ladies and some laughter from the young men ; however, when they were silent, Dioneo thus began :—Dainty my ladies, a black crow among a flock of white doves enhances their beauty more than

would a white swan ; and so, when many sages are met together,
their ripe wisdom not only shews the brighter and goodlier for
the presence of one that is not so wise, but may even derive
pleasure and diversion therefrom. Wherefore as you, my
ladies, are one and all most discreet and judicious, I, who know
myself to be somewhat scant of sense, should, for that by my
demerit I make your merit shew the more glorious, be more
dear to you, than if by my greater merit I eclipsed yours, and
by consequence should have more ample license to reveal myself
to you as I am ; and therefore have more patient sufferance on
your part than would be due to me, were I more discreet, in the
relation of the tale which I am about to tell you. 'Twill be,
then, a story none too long, wherefrom you may gather with
what exactitude it behoves folk to observe the injunctions of
those that for any purpose use an enchantment, and how slight
an error committed therein may bring to nought all the work
of the enchanter.

A year or so ago there was at Barletta a priest named Dom
Gianni di Barolo, who, to eke out the scanty pittance his church
afforded him, set a pack-saddle upon his mare, and took to going
the round of the fairs of Apulia, buying and selling merchandise.
And so it befell that he clapped up a close acquaintance with
one Pietro da Tresanti, who plied the same trade as he, albeit
instead of a mare he had but an ass ; whom in token of friendship and good-fellowship Dom Gianni after the Apulian fashion
called ever Gossip Pietro, and had him to his house and there
lodged and honourably entreated him as often as he came to
Barletta. Gossip Pietro on his part, albeit he was very poor
and had but a little cot at Tresanti that scarce sufficed for himself, his fair, young wife, and their ass, nevertheless, whenever
Dom Gianni arrived at Tresanti, made him welcome, and did
him the honours of his house as best he might, in requital of the
hospitality which he received at Barletta. However, as Gossip
Pietro had but one little bed, in which he slept with his fair
wife, 'twas not in his power to lodge Dom Gianni as comfortably
as he would have liked ; but the priest's mare being quartered
beside the ass in a little stable, the priest himself must needs
lie beside her on the straw. Many a time when the priest came,
the wife, knowing how honourably he entreated her husband at
Barletta, would fain have gone to sleep with a neighbour, one
Zita Carapresa di Giudice Leo, that the priest might share the
bed with her husband, and many a time had she told the priest
so : howbeit he would never agree to it, and on one occasion :—

" Gossip Gemmata," quoth he, " trouble not thyself about me ;
I am well lodged ; for, when I am so minded, I turn the mare
into a fine lass and dally with her, and then, when I would, I
turn her back into a mare ; wherefore I could ill brook to part
from her." The young woman, wondering but believing, told
her husband what the priest had said, adding :—" If he is even
such a friend as thou sayst, why dost thou not get him to teach
thee the enchantment, so that thou mayst turn me into a mare,
and have both ass and mare for thine occasions ? We should
then make twice as much gain as we do, and thou couldst turn
me back into a woman when we came home at night."

Gossip Pietro, whose wit was somewhat blunt, believed that
'twas as she said, approved her counsel, and began adjuring
Dom Gianni, as persuasively as he might, to teach him the
incantation.   Dom Gianni did his best to wean him of his folly ;
but as all was in vain :—" Lo, now," quoth he, " as you are both
bent on it, we will be up, as is our wont, before the sun to-
morrow morning, and I will shew you how 'tis done.   The truth
is that 'tis in the attachment of the tail that the great difficulty
lies, as thou wilt see."   Scarce a wink of sleep had either
Gossip Pietro or Gossip Gemmata that night, so great was their
anxiety ; and towards daybreak up they got, and called Dom
Gianni ; who, being risen, came in his shirt into Gossip Pietro's
little bedroom, and :—" I know not," quoth he, " that there is
another soul in the world for whom I would do this, save you,
my gossips ; however, as you will have it so, I will do it, but it
behoves you to do exactly as I bid you, if you would have the
enchantment work."   They promised obedience, and Dom
Gianni thereupon took a light, which he handed to Gossip Pietro,
saying :—" Let nought that I shall do or say escape thee ;
and have a care, so thou wouldst not ruin all, to say never a
word, whatever thou mayst see or hear ; and pray God that
the tail may be securely attached."   So Gossip Pietro took the
light, and again promised obedience ; Dom Gianni caused
Gossip Gemmata to strip herself stark naked, and stand on all
fours like a mare, at the same time strictly charging her that,
whatever might happen, she must utter no word.   Then,
touching her head and face :—" Be this a fine head of a mare,"
quoth he ; in like manner touching her hair, he said :—" Be
this a fine mane of a mare ; " touching her arms :—" Be these
fine legs and fine hooves of a mare ; " then, as he touched her
breast and felt its firm roundness, and there awoke and arose
one that was not called :—" And be this a fine breast of a mare,"

quoth he ; and in like manner he dealt with her back, belly, croup, thighs, and legs. Last of all, the work being complete save for the tail, he lifted his shirt and took in his hand the tool with which he was used to plant men, and forthwith thrust it into the furrow made for it, saying :—" And be this a fine tail of a mare." Whereat Gossip Pietro, who had followed everything very heedfully to that point, disapproving that last particular, exclaimed :—" No ! Dom Gianni, I'll have no tail, I'll have no tail." The essential juice, by which all plants are propagated, was already discharged, when Dom Gianni withdrew the tool, saying :—" Alas ! Gossip Pietro, what hast thou done ? Did I not tell thee to say never a word, no matter what thou mightst see ? The mare was all but made ; but by speaking thou hast spoiled all ; and 'tis not possible to repeat the enchantment." " Well and good," replied Gossip Pietro, " I would have none of that tail. Why saidst thou not to me :— ' Make it thou ' ? And besides, thou wast attaching it too low." " 'Twas because," returned Dom Gianni, " thou wouldst not have known, on the first essay, how to attach it so well as I." Whereupon the young woman stood up, and in all good faith said to her husband :—" Fool that thou art, wherefore hast thou brought to nought what had been for the good of us both ? When didst thou ever see mare without a tail ? So help me God, poor as thou art, thou deservest to be poorer still." So, after Gossip Pietro's ill-timed speech, there being no way left of turning the young woman into a mare, downcast and melancholy she resumed her clothes ; and Gossip Pietro plied his old trade with his ass, and went with Dom Gianni to the fair of Bitonto, and never asked him so to serve him again.

What laughter this story drew from the ladies, who understood it better than Dioneo had wished, may be left to the imagination of the fair one that now laughs thereat. However, as the stories were ended, and the sun now shone with a tempered radiance, the queen, witting that the end of her sovereignty was come, stood up and took off the crown, and set it on the head of Pamfilo, whom alone it now remained thus to honour ; and said with a smile :—" My lord, 'tis a great burden that falls upon thee, seeing that thou, coming last, art bound to make good my shortcomings and those of my predecessors ; which God give thee grace to accomplish, even as He has given me grace to make thee king." With gladsome acknowledgment of the honour :—" I doubt not," replied Pamfilo, " that, thanks to your noble qualities and those of my other subjects, I shall

win even such praise as those that have borne sway before me."
Then, following the example of his predecessors, he made all
meet arrangements in concert with the seneschal : after which,
he turned to the expectant ladies, and thus spoke :—" Enamoured my ladies, Emilia, our queen of to-day, deeming it proper
to allow you an interval of rest to recruit your powers, gave you
license to discourse of such matters as should most commend
themselves to each in turn ; and as thereby you are now rested,
I judge that 'tis meet to revert to our accustomed rule.   Wherefore I ordain that for to-morrow you do each of you take thought
how you may discourse of the ensuing theme : to wit, of such
as in matters of love, or otherwise, have done something with
liberality or magnificence.   By the telling, and (still more) by
the doing of such things, your spirits will assuredly be duly
attuned and animated to emprise high and noble ; whereby
our life, which cannot but be brief, seeing that 'tis enshrined
in a mortal body, fame shall perpetuate in glory ; which whoso
serves not the belly, as do the beasts, must not only covet, but
with all zeal seek after and labour to attain."

The gay company having, one and all, approved the theme,
rose at a word from their new king, and betook them to their
wonted pastimes, and so, according as they severally had most
lief, diverted them, until they blithely reunited for supper, which
being served with all due care and despatched, they rose up to
dance, as they were wont, and when they had sung, perhaps,
a thousand ditties, fitter to please by their words than by any
excellence of musical art, the king bade Neifile sing one on her
own account.   And promptly and graciously, with voice clear
and blithe, thus Neifile sang :—

> In prime of maidenhood, and fear and feat
> 　'Mid spring's fresh foison chant I merrily :
> Thanks be to Love and to my fancies sweet.
>
> As o'er the grassy mead I, glancing, fare,
> 　I mark it white and yellow and vermeil dight
> 　With flowers, the thorny rose, the lily white :
> And all alike to his face I compare,
> 　Who, loving, hath me ta'en, and me shall e'er
> 　Hold bounden to his will, sith I am she
> That in his will findeth her joy complete.
>
> Whereof if so it be that I do find
> 　Any that I most like to him approve,
> 　That pluck I straight and kiss with words of love,
> Discovering all, as best I may, my mind ;
> 　Yea, all my heart's desire ; and then entwined
> 　I set it in the chaplet daintily,
> And with my yellow tresses bind and pleat.

And as mine eyes do drink in the delight
 Which the flower yields them, even so my mind,
 Fired with his sweet love, doth such solace find,
 As he himself were present to the sight:
 But never word of mine discover might
 That which the flower's sweet smell awakes in me:
 Witness the true tale that my sighs repeat.

For from my bosom gentle and hot they fly,
 Not like the gusty sighs that others heave,
 Whenas they languish and do sorely grieve;
 And to my love incontinent they hie:
 Whereof when he is ware, he, by and by,
 To meward hasting, cometh suddenly,
 When:—" Lest I faint," I cry, " come, I entreat."

  The king and all the ladies did not a little commend Neifile's
song; after which, as the night was far spent, the king bade all
go to rest until the morrow.

Endeth here the ninth day of the Decameron, and beginneth the tenth, in which, under the rule of Pamfilo, discourse is had of such as in matters of love, or otherwise, have done something with liberality or magnificence.

SOME cloudlets in the West still shewed a vermeil flush, albeit those of the eastern sky, as the sun's rays smote them anear, were already fringed as with most lucent gold, when uprose Pamfilo, and roused the ladies and his comrades. And all the company being assembled, and choice made of the place whither they should betake them for their diversion, he, accompanied by Filomena and Fiammetta, led the way at a slow pace, followed by all the rest. So fared they no little space, beguiling the time with talk of their future way of life, whereof there was much to tell and much to answer, until, as the sun gained strength, they returned, having made quite a long round, to the palace ; and being gathered about the fountain, such as were so minded drank somewhat from beakers rinsed in its pure waters ; and then in the delicious shade of the garden they hied them hither and thither, taking their pleasure until breakfast-time. Their meal taken, they slept as they were wont ; and then, at a spot chosen by the king, they reassembled, where Neifile, having received his command to lead the way, blithely thus began.

NOVEL I

A knight in the service of the King of Spain deems himself ill requited. Wherefore the King, by most cogent proof, shews him that the blame rests not with him, but with the knight's own evil fortune ; after which, he bestows upon him a noble gift.

HIGHLY graced, indeed, do I deem myself, honourable my ladies, that our king should have given to me the precedence in a matter so arduous to tell of as magnificence : for, as the sun irradiates all the heaven with his glory and beauty, even so does

268

magnificence enhance the purity and the splendour of every other virtue. I shall therefore tell you a story, which, to my thinking, is not a little pretty ; and which, assuredly, it must be profitable to call to mind.

You are to know, then, that, among other honourable knights that from days of old even until now have dwelt in our city, one, and perchance the worthiest of all, was Messer Ruggieri de' Figiovanni. Who, being wealthy and magnanimous, reflecting on the customs and manner of life of Tuscany, perceived that by tarrying there he was like to find little or no occasion of shewing his mettle, and accordingly resolved to pass some time at the court of Alfonso, King of Spain, who for the fame of his high qualities was without a peer among the potentates of his age. So, being well provided with arms and horses and retinue suitable to his rank, he hied him to Spain, where he was graciously received by the King. There tarrying accordingly, Messer Ruggieri very soon, as well by the splendid style in which he lived as by the prodigious feats of arms that he did, gave folk to know his high desert.

Now, having tarried there some while, and observed the King's ways with much care, and how he would grant castles, cities, or baronies, to this, that, or the other of his subjects, he deemed that the King shewed therein but little judgment, seeing that he would give them to men that merited them not. And for that nought was given to him, he, knowing his merit, deemed himself gravely injured in reputation ; wherefore he made up his mind to depart the realm, and to that end craved license of the King ; which the King granted him, and therewith gave him one of the best and finest mules that was ever ridden, a gift which Messer Ruggieri, as he had a long journey to make, did not a little appreciate. The King then bade one of his discreet domestics contrive, as best he might, to ride with Messer Ruggieri on such wise that it might not appear that he did so by the King's command, and charge his memory with whatever Messer Ruggieri might say of him, so that he might be able to repeat it ; which done, he was on the very next morning to bid Ruggieri return to the King forthwith. The King's agent was on the alert, and no sooner was Ruggieri out of the city, than without any manner of difficulty he joined his company, giving out that he was going towards Italy. As thus they rode, talking of divers matters, Messer Ruggieri being mounted on the mule given him by the King :—" Methinks," quoth the other, it being then hard upon tierce, " that 'twere

well to give the beasts a voidance ; " and by and by, being come
to a convenient place, they voided all the beasts save the mule.
Then, as they continued their journey, the squire hearkening
attentively to the knight's words, they came to a river, and
while there they watered the beasts, the mule made a voidance
in the stream. Whereat :—" Ah, foul fall thee, beast," quoth
Messer Ruggieri, " that art even as thy master, that gave thee
to me ! " Which remark, as also many another that fell from
Ruggieri as they rode together throughout the day, the squire
stored in his memory ; but never another word did he hear
Ruggieri say touching the King, that was not laudatory to the
last degree.

On the morrow, when they were gotten to horse, and had set
their faces towards Tuscany, the squire apprised Ruggieri of
the King's command, and thereupon Ruggieri turned back.
On his arrival the King, having already heard what he had said
touching the mule, gave him gladsome greeting, and asked him
wherefore he had likened him to the mule, or rather the mule
to him. Whereto Messer Ruggieri answered frankly :—" My
lord, I likened you to the mule, for that, as you bestow your
gifts where 'tis not meet, and where meet it were, bestow them
not, so the mule where 'twas meet, voided not, and where 'twas
not meet, voided." " Messer Ruggieri," replied the King, " 'tis
not because I have not discerned in you a knight most good and
true, for whose desert no gift were too great, that I have not
bestowed on you such gifts as I have bestowed upon many
others, who in comparison of you are nothing worth : the fault
is none of mine but solely of your fortune, which would not
suffer me ; and that this which I say is true, I will make abundantly plain to you." " My lord," returned Messer Ruggieri,
" mortified am I, not that you gave me no gift, for thereof I
had no desire, being too rich, but that you made no sign of
recognition of my desert ; however, I deem your explanation
sound and honourable, and whatever you shall be pleased that
I should see, that gladly will I, albeit I believe you without
attestation."

The King then led him into one of the great halls, in which,
by his preordinance, were two chests closed under lock and key,
and, not a few others being present, said to him :—" Messer
Ruggieri, one of these chests contains my crown, sceptre and
orb, with many a fine girdle, buckle, ring, and whatever else of
jewellery I possess ; the other is full of earth : choose then,
and whichever you shall choose, be it yours ; thereby you will

discover whether 'tis due to me or to your fortune that your
deserts have lacked requital." Such being the King's pleasure,
Messer Ruggieri chose one of the chests, which at the King's
command being opened and found to be that which contained
the earth :—" Now, Messer Ruggieri," quoth the King with a
laugh, " your own eyes may warrant you of the truth of what
I say touching Fortune ; but verily your merit demands that
I take arms against her in your cause. I know that you are
not minded to become a Spaniard, and therefore I shall give
you neither castle nor city; but that chest, which Fortune
denied you, I bestow on you in her despite, that you may take
it with you to your own country, and there with your neighbours justly vaunt yourself of your deserts, attested by my
gifts." Messer Ruggieri took the chest, and having thanked
the King in a manner befitting such a gift, returned therewith, well pleased, to Tuscany.

NOVEL II

*Ghino di Tacco captures the Abbot of Cluny, cures him of a disorder
of the stomach, and releases him. The abbot, on his return
to the court of Rome, reconciles Ghino with Pope Boniface,
and makes him prior of the Hospital.*

WHEN an end was made of extolling the magnificence shewn
by King Alfonso towards the Florentine knight, the king, who
had listened to the story with no small pleasure, bade Elisa
follow suit ; and forthwith Elisa began :—Dainty my ladies,
undeniable it is that for a king to be magnificent, and to entreat
magnificently one that has done him service, is a great matter,
and meet for commendation. What then shall we say when
the tale is of a dignitary of the Church that shewed wondrous
magnificence towards one whom he might well have entreated
as an enemy, and not have been blamed by a soul ? Assuredly
nought else than that what in the king was virtue was in the
prelate nothing less than a miracle, seeing that for superlative
greed the clergy, one and all, outdo us women, and wage war
to the knife upon every form of liberality. And albeit all men
are by nature prone to avenge their wrongs, 'tis notorious that
the clergy, however they may preach longsuffering, and commend of all things the forgiving of trespasses, are more quick
and hot to be avenged than the rest of mankind. Now this, to

wit, after what manner a prelate shewed magnificence, will be made manifest to you in my story.

Ghino di Tacco, a man redoubtable by reason of his truculence and his high-handed deeds, being banished from Siena, and at enmity with the Counts of Santa Fiore, raised Radicofani in revolt against the Church of Rome, and there abiding, harried all the surrounding country with his soldiers, plundering all wayfarers. Now Pope Boniface VIII. being at Rome, there came to court the Abbot of Cluny, who is reputed one of the wealthiest prelates in the world ; and having there gotten a disorder of the stomach, he was advised by the physicians to go to the baths of Siena, where (they averred) he would certainly be cured. So, having obtained the Pope's leave, reckless of the bruit of Ghino's exploits, he took the road, being attended by a great and well-equipped train of sumpter-horses and servants. Ghino di Tacco, getting wind of his approach, spread his nets to such purpose as without the loss of so much as a boy to surround the abbot, with all his servants and effects, in a strait pass, from which there was no exit. Which done, he sent one of his men, the cunningest of them all, with a sufficient retinue to the abbot, who most lovingly on Ghino's part besought the abbot to come and visit Ghino at the castle. Whereto the abbot, very wroth, made answer that he would none of it, for that nought had he to do with Ghino ; but that he purposed to continue his journey, and would fain see who would hinder him. " Sir," returned the envoy, assuming a humble tone, " you are come to a part of the country where we have no fear of aught save the might of God, and where excommunications and interdicts are one and all under the ban ; wherefore you were best be pleased to shew yourself agreeable to Ghino in this particular." As they thus spoke, Ghino's soldiers shewed themselves on every side, and it being thus manifest to the abbot that he and his company were taken prisoners, he, albeit mightily incensed, suffered himself with all his train and effects to be conducted by the envoy to the castle ; where the abbot, being alighted, was lodged in a small and very dark and discomfortable room, while his retinue, according to their several conditions, were provided with comfortable quarters in divers parts of the castle, the horses well stabled and all the effects secured, none being in any wise tampered with. Which done, Ghino hied him to the abbot, and :—" Sir," quoth he, " Ghino, whose guest you are, sends me to entreat you to be pleased to inform him of your destination, and the purpose of your journey." The

abbot, vailing his pride like a wise man, told whither he was
bound and for what purpose. Whereupon Ghino left him,
casting about how he might cure him without a bath. To
which end he kept a great fire ever burning in the little chamber,
and had it closely guarded, and returned not to the abbot until
the ensuing morning, when he brought him in a spotless napkin
two slices of toast and a great beaker of vernaccia of Corniglia,
being of the abbot's own vintage; and :—" Sir," quoth he to
the abbot, " Ghino, as a young man, made his studies in medicine, and avers that he then learned that there is no better
treatment for disorder of the stomach than that which he will
afford you, whereof the matters that I bring you are the beginning; wherefore take them and be of good cheer."

The abbot, being far too hungry to make many words about
the matter, ate (albeit in high dudgeon) the toast, and drank the
vernaccia; which done, he enlarged on his wrongs in a high
tone, with much questioning and perpending; and above all
he demanded to see Ghino. Part of what the abbot said Ghino
disregarded as of no substance, to the other part he replied courteously enough; and having assured him that Ghino would
visit him as soon as might be, he took his leave of him; nor did
he return until the morrow, when he brought him toast and
vernaccia in the same quantity as before; and so he kept him
several days: then, having marked that the abbot had eaten
some dried beans that he had secretly brought and left there of
set purpose, he asked him in Ghino's name how he felt in the
stomach. "Were I but out of Ghino's hands," replied the
abbot, " I should feel myself well, indeed: next to which, I
desire most of all a good breakfast, so excellent a cure have his
medicines wrought on me." Whereupon Ghino caused the
abbot's servants to furnish a goodly chamber with the abbot's
own effects, and there on the morrow make ready a grand
banquet, at which all the abbot's suite and not a few of the
garrison being assembled, he hied him to the abbot, and :—
" Sir," quoth he, " 'tis time you left the infirmary, seeing that
you now feel yourself well; " and so saying, he took him by the
hand, and led him into the chamber made ready for him, and
having left him there with his own people, made it his chief
concern that the banquet should be magnificent. The abbot's
spirits revived as he found himself again among his men, with
whom he talked a while, telling them how he had been entreated,
wherewith they contrasted the signal honour which they, on
the other hand, had, one and all, received from Ghino.

Breakfast-time came, and with order meet the abbot and the rest were regaled with good viands and good wines, Ghino still suffering not the abbot to know who he was. But when the abbot had thus passed several days, Ghino, having first had all his effects collected in a saloon, and all his horses, to the poorest jade, in the courtyard below, hied him to the abbot and asked him how he felt, and if he deemed himself strong enough to ride. The abbot replied that he was quite strong enough, and that 'twould be well indeed with him, were he once out of Ghino's hands. Ghino then led him into the saloon in which were his effects and all his retinue, and having brought him to a window, whence he might see all his horses :—" Sir Abbot," quoth he, " you must know that 'tis not for that he has an evil heart, but because, being a gentleman, he is banished from his home, and reduced to poverty, and has not a few powerful enemies, that in defence of his life and honour, Ghino di Tacco, whom you see before you, has become a robber of highways and an enemy to the court of Rome. But such as I am, I have cured you of your malady of the stomach, and taking you to be a worthy lord, I purpose not to treat you as I would another, from whom, were he in my hands, as you are, I should take such part of his goods as I should think fit ; but I shall leave it to you, upon considera- tion of my need, to assign to me such portion of your goods as you yourself shall determine. Here are they before you un- diminished and unimpaired, and from this window you may see your horses below in the courtyard ; wherefore take the part or take the whole, as you may see fit, and be it at your option to tarry here, or go hence, from this hour forth."

The abbot marvelled to hear a highway robber speak thus liberally, and such was his gratification that his wrath and fierce resentment departed from him, nay, were transformed into kindness, insomuch that in all cordial amity he hasted to embrace Ghino, saying :—" By God I swear, that to gain the friendship of a man such I now deem thee to be, I would be content to suffer much greater wrong than that which until now, meseemed, thou hadst done me. Cursed be Fortune that constrains thee to ply so censurable a trade." Which said, he selected a very few things, and none superfluous, from his ample store, and having done likewise with the horses, ceded all else to Ghino, and hied him back to Rome ; where, seeing him, the Pope, who to his great grief had heard of his capture, asked him what benefit he had gotten from the baths. Whereto the abbot made answer with a smile :—" Holy Father, I found

nearer here than the baths a worthy physician who has wrought
a most excellent cure on me : " he then recounted all the circumstances, whereat the Pope laughed.   Afterwards, still pursuing
the topic, the abbot, yielding to the promptings of magnificence,
asked a favour of the Pope ; who, expecting that he would ask
somewhat else than he did, liberally promised to give him whatever he should demand.   Whereupon :—" Holy Father," quoth
the abbot, " that which I would crave of you is that you restore
Ghino di Tacco, my physician, to your favour ; seeing that
among the good men and true and meritorious that I have
known, he is by no means of the least account.   And for the
evil life that he leads I impute it to Fortune rather than to
him : change then his fortune, by giving him the means whereby
he may live in manner befitting his rank, and I doubt not that
in a little while your judgment of him will jump with mine."
Whereto the Pope, being magnanimous, and an admirer of
good men and true, made answer that so he would gladly do,
if Ghino should prove to be such as the abbot said ; and that he
would have him brought under safe conduct to Rome.   Thither
accordingly under safe conduct came Ghino, to the abbot's
great delight ; nor had he been long at court before the Pope
approved his worth, and restored him to his favour, granting
him a great office, to wit, that of prior of the Hospital, whereof
he made him knight.   Which office he held for the rest of his
life, being ever a friend and vassal of Holy Church and the
Abbot of Cluny.

NOVEL III

*Mitridanes, holding Nathan in despite by reason of his courtesy,
journeys with intent to kill him, and falling in with him unawares, is advised by him how to compass his end.   Following
his advice, he finds him in a copse, and recognizing him, is
shame-stricken, and becomes his friend.*

VERILY like to a miracle seemed it to all to hear that a prelate
had done aught with magnificence ; but when the ladies had
made an end of their remarks, the king bade Filostrato follow
suit ; and forthwith Filostrato began :—Noble ladies, great
was the magnificence of the King of Spain, and perchance a
thing unheard-of the magnificence of the Abbot of Cluny ; but
peradventure 'twill seem not a whit less marvellous to you to

hear of one who, to shew liberality towards another, did resolve artfully to yield to him his blood, nay, his very life, for which the other thirsted, and had so done, had the other chosen to take them, as I shall shew you in a little story.

Beyond all question, if we may believe the report of certain Genoese, and other folk that have been in those regions, there dwelt of yore in the parts of Cathay one Nathan, a man of noble lineage and incomparable wealth. Who, having a seat hard by a road, by which whoso would travel from the West eastward, or from the East westward, must needs pass, and being magnanimous and liberal, and zealous to approve himself such in act, did set on work cunning artificers not a few, and cause one of the finest and largest and most luxurious palaces that ever were seen, to be there builded and furnished in the goodliest manner with all things meet for the reception and honourable entertainment of gentlemen. And so, keeping a great array of excellent servants, he courteously and hospitably did the honours of his house to whoso came and went : in which laudable way of life he persevered, until not only the East, but well-nigh all the West had heard his fame ; which thus, what time he was well-stricken in years, albeit not for that cause grown weary of shewing courtesy, reached the ears of one Mitridanes, a young man of a country not far distant. Who, knowing himself to be no less wealthy than Nathan, grew envious of the renown that he had of his good deeds, and resolved to obliterate, or at least to obscure it, by a yet greater liberality. So he had built for himself a palace like that of Nathan, of which he did the honours with a lavish courtesy that none had ever equalled, to whoso came or went that way ; and verily in a short while he became famous enough.

Now it so befell that on a day when the young man was all alone in the courtyard of the palace, there came in by one of the gates a poor woman, who asked of him an alms, and had it ; but, not content therewith, came again to him by the second gate, and asked another alms, and had it, and after the like sort did even unto the twelfth time ; but, she returning for the thirteenth time :—" My good woman," quoth Mitridanes, " thou art not a little pertinacious in thy begging : " howbeit he gave her an alms. Whereupon :—" Ah ! the wondrous liberality of Nathan ! " quoth the beldam : " thirty-two gates are there to his palace, by every one of which I have entered, and asking alms of him, was never—for aught he shewed—recognized, or refused, and here, though I have entered as yet

by but thirteen gates, I am recognized and reprimanded."
And therewith she departed, and returned no more. Mitridanes,
who accounted the mention of Nathan's fame an abatement of
his own, was kindled by her words with a frenzy of wrath, and
began thus to commune with himself :—Alas ! when shall I
attain to the grandeur of Nathan's liberality, to say nought of
transcending it, as I would fain, seeing that in the veriest trifles
I cannot approach him ? Of a surety my labour is in vain, if
I rid not the earth of him : which, since old age relieves me not
of him, I must forthwith do with mine own hands. And in
the flush of his despite up he started, and giving none to know
of his purpose, got to horse with a small company, and after
three days arrived at the place where Nathan abode ; and
having enjoined his comrades to make as if they were none of
his, and knew him not, and to go quarter themselves as best
they might until they had his further orders, he, being thus
alone, towards evening came upon Nathan, also alone, at no
great distance from his splendid palace. Nathan was recreating
himself by a walk, and was very simply clad ; so that Mitridanes,
knowing him not, asked him if he could shew him where Nathan
dwelt. " My son," replied Nathan gladsomely, " that can none
in these parts better than I ; wherefore, so it please thee, I will
bring thee thither." The young man replied that 'twould be
mighty agreeable to him, but that, if so it might be, he had a
mind to be neither known nor seen by Nathan. " And herein
also," returned Nathan, " since 'tis thy pleasure, I will gratify
thee." Whereupon Mitridanes dismounted, and with Nathan,
who soon engaged him in delightsome discourse, walked to the
goodly palace. Arrived there Nathan caused one of his servants
take the young man's horse, and drawing close to him, bade
him in a whisper to see to it without delay that none in the
house should tell the young man that he was Nathan : and so
'twas done.

Being come into the palace, Nathan quartered Mitridanes in
a most goodly chamber, where none saw him but those whom
he had appointed to wait upon him ; and he himself kept him
company, doing him all possible honour. Of whom Mitridanes,
albeit he reverenced him as a father, yet, being thus with him,
forbore not to ask who he was. Whereto Nathan made answer :
—" I am a petty servant of Nathan : old as I am, I have been
with him since my childhood, and never has he advanced me to
higher office than this wherein thou seest me : wherefore,
howsoever other folk may praise him, little cause have I to do

so." Which words afforded Mitridanes some hope of carrying
his wicked purpose into effect with more of plan and less of risk
than had otherwise been possible. By and by Nathan very
courteously asked him who he was, and what business brought
him thither; offering him such counsel and aid as he might be
able to afford him. Mitridanes hesitated a while to reply: but
at last he resolved to trust him, and when with no little circum-
locution he had demanded of him fidelity, counsel and aid, he
fully discovered to him who he was, and the purpose and
motive of his coming thither. Now, albeit to hear Mitridanes
thus unfold his horrid design caused Nathan no small inward
commotion, yet 'twas not long before courageously and com-
posedly he thus made answer:—" Noble was thy father, Mitridanes, and thou art minded to shew thyself not unworthy of
him by this lofty emprise of thine, to wit, of being liberal to all
comers: and for that thou art envious of Nathan's merit I
greatly commend thee; for were many envious for a like
cause, the world, from being a most wretched, would soon
become a happy, place. Doubt not that I shall keep secret the
design which thou hast confided to me, for the furtherance
whereof 'tis good advice rather than substantial aid that I have
to offer thee. Which advice is this. Hence, perhaps half a
mile off, thou mayst see a copse, in which almost every morning
Nathan is wont to walk, taking his pleasure, for quite a long
while: 'twill be an easy matter for thee to find him there, and
deal with him as thou mayst be minded. Now, shouldst thou
slay him, thou wilt get thee home with less risk of let, if thou
take not the path by which thou camest hither, but that which
thou seest issue from the copse on the left, for, though 'tis
somewhat more rough, it leads more directly to thy house, and
will be safer for thee."

Possessed of this information, Mitridanes, when Nathan had
left him, privily apprised his comrades, who were likewise
lodged in the palace, of the place where they were to await him
on the ensuing day; which being come, Nathan, inflexibly
determined to act in all respects according to the advice which
he had given Mitridanes, hied him forth to the copse unattended,
to meet his death. Mitridanes, being risen, took his bow and
sword, for other arms he had none with him, mounted his horse,
and rode to the copse, through which, while he was yet some way
off, he saw Nathan passing, quite alone. And being minded,
before he fell upon him, to see his face and hear the sound of his
voice, as, riding at a smart pace, he came up with him, he laid

hold of him by his head-gear, exclaiming :—" Greybeard, thou
art a dead man." Whereto Nathan answered nought but :—
" Then 'tis but my desert." But Mitridanes, hearing the voice,
and scanning the face, forthwith knew him for the same man
that had welcomed him heartily, consorted with him familiarly,
and counselled him faithfully ; whereby his wrath presently
subsided, and gave place to shame. Wherefore, casting away
the sword that he held drawn in act to strike, he sprang from
his horse, and weeping, threw himself at Nathan's feet, saying :—
" Your liberality, dearest father, I acknowledge to be beyond
all question, seeing with what craft you did plot your coming
hither to yield me your life, for which, by mine own avowal,
you knew that I, albeit cause I had none, did thirst. But God,
more regardful of my duty than I myself, has now, in this
moment of supreme stress, opened the eyes of my mind, that
wretched envy had fast sealed. The prompter was your compliance, the greater is the debt of penitence that I owe you for
my fault ; wherefore wreak even such vengeance upon me as
you may deem answerable to my transgression." But Nathan
raised Mitridanes to his feet, and tenderly embraced him, saying :—" My son, thy enterprise, howsoever thou mayst denote
it, whether evil or otherwise, was not such that thou shouldst
crave, or I give, pardon thereof ; for 'twas not in malice but in
that thou wouldst fain have been reputed better than I that
thou ensuedst it. Doubt then no more of me ; nay, rest assured
that none that lives bears thee such love as I, who know the
loftiness of thy spirit, bent not to heap up wealth, as do the
caitiffs, but to dispense in bounty thine accumulated store.
Think it no shame that to enhance thy reputation thou wouldst
have slain me ; nor deem that I marvel thereat. To slay not
one man, as thou wast minded, but countless multitudes, to
waste whole countries with fire, and to raze cities to the ground
has been well-nigh the sole art, by which the mightiest emperors
and the greatest kings have extended their dominions, and by
consequence their fame. Wherefore, if thou, to increase thy
fame, wouldst fain have slain me, 'twas nothing marvellous or
strange, but wonted."

Whereto Mitridanes made answer, not to excuse his wicked
design, but to commend the seemly excuse found for it by
Nathan, whom at length he told how beyond measure he marvelled that Nathan had not only been consenting to the enterprise, but had aided him therein by his counsel. But Nathan
answered :—" Liefer had I, Mitridanes, that thou didst not

marvel either at my consent or at my counsel, for that, since I was my own master and of a mind to that emprise whereon thou art also bent, never a soul came to my house, but, so far as in me lay, I gave him all that he asked of me. Thou camest, lusting for my life; and so, when I heard thee crave it of me, I forthwith, that thou mightst not be the only guest to depart hence ill content, resolved to give it thee; and to that end I gave thee such counsel as I deemed would serve thee both to the taking of my life and the preservation of thine own. Wherefore yet again I bid thee, nay, I entreat thee, if so thou art minded, to take it for thy satisfaction: I know not how I could better bestow it. I have had the use of it now for some eighty years, and pleasure and solace thereof; and I know that, by the course of Nature and the common lot of man and all things mundane, it can continue to be mine for but a little while; and so I deem that 'twere much better to bestow it, as I have ever bestowed and dispensed my wealth, than to keep it, until, against my will, it be reft from me by Nature. 'Twere but a trifle, though 'twere a hundred years: how insignificant, then, the six or eight years that are all I have to give! Take it, then, if thou hadst lief, take it, I pray thee; for, long as I have lived here, none have I found but thee to desire it; nor know I when I may find another, if thou take it not, to demand it of me. And if, peradventure, I should find one such, yet I know that the longer I keep it, the less its worth will be; wherefore, ere it be thus cheapened, take it, I implore thee."

Sore shame-stricken, Mitridanes made answer:—" Now God forefend that I should so much as harbour, as but now I did, such a thought, not to say do such a deed, as to wrest from you a thing so precious as your life, the years whereof, so far from abridging, I would gladly supplement with mine own." " So then," rejoined Nathan promptly, " thou wouldst, if thou couldst, add thy years to mine, and cause me to serve thee as I never yet served any man, to wit, to take from thee that which is thine, I that never took aught from a soul! " " Ay, that would I," returned Mitridanes. " Then," quoth Nathan, " do as I shall bid thee. Thou art young: tarry here in my house, and call thyself Nathan; and I will get me to thy house, and ever call myself Mitridanes." Whereto Mitridanes made answer:—" Were I but able to discharge this trust, as you have been and are, scarce would I hesitate to accept your offer; but, as too sure am I that aught that I might do would but serve to lower Nathan's fame, and I am not minded to mar that in another which I cannot mend in myself, accept it I will not."

After which and the like interchange of delectable discourse, Nathan and Mitridanes, by Nathan's desire, returned to the palace ; where Nathan for some days honourably entreated Mitridanes, and by his sage counsel confirmed and encouraged him in his high and noble resolve ; after which, Mitridanes, being minded to return home with his company, took his leave of Nathan, fully persuaded that 'twas not possible to surpass him in liberality.

NOVEL IV

Messer Gentile de' Carisendi, being come from Modena, disinters a lady that he loves, who has been buried for dead. She, being reanimated, gives birth to a male child ; and Messer Gentile restores her, with her son, to Niccoluccio Caccianimico, her husband.

A THING marvellous seemed it to all that for liberality a man should be ready to sacrifice his own life ; and herein they averred that Nathan had without doubt left the King of Spain and the Abbot of Cluny behind. However, when they had discussed the matter diversely and at large, the king, bending his regard on Lauretta, signified to her his will that she should tell ; and forthwith, accordingly, Lauretta began :—Goodly matters are they and magnificent that have been recounted to you, young ladies ; nay, so much of our field of discourse is already filled by their grandeur, that for us that are yet to tell, there is, methinks, no room left, unless we seek our topic there where matter of discourse germane to every theme does most richly abound, to wit, in the affairs of love. For which cause, as also for that our time of life cannot but make us especially inclinable thereto, I am minded that my story shall be of a feat of magnificence done by a lover : which, all things considered, will, peradventure, seem to you inferior to none that have been shewn you ; so it be true that to possess the beloved one, men will part with their treasures, forget their enmities, and jeopardize their own lives, their honour and their reputation, in a thousand ways.

Know, then, that at Bologna, that most famous city of Lombardy, there dwelt a knight, Messer Gentile Carisendi by name, worshipful alike for his noble lineage and his native worth : who in his youth, being enamoured of a young gentlewoman named Madonna Catalina, wife of one Niccoluccio Caccianimico, and well-nigh despairing, for that the lady gave him but a sorry requital of his love, betook him to Modena, being called thither as Podestà. Now what time he was there, Niccoluccio being also away from Bologna, and his lady gone, for that she was with child, to lie in at a house she had some three miles or so from the city, it befell that she was suddenly smitten with a sore malady of such and so virulent a quality that it left no sign of life in her, so that the very physicians pronounced her dead. And for that the women that were nearest of kin to her professed to have been told by her, that she was not so far gone in pregnancy that the child could be perfectly formed, they, without more ado, laid her in a tomb in a neighbouring church, and after long lamentation closed it upon her.

Whereof Messer Gentile being forthwith apprised by one of his friends, did, for all she had been most niggardly to him of her favour, grieve not a little, and at length fell a-communing with himself on this wise :—So, Madonna Catalina, thou art dead ! While thou livedst, never a glance of thine might I have ; wherefore, now that thou art dead, 'tis but right that I go take a kiss from thee. 'Twas night while he thus mused ; and forthwith, observing strict secrecy in his departure, he got him to horse with a single servant, and halted not until he was come to the place where the lady was interred ; and having opened the tomb he cautiously entered it. Then, having laid down beside her, he set his face against hers ; and again and again, weeping profusely the while, he kissed it. But as 'tis matter of common knowledge that the desires of men, and more especially of lovers, know no bounds, but crave ever an ampler satisfaction ; even so Messer Gentile, albeit he had been minded to tarry there no longer, now said to himself :—Wherefore touch I not her bosom a while ? I have never yet touched it, nor shall I ever touch it again. Obeying which impulse, he laid his hand on her bosom, and keeping it there some time, felt, as he thought, her heart faintly beating. Whereupon, banishing all fear, and examining the body with closer attention, he discovered that life was not extinct, though he judged it but scant and flickering : and so, aided by his servant, he bore her, as gently as he might, out of the tomb ; and set her before him upon his horse, and brought her privily to his house at Bologna, where dwelt his wise and worthy mother, who, being fully apprised by him of the circumstances, took pity on the lady, and had a huge fire kindled, and a bath made ready, whereby she restored her to life. Whereof the first sign she gave was to heave a great sigh, and murmur:—" Alas ! where am I ? " To which the worthy lady made answer :—" Be of good cheer ; thou art well lodged." By and by the lady, coming to herself, looked about her ; and finding herself she knew not where, and seeing Messer Gentile before her, was filled with wonder, and besought his mother to tell her how she came to be there.

Messer Gentile thereupon told her all. Sore distressed thereat, the lady, after a while, thanked him as best she might ; after which she besought him by the love that he had borne her, and of his courtesy, that she might, while she tarried in his house, be spared aught that could impair her honour and her husband's ; and that at daybreak he would suffer her to return home. " Madam," replied Messer Gentile, " however I did affect you in time past, since God in His goodness has, by means of the love I bore you, restored you to me alive, I mean not now, or at any time hereafter, to entreat you either here or elsewhere, save as a dear sister ; but yet the service I have to-night rendered you merits some guerdon : and therefore lief had I that you deny me not a favour which I shall ask of you." Whereto the lady graciously made answer that she would be prompt to grant it, so only it were in her power, and consonant with her honour. Said then Messer Gentile :—" Your kinsfolk, Madam, one and all, nay, all the folk in Bologna are fully persuaded that you are dead : there is therefore none to expect you at home : wherefore the favour I crave of you is this, that you will be pleased to tarry privily here with my mother, until such time—which will be speedily—as I return from Modena. And 'tis for that I purpose to make solemn and joyous donation of you to your husband in presence of the most honourable folk of this city that I ask of you this grace." Mindful of what she owed the knight, and witting that what he craved was seemly, the lady, albeit she yearned not a little to gladden her kinsfolk with the sight of her in the flesh, consented to do as Messer Gentile besought her, and thereto pledged him her faith. And scarce had she done so, when she felt that the hour of her travail was come ; and so, tenderly succoured by Messer Gentile's mother, she not long after gave birth to a fine boy. Which event did mightily enhance her own and Messer Gentile's happiness. Then, having made all meet provision for her, and left word that she was to be tended as if she were his own wife. Messer Gentile, observing strict secrecy, returned to Modena.

His time of office there ended, in anticipation of his return to Bologna, he appointed for the morning of his arrival in the city a great and goodly banquet at his house, whereto were bidden not a few of the gentlemen of Bologna, and among them Niccoluccio Caccianimico. Whom, when he was returned and dismounted, he found awaiting him, as also the lady, fairer and more healthful than ever, and her little son doing well ; and so with a gladness beyond compare he ranged his guests at table, and regaled them with many a course magnificently served. And towards the close of the feast, having premonished the lady of his intention, and concerted with her how she should behave, thus he spoke :—" Gentlemen, I mind me to have once heard tell of (as I deem it) a delightsome custom which they have in Persia ; to wit, that, when one would do his friend especial honour, he bids him to his house, and there shews him that treasure, be it wife, or mistress, or daughter, or what not, that he holds most dear ; assuring him that yet more gladly, were it possible, he would shew him his heart. Which custom I am minded to observe here in Bologna. You, of your courtesy, have honoured my feast with your presence, and I propose to do you honour in the Persian fashion, by shewing you that which in all the world I do, and must ever, hold most dear. But before I do so, tell me, I pray you, how you conceive of a nice question that I shall lay before you. Suppose that one has in his house a good and most faithful servant, who falls sick of a grievous disorder ; and that the master tarries not for the death of the servant, but has him borne out into the open street, and concerns himself no more with him : that then a stranger comes by, is moved to pity of the sick man, and takes him to his house, and by careful tendance and at no small cost restores him to his wonted health. Now I would fain know whether the first master has in equity any just cause to complain of or be aggrieved with the second master, if he retain the servant in his employ, and refuse to restore him, when so required."

The gentlemen discussed the matter after divers fashions, and all agreed in one sentence, which they committed to Niccoluccio Caccianimico, for that he was an eloquent and accomplished speaker, to deliver on the part of them all. Niccoluccio began by commending the Persian custom : after which he said that he and the others were all of the same opinion, to wit,

that the first master had no longer any right in his servant, since
he had not only abandoned but cast him forth; and that by
virtue of the second master's kind usage of him he must be
deemed to have become his servant; wherefore, by keeping
him, he did the first master no mischief, no violence, no wrong.
Whereupon the rest that were at the table said, one and all,
being worthy men, that their judgment jumped with Niccoluccio's answer. The knight, well pleased with the answer, and
that 'twas Niccoluccio that gave it, affirmed that he was of the
same opinion; adding:—" 'Tis now time that I shew you that
honour which I promised you." He then called two of his
servants, and sent them to the lady, whom he had caused to
be apparelled and adorned with splendour, charging them to
pray her to be pleased to come and gladden the gentlemen with
her presence. So she, bearing in her arms her most lovely little
son, came, attended by the two servants, into the saloon, and
by the knight's direction, took a seat beside a worthy gentleman: whereupon:—" Gentlemen," quoth the knight, " this
is the treasure that I hold, and mean ever to hold, more dear
than aught else. Behold, and judge whether I have good
cause."

The gentlemen said not a little in her honour and praise,
averring that the knight ought indeed to hold her dear: then,
as they regarded her more attentively, there were not a few that
would have pronounced her to be the very woman that she was,
had they not believed that woman to be dead. But none
scanned her so closely as Niccoluccio, who, the knight being
withdrawn a little space, could no longer refrain his eager desire
to know who she might be, but asked her whether she were of
Bologna, or from other parts. The lady, hearing her husband's
voice, could scarce forbear to answer; but yet, not to disconcert
the knight's plan, she kept silence. Another asked her if that
was her little boy; and yet another, if she were Messer Gentile's
wife, or in any other wise his connection. To none of whom she
vouchsafed an answer. Then, Messer Gentile coming up:
" Sir," quoth one of the guests, " this treasure of yours is goodly
indeed; but she seems to be dumb: is she so?" " Gentle
men," quoth Messer Gentile, " that she has not as yet spoken
is no small evidence of her virtue." " Then tell us, you, who
she is," returned the other. " That," quoth the knight, " will
I right gladly, so you but promise me, that, no matter what I
may say, none of you will stir from his place, until I have ended
my story." All gave the required promise, and when the tables

had been cleared, Messer Gentile, being seated beside the lady, thus spoke :—" Gentlemen, this lady is that loyal and faithful servant, touching whom a brief while ago I propounded to you my question, whom her own folk held none too dear, but cast out into the open street as a thing vile and no longer good for aught, but I took thence, and by my careful tendance wrested from the clutch of death ; whom God, regardful of my good will, has changed from the appalling aspect of a corpse to the thing of beauty that you see before you. But for your fuller understanding of this occurrence, I will briefly explain it to you." He then recounted to them in detail all that had happened from his first becoming enamoured of the lady to that very hour ; whereto they hearkened with no small wonder ; after which :— " And so," he added, " unless you, and more especially Niccoluccio, are now of another opinion than you were a brief while ago, the lady rightly belongs to me, nor can any man lawfully reclaim her of me."

None answered, for all were intent to hear what more he would say. But, while Niccoluccio, and some others that were there, wept for sympathy, Messer Gentile stood up, and took the little boy in his arms and the lady by the hand, and approached Niccoluccio, saying :—" Rise, my gossip : I do not, indeed, restore thee thy wife, whom thy kinsfolk and hers cast forth ; but I am minded to give thee this lady, my gossip, with this her little boy, whom I know well to be thy son, and whom I held at the font, and named Gentile : and I pray thee that she be not the less dear to thee for that she has tarried three months in my house ; for I swear to thee by that God, who, peradventure, ordained that I should be enamoured of her, to the end that my love might be, as it has been, the occasion of her restoration to life, that never with her father, or her mother, or with thee, did she live more virtuously than with my mother in my house." Which said, he turned to the lady, saying :—" Madam, I now release you from all promises made to me, and so deliver you to Niccoluccio." Then, leaving the lady and the child in Niccoluccio's embrace, he returned to his seat.

Thus to receive his wife and son was to Niccoluccio a delight great in the measure of its remoteness from his hope. Wherefore in the most honourable terms at his command he thanked the knight, whom all the rest, weeping for sympathy, greatly commended for what he had done, as did also all that heard thereof. The lady, welcomed home with wondrous cheer, was long a portent to the Bolognese, who gazed on her as on one raised from the dead. Messer Gentile lived ever after as the friend of Niccoluccio, and his and the lady's kinsfolk.

Now what shall be your verdict, gracious ladies ? A king's largess, though it was of his sceptre and crown, an abbot's reconciliation, at no cost to himself, of a malefactor with the Pope, or an old man's submission of his throat to the knife of his enemy—will you adjudge that such acts as these are comparable to the deed of Messer Gentile ? Who, though young, and burning with passion, and deeming himself justly entitled to that which the heedlessness of another had discarded, and he by good fortune had recovered, not only tempered his ardour with honour, but having that which with his whole soul he had long been bent on wresting from another, did with liberality restore it. Assuredly none of the feats aforesaid seem to me like unto this.

NOVEL V

Madonna Dianora craves of Messer Ansaldo a garden that shall be as fair in January as in May. Messer Ansaldo binds himself to a necromancer, and thereby gives her the garden. Her husband gives her leave to do Messer Ansaldo's pleasure : he, being apprised of her husband's liberality, releases her from her promise ; and the necromancer releases Messer Ansaldo from his bond, and will take nought of his.

EACH of the gay company had with superlative commendation extolled Messer Gentile to the skies, when the king bade Emilia follow suit ; and with a good courage, as burning to speak, thus Emilia began :—" Delicate my ladies, none can justly say that 'twas not magnificently done of Messer Gentile ; but if it be alleged that 'twas the last degree of magnificence, 'twill perchance not be difficult to shew that more was possible, as is my purpose in the little story that I shall tell you.

In Friuli, a country which, though its air is shrewd, is pleasantly diversified by fine mountains and not a few rivers and clear fountains, is a city called Udine, where dwelt of yore a fair and noble lady, Madonna Dianora by name, wife of a wealthy grandee named Giliberto, a very pleasant gentleman, and debonair. Now this lady, for her high qualities, was in the last degree beloved by a great and noble baron, Messer Ansaldo Gradense by name, a man of no little consequence, and whose fame for feats of arms and courtesy was spread far and wide. But, though with all a lover's ardour he left nought undone that he might do to win her love, and to that end frequently plied her with his ambassages, 'twas all in vain. And the lady being distressed by his importunity, and that, refuse as she might all that he asked of her, he none the less continued to love her and press his suit upon her, bethought her how she might rid herself of him by requiring of him an extraordinary and, as she deemed, impossible feat. So one day, a woman that came oftentimes from him to her being with her :—" Good woman," quoth she, " thou hast many a time affirmed that Messer Ansaldo loves me above all else ; and thou hast made proffer to me on his part of wondrous rich gifts which I am minded he keep to himself, for that I could never bring myself to love him or pleasure him for their sake ; but, if I might be certified that he loves me as much as thou sayst, then without a doubt I should not fail to love him, and do his pleasure ; wherefore, so he give me the assurance that I shall require, I shall be at his command." " What is it, Madam," returned the good woman, " that you would have him do ? " " This," replied the lady ; " I would have this next ensuing January, hard by this city, a garden full of green grass and flowers and flowering trees, just as if it were May ; and if he cannot provide me with this garden, bid him never again send either thee or any other to me, for that, should he harass me any further, I shall no longer keep silence, as I have hitherto done, but shall make my complaint to my husband and all my kinsmen, and it shall go hard but I will be quit of him."

The gentleman being apprised of his lady's stipulation and promise, notwithstanding that he deemed it no easy matter, nay, a thing almost impossible, to satisfy her, and knew besides that 'twas but to deprive him of all hope that she made the demand, did nevertheless resolve to do his endeavour to comply with it, and causing search to be made in divers parts of the world, if any he might find to afford him counsel or aid, he lit upon one, who for a substantial reward offered to do the thing by necromancy. So Messer Ansaldo, having struck the bargain with him for an exceeding great sum of money, gleefully expected the appointed time. Which being come with extreme cold, insomuch that there was nought but snow and ice, the adept on the night before the calends of January wrought with his spells to such purpose that on the morrow, as was averred by eye-witnesses, there appeared in a meadow hard by the city

one of the most beautiful gardens that was ever seen, with no
lack of grass and trees and fruits of all sorts. At sight whereof
Messer Ansaldo was overjoyed, and caused some of the finest
fruits and flowers that it contained to be gathered, and privily
presented to his lady, whom he bade come and see the garden
that she had craved, that thereby she might have assurance of
his love, and mind her of the promise that she had given him
and confirmed with an oath, and, as a loyal lady, take thought
for its performance. When she saw the flowers and fruits, the
lady, who had already heard not a few folk speak of the wondrous
garden, began to repent her of her promise. But for all that,
being fond of strange sights, she hied her with many other
ladies of the city to see the garden, and having gazed on it with
wonderment, and commended it not a little, she went home the
saddest woman alive, bethinking her to what it bound her :
and so great was her distress that she might not well conceal it ;
but, being written on her face, 'twas marked by her husband,
who was minded by all means to know the cause thereof.

The lady long time kept silence : but at last she yielded to his
urgency, and discovered to him the whole matter from first
to last. Whereat Giliberto was at first very wroth ; but on
second thoughts, considering the purity of the lady's purpose,
he was better advised, and dismissing his anger :—" Dianora,"
quoth he, " 'tis not the act of a discreet or virtuous lady to give
ear to messages of such a sort, nor to enter into any compact
touching her chastity with any man on any terms. Words
that the ears convey to the heart have a potency greater than
is commonly supposed, and there is scarce aught that lovers
will not find possible. 'Twas then ill done of thee in the
first instance to hearken, as afterwards to make the compact ;
but, for that I know the purity of thy soul, that thou mayst be
quit of thy promise, I will grant thee that which, perchance,
no other man would grant, being also swayed thereto by fear
of the necromancer, whom Messer Ansaldo, shouldst thou
play him false, might, peradventure, cause to do us a mischief.
I am minded, then, that thou go to him, and contrive, if on any
wise thou canst, to get thee quit of this promise without loss of
virtue ; but if otherwise it may not be, then for the nonce thou
mayst yield him thy body, but not thy soul." Whereat the
lady, weeping, would none of such a favour at her husband's
hands. But Giliberto, for all the lady's protestations, was
minded that so it should be.

Accordingly, on the morrow about dawn, apparelled none too

ornately, preceded by two servants and followed by a chamber-maid, the lady hied her to Messer Ansaldo's house. Apprised that his lady was come to see him, Messer Ansaldo, marvelling not a little, rose, and having called the necromancer :—" I am minded," quoth he, " that thou see what goodly gain I have gotten by thine art." And the twain having met the lady, Ansaldo gave way to no unruly appetite, but received her with a seemly obeisance ; and then the three repaired to a goodly chamber, where there was a great fire, and having caused the lady to be seated, thus spoke Ansaldo :—" Madam, if the love that I have so long borne you merit any guerdon, I pray you that it be not grievous to you to discover to me the true occasion of your coming to me at this hour, and thus accompanied." Shamefast, and the tears all but standing in her eyes, the lady made answer :—" Sir, 'tis neither love that I bear you, nor faith that I pledged you, that brings me hither, but the command of my husband, who, regarding rather the pains you have had of your unbridled passion than his own or my honour, has sent me hither ; and for that he commands it, I, for the nonce, am entirely at your pleasure."

If Messer Ansaldo had marvelled to hear of the lady's coming, he now marvelled much more, and touched by Giliberto's liberality, and passing from passion to compassion :—" Now, God forbid, Madam," quoth he, " that, it being as you say, I should wound the honour of him that has compassion on my love ; wherefore, no otherwise than as if you were my sister shall you abide here, while you are so minded, and be free to depart at your pleasure ; nor crave I aught of you but that you shall convey from me to your husband such thanks as you shall deem meet for courtesy such as his has been, and entreat me ever henceforth as your brother and servant." Whereat over-joyed in the last degree :—" Nought," quoth the lady, " by what I noted of your behaviour, could ever have caused me to anticipate other sequel of my coming hither than this which I see is your will, and for which I shall ever be your debtor." She then took her leave, and, attended by a guard of honour, returned to Giliberto, and told him what had passed ; between whom and Messer Ansaldo there was thenceforth a most close and loyal friendship.

Now the liberality shewn by Giliberto towards Messer Ansaldo, and by Messer Ansaldo towards the lady, having been marked by the necromancer, when Messer Ansaldo made ready to give him the promised reward :—" Now God forbid," quoth he,

" that, as I have seen Giliberto liberal in regard of his honour, and you liberal in regard of your love, I be not in like manner liberal in regard of my reward, which accordingly, witting that 'tis in good hands, I am minded that you keep." The knight was abashed, and strove hard to induce him to take, if not the whole, at least a part of the money; but finding that his labour was in vain, and that the necromancer, having caused his garden to vanish after the third day, was minded to depart, he bade him adieu. And the carnal love he had borne the lady being spent, he burned for her thereafter with a flame of honourable affection. Now what shall be our verdict in this case, lovesome ladies? A lady, as it were dead, and a love grown luke-warm for utter hopelessness! Shall we set a liberality shewn in such a case above this liberality of Messer Ansaldo, loving yet as ardently, and hoping, perchance, yet more ardently than ever, and holding in his hands the prize that he had so long pursued? Folly indeed should I deem it to compare that liberality with this.

NOVEL VI

King Charles the Old, being conqueror, falls in love with a young maiden, and afterwards growing ashamed of his folly bestows her and her sister honourably in marriage.

WHO might fully recount with what diversity of argument the ladies debated which of the three, Giliberto, or Messer Ansaldo, or the necromancer, behaved with the most liberality in the affair of Madonna Dianora? Too long were it to tell. However, when the king had allowed them to dispute a while, he, with a glance at Fiammetta, bade her rescue them from their wrangling by telling her story. Fiammetta made no demur, but thus began:—Illustrious my ladies, I have ever been of opinion that in companies like ours one should speak so explicitly that the import of what is said should never by excessive circumscription afford matter for disputation; which is much more in place among students in the schools, than among us. whose powers are scarce adequate to the management of the distaff and the spindle. Wherefore I, that had in mind a matter of, perchance, some nicety, now that I see you all at variance touching the matters last mooted, am minded to lay it aside, and tell you somewhat else, which concerns a man

by no means of slight account, but a valiant king, being a
chivalrous action that he did, albeit in no wise thereto actuated
by his honour.

There is none of you but may not seldom have heard tell of
King Charles the Old, or the First, by whose magnificent
emprise, and the ensuing victory gained over King Manfred,
the Ghibellines were driven forth of Florence, and the Guelfs
returned thither. For which cause a knight, Messer Neri
degli Uberti by name, departing Florence with his household
and not a little money, resolved to fix his abode under no
other sway than that of King Charles. And being fain of a
lonely place in which to end his days in peace, he betook him
to Castello da Mare di Stabia ; and there, perchance a cross-
bow-shot from the other houses of the place, amid the olives
and hazels and chestnuts that abound in those parts, he bought
an estate, on which he built a goodly house and commodious,
with a pleasant garden beside it, in the midst of which, having
no lack of running water, he set, after our Florentine fashion,
a pond fair and clear, and speedily filled it with fish. And while
thus he lived, daily occupying himself with nought else but how
to make his garden more fair, it befell that King Charles in the
hot season betook him to Castello da Mare to refresh himself
a while, and hearing of the beauty of Messer Neri's garden,
was desirous to view it. And having learned to whom it
belonged, he bethought him that, as the knight was an adherent
of the party opposed to him, he would use more familiarity
towards him than he would otherwise have done ; and so he
sent him word that he and four comrades would sup privily
with him in his garden on the ensuing evening. Messer Neri
felt himself much honoured ; and having made his preparations
with magnificence, and arranged the order of the ceremonies
with his household, did all he could and knew to make the
King cordially welcome to his fair garden.

When the King had viewed the garden throughout, as also
Messer Neri's house, and commended them, he washed, and
seated himself at one of the tables, which were set beside the
pond, and bade Count Guy de Montfort, who was one of his
companions, sit on one side of him, and Messer Neri on the
other, and the other three to serve, as they should be directed
by Messer Neri. The dishes that were set before them were
dainty, the wines excellent and rare, the order of the repast
very fair and commendable, without the least noise or aught
else that might distress ; whereon the King bestowed no

stinted praise. As thus he gaily supped, well-pleased with the lovely spot, there came into the garden two young maidens, each perhaps fifteen years old, blonde both, their golden tresses falling all in ringlets about them, and crowned with a dainty garland of periwinkle-flowers ; and so delicate and fair of face were they that they shewed liker to angels than aught else, each clad in a robe of finest linen, white as snow upon their flesh, close-fitting as might be from the waist up, but below the waist ample, like a pavilion to the feet. She that was foremost bore on her shoulders a pair of nets, which she held with her left hand—carrying in her right a long pole. Her companion followed, bearing on her left shoulder a frying-pan, under her left arm a bundle of faggots, and in her left hand a tripod, while in the other hand she carried a cruse of oil and a lighted taper. At sight of whom the King marvelled, and gazed intent to learn what it might import. The two young maidens came forward with becoming modesty, and did obeisance to the King ; which done they hied them to the place of ingress to the pond, and she that had the frying-pan, having set it down, and afterward the other things, took the pole that the other carried, and so they both went down into the pond, being covered by its waters to their breasts. Whereupon one of Messer Neri's servants, having forthwith lit a fire, and set the tripod on the faggots and oil therein, addressed himself to wait, until some fish should be thrown to him by the girls. Who, the one searching with the pole in those parts where she knew the fish lay hid, while the other made ready the nets, did in a brief space of time, to the exceeding great delight of the King, who watched them attentively, catch fish not a few, which they tossed to the servant, who set them, before the life was well out of them, in the frying-pan. After which, the maidens, as pre-arranged, addressed them to catch some of the finest fish, and cast them on to the table before the King, and Count Guy, and their father. The fish wriggled about the table to the prodigious delight of the King, who in like manner took some of them, and courteously returned them to the girls ; with which sport they diverted them, until the servant had cooked the fish that had been given him : which, by Messer Neri's command, were set before the King rather as a side-dish than as aught very rare or delicious.

When the girls saw that all the fish were cooked, and that there was no occasion for them to catch any more, they came forth of the pond, their fine white garments cleaving everywhere close to their flesh so as to hide scarce any part of their delicate persons, took up again the things that they had brought, and passing modestly before the King, returned to the house. The King, and the Count, and the other gentlemen that waited, had regarded the maidens with no little attention, and had, one and all, inly bestowed on them no little praise, as being fair and shapely, and therewithal sweet and debonair ; but 'twas in the King's eyes that they especially found favour. Indeed, as they came forth of the water, the King had scanned each part of their bodies so intently that, had one then pricked him, he would not have felt it, and his thoughts afterwards dwelling upon them, though he knew not who they were, nor how they came to be there, he felt stir within his heart a most ardent desire to pleasure them, whereby he knew very well that, if he took not care, he would grow enamoured ; howbeit he knew not whether of the twain pleased him the more, so like was each to the other. Having thus brooded a while, he turned to Messer Neri, and asked who the two damsels were. Whereto : " Sire," replied Messer Neri, " they are my twin daughters, and they are called, the one, Ginevra the Fair, and the other, Isotta the Blonde." Whereupon the King was loud in praise of them, and exhorted Messer Neri to bestow them in marriage. To which Messer Neri demurred, for that he no longer had the means. And nought of the supper now remaining to serve, save the fruit, in came the two young damsels in gowns of taffeta very fine, bearing in their hands two vast silver salvers full of divers fruits, such as the season yielded, and set them on the table before the King. Which done, they withdrew a little space and fell a-singing to music a ditty, of which the opening words were as follows :—

> Love, many words would not suffice
> There where I am come to tell.

And so dulcet and delightsome was the strain that to the King, his eyes and ears alike charmed, it seemed as if all the nine orders of angels were descended there to sing. The song ended, they knelt and respectfully craved the King's leave to depart ; which, though sorely against his will, he gave them with a forced gaiety.

Supper ended, the King and his companions, having remounted their horses, took leave of Messer Neri, and conversing of divers matters, returned to the royal quarters ; where the King, still harbouring his secret passion, nor, despite

affairs of state that supervened, being able to forget the beauty
and sweetness of Ginevra the Fair, for whose sake he likewise
loved her twin sister, was so limed by Love that he could scarce
think of aught else. So, feigning other reasons, he consorted
familiarly with Messer Neri, and did much frequent his garden,
that he might see Ginevra. And at length, being unable to
endure his suffering any longer, and being minded, for that he
could devise no other expedient, to despoil their father not
only of the one but of the other damsel also, he discovered both
his love and his project to Count Guy ; who, being a good man
and true, thus made answer :—" Sire, your tale causes me not
a little astonishment, and that more especially because of your
conversation from your childhood to this very day, I have,
methinks, known more than any other man. And as no such
passion did I ever mark in you, even in your youth, when Love
should more readily have fixed you with his fangs, as now I
discern, when you are already on the verge of old age, 'tis to
me so strange, so surprising that you should veritably love,
that I deem it little short of a miracle. And were it meet for
me to reprove you, well wot I the language I should hold to
you, considering that you are yet in arms in a realm but lately
won, among a people as yet unknown to you, and wily and
treacherous in the extreme, and that the gravest anxieties and
matters of high policy engross your mind, so that you are not
as yet able to sit you down, and nevertheless amid all these
weighty concerns you have given harbourage to false, flattering
Love. This is not the wisdom of a great king, but the folly of
a feather-pated boy. And moreover, what is far worse, you say
that you are resolved to despoil this poor knight of his two
daughters, whom, entertaining you in his house, and honouring
you to the best of his power, he brought into your presence
all but naked, testifying thereby, how great is his faith in you,
and how assured he is that you are a king, and not a devouring
wolf. Have you so soon forgotten that 'twas Manfred's out-
rageous usage of his subjects that opened you the way into this
realm ? What treachery was he ever guilty of that better
merited eternal torment, than 'twould be in you to wrest from
one that honourably entreats you at once his hope and his
consolation ? What would be said of you if so you should do ?
Perchance you deem that 'twould suffice to say :—' I did it
because he is a Ghibelline.' Is it then consistent with the
justice of a king that those, be they who they may, who seek
his protection, as this man has sought yours, should be entreated

after this sort ? King, I bid you remember that exceeding great as is your glory to have vanquished Manfred, yet to conquer oneself is a still greater glory : wherefore you, to whom belongs the correction of others, see to it that you conquer yourself, and refrain this unruly passion ; and let not such a blot mar the splendour of your achievements."

Sore stricken at heart by the Count's words, and the more mortified that he acknowledged their truth, the King heaved a fervent sigh or two, and then :—" Count," quoth he, " that enemy there is none, however mighty, but to the practised warrior is weak enough and easy to conquer in comparison of his own appetite, I make no doubt ; but, great though the struggle will be and immeasurable the force that it demands, so shrewdly galled am I by your words, that not many days will have gone by before I shall without fail have done enough to shew you that I, that am the conqueror of others, am no less able to gain the victory over myself." And indeed but a few days thereafter, the King, on his return to Naples, being minded at once to leave himself no excuse for dishonourable conduct, and to recompense the knight for his honourable entreatment of him, did, albeit 'twas hard for him to endow another with that which he had most ardently desired for himself, none the less resolve to bestow the two damsels in marriage, and that not as Messer Neri's daughters, but as his own. Wherefore, Messer Neri consenting, he provided both with magnificent dowries, and gave Ginevra the Fair to Messer Maffeo da Palizzi, and Isotta the Blonde to Messer Guglielmo della Magna, noble knights and great barons both ; which done, sad at heart beyond measure, he betook him to Apulia, and by incessant travail did so mortify his vehement appetite that he snapped and broke in pieces the fetters of Love, and for the rest of his days was no more vexed by such passion.

Perchance there will be those who say that 'tis but a trifle for a king to bestow two girls in marriage ; nor shall I dispute it : but say we that a king in love bestowed in marriage her whom he loved, neither having taken nor taking, of his love, leaf or flower or fruit ; then this I say was a feat great indeed, nay, as great as might be.

After such a sort then did this magnificent King, at once generously rewarding the noble knight, commendably honouring the damsels that he loved, and stoutly subduing himself.

NOVEL VII

*King Pedro, being apprised of the fervent love borne him by Lisa,
who thereof is sick, comforts her, and forthwith gives her in
marriage to a young gentleman, and having kissed her on
the brow, ever after professes himself her knight.*

WHEN Fiammetta was come to the end of her story, and not
a little praise had been accorded to the virile magnificence of
King Charles, albeit one there was of the ladies, who, being a
Ghibelline, joined not therein, Pampinea, having received the
king's command, thus began :—None is there of discernment,
worshipful my ladies, that would say otherwise than you have
said touching good King Charles, unless for some other cause
she bear him a grudge ; however, for that there comes to my
mind the, perchance no less honourable, entreatment of one
of our Florentine girls by one of his adversaries, I am minded
to recount the same to you.

What time the French were driven forth of Sicily there dwelt
at Palermo one of our Florentines, that was an apothecary,
Bernardo Puccini by name, a man of great wealth, that by his
lady had an only and exceeding fair daughter, then of marriageable age. Now King Pedro of Arragon, being instated in the
sovereignty of the island, did at Palermo make with his barons
marvellous celebration thereof ; during which, as he tilted
after the Catalan fashion, it befell that Bernardo's daughter,
Lisa by name, being with other ladies at a window, did thence
espy him in the course, whereat being prodigiously delighted,
she regarded him again and again, and grew fervently enamoured
of him ; nor yet, when the festivities were ended, and she
was at home with her father, was there aught she could think
of but this her exalted and aspiring love. In regard whereof
that which most irked her was her sense of her low rank, which
scarce permitted her any hope of a happy issue ; but, for all
that, give over her love for the King she would not ; nor yet,
for fear of worse to come, dared she discover it. The King,
meanwhile, recking, witting nothing of the matter, her suffering
waxed immeasurable, intolerable ; and her love ever growing
with ever fresh accessions of melancholy, the fair maiden, overborne at last, fell sick, and visibly day by day wasted like snow
in sunlight. Distraught with grief thereat, her father and
mother afforded her such succour as they might with words of

good cheer, and counsel of physicians, and physic; but all to
no purpose; for that she in despair of her love was resolved
no more to live.

Now her father assuring her that there was no whim of hers
but should be gratified, the fancy took her that, if she might
find apt means, she would, before she died, make her love and
her resolve known to the King: wherefore one day she besought
her father to cause Minuccio d'Arezzo to come to her; which
Minuccio was a singer and musician of those days, reputed most
skilful, and well seen of King Pedro. Bernardo, deeming that
Lisa desired but to hear him play and sing a while, conveyed
her message to him; and he, being an agreeable fellow, came
to her forthwith, and after giving her some words of loving
cheer, sweetly discoursed some airs upon his viol, and then
sang her some songs; whereby, while he thought to comfort
her, he did but add fire and flame to her love. Presently
the girl said that she would fain say a few words to him in
private, and when all else were withdrawn from the chamber:
—" Minuccio," quoth she, " thee have I chosen, deeming thee
most trusty, to be the keeper of my secret, relying upon thee
in the first place never to betray it to a soul, and next to lend
me in regard thereof such aid as thou mayst be able; and so
I pray thee to do. Thou must know, then, Minuccio mine,
that on the day when our lord King Pedro held the great festival
in celebration of his triumph, I, seeing him tilt, was so smitten
with love of him that thereof was kindled within my soul the
fire which has brought me, as thou seest, to this pass; and
knowing how ill it beseems me to love a king, and being unable,
I say not to banish it from my heart, but so much as to bring it
within bounds, and finding it exceeding grievous to bear, I
have made choice of death as the lesser pain; and die I shall.
But should he wot not of my love before I die, sore disconsolate
should I depart; and knowing not by whom more aptly than
by thee I might give him to know this my frame, I am minded
to entrust the communication thereof to thee; which office
I entreat thee not to refuse, and having discharged it, to let
me know, that dying thus consoled, I may depart this pain."
Which said, she silently wept.

Marvelling at the loftiness of the girl's spirit and her desperate
determination, Minuccio commiserated her not a little; and
presently it occurred to him that there was a way in which
he might honourably serve her: wherefore:—" Lisa," quoth
he, " my faith I plight thee, wherein thou mayst place sure

confidence that I shall never play thee false, and lauding thy
high emprise, to wit, the setting thine affections upon so great
a king, I proffer thee mine aid, whereby, so thou wilt be of good
cheer, I hope, and believe, that, before thou shalt see the third
day from now go by, I shall have brought thee tidings which
will be to thee for an exceeding great joy; and, not to lose
time, I will set to work at once." And so Lisa, assuring him
that she would be of good cheer, and plying him afresh with
instant obsecrations, bade him Godspeed; and Minuccio, having
taken leave of her, hied him to one Mico da Siena, a very expert
rhymester of those days, who at his instant request made the
ensuing song:—

> Hence hie thee, Love; and hasting to my King,
>   Give him to know what torment dire I bear,
>   How that to death I fare,
> Still close, for fear, my passion harbouring.
>
> Lo, Love, to thee with claspèd hands I turn,
>   And pray thee seek him where he tarrieth,
>   And tell him how I oft for him do yearn,
>   So sweetly he my heart enamoureth;
>   And of the fire, wherewith I throughly burn,
>   I think to die, but may the hour uneath
>   Say, when my grievous pain shall with my breath
> Surcease; till when, neither may fear nor shame
>   The least abate the flame.
> Ah! to his ears my woeful story bring.
>
> Since of him I was first enamourèd,
>   Never hast thou, O Love, my fearful heart
>   With any such fond hope encouragèd,
>   As e'er its message to him to impart,
>   To him, my lord, that me so sore bested
>   Holds: dying thus, 'twere grievous to depart:
>   Perchance, were he to know my cruel smart,
>   'Twould not displease him; might I but make bold
> My soul to him to unfold,
>   And shew him all my woeful languishing.
>
> Love, since 'twas not thy will me to accord
>   Such boldness as that e'er unto my King
>   I may discover my sad heart's full hoard,
>   Or any word or sign thereof him bring:
>   This all my prayer to thee, O sweet my Lord:
>   Hie thee to him, and so him whispering
>   Mind of the day I saw him tourneying
> With all his paladins environèd,
>   And grew enamourèd
> Ev'n to my very heart's disrupturing.

Which words Minuccio forthwith set to music after a soft and
plaintive fashion befitting their sense; and on the third day
thereafter hied him to court while King Pedro was yet at

breakfast. And being bidden by the King to sing something to the accompaniment of his viol, he gave them this song with such sweet concord of words and music that all the folk that were in the King's hall seemed, as it were, entranced, so intent and absorbed stood they to listen, and the King rather more than the rest. And when Minuccio had done singing, the King asked whence the song came, that, as far as he knew, he had never heard it before. " Sire," replied Minuccio, " 'tis not yet three days since 'twas made, words and music alike." And being asked by the King in regard of whom 'twas made :— " I dare not," quoth he, " discover such a secret save to you alone." Bent on hearing the story, the King, when the tables were cleared, took Minuccio into his privy chamber ; and there Minuccio told him everything exactly as he had heard it from Lisa's lips. Whereby the King was much gratified, and lauded the maiden not a little, and said that a girl of such high spirit merited considerate treatment, and bade Minuccio be his envoy to her, and comfort her, and tell her that without fail that very day at vespers he would come to visit her. Overjoyed to bear the girl such gladsome tidings, Minuccio tarried not, but hied him back to the girl with his viol, and being closeted with her, told her all that had passed, and then sang the song to the accompaniment of his viol. Whereby the girl was so cheered and delighted that forthwith there appeared most marked and manifest signs of the amendment of her health, while with passionate longing (albeit none in the house knew or divined it) she awaited the vesper hour, when she was to see her lord.

Knowing the girl very well, and how fair she was, and pondering divers times on what Minuccio had told him, the King, being a prince of a liberal and kindly disposition, grew ever more compassionate. So, about vespers, he mounted his horse, and rode forth, as if for mere pleasure, and being come to the apothecary's house, demanded access to a very goodly garden that the apothecary had, and having dismounted, after a while enquired of Bernardo touching his daughter, and whether he had yet bestowed her in marriage. "Sire," replied Bernardo, "she is not yet married ; and indeed she has been and still is very ill : howbeit since none she is wonderfully amended." The significance of which amendment being forthwith apprehended by the King :—" In good faith," quoth he, " 'twere a pity so fair a creature were reft from the world so early ; we would go in and visit her." And presently, attended only by two of

his lords and Bernardo, he betook him to her chamber, where
being entered, he drew nigh the bed, whereon the girl half
reclined, half sate in eager expectation of his coming ; and
taking her by the hand :—" Madonna," quoth he, " what means
this ? A maiden like you should be the comfort of others,
and you suffer yourself to languish. We would entreat you
that for love of us you be of good cheer, so as speedily to recover
your health." To feel the touch of his hand whom she loved
above all else, the girl, albeit somewhat shamefast, was so
enraptured that 'twas as if she was in Paradise ; and as soon
as she was able :—" My lord," she said, " 'twas the endeavour,
weak as I am, to sustain a most grievous burden that brought
this sickness upon me ; but 'twill not be long ere you will see
me quit thereof, thanks to your courtesy." The hidden meaning
of which words was apprehended only by the King, who
momently made more account of the girl, and again and again
inly cursed Fortune, that had decreed that she should be the
daughter of such a man. And yet a while he tarried with her,
and comforted her, and so took his leave. Which gracious
behaviour of the King was not a little commended, and accounted
a signal honour to the apothecary and his daughter.

The girl, glad at heart as was ever lady of her lover, mended
with reviving hope, and in a few days recovered her health, and
therewith more than all her wonted beauty. Whereupon the
King, having taken counsel with the Queen how to reward
so great a love, got him one day to horse with a great company
of his barons, and hied him to the apothecary's house ; and
being come into the garden, he sent for the apothecary and his
daughter ; and there, being joined by the Queen with not a
few ladies, who received the girl into their company, they
made such cheer as 'twas a wonder to see. And after a while
the King and Queen having called Lisa to them, quoth the
King :—" Honourable damsel, by the great love that you have
borne us we are moved greatly to honour you ; and we trust
that, for love of us, the honour that we design for you will be
acceptable to you. Now 'tis thus we would honour you : to
wit, that, seeing that you are of marriageable age, we would
have you take for husband him that we shall give you ; albeit
'tis none the less our purpose ever to call ourself your knight,
demanding no other tribute of all your love but one sole kiss."
Scarlet from brow to neck, the girl, making the King's pleasure
her own, thus with a low voice replied :—" My lord, very sure
am I that, should it come to be known that I was grown en-

amoured of you, most folk would hold me for a fool, deeming, perchance, that I was out of my mind, and witless alike of my own rank and yours; but God, who alone reads the hearts of us mortals, knows that even then, when first I did affect you, I wist that you were the King, and I but the daughter of Bernardo the apothecary, and that to suffer my passion to soar so high did ill become me; but, as you know far better than I, none loves of set and discreet purpose, but only according to the dictates of impulse and fancy; which law my forces, albeit not seldom opposed, being powerless to withstand, I loved and still love and shall ever love you. But as no sooner knew I myself subjugated to your love, than I vowed to have ever no will but yours; therefore not only am I compliant to take right gladly him whom you shall be pleased to give me for husband, thereby conferring upon me great honour and dignity; but if you should bid me tarry in the fire, delighted were I to obey, so thereby I might pleasure you. How far it beseems me to have you, my King, for my knight, you best know; and therefore I say nought thereof; nor will the kiss which you crave as your sole tribute of my love be granted you save by leave of my Lady the Queen. Natheless, may you have of this great graciousness that you and my Lady the Queen have shewn me, and which I may not requite, abundant recompense in the blessing and favour of God;" and so she was silent.

The Queen was mightily delighted with the girl's answer, and deemed her as discreet as the King had said. The King then sent for the girl's father and mother, and being assured that his intention had their approval, summoned to his presence a young man, Perdicone by name, that was of gentle birth, but in poor circumstances, and put certain rings into his hand, and (he nowise gainsaying) wedded him to Lisa. Which done, besides jewels many and precious that he and the Queen gave the girl, he forthwith bestowed upon Perdicone two domains, right goodly and of ample revenues, to wit, Ceffalù and Calatabellotta, saying:—"We give them to thee for thy wife's dowry; what we have in store for thee thou wilt learn hereafter." Which said, he turned to the girl, and:—"Now," quoth he, "we are minded to cull that fruit which is due to us of thy love;" and so, taking her head between both his hands, he kissed her brow. Wherefore, great was the joy of Perdicone, and the father and mother of Lisa, and Lisa herself, and mighty the cheer they made, and gaily did they celebrate the nuptials. And, as many affirm, right well did the King keep his promise to the girl;

for that ever, while he lived, he called himself her knight, nor
went to any passage of arms bearing other device than that
which he had from her.

Now 'tis by doing after this sort that sovereigns win the hearts
of their subjects, give others occasion of well-doing, and gain
for themselves an imperishable renown. At which mark few
or none in our times have bent the bow of their understanding,
the more part of the princes having become but cruel tyrants.

NOVEL VIII

*Sophronia, albeit she deems herself wife to Gisippus, is wife to
Titus Quintius Fulvus, and goes with him to Rome, where
Gisippus arrives in indigence, and deeming himself scorned
by Titus, to compass his own death, avers that he has slain a
man. Titus recognizes him, and to save his life, alleges that
'twas he that slew the man: whereof he that did the deed being
witness, he discovers himself as the murderer. Whereby
it comes to pass that they are all three liberated by Octavianus;
and Titus gives Gisippus his sister to wife, and shares with
him all his substance.*

So ceased Pampinea; and when all the ladies, and most of all
the Ghibelline, had commended King Pedro, Filomena by command of the king thus began:—Magnificent my ladies, who wots
not that there is nought so great but kings, when they have a
mind, may accomplish it? As also that 'tis of them that
magnificence is most especially demanded? Now whoso, being
powerful, does that which it appertains to him to do, does well;
but therein is no such matter of marvel, or occasion of extolling
him to the skies, as in his deed, of whom, for that his power is
slight, less is demanded. Wherefore, as you are so profuse of
your words in exaltation of the fine deeds, as you deem them,
of monarchs, I make no manner of doubt, but that the doings
of our peers must seem to you yet more delectable and commendable, when they equal or surpass those of kings. Accordingly 'tis a transaction, laudable and magnificent, that passed
between two citizens, who were friends, that I purpose to recount
to you in my story.

I say, then, that what time Octavianus Caesar, not as yet
hight Augustus, but being in the office called Triumvirate,
swayed the empire of Rome, there dwelt at Rome a gentleman

Publius Quintius Fulvus by name, who, having a son, Titus
Quintius Fulvus, that was a very prodigy of wit, sent him to
Athens to study philosophy, and to the best of his power commended him to a nobleman of that city, Chremes by name, who
was his very old friend. Chremes lodged Titus in his own house
with his son Gisippus, and placed both Titus and Gisippus under
a philosopher named Aristippus, to learn of him his doctrine.
And the two youths thus keeping together, found each the
other's conversation so congruous with his own, that there grew
up between them a friendship so close and brotherly that 'twas
never broken by aught but death ; nor knew either rest or
solace save when he was with the other. So, gifted alike with
pre-eminent subtlety of wit, they entered on their studies, and
with even pace and prodigious applause scaled together the
glorious heights of philosophy. In which way of life, to the
exceeding great delight of Chremes, who entreated Titus as
no less his son than Gisippus, they continued for full three
years. At the end whereof, it befell (after the common course
of things mundane) that Chremes (being now aged) departed
this life. Whom with equal grief they mourned as a common
father ; and the friends and kinsfolk of Chremes were alike at
a loss to determine whether of the twain stood in need of the
more consolation upon the bereavement.

  Some months afterward the friends and kinsfolk of Gisippus
came to him and exhorted him, as did also Titus, to take a
wife, and found him a maiden, wondrous fair, of one of the most
noble houses of Athens, her name Sophronia, and her age about
fifteen years. So a time was appointed for their nuptials, and
one day, when 'twas near at hand, Gisippus bade Titus come
see the maiden, whom as yet he had not seen ; and they being
come into her house, and she sitting betwixt them, Titus, as
he were fain to observe with care the several charms of his
friend's wife that was to be, surveyed her with the closest
attention, and being delighted beyond measure with all that
he saw, grew, as inly he extolled her charms to the skies, enamoured of her with a love as ardent, albeit he gave no sign
of it, as ever lover bore to lady. However, after they had tarried
a while with her, they took their leave, and went home, where
Titus repaired to his chamber, and there gave himself over to
solitary musing on the damsel's charms, and the longer he
brooded, the more he burned for her. Whereon as he reflected,
having heaved many a fervent sigh, thus he began to commune
with himself :—Ah ! woe worth thy life, Titus ! Whom makest

thou the mistress of thy soul, thy love, thy hope? Knowest thou not that by reason as well of thy honourable entreatment by Chremes and his kin as of the whole-hearted friendship that is between thee and Gisippus, it behoves thee to have his betrothed in even such pious regard as if she were thy sister? Whither art thou suffering beguiling love, delusive hope, to hurry thee? Open the eyes of thine understanding, and see thyself, wretched man, as thou art; obey the dictates of thy reason, refrain thy carnal appetite, control thine inordinate desires, and give thy thoughts another bent; join battle with thy lust at the outset, and conquer thyself while there is yet time. This which thou wouldst have is not meet, is not seemly: this which thou art minded to ensue, thou wouldst rather, though thou wert, as thou art not, sure of its attainment, eschew, hadst thou but the respect thou shouldst have, for the claims of true friendship. So, then, Titus, what wilt thou do? What but abandon this unseemly love, if thou wouldst do as it behoves thee?

But then, as he remembered Sophronia, his thoughts took the contrary direction, and he recanted all he had said, musing on this wise:—The laws of Love are of force above all others; they abrogate not only the law of human friendship, but the law Divine itself. How many times ere now has father loved daughter, brother sister, step-mother step-son? aberrations far more notable than that a friend should love his friend's wife, which has happened a thousand times. Besides which, I am young, and youth is altogether subject to the laws of Love. Love's pleasure, then, should be mine. The seemly is for folk of riper years. 'Tis not in my power to will aught save that which Love wills. So beauteous is this damsel that there is none but should love her; and if I love her, who am young, who can justly censure me? I love her not because she is the affianced of Gisippus; no matter whose she was, I should love her all the same. Herein is Fortune to blame, that gave her to my friend, Gisippus, rather than to another. And if she is worthy of love, as for beauty she is, Gisippus, if he should come to know that I love her, ought to be less jealous than another.

Then, scorning himself that he should indulge such thoughts, he relapsed into the opposing mood, albeit not to abide there, but ever veering to and fro, he spent not only the whole of that day and the ensuing night, but many others; insomuch that, being able neither to eat nor to sleep, he grew so weak that he

was fain to take to his bed. Gisippus, who had marked his
moodiness for some days, and now saw that he was fairly sick,
was much distressed; and with sedulous care, never quitting
his side, he tended, and strove as best he might to comfort,
him, not seldom and most earnestly demanding to know of
him the cause of his melancholy and his sickness. Many were
the subterfuges to which Titus resorted; but, as Gisippus was
not to be put off with his fables, finding himself hard pressed
by him, with sighs and sobs he made answer on this wise:—
"Gisippus, had such been the will of the Gods, I were fain
rather to die than to live, seeing that Fortune has brought me
to a strait in which needs must my virtue be put to the ordeal,
and, to my most grievous shame, 'tis found wanting: whereof
I confidently expect my due reward, to wit, death, which will
be more welcome to me than to live, haunted ever by the
memory of my baseness, which, as there is nought that from
thee I either should or can conceal, I, not without burning
shame, will discover to thee." And so he recounted the whole
story from first to last, the occasion of his melancholy, its several
moods, their conflict, and with which of them the victory rested,
averring that he was dying of love for Sophronia, and that,
knowing how ill such love beseemed him, he had, for penance,
elected to die, and deemed the end was now not far off.
Gisippus, hearing his words and seeing his tears, for a while
knew not what to say, being himself smitten with the damsel's
charms, albeit in a less degree than Titus; but ere long he made
up his mind that Sophronia must be less dear to him than his
friend's life.

And so, moved to tears by his friend's tears:—" Titus," quoth
he between his sobs, " but that thou art in need of comfort, I
should reproach thee, that thou hast offended against our friendship in that thou hast so long kept close from me this most distressful passion; and albeit thou didst deem it unseemly, yet
unseemly things should no more than things seemly be withheld
from a friend, for that, as a friend rejoices with his friend in
things seemly, so he does his endeavour to wean his friend
from things unseemly: but enough of this for the nonce:
I pass to that which, I wot, is of greater moment. If thou
ardently lovest Sophronia, my affianced, so far from marvelling
thereat, I should greatly marvel were it not so, knowing how fair
she is, and how noble is thy soul, and thus the apter to be
swayed by passion, the more excelling is she by whom thou art
charmed. And the juster the cause thou hast to love Sophronia,

the greater is the injustice with which thou complainest of
Fortune (albeit thou dost it not in so many words) for giving
her to me, as if thy love of her had been seemly, had she belonged
to any other but me; whereas, if thou art still the wise man thou
wast wont to be, thou must know that to none could Fortune
have assigned her, with such good cause for thee to thank her,
as to me. Had any other had her, albeit thy love had been
seemly, he had loved her as his own, rather than as thine;
which, if thou deem me even such a friend to thee as I am,
thou wilt not apprehend from me, seeing that I mind me not
that, since we were friends, I had ever aught that was not as
much thine as mine. And so should I entreat thee herein as
in all other matters, were the affair gone so far that nought else
were possible; but as it is, I can make thee sole possessor of
her; and so I mean to do; for I know not what cause thou
shouldst have to prize my friendship, if, where in seemly sort
it might be done, I knew not how to surrender my will to thine.
'Tis true that Sophronia is my betrothed, and that I loved her
much, and had great cheer in expectation of the nuptials:
but as thou, being much more discerning than I, dost more
fervently affect this rare prize, rest assured that she will enter
my chamber not mine but thine. Wherefore, away with thy
moodiness, banish thy melancholy, recover thy lost health,
thy heartiness and jollity, and gladsomely, even from this very
hour, anticipate the guerdon of thy love, a love worthier far
than mine."

Delightful as was the prospect with which hope flattered
Titus, as he heard Gisippus thus speak, no less was the shame
with which right reason affected him, admonishing him that
the greater was the liberality of Gisippus, the less it would
become him to profit thereby. Wherefore, still weeping, he
thus constrained himself to make answer:—" Gisippus, thy
generous and true friendship leaves me in no doubt as to the
manner in which it becomes me to act. God forefend that her,
whom, as to the more worthy, He has given to thee, I should
ever accept of thee for mine. Had He seen fit that she should
be mine, far be it from thee or any other to suppose that He
would ever have awarded her to thee. Renounce not, then,
that which thy choice and wise counsel and His gift have made
thine, and leave me, to whom, as unworthy, He has appointed
no such happiness, to waste my life in tears; for either I shall
conquer my grief, which will be grateful to thee, or it will conquer me, and so I shall be quit of my pain." Quoth then

Gisippus :—" If our friendship, Titus, is of such a sort as may
entitle me to enforce thee to ensue behests of mine, or as may
induce thee of thine own free will to ensue the same, such is
the use to which, most of all, I am minded to put it ; and if
thou lend not considerate ear unto my prayers, I shall by force,
that force which is lawful in the interest of a friend, make
Sophronia thine. I know the might of Love, how redoubtable
it is, and how, not once only, but oftentimes, it has brought ill-
starred lovers to a miserable death ; and thee I see so hard
bested that turn back thou mightst not, nor get the better of
thy grief, but holding on thy course, must succumb, and perish ;
and without doubt I should speedily follow thee. And so, had
I no other cause to love thee, thy life is precious to me in that
my own is bound up with it. Sophronia, then, shall be thine ;
for thou wouldst not lightly find another so much to thy mind,
and I shall readily find another to love, and so shall content
both thee and me. In which matter, peradventure, I might
not be so liberal, were wives so scarce or hard to find as are
friends ; wherefore, as 'tis so easy a matter for me to find
another wife, I had liefer—I say not lose her, for in giving her
to thee lose her I shall not, but only transfer her to one that is
my *alter ego*, and that to her advantage—I had liefer, I say,
transfer her to thee than lose thee. And so, if aught my prayers
avail with thee, I entreat thee extricate thyself from this thy
woeful plight, and comfort at once thyself and me, and in good
hope, address thyself to pluck that boon which thy fervent
love craves of her for whom thou yearnest."

Still scrupling, for shame, to consent that Sophronia should
become his wife, Titus remained yet a while inexorable ; but,
yielding at last to the solicitations of Love, reinforced by the
exhortations of Gisippus, thus he made answer :—" Lo now,
Gisippus, I know not how to call it, whether 'tis more thy
pleasure than mine, this which I do, seeing that 'tis as thy
pleasure that thou so earnestly entreatest me to do it ; but, as
thy liberality is such that my shame, though becoming, may
not withstand it, I will even do it. But of this rest assured,
that I do so, witting well that I receive from thee, not only the
lady I love, but with her my very life. And, Fate permitting,
may the Gods grant me to make thee such honourable and
goodly requital as may shew thee how sensible I am of the boon,
which thou, more compassionate of me than I am of myself,
conferrest on me." Quoth then Gisippus :—" Now, for the
giving effect to our purpose, methinks, Titus, we should proceed

on this wise. Thou knowest that Sophronia, by treaty at length concluded between my family and hers, is become my betrothed : were I now to say that she should not be my wife, great indeed were the scandal that would come thereof, and I should affront both her family and mine own ; whereof, indeed, I should make no account, so it gave me to see her become thine ; but I fear that, were I to give her up at this juncture, her family would forthwith bestow her upon another, perchance, than thee, and so we should both be losers. Wherefore methinks that, so thou approve, I were best to complete what I have begun, bring her home as my wife, and celebrate the nuptials, and thereafter we can arrange that thou lie with her, privily, as thy wife. Then, time and occasion serving, we will disclose the whole affair, and if they are satisfied, well and good ; if not, 'twill be done all the same, and as it cannot be undone, they must perforce make the best of it."

Which counsel being approved by Titus, Gisippus brought the lady home as his wife, Titus being now recovered, and quite himself again ; and when they had made great cheer, and night was come, the ladies, having bedded the bride, took their departure. Now the chambers of Titus and Gisippus were contiguous, and one might pass from one into the other : Gisippus, therefore, being come into his room, extinguished every ray of light, and stole into that of Titus, and bade him go get him to bed with his lady. Whereat Titus gave way to shame, and would have changed his mind, and refused to go in ; but Gisippus, no less zealous at heart than in words to serve his friend, after no small contention prevailed on him to go thither. Now no sooner was Titus abed with the lady, than, taking her in his arms, he, as if jestingly, asked in a low tone whether she were minded to be his wife. She, taking him to be Gisippus, answered, yes ; whereupon he set a fair and costly ring on her finger, saying :—" And I am minded to be thy husband." And having presently consummated the marriage, he long and amorously disported him with her, neither she, nor any other, being ever aware that another than Gisippus lay with her.

Now Titus and Sophronia being after this sort wedded, Publius, the father of Titus, departed this life. For which cause Titus was bidden by letter to return forthwith to Rome to see to his affairs ; wherefore he took counsel with Gisippus how he might take Sophronia thither with him ; which might not well be done without giving her to know how matters stood.

Whereof, accordingly, one day, having called her into the chamber, they fully apprised her, Titus for her better assurance bringing to her recollection not a little of what had passed between them. Whereat she, after glancing from one to the other somewhat disdainfully, burst into a flood of tears, and reproached Gisippus that he had so deluded her; and forthwith, saying nought of the matter to any there, she hied her forth of Gisippus' house and home to her father, to whom and her mother she recounted the deceit which Gisippus had practised upon them as upon her, averring that she was the wife not of Gisippus, as they supposed, but of Titus. Whereby her father was aggrieved exceedingly, and prolonged and grave complaint was made thereof by him and his own and Gisippus' families, and there was not a little parleying, and a world of pother. Gisippus earned the hatred of both his own and Sophronia's kin, and all agreed that he merited not only censure but severe punishment. He, however, averred that he had done a thing seemly, and that Sophronia's kinsfolk owed him thanks for giving her in marriage to one better than himself.

All which Titus witnessed with great suffering, and witting that 'twas the way of the Greeks to launch forth in high words and menaces, and refrain not until they should meet with one that answered them, whereupon they were wont to grow not only humble but even abject, was at length minded that their clavers should no longer pass unanswered; and, as with his Roman temper he united Athenian subtlety, he cleverly contrived to bring the kinsfolk, as well of Gisippus as of Sophronia, together in a temple, where, being entered, attended only by Gisippus, thus (they being intent to hear) he harangued them:—" 'Tis the opinion of not a few philosophers that whatsoever mortals do is ordained by the providence of the immortal Gods; for which cause some would have it that nought either is, or ever shall be, done, save of necessity, albeit others there are that restrict this necessity to that which is already done. Regard we but these opinions with some little attention, and we shall very plainly perceive that to censure that which cannot be undone is nought else but to be minded to shew oneself wiser than the Gods; by whom we must suppose that we and our affairs are swayed and governed with uniform and unerring wisdom. Whereby you may very readily understand how vain and foolish a presumption it is to pass judgment on their doings, and what manner and might of chains they need who suffer themselves to be transported to such excess of daring. Among whom, in my judgment, you must one and all be numbered, if 'tis true, what I hear, to wit, that you have complained and do continue to complain that Sophronia, albeit you gave her to Gisippus, is, nevertheless, become my wife; not considering that 'twas ordained from all eternity that she should become, not the wife of Gisippus, but mine, as the fact does now declare.

" But, for that discourse of the secret providence and purposes of the Gods seems to many a matter hard and scarce to be understood, I am willing to assume that they meddle in no wise with our concerns, and to descend to the region of human counsels; in speaking whereof I must needs do two things quite at variance with my wont, to wit, in some degree praise myself and censure or vilify another. But, as in either case I mean not to deviate from the truth, and 'tis what the occasion demands, I shall not fail so to do. With bitter upbraidings, animated rather by rage than by reason, you cease not to murmur, nay, to cry out, against Gisippus, and to harass him with your abuse, and hold him condemned, for that her, whom you saw fit to give him, he has seen fit to give me, to wife; wherein I deem him worthy of the highest commendation, and that for two reasons, first, because he has done the office of a friend, and secondly, because he has done more wisely than you did. After what sort the sacred laws of friendship prescribe that friend shall entreat friend, 'tis not to my present purpose to declare; 'twill suffice to remind you that the tie of friendship should be more binding than that of blood, or kinship; seeing that our friends are of our own choosing, whereas our kinsfolk are appointed us by Fortune; wherefore, if my life was more to Gisippus than your goodwill, since I am, as I hold myself, his friend, can any wonder thereat?

" But pass we to my second reason; in the exposition whereof I must needs with yet more cogency prove to you that he has been wiser than you, seeing that, methinks, you wot nought of the providence of the Gods, and still less of the consequences of friendship. I say then, that, as 'twas your premeditated and deliberate choice that gave Sophronia to this young philosopher Gisippus, so 'twas his that gave her to another young philosopher. 'Twas your counsel that gave her to an Athenian; 'twas his that gave her to a Roman: 'twas your counsel that gave her to a man of gentle birth; 'twas his that gave her to one of birth yet gentler: wealthy was he to whom your counsel gave her, most wealthy he to whom his counsel gave her. Not only did he to whom your counsel gave her, love her not, but

he scarce knew her, whereas 'twas to one that loved her beyond
all other blessings, nay, more dearly than his own life, that his
counsel gave her. And to the end that it may appear more
plainly that 'tis even as I say, and Gisippus' counsel more to
be commended than yours, let us examine it point by point.
That I, like Gisippus, am young and a philosopher, my countenance and my pursuits may, without making more words
about the matter, sufficiently attest. We are also of the same
age, and have ever kept pace together in our studies. Now
true it is that he is an Athenian, and I am a Roman. But,
as touching the comparative glory of the cities, should the
matter be mooted, I say that I am of a free city, and he of a
city tributary ; that I am of a city that is mistress of all the
world, and he of one that is subject to mine ; that I am of a city
that flourishes mightily in arms, in empire, and in arts ; whereas
he cannot boast his city as famous save in arts.

"Moreover, albeit you see me here in the guise of a most
humble scholar, I am not born of the dregs of the populace of
Rome. My halls and the public places of Rome are full of the
antique effigies of my forefathers, and the annals of Rome
abound with the records of triumphs led by the Quintii to the
Roman Capitol ; and so far from age having withered it, to-day,
yet more abundantly than ever of yore, flourishes the glory of
our name. Of my wealth I forbear, for shame, to speak, being
mindful that honest poverty is the time-honoured and richest
inheritance of the noble citizens of Rome ; but, allowing for
the nonce the opinion of the vulgar, which holds poverty in
disrepute, and highly appraises wealth, I albeit I never sought
it, yet, as the favoured of Fortune, have abundant store thereof.
Now well I wot that, Gisippus being of your own city, you justly
prized and prize an alliance with him ; but not a whit less
should you prize an alliance with me at Rome, considering that
there you will have in me an excellent host, and a patron apt,
zealous and potent to serve you as well in matters of public
interest as in your private concerns. Who, then, dismissing
all bias from his mind, and judging with impartial reason, would
deem your counsel more commendable than that of Gisippus ?
Assuredly none. Sophronia, then, being married to Titus
Quintius Fulvus, a citizen of Rome, of an ancient and illustrious
house, and wealthy, and a friend of Gisippus, whoso takes um-
brage or offence thereat, does that which it behoves him not to
do, and knows not what he does.

"Perchance some will say that their complaint is not that

Sophronia is the wife of Titus, but that she became his wife
after such a sort, to wit, privily, by theft, neither friend nor
any of her kin witting aught thereof ; but herein is no matter
of marvel, no prodigy as yet unheard-of. I need not instance
those who before now have taken to them husbands in defiance
of their fathers' will, or have eloped with their lovers and been
their mistresses before they were their wives, or of whose
marriages no word has been spoken, until their pregnancy or
parturition published them to the world, and necessity sanc-
tioned the fact : nought of this has happened in the case of
Sophronia ; on the contrary, 'twas in proper form, and in
meet and seemly sort, that Gisippus gave her to Titus. And
others, peradventure, will say that 'twas by one to whom such
office belonged not that she was bestowed in marriage. Nay,
but this is but vain and womanish querulousness, and comes of
scant consideration. Know we not, then, that Fortune varies
according to circumstances her methods and her means of disposing events to their predetermined ends ? What matters it
to me, if it be a cobbler, rather than a philosopher, that Fortune
has ordained to compass something for me, whether privily or
overtly, so only the result is as it should be ? I ought, indeed,
to take order, if the cobbler be indiscreet, that he meddle no
more in affairs of mine, but, at the same time, I ought to thank
him for what he has done. If Gisippus has duly bestowed
Sophronia in marriage, it is gratuitous folly to find fault with
the manner and the person. If you mistrust his judgment,
have a care that it be not in his power to do the like again, but
thank him for this turn.

"Natheless, you are to know that I used no cunning practice
or deceit to sully in any degree the fair fame of your house in
the person of Sophronia ; and, albeit I took her privily to wife,
I came not as a ravisher to despoil her of her virginity, nor in
any hostile sort was I minded to make her mine on dishonourable
terms, and spurn your alliance ; but, being fervently enamoured
of her bewitching beauty and her noble qualities, I wist well
that, should I make suit for her with those formalities which
you, perchance, will say were due, then, for the great love you
bear her, and for fear lest I should take her away with me to
Rome, I might not hope to have her. Accordingly I made use
of the secret practice which is now manifest to you, and brought
Gisippus to consent in my interest to that whereto he was
averse ; and thereafter, ardently though I loved her, I sought
not to commingle with her as a lover, but as a husband, nor

closed with her, until, as she herself by her true witness may assure you, I had with apt words and with the ring made her my lawful wife, asking her if she would have me to husband, whereto she answered, yes. Wherein if she seem to have been tricked 'tis not I that am to blame, but she, for that she asked me not who I was.

"This, then, is the great wrong, sin, crime, whereof for love and friendship's sake Gisippus and I are guilty, that Sophronia is privily become the wife of Titus Quintius: 'tis for this that you harass him with your menaces and hostile machinations. What more would you do, had he given her to a villein, to a caitiff, to a slave? Where would you find fetters, dungeons, crosses adequate to your vengeance? But enough of this at present: an event, which I did not expect, has now happened; my father is dead; and I must needs return to Rome; wherefore, being fain to take Sophronia with me, I have discovered to you that which otherwise I had, perchance, still kept close. Whereto, if you are wise, you will gladly reconcile yourselves; for that, if I had been minded to play you false, or put an affront upon you, I might have scornfully abandoned her to you; but God forefend that such baseness be ever harboured in a Roman breast. Sophronia, then, by the will of the Gods, by force of law, and by my own love-taught astuteness, is mine. The which it would seem that you, deeming yourselves, peradventure, wiser than the Gods, or the rest of mankind, do foolishly set at nought, and that in two ways alike most offensive to me; inasmuch as you both withhold from me Sophronia, in whom right, as against me, you have none, and also entreat as your enemy Gisippus, to whom you are rightfully bounden. The folly whereof I purpose not at present fully to expound to you, but in friendly sort to counsel you to abate your wrath and abandon all your schemes of vengeance, and restore Sophronia to me, that I may part from you on terms of amity and alliance, and so abide: but of this rest assured, that whether this, which is done, like you or not, if you are minded to contravene it, I shall take Gisippus hence with me, and once arrived in Rome, shall in your despite find means to recover her who is lawfully mine, and pursuing you with unremitting enmity, will apprise you by experience of the full measure and effect of a Roman's wrath."

Having so said, Titus started to his feet, his countenance distorted by anger, and took Gisippus by the hand, and with manifest contempt for all the rest, shaking his head at them and threatening them, led him out of the temple. They that remained in the temple, being partly persuaded by his arguments to accept his alliance and friendship, partly terrified by his last words, resolved by common consent that 'twas better to have the alliance of Titus, as they had lost that of Gisippus, than to add to that loss the enmity of Titus. Wherefore they followed Titus, and having come up with him, told him that they were well pleased that Sophronia should be his, and that they should prize his alliance and the friendship of dear Gisippus; and having ratified this treaty of amity and alliance with mutual cheer, they departed and sent Sophronia to Titus. Sophronia, discreetly making a virtue of necessity, transferred forthwith to Titus the love she had borne Gisippus, and being come with Titus to Rome, was there received with no small honour. Gisippus tarried in Athens, held in little account by well-nigh all the citizens, and being involved in certain of their broils, was, not long afterwards, with all his household, banished the city, poor, nay, destitute, and condemned to perpetual exile. Thus hard bested, and at length reduced to mendicancy, he made his way, so as least discomfortably he might, to Rome, being minded to see whether Titus would remember him : and there, learning that Titus lived, and was much affected by all the Romans, and having found out his house, he took his stand in front of it, and watched until Titus came by ; to whom, for shame of the sorry trim that he was in, he ventured no word but did his endeavour that he might be seen of him, hoping that Titus might recognize him, and call him by his name : but Titus passing on, Gisippus deeming that he had seen and avoided him, and calling to mind that which aforetime he had done for him, went away wroth and desperate. And fasting and penniless, and—for 'twas now night—knowing not whither he went, and yearning above all for death, he wandered by chance to a spot, which, albeit 'twas within the city, had much of the aspect of a wilderness, and espying a spacious grotto, he took shelter there for the night ; and worn out at last with grief, on the bare ground, wretchedly clad as he was, he fell asleep.

Now two men that had that night gone out a-thieving, having committed the theft, came towards morning to the grotto, and there quarrelled, and the stronger slew the other, and took himself off. Aroused by the noise, Gisippus witnessed the murder, and deeming that he had now the means of com-passing, without suicide, the death for which he so much longed, budged not a jot, but stayed there, until the serjeants of the court, which had already got wind of the affair, came on the scene, and laid violent hands upon him, and led him away. Being examined, he confessed that he had slain the man, and had then been unable to make his escape from the grotto. Wherefore the praetor, Marcus Varro by name, sentenced him to death by crucifixion, as was then the custom. But Titus, who happened at that moment to come into the praetorium, being told the crime for which he was condemned, and scanning the poor wretch's face, presently recognized him for Gisippus, and marvelled how he should come to be there, and in such a woeful plight. And most ardently desiring to succour him, nor seeing other way to save his life except to exonerate him by accusing himself, he straightway stepped forward, and said with a loud voice :—" Marcus Varro, call back the poor man on whom thou hast passed sentence, for he is innocent. 'Tis enough that I have incurred the wrath of the Gods by one deed of violence, to wit, the murder of him whom your serjeants found dead this morning, without aggravating my offence by the death of another innocent man." Perplexed, and vexed that he should have been heard by all in the praetorium, but unable honourably to avoid compliance with that which the laws enjoined, Varro had Gisippus brought back, and in presence of Titus said to him :—" How camest thou to be so mad as, though no constraint was put upon thee, to confess a deed thou never didst, thy life being at stake ? Thou saidst that 'twas thou by whom the man was slain last night, and now comes this other, and says that 'twas not thou but he that slew him." Gisippus looked, and seeing Titus, wist well that, being grateful for the service rendered by him in the past, Titus was now minded to save his life at the cost of his own : wherefore, affected to tears, he said :—" Nay, but Varro, in very sooth I slew him, and 'tis now too late, this tender solicitude of Titus for my deliverance." But on his part :—" Praetor," quoth Titus, " thou seest this man is a stranger, and was found unarmed beside the murdered man ; thou canst not doubt that he was fain of death for very wretchedness : wherefore discharge him, and let punishment light on me who have merited it."

Marvelling at the importunity of both, Varro readily surmised that neither was guilty. And while he was casting about how he might acquit them, lo, in came a young man, one Publius Ambustus, a desperate character, and known to all the Romans for an arrant thief. He it was that had verily committed the murder, and witting both the men to be innocent of that of which each accused himself, so sore at heart was he by reason of their innocence, that, overborne by an exceeding great compassion, he presented himself before Varro, and:—" Praetor," quoth he, " 'tis destiny draws me hither to loose the knot of these men's contention; and some God within me leaves me no peace of his whips and stings, until I discover my offence: wherefore know that neither of these men is guilty of that of which each accuses himself. 'Tis verily I that slew the man this morning about daybreak; and before I slew him, while I was sharing our plunder with him, I espied this poor fellow asleep there. Nought need I say to clear Titus: the general bruit of his illustrious renown attests that he is not a man of such a sort. Discharge him, therefore, and exact from me the penalty prescribed by the laws."

The affair had by this time come to the ears of Octavianus, who caused all three to be brought before him, and demanded to know the causes by which they had been severally moved to accuse themselves; and, each having told his story, Octavianus released the two by reason of their innocence, and the third for love of them. Titus took Gisippus home, having first chidden him not a little for his faint-heartedness and diffidence, and there, Sophronia receiving him as a brother, did him marvellous cheer; and having comforted him a while, and arrayed him in apparel befitting his worth and birth, he first shared with him all his substance, and then gave him his sister, a young damsel named Fulvia, to wife, and said to him:—" Choose now, Gisippus, whether thou wilt tarry here with me, or go back to Achaia with all that I have given thee."

Partly perforce of his banishment from his city, partly for that the sweet friendship of Titus was justly dear to him, Gisippus consented to become a Roman. And so, long and happily they lived together at Rome, Gisippus with his Fulvia, and Titus with his Sophronia, in the same house, growing, if possible, greater friends day by day.

Exceeding sacred then, is friendship, and worthy not only to be had in veneration, but to be extolled with never-ending praise, as the most dutiful mother of magnificence and seemliness, sister of gratitude and charity, and foe to enmity and avarice; ever, without waiting to be asked, ready to do as generously by another as she would be done by herself. Rarely indeed is it to-day that twain are found, in whom her most holy fruits are manifest; for which is most shamefully answerable the covetousness of mankind, which, regarding only private interest, has banished friendship beyond earth's farthest bourne, there to abide in perpetual exile. How should love, or wealth, or kinship, how should aught but friendship have so quickened the soul of Gisippus that the tears and sighs of Titus should incline his heart to cede to him the fair and gracious lady that was his betrothed and his beloved? Laws, menaces, terror! How should these, how should aught but friendship, have withheld Gisippus, in lonely places, in hidden retreats, in his own bed, from enfolding (not perchance unsolicited by her) the fair damsel within his youthful embrace? Honours, rewards, gains! Would Gisippus for these, would he for aught but friendship, have made nothing of the loss of kindred—his own and Sophronia's—have made nothing of the injurious murmurs of the populace, have made nothing of mocks and scorns, so only he might content his friend? And on the other hand, for what other cause than friendship had Titus, when he might decently have feigned not to see, have striven with the utmost zeal to compass his own death, and set himself upon the cross in Gisippus' stead? And what but friendship had left no place for suspicion in the soul of Titus, and filled it with a most fervent desire to give his sister to Gisippus, albeit he saw him to be reduced to extreme penury and destitution? But so it is that men covet hosts of acquaintance, troops of kinsfolk, offspring in plenty; and the number of their dependants increases with their wealth; and they reflect not that there is none of these, be he who he may, but will be more apprehensive of the least peril threatening himself than cumbered to avert a great peril from his lord or kinsman, whereas between friends we know 'tis quite contrariwise.

NOVEL IX

*Saladin, in guise of a merchant, is honourably entreated by Messer
Torello. The Crusade ensuing, Messer Torello appoints
a date, after which his wife may marry again : he is taken
prisoner, and by training hawks comes under the Soldan's
notice. The Soldan recognizes him, makes himself known
to him, and entreats him with all honour. Messer Torello
falls sick, and by magic arts is transported in a single night
to Pavia, where his wife's second marriage is then to be
solemnized, and being present thereat, is recognized by her,
and returns with her to his house.*

So ended Filomena her story, and when all alike had commended
the magnificence shewn by Titus in his gratitude, the king,
reserving the last place for Dioneo, thus began :—Lovesome
my ladies, true beyond all question is what Filomena reports of
friendship, and with justice did she deplore in her closing words
the little account in which 'tis held to-day among mortals.
And were we here for the purpose of correcting, or even of censuring, the vices of the age, I should add a copious sequel to
her discourse ; but as we have another end in view, it has
occurred to me to set before you in a narrative, which will be
of considerable length, but entertaining throughout, an instance
of Saladin's magnificence, to the end that, albeit, by reason of
our vices, it may not be possible for us to gain to the full the
friendship of any, yet by the matters whereof you shall hear in
my story we may at least be incited to take delight in doing
good offices, in the hope that sooner or later we may come by
our reward thereof.

I say, then, that in the time of the Emperor Frederic I., as
certain writers affirm, the Christians made common emprise
for the recovery of the Holy Land. Whereof that most valiant
prince, Saladin, then Soldan of Babylonia, being in good time
apprised, resolved to see for himself the preparations made by
the Christian potentates for the said emprise, that he might
put himself in better trim to meet them. So, having ordered
all things to his mind in Egypt, he made as if he were bound
on a pilgrimage, and attended only by two of his chiefest and
sagest lords, and three servants, took the road in the guise of
a merchant. And having surveyed many provinces of Christen-
dom, as they rode through Lombardy with intent to cross the

Alps, they chanced, between Milan and Pavia, to fall in with a
gentleman, one Messer Torello d'Istria da Pavia, who with his
servants and his dogs and falcons was betaking him to a fine
estate that he had on the Ticino, there to tarry a while. Now
Messer Torello no sooner espied Saladin and his lords than he
guessed them to be gentlemen and foreigners ; and, being zealous
to do them honour, when Saladin asked one of his servants how
far off Pavia might still be, and if he might win there in time
to enter the town, he suffered not the servant to make answer,
but :—" No, gentlemen," quoth he, " by the time you reach
Pavia 'twill be too late for you to enter." " So ! " replied
Saladin, " then might you be pleased to direct us, as we are
strangers, where we may best be lodged ? " " That gladly
will I," returned Messer Torello, " I was but now thinking to
send one of these my men on an errand to Pavia ; I will send
him with you, and he will guide you to a place where you will
find very comfortable quarters." Then, turning to one of his
most trusty servants, he gave him his instructions, and
despatched him with them : after which, he repaired to his
estate, and forthwith, as best he might, caused a goodly supper
to be made ready, and the tables set in his garden ; which done,
he stationed himself at the gate on the look-out for his guests.

The servant, conversing with the gentlemen of divers matters,
brought them by devious roads to his lord's estate without their
being ware of it. Whom as soon as Messer Torello espied, he
came forth afoot to meet them, and said with a smile :—" A
hearty welcome to you, gentlemen." Now Saladin, being very
quick of apprehension, perceived that the knight had doubted,
when he met them, that, were he to bid them to his house,
they might not accept his hospitality ; and accordingly, that
it might not be in their power to decline it, had brought them
to his house by a ruse. And so, returning his greeting :—
" Sir," quoth he, " were it meet to find fault with those that
shew courtesy, we should have a grievance against you, for
that, to say nought of somewhat delaying our journey, you
have in guerdon of a single greeting constrained us to accept so
noble a courtesy as yours." Whereto the knight, who was of
good understanding and well-spoken, made answer :—" Gentlemen, such courtesy as we shew you will, in comparison of that
which, by what I gather from your aspect, were meet for you,
prove but a sorry thing ; but in sooth this side of Pavia you
might not anywhere have been well lodged ; wherefore take it
not amiss that you have come somewhat out of your way to

find less discomfortable quarters." And as he spoke, about them flocked the servants, who, having helped them to dismount, saw to their horses; whereupon Messer Torello conducted them to the chambers that were made ready for them, where, having caused them to be relieved of their boots, and refreshed with the coolest of wines, he held pleasant converse with them until supper-time. Saladin and his lords and servants all knew Latin, so that they both understood and made themselves understood very well, and there was none of them but adjudged this knight to be the most agreeable and debonair man, and therewithal the best talker, that he had ever seen; while to Messer Torello, on the other hand, they shewed as far greater magnificoes than he had at first supposed, whereby he was inly vexed that he had not been able that evening to do them the honours of company, and a more ceremonious banquet. For which default he resolved to make amends on the ensuing morning: wherefore, having imparted to one of his servants that which he would have done, he sent him to his most judicious and highminded lady at Pavia, which was close by, and where never a gate was locked. Which done, he brought the gentlemen into the garden, and courteously asked them who they were. "We are Cypriote merchants," replied Saladin, "and 'tis from Cyprus we come, and we are on our way to Paris on business." Quoth then Messer Torello:—"Would to God that our country bred gentlemen of such a quality as are the merchants that I see Cyprus breeds!" From which they passed to discourse of other matters, until, supper-time being come, he besought them to seat them at table; whereat, considering that the supper was but improvised, their entertainment was excellent and well-ordered.

The tables being cleared, Messer Torello, surmising that they must be weary, kept them no long time from their rest, but bestowed them in most comfortable beds, and soon after went to rest himself. Meanwhile the servant that he had sent to Pavia did his lord's errand to the lady, who, in the style rather of a queen than of a housewife, forthwith assembled not a few of Messer Torello's friends and vassals, and caused all meet preparation to be made for a magnificent banquet, and by messengers bearing torches bade not a few of the noblest of the citizens thereto; and had store of silken and other fabrics and fair brought in, and all set in order in every point as her husband had directed. Day came, and the gentlemen being risen, Messer Torello got him to horse with them, and having sent for his

hawks, brought them to a ford, and shewed them how the
hawks flew. By and by, Saladin requesting of him a guide to
the best inn at Pavia :—" I myself will be your guide," returned
Messer Torello, " for I have occasion to go thither." Which
offer they, nothing doubting, did gladly accept, and so with
him they set forth ; and about tierce, being come to the city,
and expecting to be directed to the best inn, they were brought
by Messer Torello to his own house, where they were forthwith
surrounded by full fifty of the greatest folk of the city, gathered
there to give the gentlemen a welcome ; and 'twas who should
hold a bridle or a stirrup, while they dismounted. Whereby
Saladin and his lords more than guessing the truth :—" Messer
Torello," quoth they, " 'twas not this that we craved of you.
Honour enough had we from you last night, and far in excess
of our desires ; wherefore thou mightst very well have left us
to go our own road." Whereto :—" Gentlemen," replied
Messer Torello, " for that which was done yestereve I have to
thank Fortune rather than you : seeing that Fortune surprised
you on the road at an hour when you must needs repair to my
little house : for that which shall be done this morning I shall
be beholden to you, as will also these gentlemen that surround
you, with whom, if you deem it courteous so to do, you may
refuse to breakfast, if you like."

Fairly conquered, Saladin and his lords dismounted, and
heartily welcomed by the gentlemen, were conducted to the
chambers which had been most sumptuously adorned for their
use ; and having laid aside their riding dress, and taken some
refreshment, repaired to the saloon, where all had been made
ready with splendour. There, having washed their hands, they
sat them down to table, and were regaled with a magnificent
repast of many courses, served with all stately and fair ceremony, insomuch that, had the Emperor himself been there,
'twould not have been possible to do him more honour. And
albeit Saladin and his lords were grandees, and used to exceeding
great displays of pomp and state, nevertheless this shewed to
them as not a little marvellous, and one of the greatest they
had ever seen, having regard to the quality of their host, whom
they knew to be but a citizen, and no lord. Breakfast done,
and the tables cleared, they conversed a while of high matters,
and then, as 'twas very hot, all the gentlemen of Pavia—so it
pleased Messer Torello—retired for their siesta, while he remained with his three guests ; with whom he presently withdrew into a chamber, whither, that there might be nought

that he held dear which they had not seen, he called his noble
lady. And so the dame, exceeding fair and stately of person,
and arrayed in rich apparel, with her two little boys, that
shewed as two angels, on either hand, presented herself before
them, and graciously greeted them. Whereupon they rose, and
returned her salutation with reverence, and caused her to sit
down among them, and made much of her two little boys. But
after some interchange of gracious discourse, Messer Torello
being withdrawn somewhat apart, she asked them courteously,
whence they came and whither they were bound, and had of
them the same answer that Messer Torello had received. " So ! "
quoth the lady with a joyful air, " then I see that my woman's
wit will be of service to you ; wherefore I pray you as a special
favour neither to reject nor to despise the little gift that I am
about to present to you ; but reflecting that, as women have
but small minds, so they make but small gifts, accept it, having
regard rather to the good will of the giver than the magnitude
of the gift." She then caused bring forth for each of them two
pair of robes, lined the one with silk, the other with vair, no
such robes as citizens or merchants, but such as lords, use to
wear, and three vests of taffeta, besides linen clothes, and :—
" Take them," quoth she. " The robes I give you are even
such as I have arrayed my lord withal : the other things, considering that you are far from your wives, and have come a long
way, and have yet a long way to go, and that merchants love
to be neat and trim, may, albeit they are of no great value, be
yet acceptable to you."

Wondering, the gentlemen acknowledged without reserve that
there was no point of courtesy wherein Messer Torello was not
minded to acquit himself towards them. And noting the lordly
fashion of the robes, unsuited to the quality of merchants, they
misdoubted that Messer Torello had recognized them. However,
quoth one of them to the lady :—" Gifts great indeed are these,
Madam, nor such as lightly to accept, were it not that thereto
we are constrained by your prayers, to which we may on no
account say, no." Whereupon, Messer Torello being now
come back, the lady bade them adieu, and took her leave of
them ; and in like manner did she cause their servants to be
supplied with equipment suitable to them. The gentlemen,
being much importuned thereto by Messer Torello, consented
to tarry the rest of the day with him ; and so, having slept,
they donned their robes, and rode a while with him about the
city ; and supper-time being come, they feasted magnificently,

and with a numerous and honourable company. And so in
due time they betook them to rest; and at daybreak, being
risen, they found, in lieu of their jaded nags, three stout and
excellent palfreys, and in like manner fresh and goodly mounts
for their servants. Which Saladin marking turned to his lords,
and:—"By God," quoth he, "never was gentleman more
complete and courteous and considerate than this Messer Torello,
and if the Christian kings are as kingly as he is knightly, there
is none of them whose onset the Soldan of Babylon might well
abide, to say nought of so many as we see making ready to fall
upon him." However, knowing that 'twas not permissible to
refuse, he very courteously thanked Messer Torello: and so
they got them to horse. Messer Torello with a numerous company escorted them far beyond the gate of the city, until, loath
though Saladin was to part from him, so greatly did he now
affect him, yet as he must needs speed on, he besought him to
turn back. Whereupon, albeit it irked him to take leave of
them:—"Gentlemen," quoth Messer Torello, "since such is
your pleasure, I obey; but this I must say to you. Who you
are I know not, nor would I know more than you are pleased
to impart; but whoever you may be, you will not make me
believe that you are merchants this while; and so adieu!"
To whom Saladin, having already taken leave of all his company,
thus made answer:—"Peradventure, Sir, we shall one day give
you to see somewhat of our merchandise, and thereby confirm
your belief: and so adieu!"

Thus parted Saladin and his company from Messer Torello,
Saladin burning with an exceeding great desire, if life should
be continued to him, and the war, which he anticipated, should
not undo him, to shew Messer Torello no less honour than he
had received at his hands, and conversing not a little with his
lords both of Messer Torello himself and of his lady, and all that
he did and that in any wise concerned him, ever more highly
commending them. However, having with much diligence
spied out all the West, he put to sea, and returned with his
company to Alexandria; and having now all needful information, he put himself in a posture of defence. Messer Torello,
his mind full of his late guests, returned to Pavia; but, though
he long pondered who they might be, he came never at or anywhere near the truth.

Then with great and general mustering of forces came the
time for embarking on the emprise, and Messer Torello, heeding
not the tearful entreaties of his wife, resolved to join therein.

So, being fully equipped and about to take horse, he said to his lady, whom he most dearly loved :—" Wife, for honour's sake and for the weal of my soul, I go, as thou seest, on this emprise : our substance and our honour I commend to thy care. Certain I am of my departure, but, for the thousand accidents that may ensue, certitude have I none of my return : wherefore I would have thee do me this grace, that, whatever be my fate, shouldst thou lack certain intelligence that I live, thou wilt expect me a year and a month and a day from this my departure, before thou marry again." Whereto the lady, weeping bitterly, made answer :—" Messer Torello, I know not how I shall support the distress in which, thus departing, you leave me ; but should my life not fail beneath it, and aught befall thee, live and die secure that I shall live and die the wife of Messer Torello, and of his memory." Whereupon :—" Wife," returned Messer Torello, " well assured I am that, so far as in thee shall lie, this promise of thine will be kept ; but thou art young, and fair, and of a great family, and thy virtue is rare and generally known : wherefore I make no doubt that, should there be any suspicion of my death, thou wilt be asked of thy brothers and kinsmen by many a great gentleman : against whose attacks, though thou desire it never so, thou wilt not be able to hold out, but wilt perforce be fain to gratify one or other of them ; for which cause it is that I ask thee to wait just so long and no longer." " As I have said," replied the lady, " so, in so far as I may, I shall do ; and if I must needs do otherwise, rest assured that of this your behest I shall render you obedience. But I pray God that He bring neither you nor me to such a strait yet a while." Which said, the lady wept, and having embraced Messer Torello, drew from her finger a ring, and gave it to him, saying :— " Should it betide that I die before I see you again, mind you of me, when you look upon it."

Messer Torello took the ring, and got him to horse, and having bidden all adieu, fared forth on his journey ; and being arrived with his company at Genoa, he embarked on a galley, and having departed thence, in no long time arrived at Acre, and joined the main Christian host ; wherein there by and by broke out an exceeding great and mortal sickness ; during which, whether owing to Saladin's strategy, or his good fortune, he made an easy capture of well-nigh all the remnant of the Christians that were escaped, and quartered them in divers prisons in many cities ; of which captives Messer Torello being one, was brought to Alexandria and there confined. Where, not being known,

and fearing to make himself known, he under constraint of
necessity, applied him to the training of hawks, whereof he was
a very great master ; and thereby he fell under the notice of
Saladin, who took him out of the prison, and made him his
falconer. The Soldan called him by no other name than
"Christian," and neither recognized, nor was recognized by,
him, who, his whole soul ever in Pavia, essayed many a time to
escape, that he might return thither, but still without success :
wherefore, certain Genoese, that were come to Alexandria as
ambassadors to the Soldan for the redemption of some of their
townsfolk, being about to return, he resolved to write to his
lady, how that he lived, and would come back to her, as soon
as he might, and that she should expect his return ; and having
so done, he earnestly besought one of the ambassadors, whom
he knew, to see that the letter reached the hands of the Abbot
of San Pietro in Ciel d'Oro, who was his uncle.

Now, such being the posture of Messer Torello's affairs, it
befell one day that, while he talked with Saladin of his hawks,
he smiled ; whereby his mouth shaped itself in a fashion, of
which Saladin had taken particular note, while he was at Pavia.
And so, recalling Messer Torello to mind, he fixed his gaze upon
him, and it seemed to him that 'twas indeed Messer Torello ;
wherefore, leaving the matter of which they were conversing :—
"Tell me, Christian," quoth he, "of what country art thou in
the West ?" "My lord," replied Messer Torello, "I am a
Lombard, of a city called Pavia, a poor man, and of humble
condition." Which when he heard, Saladin, well-nigh resolved
of his doubt, said joyfully to himself :—" God has provided me
with occasion meet to prove to this man what store I set by his
courtesy ; " and without another word he brought him into a
room where he kept all his wearing apparel, and said :—" Look,
Christian, if among these robes there be any that thou hast ever
seen before." So Messer Torello examined the robes, and espied
those which his lady had given to Saladin ; but, deeming they
could not be the same, he replied :—" My lord, there is no robe
here that I recognize, albeit 'tis true that those two robes are
such as I once wore myself, in company with three merchants
that came to my house." Whereupon Saladin could refrain
himself no longer ; but, tenderly embracing him :—" You,"
quoth he, " are Messer Torello d'Istria, and I am one of those
three merchants to whom your lady gave these robes ; and
now is the time to warrant you of the quality of my merchandise,
as, when I parted from you, I told you might come to pass."

Which to hear, Messer Torello was at once overjoyed and abashed, overjoyed to have entertained so illustrious a guest, and abashed, for that it seemed to him that he had given him but a sorry entertainment. To whom :—"Messer Torello," quoth Saladin, "since hither has God sent you to me, deem that 'tis no more I that am lord here, but you." And so they made great cheer together ; and then Saladin caused Messer Torello to be royally arrayed ; and presented him to all his greatest lords, and having extolled his merit in no stinted measure, bade all, as they hoped for grace from him, honour Messer Torello even as himself. And so from that hour did they all ; but most especially the two lords that had been with Saladin at Messer Torello's house.

The glory, to which Messer Torello thus suddenly found himself raised, somewhat diverted his mind from the affairs of Lombardy, and the more so, for that he entertained no doubt that his letter had reached his uncle's hands. But for that in the camp, or rather army, of the Christians, on the day when they were taken by Saladin, there died and was buried one Messer Torello de Dignes, an obscure knight of Provence, whereas Messer Torello d'Istria was known to all the host for a right noble gentleman, whoso heard tell that Messer Torello was dead, supposed that 'twas Messer Torello d'Istria, and not Messer Torello de Dignes ; nor did what happened after, to wit, the capture, avail to undeceive them ; for not a few Italians had carried the report home with them ; among whom there were some who made bold to say that they had seen Messer Torello d'Istria's dead body, and had been present at its interment. Which rumour coming to the ears of his lady and his kinsfolk, great indeed, nay, immeasurable was the distress that it occasioned not only to them, but to all that had known him. The mode and measure of his lady's grief, her mourning, her lamentation, 'twere tedious to describe. Enough that, after some months spent in almost unmitigated tribulation, her sorrow shewed signs of abatement ; whereupon, suit being made for her hand by some of the greatest men of Lombardy, her brothers and other kinsfolk began to importune her to marry again. Times not a few, and with floods of tears, she refused ; but, overborne at last, she consented to do as they would have her, upon the understanding that she was to remain unmarried until the term for which she had bound herself to Messer Torello was fulfilled.

Now the lady's affairs being in this posture at Pavia, it befell that some eight days or so before the time appointed for her marriage, Messer Torello one day espied in Alexandria one that he had observed go with the Genoese ambassadors aboard the galley that took them to Genoa ; wherefore he called him, and asked him what sort of a voyage they had had, and when they had reached Genoa. "My lord," replied the other, "the galley made but a sorry voyage of it, as I learned in Crete, where I remained ; for that, while she was nearing Sicily, there arose a terrible gale from the North that drove her on to the shoals of Barbary, and never a soul escaped, and among the rest my two brothers were lost." Which report believing—and 'twas indeed most true—and calling to mind that in a few days the term that he had asked of his wife would be fulfilled and surmising that there could be no tidings of him at Pavia, Messer Torello made no question but that the lady was provided with another husband ; whereby he sank into such a depth of woe that he lost all power to eat, and betook him to his bed and resigned himself to die. Which when Saladin, by whom he was most dearly beloved, learned, he came to him, and having plied him with many and most instant entreaties, learned at length the cause of his distress and sickness ; and, having chidden him not a little that he had not sooner apprised him thereof, he besought him to put on a cheerful courage, assuring him, that, if so he did, he would bring it to pass that he should be in Pavia at the time appointed, and told him how. Believing Saladin's words the more readily that he had many times heard that 'twas possible, and had not seldom been done, Messer Torello recovered heart, and was instant with Saladin that he should make all haste.

Accordingly Saladin bade one of his necromancers, of whose skill he had already had proof, to devise a method whereby Messer Torello should be transported abed in a single night to Pavia : the necromancer made answer that it should be done, but that 'twere best he put Messer Torello to sleep. The matter being thus arranged, Saladin hied him back to Messer Torello, and finding him most earnestly desirous to be in Pavia at the time appointed, if so it might be, and if not, to die :—"Messer Torello," quoth he, "if you dearly love your lady, and misdoubt that she may become the bride of another, no wise, God wot, do I censure you, for that, of all the ladies that ever I saw, she, for bearing, manners, and address—to say nought of beauty, which is but the flower that perishes—seems to me the most worthy to be lauded and cherished. Much had I been gratified, since Fortune has sent you hither to me, that, while you and I yet live, we had exercised equal lordship in the governance of this my realm, and, if such was not God's will, and this must needs come upon you, that you are fain either to be at Pavia at the time appointed or to die, I had desired of all things to have been apprised thereof at such a time that I might have sent you home with such honourable circumstance and state and escort as befit your high desert; which not being vouch-safed me, and as nought will content you but to be there forth-with, I do what I can, and speed you thither on such wise as I have told you." "My lord," replied Messer Torello, "had you said nought, you have already done enough to prove your good-will towards me, and that in so high a degree as is quite beyond my deserts, and most assured of the truth of what you say shall I live and die, and so had done, had you not said it; but, seeing that my resolve is taken, I pray you that that, which you pro-mise to do, be done speedily, for that after to-morrow I may no longer count on being expected."

Saladin assured him that 'twas so ordered that he should not be disappointed. And on the morrow, it being his purpose to speed him on his journey that same night, he caused to be set up in one of his great halls a most goodly and sumptuous bed composed of mattresses, all, as was their wont, of velvet and cloth of gold, and had it covered with a quilt, adorned at certain intervals with enormous pearls, and most rare precious stones, insomuch that 'twas in after time accounted a priceless treasure, and furnished with two pillows to match it. Which done, he bade array Messer Torello, who was now quite recovered, in a robe after the Saracenic fashion, the richest and goodliest thing of the kind that was ever seen, and wrap about his head, accord-ing to their wont, one of their huge turbans. Then, at a late hour, Saladin, attended by certain of his lords, entered the chamber where Messer Torello was, and seating himself beside him, all but wept as thus he began:—"Messer Torello, the time is nigh at hand when you and I must part; wherefore, since I may neither give you my own, nor others' company (the journey that you are about to make not permitting it), I am come here, as 'tis fitting, in this chamber to take my leave of you. Wherefore, before I bid you adieu, I entreat you, by that friendship, that love, which is between us, that you forget me not, and that, if it be possible, when you have settled your affairs in Lombardy, you come at least once, before our days are ended, to visit me, that thereby I may both have the delight of seeing you again, and make good that omission which, by reason of your haste, I must needs now make ; and that in the meanwhile it irk thee not to visit me by letter, and to ask of me whatever you shall have a mind to, and be sure that there lives not the man whom I shall content more gladly than you." Messer Torello could not refrain his tears, and so, with words few, and broken by his sobs, he answered that 'twas impossible that the Soldan's generous deeds and chivalrous character should ever be forgotten by him, and that without fail he would do as he bade him, so soon as occasion should serve him. Whereupon Saladin tenderly embraced and kissed him, and with many a tear bade him adieu, and quitted the chamber. His lords then took leave of Messer Torello, and followed Saladin into the hall, where he had had the bed made ready.

'Twas now late, and the necromancer being intent to hasten Messer Torello's transit, a physician brought him a potion, and having first shewn him what he was to give him by way of viaticum, caused him to drink it ; and not long after he fell asleep. In which state he was carried by Saladin's command and laid on the goodly bed, whereon he set a large and fair and most sumptuous crown, marking it in such sort that there could be no mistake that it was sent by Saladin to Messer Torello's wife. He next placed on Messer Torello's finger a ring, in which was set a carbuncle of such brilliance that it shewed as a lighted torch, and of well-nigh inestimable value. After which he girded on him a sword, the appointments of which might not readily be appraised. And therewithal he adorned him in front with a pendant, wherein were pearls, the like of which had never been seen, and not a few other rare jewels. And, moreover, on either side of him he set two vast basins of gold full of pistoles ; and strings of pearls not a few, and rings and girdles, and other things, which 'twere tedious to enumerate, he disposed around him. Which done, he kissed Messer Torello again, and bade the necromancer speed him on his journey. Whereupon, forthwith, the bed, with Messer Torello thereon, was borne away from before Saladin's eyes, and he and his barons remained conversing thereof.

The bed, as Messer Torello had requested, had already been deposited in the church of San Piero in Ciel d'Oro at Pavia, and Messer Torello, with all the aforesaid jewels and ornaments upon and about him, was lying thereon, and still slept, when, upon the stroke of matins, the sacristan came into the church, light in hand, and presently setting eyes on the sumptuous bed, was

not only amazed, but mightily terrified, insomuch that he
turned back, and took to flight. Which the abbot and monks
observing with no small surprise, asked wherefore he fled ; and
he told them. Whereupon :—" Oh," quoth the abbot, " thou
art no longer a child, nor yet so new to this church, that thou
shouldst so lightly be appalled : go we now, and see who it is
that has given thee this childish fright." So, with a blaze of
torches, the abbot, attended by his monks, entered the church,
and espied this wondrous costly bed whereon the knight slept,
and while, hesitant and fearful, daring not to approach the bed,
they scanned the rare and splendid jewels, it befell that, the
efficacy of the potion being exhausted, Messer Torello awoke and
heaved a great sigh. Whereat the monks and the abbot quaking
and crying out :—" Lord, help us ! " one and all took to flight.
Messer Torello, opening his eyes and looking about him, saw, to
his no small satisfaction, that without a doubt he was in the
very place where he had craved of Saladin to be ; so up he sate,
and taking particular note of the matters with which he was
surrounded, accounted the magnificence of Saladin to exceed
even the measure, great though it was, that he already knew.
However, he still kept quiet, save that, perceiving the monks
in flight, and surmising the reason, he began to call the abbot
by name, bidding him be of good courage, for that he was his
nephew, Torello. Whereat the abbot did but wax more terrified,
for that he deemed Torello had been many a month dead ;
but, after a while, as he heard himself still called, sound judgment got the better of his fears, and making the sign of the cross,
he drew nigh Torello ; who said to him :—" Father, what is't
you fear ? By God's grace I live, and hither am come back
from overseas." Whom, for all he had grown a long beard
and was dressed in the Saracenic fashion, the abbot after a while
recognized, and now, quite reassured, took by the hand, saying :
—" Son, welcome home : " then :—" No cause hast thou to
marvel at our fears," he went on, " seeing that there is never a
soul in these parts but firmly believes thee to be dead, insomuch
that I may tell thee that Madonna Adalieta, thy wife, overborne by the entreaties and menaces of her kinsfolk, and against
her will, is provided with another husband, to whom she is this
morning to go, and all is made ready for the nuptials and the
attendant festivities."

Whereupon Messer Torello, being risen from the sumptuous
bed, did the abbot and the monks wondrous cheer, and besought
them, one and all, to tell never a soul of his return, until he had

completed something that he had on hand. After which, having put the costly jewels in safe keeping, he recounted to the abbot all the story of his adventures to that very hour. The abbot, rejoicing in his good fortune, joined with him in offering thanks to God. Messer Torello then asked him who might be his wife's new husband, and the abbot told him. Quoth then Messer Torello :—" Before my return be known, I purpose to see how my wife will comport herself at the nuptials : wherefore, though 'tis not the wont of men of religion to go to such gatherings, I had lief that for love of me you arranged for us to go thither together." The abbot answered that he would gladly do so, and as soon as 'twas day, he sent word to the bridegroom that he had thoughts of being present at his nuptials, accompanied by a friend ; whereto the gentleman made answer that he was much gratified. So, at the breakfast hour Messer Torello, dressed as he was, hied him with the abbot to the bridegroom's house, as many as saw them gazing on him with wonder, but none recognizing him, and the abbot giving all to understand that he was a Saracen sent by the Soldan as ambassador to the King of France. Messer Torello was accordingly seated at a table directly opposite that of his lady, whom he eyed with exceeding great delight, the more so that he saw that in her face which shewed him that she was chagrined by the nuptials. She in like manner from time to time bent her regard on him ; howbeit, what with his long beard, and his foreign garb, and her firm persuasion that he was dead, she had still no sort of re-collection of him. However, Messer Torello at length deemed it time to make trial of her, whether she would remember him ; wherefore he took the ring that the lady had given him on his departure, and keeping it close in the palm of his hand, he called to him a page that waited upon her, and said to him :—" Tell the bride from me that 'tis the custom in my country, that, when a stranger, such as I, eats with a bride, like herself, at her wedding-feast, she, in token that he is welcome to her board, sends him the cup from which she herself drinks, full of wine ; and when the stranger has drunk his fill, he closes the cup, and the bride drinks what is left therein."

The page carried the message to the lady, who, being of good understanding and manners, and supposing him to be some very great man, by way of shewing that she was gratified by his presence, commanded that a gilt cup, that was on the table before her, should be rinsed, and filled with wine, and borne to the gentleman. Which being done, Messer Torello, having privily conveyed her ring into his mouth, let it fall (while he drank) into the cup on such wise that none wist thereof; and leaving but a little wine at the bottom, closed the cup and returned it to the lady; who, having taken it, that she might do full honour to the custom of her guest's country, lifted the lid, and set the cup to her mouth; whereby espying the ring, she thereon mutely gazed a while, and recognizing it for that which she had given Messer Torello on his departure, she steadfastly regarded the supposed stranger, whom now she also recognized. Whereupon well-nigh distracted, oversetting the table in front of her, she exclaimed :—" 'Tis my lord, 'tis verily Messer Torello;" and rushing to the table at which he sate, giving never a thought to her apparel, or aught that was on the table, she flung herself upon it; and reaching forward as far as she could, she threw her arms about him, and hugged him; nor, for aught that any said or did, could she be induced to release his neck, until Messer Torello himself bade her forbear a while, for that she would have time enough to kiss him thereafter. The lady then stood up, and for a while all was disorder, albeit the feast was yet more gladsome than before by reason of the recovery of so honourable a knight : then, at Messer Torello's entreaty, all were silent, while he recounted to them the story of his adventures from the day of his departure to that hour, concluding by saying that the gentleman who, deeming him to be dead, had taken his lady to wife, ought not to be affronted, if he, being alive, reclaimed her. The bridegroom, albeit he was somewhat crestfallen, made answer in frank and friendly sort, that 'twas for Messer Torello to do what he liked with his own. The lady resigned the ring and the crown that her new spouse had given her, and put on the ring she had taken from the cup, and likewise the crown sent her by the Soldan; and so, forth they hied them, and with full nuptial pomp wended their way to Messer Torello's house; and there for a great while they made merry with his late disconsolate friends and kinsfolk and all the citizens, who accounted his restoration as little short of a miracle.

Messer Torello, having bestowed part of his rare jewels upon him who had borne the cost of the wedding-feast, and part on the abbot, and many other folk; and having by more than one messenger sent word of his safe home-coming and prosperous estate to Saladin, acknowledging himself ever his friend and vassal, lived many years thereafter with his worthy lady, acquitting himself yet more courteously than of yore. Such, then,

was the end of the troubles of Messer Torello and his dear lady,
and such the reward of their cheerful and ready courtesies.

Now some there are that strive to do offices of courtesy, and
have the means, but do them with so ill a grace, that, ere they
are done, they have in effect sold them at a price above their
worth : wherefore, if no reward ensue to them thereof, neither
they nor other folk have cause to marvel.

NOVEL X

*The Marquis of Saluzzo, overborne by the entreaties of his vassals,
consents to take a wife, but, being minded to please himself in
the choice of her, takes a husbandman's daughter. He has
two children by her, both of whom he makes her believe that he
has put to death. Afterward, feigning to be tired of her, and
to have taken another wife, he turns her out of doors in her
shift, and brings his daughter into the house in guise of his
bride ; but, finding her patient under it all, he brings her
home again, and shews her her children, now grown up, and
honours her, and causes her to be honoured, as Marchioness.*

ENDED the king's long story, with which all seemed to be very
well pleased, quoth Dioneo with a laugh :—" The good man that
looked that night to cause the bogey's tail to droop, would scarce
have contributed two pennyworth of all the praise you bestow
on Messer Torello : " then, witting that it now only remained
for him to tell, thus he began :—Gentle my ladies, this day,
meseems, is dedicate to Kings and Soldans and folk of the like
quality ; wherefore, that I stray not too far from you, I am
minded to tell you somewhat of a Marquis ; certes, nought
magnificent, but a piece of mad folly, albeit there came good
thereof to him in the end. The which I counsel none to copy,
for that great pity 'twas that it turned out well with him.

There was in olden days a certain Marquis of Saluzzo, Gualtieri by name, a young man, but head of the house, who, having
neither wife nor child, passed his time in nought else but in
hawking and hunting, and of taking a wife and begetting children
had no thought ; wherein he should have been accounted very
wise : but his vassals, brooking it ill, did oftentimes entreat
him to take a wife, that he might not die without an heir, and
they be left without a lord ; offering to find him one of such a
pattern, and of such parentage, that he might marry with good

hope, and be well content with the sequel. To whom:—
" My friends," replied Gualtieri, " you enforce me to that which
I had resolved never to do, seeing how hard it is to find a wife,
whose ways accord well with one's own, and how plentiful is
the supply of such as run counter thereto, and how grievous a
life he leads who chances upon a lady that matches ill with
him. And to say that you think to know the daughters by the
qualities of their fathers and mothers, and thereby—so you
would argue—to provide me with a wife to my liking, is but
folly ; for I wot not how you may penetrate the secrets of their
mothers so as to know their fathers ; and granted that you do
know them, daughters oftentimes resemble neither of their
parents. However, as you are minded to rivet these fetters
upon me, I am content that so it be ; and that I may have no
cause to reproach any but myself, should it turn out ill, I am
resolved that my wife shall be of my own choosing ; but of this
rest assured, that, no matter whom I choose, if she receive not
from you the honour due to a lady, you shall prove to your great
cost, how sorely I resent being thus constrained by your importunity to take a wife against my will."

The worthy men replied that they were well content, so only
he would marry without more ado. And Gualtieri, who had
long noted with approval the mien of a poor girl that dwelt on
a farm hard by his house, and found her fair enough, deemed
that with her he might pass a tolerably happy life. Wherefore
he sought no further, but forthwith resolved to marry her ; and
having sent for her father, who was a very poor man, he contracted with him to take her to wife. Which done, Gualtieri
assembled all the friends he had in those parts, and :—" My
friends," quoth he, " you were and are minded that I should
take a wife, and rather to comply with your wishes, than for
any desire that I had to marry, I have made up my mind to
do so. You remember the promise you gave me, to wit, that,
whomsoever I should take, you would pay her the honour due
to a lady. Which promise I now require you to keep, the time
being come when I am to keep mine. I have found hard by here
a maiden after mine own heart, whom I purpose to take to wife,
and to bring hither to my house in the course of a few days.
Wherefore bethink you, how you may make the nuptial feast
splendid, and welcome her with all honour ; that I may confess
myself satisfied with your observance of your promise, as you
will be with my observance of mine." The worthy men, one
and all, answered with alacrity that they were well content,

and that, whoever she might be, they would entreat her as a lady, and pay her all due honour as such. After which, they all addressed them to make goodly and grand and gladsome celebration of the event, as did also Gualtieri. He arranged for a wedding most stately and fair, and bade thereto a goodly number of his friends and kinsfolk, and great gentlemen, and others, of the neighbourhood; and therewithal he caused many a fine and costly robe to be cut and fashioned to the figure of a girl who seemed to him of the like proportions as the girl that he purposed to wed; and laid in store, besides, of girdles and rings, with a costly and beautiful crown, and all the other paraphernalia of a bride.

The day that he had appointed for the wedding being come, about half tierce he got him to horse with as many as had come to do him honour, and having made all needful dispositions:— " Gentlemen," quoth he, " 'tis time to go bring home the bride." And so away he rode with his company to the village; where, being come to the house of the girl's father, they found her returning from the spring with a bucket of water, making all the haste she could, that she might afterwards go with the other women to see Gualtieri's bride come by. Whom Gualtieri no sooner saw, than he called her by her name, to wit, Griselda, and asked her where her father was. To whom she modestly made answer:—" My lord, he is in the house." Whereupon Gualtieri dismounted, and having bidden the rest await him without, entered the cottage alone; and meeting her father, whose name was Giannucolo:—" I am come," quoth he, " to wed Griselda, but first of all there are some matters I would learn from her own lips in thy presence." He then asked her, whether, if he took her to wife, she would study to comply with his wishes, and be not wroth, no matter what he might say or do, and be obedient, with not a few other questions of a like sort: to all which she answered, ay. Whereupon Gualtieri took her by the hand, led her forth, and before the eyes of all his company, and as many other folk as were there, caused her to be stript naked, and let bring the garments that he had had fashioned for her, and had her forthwith arrayed therein, and upon her unkempt head let set a crown; and then, while all wondered:—" Gentlemen," quoth he, " this is she whom I purpose to make my wife, so she be minded to have me for husband." Then, she standing abashed and astonied, he turned to her, saying:—" Griselda, wilt thou have me for thy husband?" To whom:—" Ay, my lord," answered she.

" And I will have thee to wife," said he, and married her before them all. And having set her upon a palfrey, he brought her home with pomp.

The wedding was fair and stately, and had he married a daughter of the King of France, the feast could not have been more splendid. It seemed as if, with the change of her garb, the bride had acquired a new dignity of mind and mien. She was, as we have said, fair of form and feature; and therewithal she was now grown so engaging and gracious and debonair, that she shewed no longer as the shepherdess, and the daughter of Giannucolo, but as the daughter of some noble lord, insomuch that she caused as many as had known her before to marvel. Moreover, she was so obedient and devoted to her husband, that he deemed himself the happiest and luckiest man in the world. And likewise so gracious and kindly was she to her husband's vassals, that there was none of them but loved her more dearly than himself, and was zealous to do her honour, and prayed for her welfare and prosperity and aggrandisement, and instead of, as erstwhile, saying that Gualtieri had done foolishly to take her to wife, now averred that he had not his like in the world for wisdom and discernment, for that, save to him, her noble qualities would ever have remained hidden under her sorry apparel and the garb of the peasant girl. And in short she so comported herself as in no long time to bring it to pass that, not only in the marquisate, but far and wide besides, her virtues and her admirable conversation were matter of common talk, and, if aught had been said to the disadvantage of her husband, when he married her, the judgment was now altogether to the contrary effect.

She had not been long with Gualtieri before she conceived; and in due time she was delivered of a girl; whereat Gualtieri made great cheer. But, soon after, a strange humour took possession of him, to wit, to put her patience to the proof by prolonged and intolerable hard usage; wherefore he began by afflicting her with his gibes, putting on a vexed air, and telling her that his vassals were most sorely dissatisfied with her by reason of her base condition, and all the more so since they saw that she was a mother, and that they did nought but ruefully murmur at the birth of a daughter. Whereto Griselda, without the least change of countenance or sign of discomposure, made answer:—" My lord, do with me as thou mayst deem best for thine own honour and comfort, for well I wot that I am of less account than they, and unworthy of this honourable

estate to which of thy courtesy thou hast advanced me." By
which answer Gualtieri was well pleased, witting that she was
in no degree puffed up with pride by his, or any other's, honourable entreatment of her. A while afterwards, having in general
terms given his wife to understand that the vassals could not
endure her daughter, he sent her a message by a servant. So
the servant came, and :—" Madam," quoth he with a most
dolorous mien, " so I value my life, I must needs do my lord's
bidding. He has bidden me take your daughter and . . ."
He said no more, but the lady by what she heard, and read in
his face, and remembered of her husband's words, understood
that he was bidden to put the child to death. Whereupon she
presently took the child from the cradle, and having kissed
and blessed her, albeit she was very sore at heart, she changed
not countenance, but placed it in the servant's arms, saying :—
" See that thou leave nought undone that my lord and thine
has charged thee to do, but leave her not so that the beasts and
the birds devour her, unless he have so bidden thee." So the
servant took the child, and told Gualtieri what the lady had
said ; and Gualtieri, marvelling at her constancy, sent him with
the child to Bologna, to one of his kinswomen, whom he besought
to rear and educate the child with all care, but never to let it
be known whose child she was.

Soon after it befell that the lady again conceived, and in due
time was delivered of a son, whereat Gualtieri was overjoyed.
But, not content with what he had done, he now even more
poignantly afflicted the lady ; and one day with a ruffled mien :
—" Wife," quoth he, " since thou gavest birth to this boy, I
may on no wise live in peace with my vassals, so bitterly do
they reproach me that a grandson of Giannucolo is to succeed
me as their lord ; and therefore I fear that, so I be not minded
to be sent a-packing hence, I must even do herein as I did
before, and in the end put thee away, and take another wife."
The lady heard him patiently, and answered only :—" My
lord, study how thou mayst content thee and best please thyself,
and waste no thought upon me, for there is nought I desire save
in so far as I know that 'tis thy pleasure." Not many days after,
Gualtieri, in like manner as he had sent for the daughter, sent
for the son, and having made a shew of putting him to death,
provided for his, as for the girl's, nurture at Bologna. Whereat
the lady shewed no more discomposure of countenance or speech
than at the loss of her daughter : which Gualtieri found passing
strange, and inly affirmed that there was never another woman

in the world that would have so done. And but that he had
marked that she was most tenderly affectionate towards her
children, while 'twas well pleasing to him, he had supposed that
she was tired of them, whereas he knew that 'twas of her discretion that she so did. His vassals, who believed that he had
put the children to death, held him mightily to blame for his
cruelty, and felt the utmost compassion for the lady. She,
however, said never aught to the ladies that condoled with her
on the death of her children, but that the pleasure of him that
had begotten them was her pleasure likewise.

Years not a few had passed since the girl's birth, when
Gualtieri at length deemed the time come to put his wife's
patience to the final proof. Accordingly, in the presence of a
great company of his vassals he declared that on no wise might
he longer brook to have Griselda to wife, that he confessed that
in taking her he had done a sorry thing and the act of a stripling,
and that he therefore meant to do what he could to procure
the Pope's dispensation to put Griselda away, and take another
wife : for which cause being much upbraided by many worthy
men, he made no other answer but only that needs must it so
be. Whereof the lady being apprised, and now deeming that
she must look to go back to her father's house, and perchance
tend the sheep, as she had aforetime, and see him, to whom she
was utterly devoted, engrossed by another woman, did inly
bewail herself right sorely : but still with the same composed
mien with which she had borne Fortune's former buffets, she
set herself to endure this last outrage. Nor was it long before
Gualtieri by counterfeit letters, which he caused to be sent to
him from Rome, made his vassals believe that the Pope had
thereby given him a dispensation to put Griselda away, and
take another wife. Wherefore, having caused her to be brought
before him, he said to her in the presence of not a few :—" Wife,
by license granted me by the Pope, I am now free to put thee
away, and take another wife ; and, for that my forbears have
always been great gentlemen and lords of these parts, whereas
thine have ever been husbandmen, I purpose that thou go back
to Giannucolo's house with the dowry that thou broughtest
me ; whereupon I shall bring home a lady that I have found,
and who is meet to be my wife."

'Twas not without travail most grievous that the lady, as she
heard this announcement, got the better of her woman's nature,
and suppressing her tears, made answer :—" My lord, I ever
knew that my low degree was on no wise congruous with your

nobility, and acknowledged that the rank I had with you was
of your and God's bestowal, nor did I ever make as if it were
mine by gift, or so esteem it, but still accounted it as a loan.
'Tis your pleasure to recall it, and therefore it should be, and is,
my pleasure to render it up to you. So, here is your ring, with
which you espoused me ; take it back. You bid me take with
me the dowry that I brought you ; which to do will require
neither paymaster on your part nor purse nor pack-horse on
mine ; for I am not unmindful that naked was I when you first
had me. And if you deem it seemly that that body in which
I have borne children, by you begotten, be beheld of all, naked
will I depart ; but yet, I pray you, be pleased, in guerdon of
the virginity that I brought you and take not away, to suffer
me to bear hence upon my back a single shift—I crave no more
—besides my dowry." There was nought of which Gualtieri
was so fain as to weep ; but yet, setting his face as a flint, he
made answer :—" I allow thee a shift to thy back ; so get thee
hence." All that stood by besought him to give her a robe,
that she, who had been his wife for thirteen years and more,
might not be seen to quit his house in so sorry and shameful a
plight, having nought on her but a shift. But their entreaties
went for nothing : the lady in her shift, and barefoot and bare-
headed, having bade them adieu, departed the house, and went
back to her father amid the tears and lamentations of all that
saw her. Giannucolo, who had ever deemed it a thing incredible
that Gualtieri should keep his daughter to wife, and had looked
for this to happen every day, and had kept the clothes that she
had put off on the morning that Gualtieri had wedded her, now
brought them to her ; and she, having resumed them, applied
herself to the petty drudgery of her father's house, as she had
been wont, enduring with fortitude this cruel visitation of
adverse Fortune.

Now no sooner had Gualtieri dismissed Griselda, than he gave
his vassals to understand that he had taken to wife a daughter
of one of the Counts of Panago. He accordingly made great
preparations as for the nuptials, during which he sent for
Griselda. To whom, being come, quoth he :—" I am bringing
hither my new bride, and in this her first home-coming I purpose
to shew her honour ; and thou knowest that women I have
none in the house that know how to set chambers in due order,
or attend to the many other matters that so joyful an event
requires ; wherefore do thou, that understandest these things
better than another, see to all that needs be done, and bid hither

such ladies as thou mayst see fit, and receive them, as if thou wert the lady of the house, and then, when the nuptials are ended, thou mayst go back to thy cottage." Albeit each of these words pierced Griselda's heart like a knife, for that, in resigning her good fortune, she had not been able to renounce the love she bore Gualtieri, nevertheless :—" My lord," she made answer, " I am ready and prompt to do your pleasure." And so, clad in her sorry garments of coarse romagnole, she entered the house, which, but a little before, she had quitted in her shift, and addressed her to sweep the chambers, and arrange arras and cushions in the halls, and make ready the kitchen, and set her hand to everything, as if she had been a paltry serving-wench : nor did she rest until she had brought all into such meet and seemly trim as the occasion demanded. This done, she invited in Gualtieri's name all the ladies of those parts to be present at his nuptials, and awaited the event. The day being come, still wearing her sorry weeds, but in heart and soul and mien the lady, she received the ladies as they came, and gave each a gladsome greeting.

Now Gualtieri, as we said, had caused his children to be carefully nurtured and brought up by a kinswoman of his at Bologna, which kinswoman was married into the family of the Counts of Panago ; and, the girl being now twelve years old, and the loveliest creature that ever was seen, and the boy being about six years old, he had sent word to his kinswoman's husband at Bologna, praying him to be pleased to come with this girl and boy of his to Saluzzo, and to see that he brought a goodly and honourable company with him, and to give all to understand that he brought the girl to him to wife, and on no wise to disclose to any, who she really was. The gentleman did as the Marquis bade him, and within a few days of his setting forth arrived at Saluzzo about breakfast-time with the girl, and her brother, and a noble company, and found all the folk of those parts, and much people besides, gathered there in expectation of Gualtieri's new bride. Who, being received by the ladies, was no sooner come into the hall, where the tables were set, than Griselda advanced to meet her, saying with hearty cheer :—" Welcome, my lady." So the ladies, who had with much instance, but in vain, besought Gualtieri, either to let Griselda keep in another room, or at any rate to furnish her with one of the robes that had been hers, that she might not present herself in such a sorry guise before the strangers, sate down to table ; and the service being begun, the eyes of all were set on the girl, and every one said that Gualtieri had made a good exchange, and Griselda joined with the rest in greatly commending her, and also her little brother. And now Gualtieri, sated at last with all that he had seen of his wife's patience, marking that this new and strange turn made not the least alteration in her demeanour, and being well assured that 'twas not due to apathy, for he knew her to be of excellent understanding, deemed it time to relieve her of the suffering which he judged her to dissemble under a resolute front ; and so, having called her to him in presence of them all, he said with a smile :—" And what thinkst thou of our bride ? " " My lord," replied Griselda, " I think mighty well of her ; and if she be but as discreet as she is fair—and so I deem her—I make no doubt but you may reckon to lead with her a life of incomparable felicity ; but with all earnestness I entreat you, that you spare her those tribulations which you did once inflict upon another that was yours, for I scarce think she would be able to bear them, as well because she is younger, as for that she has been delicately nurtured, whereas that other had known no respite of hardship since she was but a little child." Marking that she made no doubt but that the girl was to be his wife, and yet spoke never a whit the less sweetly, Gualtieri caused her to sit down beside him, and :—" Griselda," said he, " 'tis now time that thou see the reward of thy long patience, and that those, who have deemed me cruel and unjust and insensate, should know that what I did was done of purpose aforethought, for that I was minded to give both thee and them a lesson, that thou mightst learn to be a wife, and they in like manner might learn how to take and keep a wife, and that I might beget me perpetual peace with thee for the rest of my life ; whereof being in great fear, when I came to take a wife, lest I should be disappointed, I therefore, to put the matter to the proof, did, and how sorely thou knowest, harass and afflict thee. And since I never knew thee either by deed or by word to deviate from my will, I now, deeming myself to have of thee that assurance of happiness which I desired, am minded to restore to thee at once all that, step by step, I took from thee, and by extremity of joy to compensate the tribulations that I inflicted on thee. Receive, then, this girl, whom thou supposest to be my bride, and her brother, with glad heart, as thy children and mine. These are they, whom by thee and many another it has long been supposed that I did ruthlessly to death, and I am thy husband, that loves thee more dearly than aught else, deeming that other there is none that has the like good cause to be well content with his wife."

Which said, he embraced and kissed her; and then, while she wept for joy, they rose and hied them there where sate the daughter, all astonied to hear the news, whom, as also her brother, they tenderly embraced, and explained to them, and many others that stood by, the whole mystery. Whereat the ladies, transported with delight, rose from table and betook them with Griselda to a chamber, and, with better omen, divested her of her sorry garb, and arrayed her in one of her own robes of state; and so, in guise of a lady (howbeit in her rags she had shewed as no less) they led her back into the hall. Wondrous was the cheer which there they made with the children; and, all overjoyed at the event, they revelled and made merry amain, and prolonged the festivities for several days; and very discreet they pronounced Gualtieri, albeit they censured as intolerably harsh the probation to which he had subjected Griselda, and most discreet beyond all compare they accounted Griselda.

Some days after, the Count of Panago returned to Bologna, and Gualtieri took Giannucolo from his husbandry, and established him in honour as his father-in-law, wherein to his great solace he lived for the rest of his days. Gualtieri himself, having mated his daughter with a husband of high degree, lived long and happily thereafter with Griselda, to whom he ever paid all honour.

Now what shall we say in this case but that even into the cots of the poor the heavens let fall at times spirits divine, as into the palaces of kings souls that are fitter to tend hogs than to exercise lordship over men? Who but Griselda had been able, with a countenance not only tearless, but cheerful, to endure the hard and unheard-of trials to which Gualtieri subjected her? Who perhaps might have deemed himself to have made no bad investment, had he chanced upon one, who, having been turned out of his house in her shift, had found means so to dust the pelisse of another as to get herself thereby a fine robe.

So ended Dioneo's story, whereof the ladies, diversely inclining, one to censure where another found matter for commendation, had discoursed not a little, when the king, having glanced at the sky, and marked that the sun was now low, insomuch that 'twas nigh the vesper hour, still keeping his seat, thus began:—" Exquisite my ladies, as, methinks, you

wot, 'tis not only in minding them of the past and apprehending
the present that the wit of mortals consists ; but by one means
or the other to be able to foresee the future is by the sages
accounted the height of wisdom. Now, to-morrow, as you
know, 'twill be fifteen days since, in quest of recreation and
for the conservation of our health and life, we, shunning the
dismal and dolorous and afflicting spectacles that have ceased
not in our city since this season of pestilence began, took our
departure from Florence. Wherein, to my thinking, we have
done nought that was not seemly ; for, if I have duly used my
powers of observation, albeit some gay stories, and of a kind to
stimulate concupiscence, have here been told, and we have
daily known no lack of dainty dishes and good wine, nor yet of
music and song, things, one and all, apt to incite weak minds
to that which is not seemly, neither on your part, nor on ours,
have I marked deed or word, or aught of any kind, that called
for reprehension ; but, by what I have seen and heard, seemliness
and the sweet intimacy of brothers and sisters have ever reigned
among us. Which, assuredly, for the honour and advantage
which you and I have had thereof, is most grateful to me.
Wherefore, lest too long continuance in this way of life might
beget some occasion of weariness, and that no man may be able
to misconstrue our too long abidance here, and as we have all
of us had our day's share of the honour which still remains in
me, I should deem it meet, so you be of like mind, that we now
go back whence we came : and that the rather that our company, the bruit whereof has already reached divers others that
are in our neighbourhood, might be so increased that all our
pleasure would be destroyed. And so, if my counsel meet with
your approval, I will keep the crown I have received of you
until our departure, which, I purpose, shall be to-morrow
morning. Should you decide otherwise, I have already determined whom to crown for the ensuing day."

Much debate ensued among the ladies and young men ; but
in the end they approved the king's proposal as expedient and
seemly ; and resolved to do even as he had said. The king
therefore summoned the seneschal ; and having conferred with
him of the order he was to observe on the morrow, he dismissed
the company until supper-time. So, the king being risen, the
ladies and the rest likewise rose, and betook them, as they were
wont, to their several diversions. Supper-time being come,
they supped with exceeding great delight. Which done, they
addressed them to song and music and dancing ; and, while

Lauretta was leading a dance, the king bade Fiammetta give
them a song ; whereupon Fiammetta right debonairly sang on
this wise :—

> So came but Love, and brought no jealousy,
>   So blithe, I wot, as I,
>   Dame were there none, be she whoe'er she be.
>
> If youth's fresh, lusty pride
>   May lady of her lover well content,
>   Or valour's just renown,
>   Hardihood, prowess tried,
>   Wit, noble mien, discourse most excellent,
>   And of all grace the crown ;
>   That she am I, who, fain for love to swoun,
>   There where my hope doth lie
>   These several virtues all conjoined do see.
>
> But, for that I less wise
>   Than me no whit do other dames discern,
>   Trembling with sore dismay,
>   I still the worst surmise,
>   Deeming their hearts with the same flame to burn
>   That of mine maketh prey :
>   Wherefore of him that is my hope's one stay
>   Disconsolate I sigh,
>   Yea mightily, and daily do me dree.
>
> If but my lord as true
>   As worthy to be loved I might approve,
>   I were not jealous then :
>   But, for that charmer new
>   Doth all too often gallant lure to love,
>   Forsworn I hold all men,
>   And sick at heart I am, of death full fain ;
>   Nor lady doth him eye,
>   But I do quake, lest she him wrest from me.
>
> 'Fore God, then, let each she
>   List to my prayer, nor e'er in my despite
>   Such grievous wrong essay ;
>   For should there any be
>   That by or speech or mien's allurements light
>   Of him to rob me may
>   Study or plot, I, witting, shall find way,
>   My beauty it aby !
>   To cause her sore lament such frenesie.

As soon as Fiammetta had ended her song, Dioneo, who was
beside her, said with a laugh :—" Madam, 'twould be a great
courtesy on your part to do all ladies to wit, who he is, that he
be not stolen from you in ignorance, seeing that you threaten
such dire resentment." Several other songs followed ; and it
being then nigh upon midnight, all, as the king was pleased to
order, betook them to rest. With the first light of the new day

they rose, and, the seneschal having already conveyed thence all their chattels, they, following the lead of their discreet king, hied them back to Florence; and in Santa Maria Novella, whence they had set forth, the three young men took leave of the seven ladies, and departed to find other diversions elsewhere, while the ladies in due time repaired to their homes.

THE AUTHOR'S EPILOGUE

MOST noble damsels, for whose solace I addressed me to this long and toilsome task, meseems that, aided by the Divine grace, the bestowal whereof I impute to the efficacy of your pious prayers, and in no wise to merits of mine, I have now brought this work to the full and perfect consummation which in the outset thereof I promised you. Wherefore, it but remains for me to render, first to God, and then to you, my thanks, and so to give a rest to my pen and weary hand. But this I purpose not to allow them, until, briefly, as to questions tacitly mooted—for well assured I am that these stories have no especial privilege above any others, nay, I forget not that at the beginning of the Fourth Day I have made the same plain—I shall have answered certain trifling objections that one of you, maybe, or some other, might advance. Peradventure, then, some of you will be found to say that I have used excessive license in the writing of these stories, in that I have caused ladies at times to tell, and oftentimes to list, matters that, whether to tell or to list, do not well beseem virtuous women. The which I deny, for that there is none of these stories so unseemly, but that it may without offence be told by any one, if but seemly words be used; which rule, methinks, has here been very well observed. But assume we that 'tis even so (for with you I am not minded to engage in argument, witting that you would vanquish me), then, I say that for answer why I have so done, reasons many come very readily to hand. In the first place, if aught of the kind in any of these stories there be, 'twas but such as was demanded by the character of the stories, which let but any person of sound judgment scan with the eye of reason, and 'twill be abundantly manifest that, unless I had been minded to deform them, they could not have been otherwise recounted. And if, perchance, they do, after all, contain here and there a trifling indiscretion of speech, such as might ill sort with one of your precious prudes, who

weigh words rather than deeds, and are more concerned to
appear, than to be, good, I say that so to write was as permissible to me, as 'tis to men and women at large in their
converse to make use of such terms as *hole*, and *pin*, and *mortar*,
and *pestle*, and *sausage*, and *polony*, and plenty more besides of
a like sort. And therewithal privilege no less should be allowed
to my pen than to the pencil of the painter, who without in-
curring any, or at least any just, censure, not only will depict
St. Michael smiting the serpent, or St. George the dragon, with
sword or lance at his discretion ; but male he paints us Christ,
and female Eve, and His feet that for the salvation of our race
willed to die upon the cross he fastens thereto, now with one,
now with two nails.

Moreover, 'tis patent to all that 'twas not in the Church, of
matters whereto pertaining 'tis meet we speak with all purity
of heart and seemliness of phrase, albeit among her histories
there are to be found not a few that will ill compare with my
writings ; nor yet in the schools of the philosophers, where, as
much as anywhere, seemliness is demanded, nor in any place
where clergy or philosophers congregate, but in gardens, in
pleasaunces, and among folk, young indeed, but not so young
as to be seducible by stories, and at a time when, if so one
might save one's life, the most sedate might without disgrace
walk abroad with his breeches for headgear, that these stories
were told. Which stories, such as they are, may, like all things
else, be baneful or profitable according to the quality of the
hearer. Who knows not that wine is, as Cinciglione and
Scolaio [1] and many another aver, an excellent thing for the
living creature, and yet noxious to the fevered patient ? Are
we, for the mischief it does to the fever-stricken, to say that 'tis
a bad thing ? Who knows not that fire is most serviceable, nay,
necessary to mortals ? Are we to say that, because it burns
houses and villages and cities, it is a bad thing ? Arms, in like
manner, are the safeguard of those that desire to live in peace,
and also by them are men not seldom maliciously slain, albeit
the malice is not in them, but in those that use them for a
malicious purpose. Corrupt mind did never yet understand
any word in a wholesome sense ; and as such a mind has no
profit of seemly words, so such as are scarce seemly may as
little avail to contaminate a healthy mind as mud the radiance
of the sun, or the deformities of earth the splendours of the
heavens. What books, what words, what letters, are more

1 Noted topers of the day.

sacred, more excellent, more venerable, than those of Holy Writ? And yet there have been not a few that, perversely construing them, have brought themselves and others to perdition. Everything is in itself good for somewhat, and being put to a bad purpose, may work manifold mischief. And so, I say, it is with my stories. If any man shall be minded to draw from them matters of evil tendency or consequence, they will not gainsay him, if, perchance, such matters there be in them, nor will such matters fail to be found in them, if they be wrested and distorted. Nor, if any shall seek profit and reward in them, will they deny him the same; and censured or accounted as less than profitable and seemly they can never be, if the times or the persons when and by whom they are read be such as when they were recounted. If any lady must needs say paternosters or make cakes or tarts for her holy father, let her leave them alone; there is none after whom they will run a-begging to be read: howbeit there are little matters that even the beguines tell, ay, and do, now and again.

In like manner there will be some who will say that there are stories here which 'twere better far had been omitted. Granted; but 'twas neither in my power, nor did it behove me, to write any but such stories as were narrated; wherefore, 'twas for those by whom they were told to have a care that they were proper; in which case they would have been no less so as I wrote them. But, assuming that I not only wrote but invented the stories, as I did not, I say that I should take no shame to myself that they were not all proper; seeing that artist there is none to be found, save God, that does all things well and perfectly. And Charlemagne, albeit he created the Paladins, wist not how to make them in such numbers as to form an army of them alone. It must needs be that in the multitude of things there be found diversities of quality. No field was ever so well tilled but that here and there nettle, or thistle, or brier would be found in it amid the goodlier growths. Whereto I may add that, having to address me to young and unlearned ladies, as you for the most part are, I should have done foolishly, had I gone about searching and swinking to find matters very exquisite, and been sedulous to speak with great precision. However, whoso goes a-reading among these stories, let him pass over those that vex him, and read those that please him. That none may be misled, each bears on its brow the epitome of that which it hides within its bosom.

Again, I doubt not there will be such as will say that some of the stories are too long. To whom, once more, I answer, that whoso has aught else to do would be foolish to read them, albeit they were short. And though, now that I approach the end of my labours, 'tis long since I began to write, I am not, therefore, oblivious that 'twas to none but leisured ladies that I made proffer of my pains ; nor can aught be long to him that reads but to pass the time, so only he thereby accomplish his purpose. Succinctness were rather to be desired by students, who are at pains not merely to pass, but usefully to employ, their time, than by you, who have as much time at your disposal as you spend not in amorous delights. Besides which, as none of you goes either to Athens, or to Bologna, or to Paris to study, 'tis meet that what is meant for you should be more diffuse than what is to be read by those whose minds have been refined by scholarly pursuits.

Nor make I any doubt but there are yet others who will say that the said stories are too full of jests and merry conceits, and that it ill beseems a man of weight and gravity to have written on such wise. To these I am bound to render, and do render, my thanks, for that, prompted by well-meant zeal, they have so tender a regard to my reputation. But to that, which they urge against me, I reply after this sort :—That I am of weight I acknowledge, having been often weighed in my time ; wherefore, in answer to the fair that have not weighed me, I affirm that I am not of gravity ; on the contrary I am so light that I float on the surface of the water ; and considering that the sermons which the friars make, when they would chide folk for their sins, are to-day, for the most part, full of jests and merry conceits, and drolleries, I deemed that the like stuff would not ill beseem my stories, written, as they were, to banish women's dumps. However, if thereby they should laugh too much, they may be readily cured thereof by the Lament of Jeremiah, the Passion of the Saviour, or the Complaint of the Magdalen.

And who shall question but that yet others there are who will say that I have an evil tongue and venomous, because here and there I tell the truth about the friars ? Now for them that so say there is forgiveness, for that 'tis not to be believed but that they have just cause ; seeing that the friars are good folk, and eschew hardship for the love of God, and grind intermittently, and never blab ; and, were they not all a trifle malodorous, intercourse with them would be much more agreeable. Nevertheless, I acknowledge that the things of this world have no stability, but are ever undergoing change ; and this may have befallen my tongue, albeit, no great while ago, one of my fair neighbours—for in what pertains to myself I trust not my own judgment, but forgo it to the best of my power—told me 'twas the goodliest and sweetest tongue in the world ; and in sooth, when this occurred, few of the said stories were yet to write ; nor, for that those who so tax me do it despitefully, am I minded to vouchsafe them any further answer.

So, then, be every lady at liberty to say and believe whatever she may think fit : but 'tis now time for me to bring these remarks to a close, with humble thanks to Him, by whose help and guidance I, after so long travail, have been brought to the desired goal. And may you, sweet my ladies, rest ever in His grace and peace ; and be not unmindful of me, if, peradventure, any of you may, in any measure, have been profited by reading these stories.

Endeth here the tenth and last day of the book called Decameron, otherwise Prince Galeotto.

THE END